HER CASUAL SLAUGHTERS

Don Shaw

Published by Tideswell Press
Mickleover DE3 0TF
Copyright @ Don Shaw 2020
All rights reserved
The moral right of the author has been asserted

Don Shaw asserts his right to be identified as the author of his Work in accordance with the Copyright Designs and PatentsAct1988

No part of this publication may be reproduced, stored in a System, or transmitted in any form or, by any means without prior permission in writing of the publisher, nor otherwise circulated in any form of binding or cover other than that in it is published and without a similar condition including this condition being imposed on the subsequent purchaser

REVIEWS

Benjamin Evans, literary-critic of The Guardian, showered this novel with superlatives in the form of a review. Unfortunately, I am unable to emblazon them upon the book covers as it was part of an editorial process on behalf of a literary consultancy.

***

Her Casual Slaughters is a high-quality literary thriller. The Shakespeare Institute library will be proud to have it on its shelves.
Professor Michael Dobson, Director of The Shakespeare Institute, University of Birmingham

From the very first page, this exciting novel is full of sizzling possibilities with the world-renowned Shakespeare Institute as the backdrop for a scintillating mystery. Don Shaw weaves an atmosphere so heart-stoppingly evocative that it holds the reader completely captivated from start to finish. A great literary thriller from a highly accomplished and master story-teller that, together with fascinating American students, should surely create a huge demand.
Dr Chris Laoutaris, lecturer at The Shakespeare Institute and author of *Shakespeare and the Countess*

*And let me speak to the yet unknowing world
How these things came about: so shall you hear
Of carnal, bloody and unnatural acts,
Of accidental judgments, casual slaughters
Hamlet, Act V, sc. ii*

THE BOSTON GLOBE

Tuesday, December 18, 2018

American student murdered at the home of Shakespeare, Stratford-upon-Avon, England. Four students held by police.

Police in Warwickshire, England, have until tomorrow morning to charge or release four American students being questioned over the brutal slaying of a fellow student. Detective Chief Inspector Rees, leading the inquiry, stated that the body was discovered at The Shakespeare Institute in Stratford-upon-Avon early on Monday morning of this week. Police have not revealed the gender or identity of the victim, except to say that the death was the result of a ferocious attack. The identities of the arrested students have been withheld by the police.

Chapter One

Three months earlier

'So, is there beauty in death?' asked Professor Woodbridge, the visiting lecturer from Harvard University. 'Personally, I'd rather be ugly and not there when it happens.'

To some laughter and the humming of flies, the professor finally sat down, mopping his brow on yet another day of the "Indian" summer. Mid-fifties, slim, with a grey beard and sharply penetrating eyes, he was pleased with the way the seminar was developing and relieved that the old Woody Allen joke seemed to have gone down without eliciting groans.

The decision to sit outside had been made late. Two hours earlier the garden of The Shakespeare Institute in Stratford-upon-Avon had been shrouded in fog, the grass sparkling with the dew of dawn.

Now, with the garden dipped in warm sunshine, the students were spread out around him, ensuring they could see each other, some propping themselves up on their elbows, others sitting with legs akimbo or crossed. One sat next to a bust of Shakespeare, which had pride of place at the side of the lawn.

The seminar dealt with the theme of tragic death in Shakespeare. They had talked about Macbeth and Hamlet, his obsession with death along with the universality of the play's timeless themes.

One student, Franky O'Tierney, decided to throw a spanner in the works. 'When all's said and done, isn't Shakespeare saying "Come on, what do we know about *anything*?"'

Having sensitive skin, Franky wore a straw hat while sitting in the shade of a rhododendron bush, her freckled arms covered by the long sleeves of a flimsy blue top. Since her arrival she would only sit outside on a cloudy day, or in the late afternoon, when her red tresses would glisten from the splintering rays of the sun, descending behind the large copper beech.

Woodbridge, adept at locating American accents, gave her a bright smile. 'Now, you're from Massachusetts – Boston, per chance?'

'Yes, I am.'

'What's the mafia family called in Boston?'

'The Patriarca, or New England mob.'

'They could even figure in *Hamlet*, then.' He looked around his flock with a smile.

'Oh? How's that?' She felt rather teased and uncomfortable.

'Well, aren't the deaths in *Hamlet* beautiful? Not in themselves but in the mafia-like way Shakespeare bumps everyone off?'

She caught her breath and failed to join in the laughter, having suddenly recognised him from a previous encounter.

She had been wandering around Stratford, the perfect English market town, and found herself in the aptly named Sheep Street, its width conjuring up the image of a shepherd in a flapping white gown, driving his flock down to the riverside.

She'd been trying to remember how to sense what the Romans called the *genius loci*, or "spirit of place." A book she'd bought online recommended that, when in Stratford, you stood on the riverbank with your back to the Royal Shakespeare Company Theatre.

Slowly, you transferred your gaze from the riverside to the colourful boats in the marina, round to the large green sward, then Sheep Street with its overhanging black-and-white Tudor houses and from there to the row of historic almshouses and back to the theatre. Then, by closing your eyes and breathing deeply, you might feel the vibrations of that spirit.

She'd already tried it once and failed. Irritated, she went into the theatre booking office and paid £5 for a ticket to see *Richard III*, the huge discount being a privilege granted to students of The Shakespeare Institute.

After scanning the bookshelves in the adjacent shop, she swung quickly into the aisle, only to collide with a grey-bearded man passing through.

'Hah!' he exclaimed, grimacing in pain, bending low and clutching the point of his elbow.

Franky put out a hand in deep concern. 'Oh, I'm so sorry,' she said.

'You should be,' he grimaced, gritting his teeth. 'You came out like a whirl—' He glanced at her hair and broke into a pained grin. 'I should have looked, shouldn't I? Red sky in the morning is the shepherd's warning?'

'I'm so sorry. I really am.'

'Yes ... I'll ... I'll be all right.'

'You're sure?'

'Yes...' He took a few steps away, still gripping his elbow, then turned back. 'Just a joke about—he waved a hand at her hair— 'your...' he dithered a little before going to the booking desk, still holding his elbow.

She left the theatre to stand on the riverbank and watch a number of swans sail downstream, the flotilla poised and coordinated in its majesty.

Nearby, a cellist played Bach's refined and sonorous cello sonata, but the deep and melodious tones were completely lost to her rising anger. And why was she so incensed?

She took a deep breath. Because the moment, the memory of her pleasant wander, the *day* even, had been spoiled entirely and irrevocably by his unforgivable remark about her *fucking* hair.

While the seminar was still in the discussion stage Franky, with her voice-recorder switched on, observed her classmates at leisure. She had plenty of time in which to make up for any work material lost.

Unlike most students, she had no need to earn money in the evenings or at weekends. Stratford was an expensive place in terms of lodgings so, while working zealously at their studies, students were forced to take part-time jobs in order to rent an apartment or bedsit in town. To this end they dispensed coffee in Starbucks or Costa, waited on tables at the numerous restaurants, pulled pints in the ancient taverns, sold tickets at Shakespeare's Birthplace or collected deckchair fees.

Franky, having plenty of time in which to work, relax and have fun, was pleased to be excused such drab, pedestrian jobs. However, she lacked friends who might have enjoyed, along with her, the delights that Stratford had to offer.

Franky was never adept at making overtures. Her reserve stemmed from childhood, the redness of her hair seeming to produce suspicion or outright hostility from other kids. At fourteen she'd started a poem with: *'The vibrations that my hair gives forth'*, but then junked it having failed to come up with a second line.

Her wariness of other people was justified by her continued experience of disrespectful behaviour into her late teens and beyond. She had even encountered it on induction day at the Institute when a fellow student came up to her in reception…

'Hi. I'm Alicia. I heard your name called. "Françoise O'Tierney". Great name. The new entente cordiale, huh?' She laughed easily.

'That's right. My Mom's French, Dad Irish.' Franky took in the girl's athletic frame, a cloud of frizzy dark hair, an unblemished face and what appeared to be Botoxed lips. 'I'm from Boston. You?'

'Miami. Hey, I heard you say you'd been here a few days already?'

'Yes, I have.'

'I'm still bushed. We were diverted to Amsterdam. Heathrow was closed for a drone. Can you help? I have to make frequent calls home. What's the best and cheapest way, do you know?'

'Sure,' said Franky. 'You have a number of choices. You go to the store – I'll tell you where to go – and ask for a SIM card that fits, okay? Is yours a GSM cell?'

'Yes, it is.'

'If it doesn't fit, you can set up an international calling plan. Call them to change your service. If all this fails – which it shouldn't – you can get one for about £25. I've got one. Now, there are two other things you have to watch out for…'

As Franky was talking, she became aware that Alicia was looking at her, but no longer listening. Instead, her head was cocked slightly to the right, in an attempt to catch what a well-built and good-looking guy was saying to the Institute administrator.

'Craig Muirhaven.'

Franky heard him repeat his name. At a glance she guessed he was in his early-thirties. She took in his shapeless, grey tweed suit, tartan shirt and chocolate-brown woollen tie. His deep, gravelly voice and square jaw matching that of an old Hollywood screen idol, made him seriously attractive by anyone's measure.

Alicia turned to take a peep at him and then suddenly excused herself. 'Franky—just need to ask a question.'

She turned away, leaving Franky open mouthed halfway through a sentence and blinking in outright disbelief.

So, what did sweet and friendly Alicia fail to do? While waiting for Craig's conversation with the administrator to end, she had plenty of time in which to turn back and apologise – but did she hell!

When Alicia finally managed to ask her question, Franky's mouth was still open, her blue eyes dancing.

'I think her death is a fantasy, a metaphor for Shakespeare's erotic imagination,' said Tom Vantusian, a thirty-two-year-old from a wealthy part of Stamford, Connecticut. After a short break the seminar had introduced a new dynamic, Shakespeare the man.

'The flowing white virginal dress, wrapped around Ophelia's drowned body, her nipples showing,' he continued, 'all it does is cloud an audience's ability to see what a dark tragedy it really is. That was either silly or brave of him to do that.'

Franky gazed at Tom, admiring him for his dress sense. They'd chatted occasionally. He reminded her of a rich uncle she had, from the same neck of the woods. Wearing an expensive dark blue Ralph Lauren shirt, Diesel jeans and Gucci loafers, he looked every inch the offspring of a Stamford family in which the pursuit of intellect and good manners seemed hereditary.

I'll give another instance,' he continued in his educated British manner and with a slight nasal intonation. 'In making the Pyramus and Thisbe story like Romeo and Juliet, it's as if he's mocking their tragic love story with a comedy. Wasn't he risking the integrity of both plays? So, if he were that brave, we have to ask what kind of man does it make him?'

'Well, you put the question Tom, have you an answer?' Adjusting her sitting position, Franky made a display of giving him her full attention.

'Yes. A genius. If anything at all marks him as that, it's got to be making fun of himself. What other writer would dare – or risk – doing that? As I see it *A Midsummer Night's Dream* is basically *Romeo and Juliet* in another key. The play within the play highlights what could have been in the '*Dream*', and we laugh at it because it didn't happen.'

Franky continued to stare, both impressed and intrigued. She saw Tom as a patrician, despite resembling a peering John Lennon with a replica of the wire-framed National Health spectacles perched on his nose. Luminously intelligent, she'd seen him more than once dressed in a dark suit and tie, sometimes carrying a long black umbrella. His quiet, aloof personality, backed up by a steely self-confidence, was impressive.

'There are more than twenty suicides in Shakespeare's plays,' said Franky, keen to make her mark. 'Maybe he creates beauty in death by metaphor sometimes, just to ring the changes.'

'Agreed,' said Tom. 'But, overall, he's exploring the three great themes of life: love, war and death, death being the most interesting, but hardly beautiful?'

'Well can it be beautiful for the dying,' said Franky, 'an escape from all the fardels we have to bear?'

A few chuckles broke out, bringing forth a smug little smile. Since her childhood, she'd never felt part of any kind of social group and so impressing "insiders" was some form of point-scoring. From the age of six, Franky had always stayed hurt by kids who slighted her as Alicia had on induction day.

"Alicia." Just the thought of the name provoked her into a murderous rage. She revenged herself four times within hours of the slight, first by chopping open her head with an axe, then strangulation, followed by a stabbing frenzy and then by deploying a wire garotte, the latter also serving to dispatch the bookshop man. The problem was that the pleasure derived from these fantasy attacks was always short lived. One —two—three seconds —gone.

Whereas most people got over episodes of rudeness, she didn't. Following each incident her anger would coil up, nestling in her head like a snake, one that could rise up and strike at any moment. The only way to prevent that happening was for the perpetrator to apologise – *and mean it*. Now Alicia hadn't apologised, nor had the bookshop man, not properly, hence their punishment. The problem, of course, was that it was a waste of time, as it always ended with Franky hating herself, this having the unfortunate effect of intensifying her frustration.

So why the hell did she carry on doing it! She asked the same rhetorical question time after time. But it made no difference. No slight dropped out of her mind and none fell to supine forgetfulness. Each fresh incident joined dozens from many moons past, each occupying a dark place in her memory.

Her "little difficulty" – as Yvette, her mother, would put it – had its origins early in life. As a child, her pent-up and never-ending upsets were partially offset when she reached ninth grade in junior high. It was around that time when a few kids seemed to like her, well, at least respect her. Not one of them would she elevate to the rank of "friend", but getting them to do things on her behalf gave some satisfaction, compensating in some degree for her depressing fantasy attacks.

One of them, Mary Jo, her most likeable and sympathetic follower, once showed her a book about World War II. It told of a red-haired woman from Stalingrad who, in the spring of 1942, formed a 'bandit' battalion of women. Mary Jo explained that they hid in piles of hay, and when German soldiers marched by, they'd spring out and shoot them all dead.

'Oh, great story, terrific,' Franky said with a slow shake of the head. 'Wonderful. Well done.'

'Oh.' Mary Jo was devastated. 'Oh, sorry, Franky. I thought you'd be pleased with what a redhead did to the Nazis.'

'Well, no,' said Franky, taking a deep and patient breath. She put an arm around Mary Jo's shoulders giving them a squeeze. 'It's like this. The idea is we cut out references to redheads as being separate from humanity, which is exactly what you're not doing.' She squeezed her tighter. 'Why not a brown head or blonde head or a dickhead like you – why pick out a redhead? Can I kindly get through to you that my sole aim in life is to just ask the world very nicely to join me in condemning all this stereotypical red-haired apartheid, fucking bullshit!'

At Mary Jo's shocked and startled look, she burst out laughing and then sighed, having no wish to inflict pain. Instead she gave Mary Jo a warm hug. 'Sorry, just kidding. I'm sorry. Okay? It was good of you. Friends again?'

'Yes. That's okay.' Mary Jo smiled weakly.

It left Franky grimacing, all mixed up and hating herself, as per usual.

"*Slighted*" was a term that sixteen-year-old Franky first heard when Yvette took her to see a psychotherapist. She spent forty-five minutes talking with Franky, before going out for a quiet chat with Yvette.

'Tell me, how did you come to first notice it? she asked.

'Oh, I think it was when a few kids called her 'ginger.' She's always been sensitive about her hair. She'd shout back something like, "John Black, you think I'm weird but you're weirder because you've got green eyes, and you, Helen Bookbinder, you're a wart's troll." I remember that very well because she kept on about it. Even days later she'd suddenly say something about it and look miserable. I asked what was wrong and she clammed up. What causes it, do you know? Is it a kind of mental illness, or what?'

'No, not illness. It's a recognised personality disorder. Hypersensitivity to slights usually starts through lack of self-confidence, one's ego trampled on, that kind of thing. Each slight pops up in her mind from time to time. She sees it, feels it exactly like when it first happened. We're all upset by a slight, aren't we? But hers digs so deep that it stays stuck in her memory. It's like a video loop that gets played over and over again. The more she replays it the hotter she gets, literally. Then suddenly, bang, she hits back in a form of fantasy attack. From start to finish it's over in a flash.'

'Well I'm relieved she's not on her own in this. Do the others grow out of it?'

'Erm, yes, some. I hate saying this, but some sufferers can grow up to become, well, rather difficult.'

'Difficult?'

'I'm afraid sometimes even violent. It can develop into paranoia.'

'Dear God,' murmured Yvette, clutching her handbag tightly.

'Tell me, have there been any moments that you were afraid for her ... or *of* her?' The therapist tilted her head back slightly, as if nervous of the answer.

'Well ... yes, there was one time. She read the *Harry Potter* books and one day asked for her father's shotgun. She said that Harry's best friends were called Weasley, a family of red-headed wizards and witches, and they were troublemakers in the books. She hated it, kept saying why couldn't they be blonde or black? It proved that redheads were outcasts. She said she wanted to go in the woods and kill every pine martin, bobcat and stoat for preying on red squirrels.'

Afterwards, Yvette told Franky something of what the therapist had said. 'You have these loops of memory going round and round, and they sometimes explode and you hate it but you can't stop them. Is that how you feel?'

'Yes.' Franky lapsed into a gloomy silence.

'Well, let's take a step at a time. And see how we go on.'

Following the next session Yvette was greatly relieved to hear that Franky was showing signs of improvement. In terms of blood pressure, her systolic average – fifty per cent above normal in the first session – was now only thirty per cent. At this point Franky was shown how to "objectify" her complaint by writing down why she felt slighted and then read aloud what she'd written. By observing herself from the outside – and by debating with that "other person" – she would hopefully block out negative and troubling thoughts.

On their return journey they had nearly reached home when a heavy thunderstorm caused Yvette to pull over at the roadside. Franky stared through the thumping wipers for some time and then spoke suddenly.

'Why doesn't Dad love me?'

Yvette pivoted to fully face her. 'What?'

'He teaches drama. Drama's all about feelings, isn't it? So how come he hasn't got any?'

Yvette sank back in her seat and, with the rain still bucketing down, explained that his mother had died when he was only two years old. 'His brother and sister brought him up.'

Back home, Franky searched the web and read that unloved children, fearing rejection and failure, often found it difficult to trust or love anyone. It was certainly true in her case.

As she grew into her late teens, her thinking matured. It was then she realised that her father was a full-blooded psychopath. So that was why he'd left her to be jealous of other kids having fun with Dads tousling their hair and throwing the ball and laughing as they did so and being happy and carefree – not cold and remote like *him*.

It was *he* who was ultimately responsible for her slights. He'd made her feel an outcast. But he was intelligent, so why in hell didn't he realise what he was doing to her and make a goddamned effort? She got so angry that she vowed never to visit the therapist again. She'd been branded for life and by her own miserable excuse of a father.

She also reached the conclusion that Yvette, also, was incapable of showing her love – not *real* love like cuddling her when she was upset. This was proved when Fergal, her father, smacked her really hard and she'd run to Mom for sympathy. And what was Yvette's reaction? She gave a mere shrug of the shoulders with a brief and dismissive, "Aux grands maux les grands remèdes."

Franky's insight into her father's dark soul was confirmed when she turned twenty, when she began to look back, to probe into the recesses of her mind, to try and find out why she'd turned out the way she had, wary of strangers and socialising. It was all his fault.

She remembered a day when she was ten years old. He'd invited a priest "to come visit her as she was difficult to deal with." No sooner had he arrived when her father made some excuse to leave her alone with him. Their meeting didn't last long as the priest had her sitting on his knee 'for a little talk' but then had placed his hand on her thigh, stroking it, causing her to wriggle away.

When she told her father he just looked embarrassed, mumbled a little and pretended to be distracted by something.

Years later, she came across the priest's name in *The Boston Globe*, convicted of the sexual abuse of minors. He joined 248 priests in the diocese who, since 2002, had been arrested for crimes of paedophilia. From that point on, aged seventeen, she declared that she would no longer go to another therapy session, despite his threat to cut off her inheritance, should she refuse. It made her dig her heels in even further.

One day Yvette pestered her so much that she, finally, exploded: 'It's him! He's done this to me. Isn't that what psychotherapy is supposed to be all about? Once you know what's happening *and why*, you can do something about it, can't you? Who needs therapy anymore!'

No amount of persuasion and warnings could get her to continue with the sessions.

Then there was the day her father came home, glowering after some road-rage incident. He never stated precisely what had happened, but he was full of hatred for the guy who had given him 'the finger' from the safety of his car. Days later he was still muttering about it.

It suddenly dawned on her. He had the hypersensitivity-to-slight gene, without any question or doubt and had passed it on to her.

The bastard.

Sitting in the shade of the copper beech, she gave up contemplating her troubled past and tried to concentrate on what Professor Woodbridge was saying. However, he was cracking yet another joke. Deciding that he was more concerned with being a comedian than a lecturer, she allowed her thoughts to drift back to Tom, the studious one. One day, in the library, their eyes had met, at which he'd smiled a little and nodded as if to say that all was well with the world. At this point she decided to get to know him better. She had something rather exciting in mind.

'So "What a piece of work is a man!" The professor's voice rose in challenge. "How noble in reason? How infinite in faculties?" He lifted his eyebrows in query.

'What a piece of work is Shakespeare?' It was Alicia who spoke. 'Could it be another instance of making fun of himself as Tom suggests?'

'No,' said Tom. 'He's not boasting, neither is he mocking himself. In context he's expressing his melancholy over the difference between the best that men aspire to be, and how they actually behave. It's the great divide that depresses him. In that speech he actually sums up man as nothing but dust.'

'Well, I think – and it may sound crazy – but could his work show Shakespeare as something of a games player?' Craig shrugged self-deprecatingly as if to say, 'just a guess.'

There were a few chuckles.

'What do you mean by "games player"? said a student sitting behind Craig.

'Okay. Let me think — *w*hy did I say that?' Craig put his head back, grinning at the outburst of laughter.

Franky smiled. How could she not like him, he was that easy-going? His coat pockets slumped, loaded with a stapler, ballpoint pens, cell phone, notebook, memory sticks, coins and parking tickets. Over one eye hung a forelock of sandy hair which he flipped away from time to time. He had a slow, shy smile when being introduced, but when he knew you better would tease you with 'Do you remember when we…', and you would have to laugh with him at the incident. He was the type who could laugh at jokes about his home town, Oklahoma City, where men were said to hold up their pants with a bible belt.

However, he hadn't laughed much since his wife died, and tragically, later that same year, his four-year-old son, Daniel, from cancer. Franky knew his story, as did most on the course. She'd overheard a fellow student say that she'd seen him walking through town with tears in his eyes. Another student had visited him at his bedsit and found him weeping as he listened to Ella Fitzgerald singing the achingly beautiful 'Every Time We Say Goodbye'.

Faced with such overwhelming sympathy he'd felt it right he should explain himself, which he did once, in a seminar. He'd had to escape, he said, get away for a year and lose himself in some project. As an English teacher, where better to spend time than at the world-renowned Shakespeare Institute in Stratford-upon-Avon?

In the ten seconds it took Craig to work out his answer, Woodbridge caught Franky's eye and quickly looked away. He'd recognised her as soon as the group gathered on the lawn. The incident had left him remorseful. He thought she'd not recognised him, and made a mental note to apologise sincerely for his remark about her hair.

Craig finally delivered his thoughts, referencing Tom's comment about Shakespeare. 'Well, if he is making fun of his work, it shows him as no egotist, he's a man of the people. That's what games players are, aren't they? The best, are often humble. It's for others to say if their work's good or not?'

Woodbridge smiled. 'A humble man. "This above all— to thine own self be true". Can we say humble, or might we say modest?'

'I'd say both,' said Craig. 'He wouldn't have had such insight into the human condition if he weren't. He doesn't pretend to know the answers.'

'I think that's right,' said Franky. 'Take two things. He's asking questions of the past as well as the future – what makes a good king or ruler? Also, what are the priorities of government? These are questions for today, aren't they? I say that, thinking I may have voted for the wrong candidate in the Presidential election.'

This brought forth a few comments and chuckles of agreement, and Franky was pleased to see Craig turn his head to give her a gentle smile. She had cause for liking him, not just because of his relaxed manner, but for that moment on induction day when Alicia had slighted her. She wouldn't forget his wince of sympathy towards her, something warm passing between them, something she'd never experienced in her life before.

Yes, surveying Craig, she made up her mind. He was on her list, next to Tom. She now needed two more – they would be female – to participate in her venture. For the last day or two she'd toyed with the idea of renting a top-grade Tudor cottage that she knew was available for the academic year. It was expensive, *very* expensive. She reckoned on having to shell out far more than the four others she intended to recruit. However, wanting to live with other people in the hope of cutting short the time when prey to her 'loops', she'd decided to pay up and pursue it. *Keep busy*. That was what the therapist had recommended, wasn't it?

She had other reasons for inviting them both. Craig was a big guy who might be useful should a burglar try to disturb their idyll. And with Tom on board he had his polar opposite. This suited her book, literally, and made for a third reason for having both men there.

At sixteen she'd won a school prize in a short-story competition.

Incentivised by this, she'd started to write a novel, ploughing on until she realised that far more was needed in the way of character and plot than she'd bargained for. Her problem, she'd diagnosed, was lack of knowledge about people, the way they behaved, their body language, prejudices and motivations. She'd not been mature or old enough to become a serious writer.

Turning twenty she'd delved into Dickens and the Brontës, as well as Hemingway, Steinbeck and Roth. And how she loved Bret Easton Ellis, dark and satirical. But then she recalled the general advice given by most published authors: 'If you want to write, then *write about what you know.*' It stuck.

Simply put, she needed experience of behaviour patterns and the vicissitudes of life in general. She had memories of her own ups and downs from childhood onwards, but had no experience of living with adults other than her, mostly boring, relatives.

Yes, drama was all about conflict of one type or another, and with housemates she'd have continual interaction, from which she'd learn. In considering Tom and Craig, each different from the other in so many ways, she thought it would be interesting to chart their relationship. She might even initiate a little friction between them here and there, that could help in developing her imagination?

There would be another benefit. Tom, with his graceful airs and steely intellect could prove amusing. Life with her parents had been empty of humour, and Tom could easily provide it.

He was also an interesting enigma. He'd pronounce something on a subject that you would think was his considered opinion, when suddenly he'd qualify it with something out of left field, like when they were talking about a long-term serial killer and he'd raised something of a technical nature.

He had other gifts; it turned out that he was fluent in both French and German. With him in the fold, surely life would never be dull? Could he be touched by Asperger's syndrome, a form of autism, she wondered. It would account for his amazing general knowledge, reserve and sharp focus.

As it grew warmer, Woodbridge took out a handkerchief and pressed it against his brow. 'Okay.' He opened out his arms. 'We have to ask if there's any other reason for Shakespeare juxtaposing Pyramus with Romeo. Is there?'

A new voice chirped up, bright and cheerful, 'Is it, maybe, that if we could see Pyramus and Thisbe first, then we'd really appreciate how solemn Romeo's and Juliet's deaths are in comparison?'

The speaker was Hannah Bron. Small and slim, with blond hair cut short, she was pretty in a snub-nosed, good natured way. Her light blue eyes had settled on Franky on the second day of term and saw her looking downcast. Hannah, always ready to help anyone in need, followed Franky into the Institute garden, where she sat looking a shade melancholic. Feeling curious, as well as sorry for her, she just had to make an approach.

'Hi, I'm Hannah,' she said. 'Hannah Bron.'

'Franky. Franky O'Tierney.' She gave her a flicker of a smile.

They got chatting. Later, they gravitated into the conservatory for coffee.

When meeting strangers, Franky's attitude was to show caution, but she soon became intrigued as to why Hannah wanted to latch on to her. But any suspicion that she felt had been quickly dismissed by the bright and bubbly girl from Detroit. She could imagine her as a college cheerleader, stomping around in knee-length socks and miniskirt, while shaking wrist-clamped pompoms.

It was Hannah's total lack of reserve, while demonstrating a pure innocence along with a complete lack of guile and cynicism, that grabbed Franky. She could be the sunshine in her life. They got along fine that day – even to the point of recounting their life stories.

Hannah told hers, sitting on a bench by the riverside.

'My dad's Polish,' she said, munching an apple, 'called Bronowski. He shortened it to "Bron" after arriving in America when the Soviet Union collapsed. He got married in '91 but changed his name to escape all the "Polack" jokes. They christened me Beverly. Hannah was my second name and I decided it was more me. There's another reason. They still call me Bev, relatives and the like. Say it quick and "Bevbron" sounds like Hebron, a town in Palestine, had to junk it.'

It hadn't taken long for her cheerful spontaneity to become irresistible. Clearly, she wasn't after something *like money* – Franky had briefly entertained that possibility. Hannah, it seemed, was there for her, ready to drag any monkey of depression off her back. How could she not invite her into the Tudor fold? Life on campus with Hannah close by, was an appealing prospect.

But then something happened to give Franky pause: Alicia. She began to notice that, whenever Craig was around, she'd show a sexy confidence, her worldly-wise smile saying: 'I'm not here to fall for you, big guy. If we get together it's on my terms. You're there for my amusement, not yours.'

Deciding that sexual tension and jealousy were, in terms of fiction, something she'd like to explore, Franky began to compare Alicia's body language with that of Hannah, who was far more overt. Sometimes when Craig showed up, she would blush, giving a little shimmy shake of the shoulders as if spreading out her antennae to pick up Craig's vibes, so blocking out Alicia's. Oh yes, Hannah was definitely aware she might have a competitor. It suggested potential theatre. Could it be the type that would be readily on tap in their new abode?

However, caution showed itself. She must not be impetuous in her choice of housemates. While looking for dramatic fodder, she had to keep the four rubbing along together. Hannah, having the hots for the cowboy from Oklahoma, up against Alicia, could produce fireworks. *Difficult* one to think about. She didn't want to lose out in a battle between two of the four. She could also envisage Hannah's high-intensity mojo being too much for the likes of the relaxed Craig, as well as the elegant and studious Tom.

It could all produce great chemistry. But what if it went haywire?

It put her in a quandary. She would have to think about it.

Carefully.

The following day she made a decision. She, being boss of the outfit, would draw up a list of rules that forbade certain types of behaviour, and the four, whether they liked it or not, would have to sign a pledge to abide by them. She would talk to Hannah about it, but decide to bide her time until the moment when she could bring up the subject of Alicia. She needed Hannah's promise that, come what may, she would remain in control of her feelings over Craig.

Oddly – and conveniently – it was Hannah, herself who brought Franky up to speed on that matter. Out walking, a rainstorm sent them scurrying into an Elizabethan pub. Sprawled out in front of the log fire, Hannah opened up.

'I flew from Newark to London. I was sitting next to this guy and we got talking, said he was from Oklahoma, also going there. He'd had to get a Newark connection because his direct flight was cancelled at the last minute. So, we talked. He asked where I was heading and I said Stratford-upon-Avon. He just stared at me, looked amazed – and so did I when I found we were both going to the Institute! Talk about being blown away. So, we talked about lots of things. He'd lost his wife, and his son who was only four. Lost them both in the same year. I cried for him … I really did.'

Hannah paused a moment. 'So, the cabin lights dimmed. I snuggled down with my teddy bear. He asked me about it. I said Bernard was my Grandpa's in World War II, a bomber pilot with a Polish squadron – the crew's mascot. Never flew without him. He was shot down and escaped back to England, still with Bernard.'

'Wow,' said Franky quietly. 'Some story.'

'Yes. Craig made me laugh. He said, "So the cabin steward won't have to fly the plane." It fazed me. What's this guy sitting next to me on about? I said to him, 'Come again?' "He's our lucky bear for the flight," he said. 'What am I, Franky? A dumbo.' Hannah grimaced, sticking a finger at her head.

Franky, taking a sip of rum and Coke, put down the glass. 'Great story. Serendipity, family bonds, romance at 40,000 feet … what more does anybody want?'

'You're right. Did you ever see that Brit movie *Brief Encounter*?'

'No, I didn't.'

'It was made not long after World War II. In the days of romance, not sex. A couple meet, nearly do it but don't – married, both of them. And that's it. If you accept the high moralistic tone set in a world of the stiff upper lip, as I did, it was great.' Hannah fell into reflection, the firelight reddening her face. 'By the way, talking about bears, do you know the teddy bear shop in Henley Street?'

'Teddy bear shop?'

'Yes. I went in and told them mine hadn't been valued for ages. I thought it was a Steiff. They examined him but couldn't find the hole in his ear where a button used to be. So, he's not. If it had been there, he could have been worth over $100,000.'

'Wow. All for a hole. Couldn't you have made one?' Seeing Hannah hesitate — 'Joke,' she added quickly.

'I know, but you've no idea. There are forgeries, lots from Eastern Europe and the Far East. I couldn't live with myself … especially when Grandpa was a war hero. He actually pinned his medal on Bernard, and that's where it stayed until Grandpa died. I wouldn't sell him for a million dollars. You'd be surprised how many actors have one. I read that Trump's still got his. Can you imagine him hunkering down with a bear?'

'Yes.' Franky laughed. 'I could.'

'Trump's bear.' Hannah giggled. 'Can you imagine?'

Shakespeare would have loved him.'

'Who, Trump or Bernard?'

They both laughed.

'Trump.' Hannah, looking round surreptitiously, leaned sideways to steal a log from the basket and stick it quickly on the fire. 'He's our Richard III. All those battered by his bullying, but thinking they could control him, they were first to be fired. How can they possibly accept him as President — or, by the same token, Richard as King?'

'You're right.' Franky paused, feeling now was the moment to bring up the subject of Craig.

'Hannah?' She paused too long. 'About Craig—'

'Isn't there something in us that enjoys their horrible climb to power?' Hannah was still bent on her theme. 'And King Lear as well!' she said suddenly, steadying her glass of wine.

'Yes, absolutely. Erm, Hannah. About Craig—'

'The questions keep coming,' said Hannah, still absorbed in her thoughts. 'What happens when a king is mentally and emotionally unfit? What do you do? It's the same question for Trump, isn't it?'

'And Horatio in *Hamlet*,' said Franky. 'What does he talk about? Erm … "accidental judgments", and what else was it …?' She jabbed out her arm. "Casual …?'

'Slaughters—"Casual slaughters!" Hey.' Hannah's eyes lit up. 'Great title for a dissertation.' She paused, with her mouth open. 'Erm … got it! "Casual Slaughters. Violence and Guilt in Shakespeare" da-dah!' She thrust her arm triumphantly in the air.

Franky chuckled. Normally she'd be bored by non-stop chatter but it was all down to Hannah's unassailable innocence. She felt that most people she met had something to hide, but not her. She gave up trying to discuss the matter of Craig with her. It wasn't the moment. Hannah was effervescing, far too excited.

'Did you have a bear?' Hannah said, rapidly munching potato crisps.

'Yes, I did. Dad burnt it when I was six, saying it was dirty. He bought me another one, but it didn't smell right, so I conveniently lost him.'

'Quite right. I would have too.' Hannah suddenly exhaled. 'You know, Craig's the nicest guy. On the plane I felt safe, really safe. I felt warm.'

Now was the moment. 'Hannah, about Craig—'

'It wasn't something I thought about,' continued Hannah, oblivious. 'I just did. I think about him all the time. And it hurts. It. really does.'

Franky sighed to herself. No, now was definitely not the time.

The seminar on the lawn was drawing to a close. After summing-up, Professor Woodbridge glanced at his watch. 'And, with that, I think it's lunchtime,' he said, beaming. 'A progressive, dynamic, good session, everyone. Thank you all.' He shuffled his notes together.

Franky spoke up. 'May I ask you something?'

'Yes?' Woodbridge looked up with a smile.

'I just want to ask briefly about *The Tempest* and how Shakespeare focused on the supernatural issues to undermine the philosophical standpoint on the traditional romances and new areas of metaphysical speculation.' Franky rattled out the words, her blue eyes wide open and staring.

Woodbridge slowly put the notes back in his briefcase, thinking of an appropriate reply. Discretion, he thought, was advisable. Clearly, she'd identified him from the incident in the theatre bookshop and was trying to tie him up out of petty revenge.

The other students sat open-mouthed in disbelief as they looked at Franky, her eyes sparkling. *Why* was she doing it? For everyone it produced nothing but toe-curling embarrassment.

'A rather complex question that I'm afraid I can't answer now,' said Woodbridge. 'Talk to your tutor. And we did talk about the supernatural, didn't we? How it provides insight into *Hamlet*.' Woodbridge snapped shut his briefcase.

'Yes.' Franky gave him a sweet smile. 'We did. But even then, you didn't say what was the effect of the supernatural on the ordinary people of the time.'

'Well, you only have to see the witchcraft symbols that joiners inscribed on doors: two rings locked together trying to stop demons from entering a room. It gives you some notion, some idea.' He took a deep breath, eager to leave but formally, without making a scene.

'Yes, okay, so how did it influence the people in power, the Queen, politics? You didn't mention that.'

'I'm sorry. That's for you to find out and me to get a sandwich and a nice mug of British tea. Okay? Thank you all.' His smile faded as he walked quickly into the conservatory, now having no intention of making a fulsome apology. None whatsoever.

Tom planted his hands on the grass behind him, straightened his arms and tilted back his head to take in the sun.

As he did so, a wispy tip of cumulonimbus peeked above the copper beech tree in the garden, dimming the sun's glare.

"Arise, fair sun, and kill the envious moon", he murmured.

'No, kill the sun,' said Franky. 'I hope it pisses down.' It wasn't Woodbridge she hated. It was herself through *him*. Her gift for being vengeful was handed down by *her father*.

She made her way towards the conservatory, her face lowered darkly under the straw hat.

Chapter Two

The next day, as on most mornings before lectures, the students gravitated into the conservatory for general chat.

Without Hannah present, Franky stood apart, not wanting to join in conversation that seemed limited to the cost of bedsit rentals when, having arrived early, she'd already grabbed one of the best apartments in town.

She broke into a smile as Craig appeared at her side.

'I was told to find you. Dr Manson's been taken ill.'

'Oh?'

'Apparently he's going to be off for some time.'

'What's wrong with him?'

'Don't know. In the meantime, you've got Dr Lloyd. She wants to fix a meeting, okay?'

'Yes, I'll text her. Thanks.'

As Craig moved away, Hannah appeared among the red leather chairs carrying a tray with two coffees – and a surprise cookie for Franky.

'Hey, you're a star.' Franky realising, added 'Aren't you having one?'

'No, I'm a cookie junky,' said Hannah perkily. 'Cutting down.'

'Well, how's the bedsit? Keeping warm now?'

'Yes. The landlord fixed the radiator – *at last*! But it's still, you know, I go there, dump my stuff and sleep. And then what happens? They've opened a gastropub right underneath – would you believe that? As a rental online it looked great. And now?' She put an imaginary pistol to the side of her head. 'Bang.' She sat down and picked up her coffee. 'Decided on your dissertation yet?'

'Not yet. I fancy the sense of loss in the tragic heroes. How about yours? You said you might go for pop culture?'

'Yeah. I was thinking of it. Did you ever see Joss Whedon's *Much Ado*? The film, I mean.'

'Yes, I saw it. Interesting, but I don't go along with pop Shakespeare. I know the angle and I take all the hype, but it does nothing for me.'

'No, but what got me was that core darkness he found. You know he shot it in twelve days in his own home? He went from indie cult to mainstream, don't forget.'

'I guess I'm a traditionalist,' said Franky. 'If it brings people to watch Shakespeare at Blackfriars that's great. No problem, let Whedon carry on.'

'He's got loads of fans. He really got me with the line "Shakespeare knew how to throw a party." You know, I was thinking I might do my own vlogging. But no. Hey ho. That's me again.' She paused. 'So, what do you want to do with your MA?'

'Me? Teach. I figure it's best. You too?'

'No. Well, yes, in a way. I want to bring something to people that's not been done and should be done.'

Franky saw Hannah's eyes take on a bright sparkle as though energised by something wonderful to come. 'What's that?'

'I want to form my own group of actors performing Shakespeare. I want to take it to really poor places all over America.'

Franky looked at her, suddenly impressed. 'Hannah the missionary.' She said it without a trace of cynicism.

Hannah caught her wonderment. 'I mean it. I belong to a church group back home. So, we're kind of, you know—'

'Preaching Shakespeare?'

'No.' Hannah laughed.

'But aren't people already doing it out there? There are groups all over America—'

'Sure, there are. There's Shakespeare in subways, street theatre — even parking lots, but mine would be different.'

'But isn't Nancy Bell adapting Shakespeare for different neighbourhoods?

She did the whole of St Louis, remember?'

'Yes, but it wasn't real Shakespeare. She wrote and performed *Blow Winds*, an adaptation of *King Lear*. Know it?'

'Yes, but will the poor turn up? If it were me sleeping in doorways, Shakespeare isn't going to shake my tree much, I know that. I guess if you turned up as a bunch of strolling players with scenery in trucks, parked up somewhere you'd get folk out of curiosity, sure. Hey, have I said the wrong thing? I—'

'No. I know what you're saying. Let me explain. I got the idea last year in Blackwater, Arizona. I don't think you'll ever go there. I went with my church group, helping out. Met one or two bright kids. One young guy came up with a copy of *Hamlet*. It had stains all over it, may have found it in a trash can. He wanted to understand something ... I can't remember what it was. When I explained, it was happy days for us both. I found out later he was a drug runner. I thought "There but for the grace of God", you know? I got his address and cell number. If I get the chance, I'll do something for him. I was fired up, got such a kick out of it, little ole me.' Hannah grinned. 'Seeing me standing outside a clapboard house on a mud road as it started to rain. Yeah...'

She gave an apologetic flick of the hand. 'Well, that's me trying to be the hero, I guess. But it was that young guy who got me thinking about how to do it. So, I've decided to approach three companies on the web – they've got all the plays translated into modern English, free to download. My idea is to feed Shakespeare's original text back in, wherever possible. Those who want to read it can do that before seeing it. I think there's lots I can do without destroying meaning.'

'Sounds great.'

'If I get them to agree and it becomes viable, they'll get credits and publicity, so advertisers will go to them. If I help them make money, I hope they'll freely print off the scripts, if they won't I'll do it myself.'

'I think it's a terrific idea. Even if you don't grab anyone immediately, you're raising a cultural awareness. You're —'

'That's it! That's the idea. If it raises awareness in just one or two that life has got something better to offer —like with the drug runner. It's got to be good. Hasn't it? It's offering life opportunities. I believe there's lots of folk who have talents that are never recognised, either by themselves, or by others. Look, I'm working on it. Let's leave it at that, else I'll get screwed up. I'll solve it, somehow. What do you think? Like it?'

'No, I don't just like it. I've come to the conclusion that it's great.'

'You really mean it?'

'Yes, I do. If anybody can do anything it's you. Blackwater, you said? You're right, I've never been there. So that's where you got the Eureka moment?'

'Yes. But it was my Grandpa, me thinking about him that really got me going. He was the bomber pilot with the teddy bear. After the war he flew a plane to relieve missionaries stranded in Africa. Then he helped form a group to fly food to the poor in the Caribbean and Latin America.'

'Hah,' murmured Franky quietly. 'In the family.' For a moment she felt a stab of jealousy, not for what Hannah intended to do, but for *being her*. 'But you'd need loads of money. Just think of the problems, travel, money, logistics. The website advertising won't pay for all that.'

'I know.' Hannah leaned forward, keeping her voice down. 'I'm going to the NEA in Washington. They fund projects of excellence. I think mine is. Isn't it?'

'Absolutely. What will you call it, "Hannah's Troupe"?

"Hannah's Troupe"? Maybe.' Hannah put a hand down to push herself up from the settee. 'Good for another cookie?'

'No - listen. Don't like to tell you this '— Franky pulled a pained face — 'our great President's threatening to shut down the NEA in next year's budget. Know about that?'

'Yes, I did. That's why I've already emailed the NEA theatre director. If I get in now, I hope to beat it. I'm going to try and list it as an educational organisation. "Internal Revenue Code Section 501. Organisations operating exclusively for educational purposes are tax exempt."'

'You've got it all worked out. Quoting the IRS. You're getting like Tom, wow.'

Hannah chuckled. 'No. Let's be realistic. It's an idea and I'll do my darndest to get it going. If it doesn't work I'll think of something else in Shakespeare land.'

'Meantime you won't be doing Titus and Dronicus for the dissertation.'

'No, so how about Mac and Beth?' Hannah put on a fixed smirk and, puppet-like, jerked her head from side to side, while giggling.

Franky chuckled. 'You've not decided.'

'Yes. I think so. "Insanity in the tragedies."'

'Well,' said Franky, picking up and studying her iPhone. 'I heard my dad say insanity was hereditary, you get it from your kids.'

Hannah laughed, then suddenly glanced at her watch. 'Hey.' She scrambled to her feet. 'C'mon. Gotta go – seminar.'

The seminar was billed *Shakespeare and Love* and was held in the Reading Room off the reception hall. Franky had to smile at the label on the door as she'd not seen anyone actually reading in there, equipped as it was with a projection screen.

She entered the room with Hannah, wondering if she would ever fall in love, but not like Hannah who was all-giving but not receiving. Love? For her it was an emotion too far, as she'd loved nobody, apart from her dog. She sat at the back of the room, idly surveying Alicia and Hannah. Alicia, so far, had not even looked at Craig. But Hannah had - she noted – three times already.

'Take the relationship between Benedict and Beatrice,' said the lecturer, 'and consider how the confused pair were frightened of their attraction to each other.'

This led into a discussion dealing with Shakespeare's treatment of four kinds of love – courtly, unrequited, compassionate and sexual.

It was Tom who cut to the chase. 'I think Shakespeare shows them appreciating each other's inner beauty,' he intoned. 'Their love is idealistic, and that between Claudio and Hero is more realistic and physical. Shakespeare is showing each type of love to his audience, isn't he?'

Franky decided to liven it up a little. 'Look,' she said. 'Hasn't pure love been impossible in any age? Girls today, more of them are keeping their virginity because they're scared of what they've seen of pornography. And isn't Shakespeare showing that, for true love, a couple needs friends, family and the community around them. Love doesn't exist in a vacuum – does it?'

It was Tom who was quick to respond. 'That's fine when judged by the real world today, but isn't it the case that Shakespeare deliberately kept sex in the background through Hero, knowing it could actually cost a lady her life?'

Franky stared at him. She suddenly felt dismayed, her knowledge of *Much Ado About Nothing,* among some other plays was, at the best, only sketchy. It gave way to a bout of irritation. 'Well, I think Benedick's a smart-ass and too clever by half to be loveable,' she snapped out, then grinned as it raised a few laughs. She was particularly pleased when Alicia gave her a smile and nod of approval.

Franky was first out at the end of the seminar and, with Hannah going for a tutorial, went into the Great Hall to make sense of the notes she'd made during the lecture.

Having completed the work, she allowed her eyes to settle on a framed portrait pinned to the wall on the right of the low stage. She'd been told it was the Moroccan ambassador to the court of King Henry VIII. She'd glanced at him a number of times since she'd arrived, but only now wondered why he was there when, apparently, he had nothing to do with the Bard. The ambassador wore a tribal dress and turban. With his right hand resting on a sword, his stare seemed to be aimed directly at her. It was as though he'd joined her in brooding on "things rank and gross in nature".

She gave a short grunt of frustration and went back into the conservatory, determined to come to some conclusion regarding her cottage dilemma. She wanted Hannah, of course she did. But was it wise to invite the insensitive Alicia as well? Her book might benefit but at what price collateral damage? She decided that, on balance, it was better to wait. There was "many a slip betwixt cup and lip."

She returned to the Great Hall, determined not to look at the ambassador. She positioned herself on one of the red chairs around the lengthy oak-panelled walls, fronted by a massive, wide-arched window.

From balancing the pros and cons of having Alicia, as well as Hannah in the cottage, her mind drifted back to the events that had led her to the Institute rather than one of the two outstanding Shakespeare centres back home.

Fergal her father, was mean, despite his wealth, so why hadn't he sent her to Harvard or Ashland? Why go to all that expense? It was a rhetorical question. She knew the answer, but she still thought about it, dreamt about it, went into spasms of rage and guilt about it. So why keep banging on about it, causing her pain? It was because her father was behind all the angst that she suffered, every single bit of it. What he'd done, that Saturday afternoon in April last year, was so shocking that it rendered as nothing all the slights sustained in her life put together and multiplied to the nth degree.

Normally, on arriving home at a weekend, she would hear Fergal playing music in his study. He'd had the room fitted out with all the equipment of the professional market trader, six screens displaying the prices on the major financial and commodity markets around the world. He'd put on red trouser-braces and bow tie for a selfie, showing him sitting proudly at his desk. He'd sent it to all his friends and colleagues. It was the place where he spent time short-selling the stock of companies in trouble. He did it by searching out bad news stories about them, then thinking of ways of cashing in on the falling stock. He was good at trading. Never rash or impetuous, in ten years he'd made three times what he made from teaching.

However, he was not there on that particular afternoon, a day earlier than the start of Boston University's spring break. She'd found him engaged on something more exciting than just making money. Yvette was away visiting her parents who'd retired to live by the sea at La Rochelle.

Franky had written down what happened that day as a blow-by-blow account and had saved it on two memory sticks as well as locking the original in an online vault. She had two reasons for these precautions. Firstly, should her father face arrest at any time, she would have the evidence against him ready in the form of a detailed witness statement. Secondly, because she had a yen for writing, she'd written it in the first person so as to give it a sense of immediacy. After all, it might form part of the novel that she intended to write someday. If she were to be accused of over-dramatising the events she'd witnessed, she would insist that it was an exact narrative, seen and felt through her own eyes and senses, of what had actually taken place:

I climbed the stairs, intending to enter my room, when I heard what sounded like a boy's voice moaning in pain. It seemed to come from my parents' bedroom. I tiptoed across the landing to glance inside the half-open door and saw my father, pants around his ankles, leaning over the back of a naked boy whose hands rested on the foot of the bed. I must have uttered a spontaneous gasp as the boy swivelled his head towards me, his face etched in distress. But it was nothing compared with my father's reaction.

It sent me racing downstairs, distraught, panting heavily. I looked up to see my father on the landing trying to pull up his pants, but then stumbled and cried out as he fell flat on his face. The scene became even more surreal, watching him crawl his way to the balustrade to look down at me, blood pouring from his nose. He tried to address me in teacher mode, but sounded like an alien speaking underwater. I could just make out a few phrases.

'Should ... warned you ... rehearsing ... Roman drama...'

Drops of blood began to splash on to the mahogany floor. Nauseated, I stared down at them as he tried to carry on.

'Sex with males...' he whimpered. 'Jason here ... Imperial period ... are you ... okay ... huh? Don't tell Mom ... sure to ... wrong.'

At this point he realised the futility of it all, for he suddenly let out a loud groan followed by a long and terrible shudder, at which I fled outside as if part of a nightmare movie. With a great bang of thunder and dense black clouds gathering, I raced breathlessly across a large expanse of grass to enter woodland, there to hurry through its dark and forbidding interior to a clearing where, as a child, I'd made up imaginary friends in fighting monsters. I took hold of one of the ropes that was secured to an overhead branch. Hand over hand and with feet locked, I hauled myself up to reach the branch from which I climbed towards the sky.

There, among the treetops, I stared at the house, a sharp ink-black silhouette. The first time I watched the Godfather trilogy I'd imagined home as the kind of place Don Corleone would have chosen, with its dark rooms and dominant square tower overlooking the high, church-like frontage, a Gothic, funereal place.

I stared at The Stars and Stripes fluttering lazily on a side roof and then, as the sky grew darker, hung motionless. At that moment I felt like letting loose with a high-velocity automatic gun, raking the doors and windows of the house until the magazine, as well as my rage, was spent. I stayed to watch the clouds gather into a grey mass. After a ripple of thunder, fat raindrops spattered on the surrounding canopy and, with my head raised, I welcomed them until I was saturated. Then I started my descent, shimmying down the rope to let go and land softly on the thick sponge of decaying leaves.

I left the wood to stand out on the grassy sward and greet the thundering downpour with my legs and arms apart, an exercise punctuated by an occasional scream at the heavens. I thought of suicide, of staging it so it looked like he'd murdered me, and how wonderful, superbly fitting that would be, my father left with more blood on his hands. I would post a letter to the police beforehand, telling them what I'd witnessed and giving the name of the boy, Jason.

I walked back towards the house and flinched at a crack of lightning, followed shortly by another bang of thunder. I saw that his car was not in its usual parking space. He'd fled, taking the boy with him. I went up to my room and found a bloodstained note lying on the bed:

The Shakespeare Institute, England, has a one-year course for an MA or PhD. One of my students went there. You love Shakespeare. It's made for you. If you go I'll give you $25,000 plus the course fee. But this is between the two of us. No one else must know.

Lingering under the hot shower, I found the idea exciting. A year in Stratford-upon-Avon. He was right about my love of Shakespeare. Although my ambition was to go to Harvard, I thought of the lifestyle I would have in England. I would need plenty of money, of course. His attempt at bribery was only an opening bid, obviously. He'd have to raise it substantially. The beauty of it all was that not one iota of guilt would lie on my conscience. A bribe can't be construed as blackmail, and so I replied with a note asking for $35,000, a fair compensation for the shock I'd received and pointing out that it would be at no cost to him if I failed to report him to the police.

I placed the note on his bed then went down to the kitchen to start making *myself a meal. Suddenly I stopped, sickened by what I'd witnessed. Instead, I took a bottle of wine to my room. He was back within the hour. A few minutes later I heard him push a note under my door. It said that he agreed to my terms, adding that he "had a bad headache" and so wouldn't be joining me for a meal that evening. I felt like sending it back saying "Then starve."*

He never looked me in the eye after that, only to reply tersely to domestic questions.

After reading it twice Franky deleted all reference to "*money*" and "*compensation*" – far too dangerous.

Nine months after the boy's rape, Franky was on her way to England, thinking what she could do with all that spending money. She went to sleep over Canada and woke up somewhere over the Scottish isles.

It was then that a little spike of conscience penetrated her feel-good sensation. She had to be honest with herself. Yes, he'd bribed her, but she'd upped the ante, as well as failing to inform the police. She'd freed him to go on assaulting other young victims. Wasn't she aiding him in his crimes? Okay, but what if the victim she saw was the *only one*? Oh, that was comforting. Yes, it was likely, because he would have known that creating multiple victims would increase the risk of being caught. On the heels of that encouraging thought came one even better: wouldn't he have been so scared of what his daughter might do that it could have curtailed his abominations?

It was permissible to go on taking his money.

Conscience satisfied.

Chapter Three

Franky stood outside an office on the first landing of the spiral staircase that led up from reception. The door opened and out came a student who exchanged a quick smile with her, before trotting downstairs. The person remaining in the room was a forty-year-old woman dressed entirely in black, but whose smile was immediately warm and welcoming.

Dr Lloyd put out her hand. 'Francoise. Come in.'

'Thank you, Doctor.'

She was invited to sit in a worn, but comfortable-looking leather armchair. As she did so, she was conscious of a faintly sweet and musky perfume, an echo of a summer evening spent in a Tuscan vineyard, the balmy air carrying traces of sage and rosemary.

'I'm so sorry you've had to switch tutors,' said Dr Lloyd, closing the door. 'But I'll try and make the transition easy.' She sat down at her desk. 'Now, I like first names. You like to be called?'

'Franky.'

'Franky, of course. I'm Annabelle.'

Franky was charmed by her dulcet voice, the large dark eyes and soulful face. Almost tangible was the calm that seemed to flow from her.

'So, Franky, as I'm also your welfare may I ask where you're staying?'

'I've got an apartment in High Street. And everything's fine.'

'Good. Are you all right for money, have you a part-time job?'

'No need. I'm good for money.'

'Even better. May I ask what your parents do?'

'Mom stays home. She does volunteer work. Dad teaches English and drama. He specialises in Shakespeare. He, erm…' She was about to add something, but checked herself in time.

Annabelle waited a moment, smiling expectantly. 'Yes? You were going to say?' She put up a hand against a beam of sunshine in her eyes. 'You were going to say something about your father.' She stood up to draw the curtain over part of the window. 'Is there a problem?'

'Oh no. All I meant to say was that's why he sent me here. Shakespeare. He knew I loved it.'

'So why did you hesitate?' Annabelle's smile widened in anticipation. As she sat down, she gave a self-deprecating shake of her hands. 'Stop prying, Annabelle. I'm sorry, I'm only trying to help.'

'Erm, it's just that he makes a lot of money.' Franky paused. 'In fact, I can afford to go on for the PhD,' she added quickly.

'Oh, that would be wonderful!' Annabelle's face lit up. Then it dissolved a little as she put her head to one side, her features settling into a solicitous expression. 'But do say. *Is* there a problem with your father?' Her voice remained soft and gentle. 'Is there something bothering you? That's what I'm here for. If there is, it's best to share it with someone, don't you think?'

'No. There isn't anything – really. I saw on the website that you're studying the cultural history of emotions, especially sadness in Shakespeare's time?'

'Yes. "How weary, stale, flat, and unprofitable seem to me all the uses of this world!" Annabelle chuckled lightly.

'Yes.' Franky smiled back. 'Pretty shitty at times.'

'Are *you* sad, Franky?'

'No – I'm fine.'

'I only ask because you were quick to change the subject.' Annabelle smiled sympathetically. 'There *is* something, isn't there? Don't be afraid. I'm not qualified in counselling, but it's all about listening. Nothing you tell me will leave this room. I promise.'

Franky took a deep breath, then exhaled. 'I, erm …'

'Relax.' Annabelle instinctively stretched out her arm. 'Take your time.'

'Well, yes … it's just that he never loved me. I don't exist in his universe. He never talks to me. He's locked up in himself. It kind of makes me depressed at times.'

'I'm sure it does. I'm so sorry. *That* is really sad. I had wonderful parents. And children need to be loved, don't they?'

'Yes,' said Franky, unsure as to where all this was going. She wished she'd not mentioned her father. 'The worst thing is…' her lips moved a little, trying to find words … 'it's my hair.'

'Your hair?'

'Yes. It's screwed me up since childhood. People calling me names, you know the kind of thing?'

'The colour of your hair, you mean?'

'Yes.'

'Oh.' Annabelle frowned and sat back. 'I've never come across that before.'

'Oh, yes. I've been called "ginger" many times — even "Red." Because I'm the only one in the family with red hair I did feel, you know…'

'Isn't that amazing? I know there's a myth that redheads are hot-tempered but it's never been proved. Look.' Annabelle held out the flat of her hands, closing the subject. 'Let's leave that for now.' She looked at her desk diary. 'Let's leave it until our welfare meeting. Would you like that?

'Yes, I would.'

'Let's see.' Annabelle scanned the diary. 'Okay, I have a tutorial with you next Monday at half past ten. The welfare session, shall we say the following Friday afternoon at two thirty? Is that all right?'

'Yes.' Franky made a note.

Annabelle leaned forward, planting a hand firmly on the desk, in emphasis. 'I will promise you complete confidentiality. Is that all right with you?'

'Yes. Yes, of course it is.'

Annabelle stood up. 'Good. Write down all that worries you. Try to be as objective as possible so we can deal with whatever it is. Now, if you want to cancel that's fine. I won't hassle you, I promise.'

'Yes. I'm really grateful. Thank you, so much.'

Franky went down the stairs in a glorious daze. Clearly Annabelle didn't need colourful clothes to impress. She had a face that drew you in, not exactly beautiful but, framed by lustrous black hair, with flawless skin and large dreamy eyes, she was attractive and warmly appealing.

Franky had been told by another student, who knew someone from the previous course, that the joke at the Institute was that she wore black in celebration of the late Elizabethan cult of melancholy. It fitted. She thought that Annabelle was so sensitive, that she could well suffer from sadness, the very subject she was studying and saw in her a soul mate, perhaps?

She continued descending the stairs, marvelling at her discovery. Annabelle was going to be a treasure. A bolt of euphoria surged through her body. She wanted to lose herself, to find fresh air and countryside, to romp in fields, to run on grass, slip through trees.

She went into the kitchen.

'Coffee?' Hannah stood there, waiting for the kettle to boil.

'No, thanks. I need water.' She made for the sink, but Hannah was there first, sticking a glass under the cold water tap and quickly filling it. 'There you go,' she said, handing it over.

'Thanks.' Franky took a long, greedy gulp.

'Sorted out your new tutor yet?' With the click of the boiling kettle, Hannah pulled forward a mug and slipped in a teaspoon of coffee.

'Have I!' she gasped, putting the glass down. 'I've got Annabelle. I'm so excited. She's fabulous.'

'I'm really glad for you.' Hannah poured hot water into her mug. 'I like her lots.'

'Hey. I'm free this afternoon. Want to come for a walk in the country? I'm going now.'

'No, I can't. I've got a tutorial.'

'Oh, of course, yeah.' She drained the glass. 'What time does it finish?'

'About five.'

'Okay. I'm taking you to a cafe to die for. I'll treat you to an old-fashioned English tea, scone, cream and jam and don't talk about calories.' She poked a finger. 'You're thin enough. Fancy it?'

'Oh, yes, that would be great.' Hannah put milk in her coffee. 'But I'm paying.'

'No. You are not paying. My treat.'

'You've got to stop this.'

'Stop what?'

'Being good to me.'

For some reason they both laughed.

Franky took a bus towards the village of Snitterfield, getting off a stop early. She crossed the road to where a stile stood in the hedgerow. She stepped up, eased herself through its narrow gap and took a step down into the field. There, she checked an Ordnance Survey map that she'd bought but, so far, had never used.

With a big smile on her face, she strode quickly along a worn footpath, the sun low, its rays shining golden among the trees. It cast a long shadow ahead as she walked.

Halfway across the field she stopped to look around. The smell of burning leaves reminded her of the time when her father, oddly for him, arranged a fabulous Halloween party at home. Normally she was taken elsewhere. It was the feel and smell of a particular autumnal evening that she remembered, a big starry sky, a roaring fire, warm slices of juicy pumpkin pie, carpets of crackly dried leaves, the pungent smell of cinnamon and cloves, a scarecrow on the porch, jack-o'-lanterns ... voluptuous and intoxicating.

During that same evening she'd gone into the house to use the bathroom and saw her father through the open door of his study. He was with the father of two children he'd brought to the party. The jargon they used – "scalping", "spot price" and "cross hedge" – were three terms that she later googled, coming up with "Commodity Market Futures."

The following day she had the temerity to ask her father who the guy was. He looked pleased by the question and responded with a fat smile.

'He's the Director of the US Commodity Futures Trading Commission.'

So that was great. The party hadn't been for her, but for him.

Typical.

After a few more fields the path led towards a wood. It was there that she stopped to gaze at what had once been a signpost. It stood by a stile, now just a footstep with jagged pieces of wood jutting upwards.

She hesitated and checked her map. It showed red-dotted symbols of a footpath skirting the wood, whereas it seemed in reality to go straight through it. She stared into its dark interior ... uninviting. It reminded her of that day — the boy— *him*.

She turned to retrace her steps when, suddenly, out from the wood came the shrill bark of a dog, followed immediately by the snap of a woman's voice.

'Rufus! Come back!'

From out of the wood a small dog raced through shadows into light and was now making a beeline for her.

'Aagh!' Franky rammed her legs together, her arms wrapped round her stomach.

'Rufus!'

A woman was hurrying towards her, but Franky's fearful eyes were fixed on the dog, its ears pinned back as it eagerly forced itself under the stile footstep.

'Stop it! *Rufus!*'

The dog, its ears freed, began to race around Franky, still barking.

'You little devil! You're safe with me my lover, don't worry.' The woman spoke in a curly and attractive West Country accent. 'He gets himself all of a quiver. Never sees nobody. When he does, he makes a fuss.'

It was a tiny lady who stepped awkwardly over the stile. She wore a black chimney-pot hat banded with leopard-print, the dog's lead in her hands.

'Rufus! Here, boy!' She grabbed hold of its ruff and attached the lead. Standing upright, she tipped her hat back to reveal large brown eyes outlined in thick, black mascara.

'Did he give you a fright?'

'He did, yes.' Franky was out of breath.

'Sorry. I let him off the lead as there's nobody around, except at weekends. Coming for a reading, was you?'

'Pardon me?'

'Obviously not. You sound American. Are you?'

'Yes, I am.'

'Where you heading to?'

'Nowhere. I'm just walking. I'm going back to the road.'

The woman stared at Franky, her eyes growing bigger. 'For your sake,' she said, 'it's wise not to take too many risks. Take care, my lover. You take care in your life.'

She nodded firmly, before turning round to cross the stile, retracing her steps. 'Now, Rufus, no more … I'll give it you, upsetting my lady.'

Franky stood still, regaining her breath and listening to the chattering voice until she was out of sight.

'Annabelle.' As she waited at the bus stop, she kept repeating her name, letting it ripple softly through her head. She would be her therapist, her safe haven. But then, as before, she reminded herself not to be seduced by her charm. She needed to stay vigilant, to remain secretive about the large amount of money she'd deposited in the local Lloyds Bank. She would not talk about her father's rape of the boy, nor the note that she'd written to him demanding a legal 'power of attorney', ensuring that she had control of his finances when he reached seventy.

She was pleased with herself. She had the whip hand. He was dancing to her tune, and why not? It was some recompense for her trauma and no less deserved. Bolstering her confidence was the knowledge that, under the Massachusetts penal statutes, the crime of child rape was punishable by life imprisonment without parole. She would never forget the boy's name or face. She could destroy him at any moment. It gave her the kind of replete feeling she got following a delicious meal.

The bus arrived and stopped for her, alone. After paying, she sat down in the warmth, picturing *him* again, as she had so many times, peering down at her through the gallery rails, while globules of blood fell to splat on the mahogany floor. It was ironic to recall that, at one time in her short life, she'd wanted him to love her as a father should, so making it easy for her to love him, in which case she would not have grown up to be the wounded person she was.

How she hated and despised him.

Stepping off the bus she walked into Church Street, approaching the Institute. It reminded her of the day she first set eyes on Mason Croft, as it was known prior to it becoming the Institute in 1951. It was now the world centre of postgraduate Shakespearean study where, by custom and tradition, nearly half the students were American. At college she'd written an essay on Marie Corelli, the British best-selling novelist who came to live there in 1900. It was said that she'd entertained a visitor, who claimed to have seen the ghost of a woman in Tudor style clothing pass through the Great Hall. Franky recalled the frisson of excitement she'd felt on her first glimpse of the odd, pointed gables above the large eighteenth-century facade.

She had time to kill before she met Hannah. Sitting in the Great Hall she watched dust motes floating in a shaft of light that pierced the immense single window.

The red exit-lighting above the doors gave the place the feeling of an auditorium, for that was its function during the staging of the annual production by the Institute Players, the amateur dramatic society to which all students were expected to belong. She was particularly keen to perform as, in this academic year, it promised not only a Shakespeare production but also "an exciting, innovative, and creative interpretation of plays of the Renaissance period, otherwise known as the "early modern."

There was nothing of that youthful enthusiasm now in the Great Hall, just a heavy, sobering silence, impregnated with the faint smell of musty air.

She breathed slowly, trying to think of her mind as separate from her body, aiming to become a "self-observer," as the therapist had advised.

Her thoughts turned to Annabelle and how good their session had made her feel.

Chapter Four

It was Monday morning and, as arranged, Franky was invited into Annabelle's office to discuss ideas for her dissertation.

'Before we begin, Franky, have you been writing down your feelings for our welfare session on Friday?'

'Yes, I have, thanks,' said Franky, sitting down in the worn and crackly leather armchair.

'And?' Annabelle smiled enquiringly. 'How did you feel— or how are you *still* feeling?'

'I felt better, more in control. Yes, I'm fine.'

'Oh, that's good. I had a student last year who was depressed, and the business of writing down everything that troubled her, followed by talking about it, really worked. It really did. I'm pleased for you.'

'And I'm really grateful, thanks.'

'Good. So, back to dissertation mode … where are we…'

As Annabelle studied her screen, Franky felt it was like lying on a warm Caribbean beach listening to the rhythmic hiss of low breaking waves. How was it that she could radiate such magnetism? Was it from a combination of voice and looks? The day before, she'd searched for a word to mean a sense of repleteness, contentment and calm. She'd come up with the word "sukha", a term used in the Indian subcontinent.

'Sukha'… she breathed the word. It was a gentle sound. And did it come from the soul, with powers of healing the mind? If so, Annabelle had got it in bundles. She felt completely relaxed in the company of her new-found saviour.

'Yes, your topic.'

Annabelle's voice jerked her back to awareness.

'You want to examine two tragic heroes, their vision of the world as well as yours. Through that prism their sense of loss and yours would be examined in relation to Shakespeare's existentialism.'

'Yes. I'd like to choose Hamlet and —'

'Oh, I'm sorry Franky.' Annabelle broke in, with an apologetic grimace. 'You wouldn't have space for two, I'm afraid. A dissertation is only 15,000 words. You can only deal with one tragic hero.'

'Then it's Hamlet. I feel closer to him than any other character in Shakespeare, in terms of sense of loss, I mean.'

'Oh. Oh dear. That's a pity.'

'A pity, why?'

'We do have a problem, I'm afraid. Amazing though it is, we've another student who's come up with a similar topic. He's also talking about his sense of loss, but in a different way. You know we encourage students to discuss their ideas with one another, but he's been through an awful experience and wants to deal with it privately.'

Franky stared at her, blinking rapidly, knowing exactly who she meant. 'Oh. But, if his is done in a different way, as you put it, why can't mine …' she tailed off at Annabelle's pained and sympathetic expression.

'Unfortunately,' she said, 'I don't make the decision about dissertations, not on my own. All the staff discuss each proposal. We consider the personalities and the strengths of students when allocating them, and I doubt it would get through in this case.'

'But the decision's not been made yet?'

'No. But, as I say—'

'But after I sent it, you emailed back to say the topic was interesting and you wanted to talk …' Franky faltered.

'I know. Yes, I did. I did indeed. It's just that his came in after that. I'm pretty certain his will take precedence, I'm sorry to say. It's no reflection on you, believe me.' She hesitated at Franky's expression. 'I know you're disappointed. Don't be. I've another idea that could be just as enticing.'

'Oh.' Franky's brows softened.

'But first, there's something I must say about this submission. Not that I expect it will be passed.' She gestured at her screen. 'I'm slightly worried. It paints your father in a rather unpleasant light, doesn't it?'

'I was talking about my feelings towards him so I had to—'

'Yes, of course. I understand that but—'

'Is that the reason for dropping it?'

'Oh, no. I'm mentioning this just in case your father gets to hear of it or, God forbid, he actually reads it. I'm now wearing my welfare hat. Don't you think it could land you in trouble?' she added tentatively. 'With him, I mean.'

'I don't think so. I know him. He wouldn't want to read it.'

'Maybe not. But what if others pointed it out to him?'

'It wouldn't worry me, Annabelle. I promise. And he won't get to read it, I promise.'

'Oh. Well, that's good.' I don't think it will be given the nod so …' she gave Franky a reassuring smile … 'onwards and upwards.' She went back to her screen.

Now,' she tapped the keyboard, 'let's go to sunnier uplands. Your essay, "A Shakespeare Performance" is impressive.'

'Oh, thank you.'

Why is she bothered about my father?

'You dealt with Henry Goodman's Shylock in a National Theatre production some years ago. Now, why not consider Shylock for your dissertation? You know that some actors who play him, report real problems? He could have been a Russian Jew facing the pogroms, or in Germany with the Nazis. He's the universal Jew in terms of being outcast, an outsider. It led to a study being carried out. Some actors playing Shylock reported that it affected them offstage. Some said that the more compelling their performance, the more teasing they got from other members of the cast. And not just teasing — sometimes they'd even been ostracised. I find it astonishing.'

'As I do,' said Franky, frowning. 'Unbelievable.'

'It shows how Antisemitism is still embedded in this world. When I was at school it was common for kids to say "You've been jewed," conned out of something. And now, despite the Holocaust, there's the issue of how we deal with it *now*, today. The British Labour Party has problems with its hard left, simply because their support for Palestinian Arabs is often equated with an inbred dislike of the Jewish race as a whole, seeing Israel as an outpost of western capitalism, and they want to get rid of it. I find that appalling, too, considering that Israel was built on socialist principles. The kibbutzim were actually communist in practice.'

'Erm, do you mean I'd be dealing with Shylock, how I relate to him in a social and historic context?'

'Yes. Think about it. It could be that you and Shylock may produce a synergy worth exploring. Is that something you'd like to do? Don't feel forced. We've plenty of time to decide.'

'Yes. Sure, I'll think about it.'

'Well, good.' Annabelle looked at her diary. 'So then, we meet for welfare on Friday at two thirty.'

'Yes.'

'Remember,' said Annabelle, tapping out another note on the keyboard, 'if you need to see me earlier, if anything interferes with your work, don't be afraid to text me. I'm always there for you. Well, you know that.' She gave Franky a further, reassuring smile.

Franky walked towards the library, a modern building reached by a footpath, leading from the conservatory to meander through tall shrubbery. She felt relieved, as she'd started to panic when Annabelle dismissed her topic, but now she felt secure again, wrapped in her warm cloak of concern and compassion.

But, why was she *concerned* about her father? When she mentioned him, there seemed a glint in her eye that, together with a forward movement of the head, betokened some kind of personal involvement, displaying a scintilla of urgency that went beyond what was supposed to be a purely scholastic discussion.

And then there was Craig. She knew about his loss, as did most. but she'd never seen him as anything but easy-going. Had she missed something? To her he seemed as happy as a sand boy. Of course, he'd lost his wife and child together in horrid circumstances, two grievous events. But the pain of losing loved ones diminishes with time, whereas her pain, she was convinced, would never diminish. At least Craig had experienced love that was received and given, a blessing that she'd never enjoy. He would surely meet someone again, someone he could love, so easing his burden, whereas she'd sustained a shock of such magnitude that it would remain with her for the rest of her life.

She could kick herself. Why hadn't she placed the child rape at the centre of her submission? Hardly a day passed by without seeing the boy's face, inflicted by the sheer horror of what she'd witnessed. It might have swung the decision back in her favour. At that moment, she'd willingly exchange her sense of loss for Craig's bereavement. Time would never heal the gaping wound in *her* psyche.

She entered the library, clicking through the chrome turnstile. There was the librarian looking up from her desk, a bright-faced young woman, her hair in flaxen ringlets. She readily took her request for literature on the subject of actors playing Shylock while pointing to a source that she could research herself. In the meantime, she would try to produce copies of newspaper and magazine articles that might be of assistance.

Franky was impressed. She could now appreciate why the library was considered to be the best in the world of Shakespearean studies. If anything deemed worthwhile was published, it would reside there.

After some searching, she found what she was looking for, quotes from actors who had played Shylock. The first, that she read, confirmed what Annabelle had said:

Patrick Stewart. *Royal Shakespeare Company: I've found, while playing Shylock, that others playing him say much the same thing, that in the company of the other actors they find themselves being treated as an outsider: I've never been teased and made fun of more than I have on those occasions. People gang up on you, all very odd and a little sinister.*

Having read one or two quotes she was led to understand that the "Hath not a Jew eyes?" speech was not just a cry of pain from an oppressed man; it also posed the question as to how the persecuted could become the persecutor, as alluded to by Anthony Sher, who had also played Shylock with the RSC. He admitted that his South African upbringing had given him "a syndrome that worried him all his life."

With a strong 'entry point' to the topic she worked hard in getting down her thoughts. An hour later, she began to relax.

She looked into the opposite alcove across the aisle. There sat Maggie, an elderly English lady with silvery hair and a trim figure. She was reading a book, her notes and pen placed neatly on the table. Franky had met her in the kitchen a few times and they'd chatted while preparing lunch.

As she lived in Stratford, Maggie's expenses were limited to the course fees. Her husband, Jack, a retired local solicitor, was still working as a public notary in the mornings and, on two afternoons a week, was a keen active member of the Stratford Boat Club, a frequent competitor in local regatta.

Their lifestyle, according to Maggie, was "superb." She had never been so happy. With a Mediterranean diet, meditation, lots of exercise and scholastic study, she had all the necessary ingredients for a healthy mind and body in old age.

Franky envied her, wishing that she, herself, was old and happily working on something she loved, the passing of the years easing her discontent.

Maggie caught Franky's gaze and gave a smile, but then it faded as she seemed to be staring through her. 'Franky. Are you all right?' She leaned forward a little. 'You okay?' she half-whispered.

Franky suddenly blinked hard. 'Oh – yes.' It came out stilted. 'Oh, I'm sorry, Maggie. I was just thinking of something. Got to go.'

She gathered up her books and cuttings file. Why be depressed? She was going to see out the academic year in style, wasn't she? And with Annabelle's assistance and four students joining her in a gorgeous cottage, she'd be cutting down the time she was prey to loops. Wasn't that the aim given her by the psychotherapist?

She gave Maggie a quick smile and, before leaving, thanked the librarian for her great service.

A minute later she entered the conservatory to find Hannah, its sole occupant, sat in one of the armchairs and reading a book.

She looked up as Franky approached.

'Coffee?' said Franky. 'My turn, I think.'

'No, it isn't. It's mine.' Hannah got up quickly to go into the narrow passageway. 'Got something to tell you.'

Franky followed her into the kitchen, annoyed with herself. Why worry about inviting Alicia and Hannah into her fold? If she was serious about writing a novel then a little drama now and then, if not providing literary inspiration, wouldn't be allowed to get out of control, she'd make sure of that.

But she still worried. Was she being idiotic, kidding herself that writing fiction would be less stressful than teaching? Authors came in all sizes and colours, but few reached a healthy old age. While in the library she'd looked up age expectancy for authors. A Dr Kaufman of California State University reported that, of the last 1,987 novelists to die around the world, their life expectancy had been a mere sixty-six years. Their problem, apparently, was that they didn't exercise enough to combat the ill effects of sitting at a desk all day.

She would take up jogging – yes, she would. It was also supposed to help cure depression as well as maintain an active brain. But why was her heart beating fast? It was happening at least once a day. She would mention it to Annabelle. If sitting with her was a calming experience then she would need to see her more often. Hannah had the opposite effect by livening her up, but in a good way. She was important, as was Annabelle, in her life. Keeping the friendship of both of them was a priority above everything else, she decided.

Hannah showed her the cookie tin.

'Thanks,' she said, taking one.

'Take two, if you want.'

'Okay, I will. So, what's the news?'

'I had an email back from the NEA theatre director.' Hannah switched on the kettle. 'She says that grants are guaranteed to be available until the President's next budget, and that's a year away.'

'So that gives you time.'

'Yes, and get this, she says no one individual or group has submitted to date anything along the lines I propose.'

'That's great.' Franky waved a cookie as she munched. 'They like it.'

'I hope so. You see, I have to apply as an organisation because individual grants are only for creative writing.'

'Oh. That's bad.'

'It is. It means a heck of a lot more work.'

'So, what's next?'

'She says as soon as I have the organisation worked out, the prospectus and so on, I should apply. Know something? I nearly didn't come here, but now I'm glad I did. You've helped me Franky, you really have.'

'Have I, how?'

'By being you.' Hannah raised her eyebrows with a smile.

Franky stared at her for a moment. Then, suddenly, she pulled out a tissue from under her sleeve.

'What?' Hannah put her head to one side, her smile fading. 'Hey, what have I said?' She put down her coffee. 'You okay?'

'Yep.' Impulsively Franky grabbed hold of her and gave her a hug.

'Hey,' said Hannah, laughing. 'What's going on here?'

'Listen.' Franky, still hugging her, talked quickly over her shoulder. 'How would you like to swap your benighted dump for a cottage? A genuine wow Elizabethan four-bedroom with original oak beams.' She pulled away from Hannah, grinning at her, a tear on her cheek.

'What!' Hannah's frown grew intense. '*What* did you say?'

'It's not far from Anne Hathaway's cottage.'

'Franky what—'

'A Tudor cottage, sister girl!' Franky shook her shoulders. 'It's for rent. Wanna come?'

'Yes! Sure. Tomorrow? What *is* this?'

'You don't fancy it?'.

'Franky. You're a razz. Pull somebody else's chain. I haven't a clue what you're—'

'Okay, okay.' Franky put a finger to her mouth. 'Shh. Let's sit down and I'll tell you.'

Hannah followed Franky into the conservatory, her brows knitted.

'How much do you pay a month for your place?' Franky put down her coffee on a low table, before sitting.

'Six hundred pounds.' Hannah regained her armchair opposite, carefully placing the coffee mug on its wide arm.

When she looked up Franky was busy tapping a calculator. 'What are you doing?'

'I'm thinking of recruiting three others… Would they pay on average the same for theirs?'

'Yes, I think so but, come on, hey, stop. I can't—'

'Nearly there.' Franky put up a hand, clicking the result. 'Okay.' She did another calculation.

'Franky.' Hannah shook her head. 'What the heck are you doing?'

'Right … okay, you're outta there.'

Hannah stared in bewilderment.

'You four each pay what you're paying now, around £3,600 for the year. I pay the rest.'

'Franky, you're goofing on me. C'mon!'

'No, I'm telling you.' Franky spoke firmly. 'I want the pleasure of your company, all four of you. If it costs me, that's my problem not yours.'

Hannah, still staring, lowered her voice, daring herself to say it. 'Franky,' she said slowly. 'Are your parents that rich?'

'No. I've just had money left me by an aunt. I can afford it.'

'Oh my God.' Hannah sat upright, straight-faced. 'You mean it. Now I know why you aren't having to work nights and weekends like us. You *are* rich.'

'Not rich. It was a one-off sum from a trust fund.' Franky took a sip of coffee. 'Are you in?'

'I… this is crazy. You're actually going to subsidise me. Why, what for?'

'Because I *want* you there. It's going to be fun.' She leaned forward, putting up an arm for a high-five.

Hannah's face broke into a huge grin. '*Yes!*' she exploded, slapping Franky's palm.

'Now God be praised, that to believing souls comes light from darkness.'

'Oh my God, I can't believe it. Who are the other three?' Hannah's voice, though thrilled, suddenly became hushed.

'I don't know yet. I'll have them by the end of the day. But they'll be interesting. I want it to be fun.'

'Just a minute. Five? Five people in a tiny cottage?'

'No, it's not tiny. There's an extension. It's got four bedrooms, one with twin beds, two bathrooms, two separate toilets— they call them loos over here. The one downstairs is a cloakroom and there's a laundry room as well.'

'I can't believe it.'

'But the *pièce de résistance*. Guess what?'

Hannah shook her head.

'A massive fireplace.'

Hannah clapped a hand to her mouth. 'You mean a Tudor inglenook?'

'Tudor kosher. Thin red-brick and half a tree across its top. Two people can actually sit inside it, either side of the fire.'

'Oh my!' Hannah's mouth was wide open. 'I don't believe this. Swear you mean it.'

'I've told you—'

'No, swear!'

'I swear.' Franky put up her hand. "On my honour I will try to serve God, my country and be a sister to every Girl Scout."

'And make the world a better place.' Hannah, giggling, slapped it. 'I was in the Girl Scouts. Tell me more about our fantastical new abode.' She eagerly dunked her cookie into her mug.

'Okay. Picture this. In summer nasturtiums are in pots outside a front door that's wreathed in roses. Sheep in the next field. It's magic.'

Hannah stared at her. 'Ye gods and little fishes,' she breathed.

'So? Yes or no?' Franky popped the rest of the cookie into her mouth. 'Well, go on, yes or no?' She was suddenly convulsed in laughter, spitting out crumbs. 'Sorry!'

'Yes! Good grief, *of course yes*! I'm still pole axed. Erm, were you going to ask Craig? He's easy-going, he'd be no trouble.'

Franky smiled. 'Guess what? Now you've mentioned him, he's my next port of call.'

'What else has the cottage got?' Hannah was eager to skate over Craig as a subject.

'Fabulous decor. Built-in furniture. And wait till you see the bathrooms. One's got a whirlpool.'

'No more, book me in!' Hannah's voice and manner suddenly became urgent. 'But don't, I mean, don't mention me to Craig. Unless he asks, and if he's in. I don't want to, you know…'

'I promise. Don't worry.'

'I've got a tutorial. Must go.'

Hannah packed and zipped her bag and then, as Franky stood up, impulsively threw both arms around her neck.

'I was at Ohio Uni for three years,' she whispered, 'living in a real dump and working for three dollars an hour, waiting tables.' She released Franky and stood back, a sparkle of tears in her eyes. 'Tis a consummation devoutly to be wished.'

Franky manfully grasped her shoulders. 'And guess what?'

'What?'

'If I get the other three, I'm taking you all out for a meal, tonight. If not, tomorrow.'

'Oh, Franky that's fantastic but I can't let you pay for a meal as well!'

''Tis no matter.' Franky raised a hand beatifically, halting her protest. 'Now go to my lord.'

'Oh, gladly, kind sir!'

Hannah gave a little skip and hurried through the doorway to the Great Hall, but then stopped dead.

She turned round and came back, shaking her head in embarrassment. 'I forgot to tell you, I'm diabetic.' She stood there, a picture of dejection. 'I should have said. '

'Hannah. You told me.'

'Oh … oh yes, I remember. Sorry.'

'Calm down. You're all ordering what you want. Any problems, I pay.'

'Oh, thanks.' Hannah exhaled. 'That's great. Simply great … yes …' She put on a bright smile. '*Right*, I go to my kind lord!' She went quickly, nearly tripping over Franky's bag in her excitement.

Franky, watching Hannah disappear, felt a trifle disappointed. She'd offered her a magical year at her own expense, and she'd made her answer partly dependent on her choosing Craig. Well, she was sick with love for him and for that could be forgiven. Nevertheless, it had taken away a little bit of pleasure. But then what did she expect? To be lauded, worshipped? She'd got what she sought, happiness and ease, the feel-good that had been lacking all her life, hadn't she? She could have been Scrooge, waking up on Christmas morning, ready to give the "intelligent and delightful" boy half a crown to buy the prize turkey.

She sighed and took the coffee mugs back to the kitchen. Yes, she did envy Hannah as she, herself, would never learn to love anyone, of that she felt certain. Fond of, yes, but that was about her limit.

As she washed up, she felt really good about herself. At that moment in time, she had the strong chance of getting the continuing gratitude from four people over a period of ten months and that was uplifting in itself, wasn't it?

At least it was more appealing than cutting throats, stabbing or beheading people, that was for sure.

Chapter Five

After the lecture, Franky went out for a walk around the two-and-a-half-acre garden and came across Tom, hidden behind a bush, by the brick wall. He had a cigarette in his hand. He winced on seeing her.

'Oh. I didn't know you smoked, Tom?'

He raised a hand in surrender and sighed, before stubbing the butt against brickwork. 'Caught … exposed, a capital offence.'

She watched ants behind his lowered head crawling like a brown thread along the red-bricked wall.

'Tom. May I ask you something?'

He stood up, smacking his hands together. 'Hah. "May I." I'm usually suspicious when I hear those words.'

'Really? Why?' It was difficult not to laugh.

'Because it betokens the possibility of extracting something from me and so I'm cautious.'

'No, not this, I promise — well, I suppose it is in a way.'

'*There,* you see!' He poked a finger at her.

'It's just curiosity – no – it's not. It's plain nosiness. It's just that I heard you majored in forensics at Florida State. Is that true?'

'Another confession. Yes. At their College of Criminology and Criminal Justice.'

'Oh. So why? I mean what are you doing here? Why aren't you helping to solve homicides?'

'I decided that human nature was more interesting than human bodies.'

She frowned. 'Okay, they take you here with a forensic degree, for *Shakespearean* studies?'

'I took a diversionary route. I decamped to Harvard to do English literature.'

'Hey. You have two degrees?' She squinted at him in disbelief.

'I like to play the dilettante.'

'What did you get – no, don't tell me. You got a Masters.'

'I was lucky.' His eyes twinkled above the rim of his round spectacles.

'Of course. Routine. Don't tell me, the same in forensics?'

'By God's good grace.'

'Hah!' She let out a laugh of incredulity. 'Amazing.'

'Now the interview is concluded shall we repair for coffee?'

'Yes. Let's.'

They strolled back to the sound of a tennis ball being struck against a wall somewhere.

'You were like a boy caught smoking behind the bike sheds, you know that?' She grinned at him.

'Caught in the act. Pants down. Six of the best.'

'Though I'm glad to see you've got a weakness. I thought you were unassailable.'

'Hah. "But no perfection is so absolute that some impurity doth not pollute." Poem, not the play.'

She stared. 'Oh God. No idea.' She knitted her brows. 'Erm … give me a clue.'

'Tarquin's ravishing strides?'

'*Macbeth.*'

'I said the poem, not the play.'

'Oh, of course. *The Rape of Lucrece.*'

'You have won today's star prize.'

Franky glanced at him just before they entered the conservatory, trying to make up her mind. Yes, life would never be dull with him around, but she still felt the need to know more.

The kitchen was empty as they entered.

She began to fill the kettle as Tom took a tin from a shelf, one with his name stuck on its side.

'Now then,' he said, opening it. 'My father works at MIT constructing a language for humans to use with robots. We meet. I ask how's it going, and he replies, "By steam. The next train is at three forty."'

Franky chuckled. 'So, how's work going?'

'You mean my dissertation?' He took a biscuit from the tin. 'Like one?'

She shook her head. 'What is it you're submitting? I've forgotten.'

'"The influence of Shakespeare in the Gothic Tradition." Castles, darkness, violence and the devil.'

'Into the satanic, eh?'

'Aren't we all? Isn't that the eternal battle?'

'What's all this about your father, this robot stuff?'

'He has a problem. They tend to get confused.'

'What do?'

'He finds synapses not connected.'

'Do robots have synapses?'

'I meant Dad's.'

She laughed out loud — and in that instant made up her mind. 'Tom. Tell me. Do you like old cottages, the kind with beams and an inglenook? I'm thinking of renting one and I need four housemates.'

'Hmm.' He peered at her with a faint smile. 'And a cat.'

'A cat?'

'Yes. You'd need a good mouser. I'm intrigued by them. You see them staring at you, with insight. It's no wonder the Egyptians worshipped them. That's why there was a musical. Difficult to do one about dogs.' He paused. 'Are you inviting me?'

'Are you interested?'

'I am extremely interested.'

She grimaced to herself. Had her impetuous offer been a mistake? His repartee, though amusing, was on the sly side, poking fun at people, reinforced by the occasional stiff finger. And he had other weird habits, like suddenly going into monologues on all kinds of subjects, as well as answering a question well after it had been put. Did he get a kick from unnerving people?

She remembered strolling with him on High Street when two small boys in school uniform approached, smirking at the sight of Tom wearing his John Lennon spectacles, a floppy black hat, a flapping overcoat down to his ankles and a ship's mooring length of blue-and-white college scarf wrapped several times round his neck and dropping to his knees.

As they drew level, one had grinned at the other while muttering some snide remark. It included the clearly heard "round eyes," at which they'd started to giggle, dipping their heads towards each other.

'Better than square eyes.'

Tom's riposte had cut dead their humour, the boy turning sharply to find a dark narrow face looming over him, at which the boy had dropped all posturing and went on quickly, looking scared.

'A Tudor cottage,' said Tom. 'Tell me all.'

She gave him the pitch. 'There's only one possible drawback,' she said at the conclusion.

'Let me think,' he said. 'One occupant is boredom, two is heaven, five a coup d'etat?' Tom munched a second biscuit while pouring milk in his coffee. 'You're saying you'll subsidise four people to live with you. Why?' He narrowed his eyes at her.

'First, I have the money, and second, because I want to.'

'Certainly not. I'd pay my share.'

'No. I can't do that with one and not the others. It's not fair.'

'Hah. I see.' He poked another finger. 'You want us indebted. It gives you the whip hand. You have to be the master of the house, sadistic and cruel.'

'You do like to tease, go on, admit it.' She picked up her coffee.

'Me? Goodness gracious. Tease?' He pretended to think about it. 'Hmm.'

She laughed, beginning to feel easier with him. 'Yes, people amuse you. Look, I'm trying to get five people together. I thought it would be more fun if they were all different. That's all.' She picked up her mug and took a sip.

'Hah, but … you've not told me what the drawback is. Cold showers each morning after a three-mile run, half-naked?'

'No!' she laughed. 'Look. You don't have to accept now and feel you're contracted. You can withdraw anytime.'

'Hah well, on that proviso I am inclined. It does sound fascinating.'

'So ... are you in?'

'It seems a benefit not to be missed. Tell me, what brought you here?'

'What brought me here? For the same reasons as everybody else, I'd guess. Why?'

'Well, I saw you in a seminar looking like you couldn't wait to get away.'

'I looked bored?'

'Erm, maybe pensive? Reflective, possibly?'

'Okay. I guess you're right. I do get bored occasionally. Have you read *Shadowplay*? The book by Clare, erm?'

'Clare Asquith?'

'Yes. You asked what brought me here, and it was that book. About Shakespeare planting secret Catholic code words in his plays. I got so excited. I wanted to come over and explore. Dig into dusty archives and make great discoveries.'

'I do admit I read half of it. But then it got slated by academia. After that, for me, it didn't hold water.' He adjusted his spectacles. 'You could be a prime example of the American non-fiction reader. Do you know that?'

'Really?' Franky gave him a screwy smile. 'Why?'

'Ask yourself, why are Americans the last people on earth to disbelieve a published book? Have you read Richard Hofstadter's *The Paranoid Style in American Politics*?'

'No. Go on, *interesting* Tom.'

He jabbed a playful finger at her stomach, causing her to laugh and flinch a little.

'Oh, of course. Hofstadter, I remember. Didn't he say conspiracy theories are a favourite pastime of Americans?'

'Yes. And why? Because we have the sneaking suspicion that somebody's out to get us – freemasons, Catholics and communists. With every tragedy we get a round of stories and fake news about "false flag" attacks and "crisis actors". Trump's full of it but he's not on his own. They're not just theories but arguments for the existence of a completely alternative version of reality.

'We are such stuff as dreams are made on—not "made *of*" — I get really irritated when people misquote it, don't you?'

'And our little life is rounded with a sleep,' she said, nodding with a smile. She remembered quoting that line to Hannah. "Coincidences." Things like that kept happening. Or *were* they coincidences? She puckered her brows at the thought.

He continued. 'Clare Asquith was wrong because she ignored how Elizabethan drama worked. Actors wouldn't have been in the dark about Catholic coded messages and Shakespeare would never have put them there had they been dangerous. Agreed?'

'Yes, I do. I do agree. Tom?' She faced him. 'The cottage. Are you in or not? You have a let-out. So, what is it to be?'

'These tight rules you're drawing up? Will they cover *all* disputes and behaviour?'

'Yes. Are you in!'

'Smoking?'

'Banned. It's in the rental contract.' She took a deep breath. 'You'll have to go outside and do it. *In or out*?' She suddenly laughed. 'Oh Tom, come on man!'

'Well, it seems an opportunity not to be missed. And I still can't understand your amazing generosity. Disregarding that, I say yes. I'm in.'

'Oh,' she exhaled, closing her eyes. 'Thank God for small mercies. Okay. Come to The White Swan tonight and you'll find out who your fellow tenants are. If you don't fancy them, then drop out.'

'The White Swan. That's in…?'

'Rother Street.'

His face suddenly lit up, breaking into a broad, smile, surprising her. 'I'm definitely in. After having just gruel and porridge, one coal burning in the grate, a wicked landlord, who'd refuse?'

'Tom,' she chuckled, shaking her head.

She left the kitchen, only to encounter Hannah coming downstairs. She looked worried.

Glancing uneasily around, she spoke in a hushed voice. 'Franky, look. I mean, can I ask … will Alicia be one? I really don't think I can if she's there. I'm so sorry.'

Franky paused a moment. 'Look, I don't want to talk about who I want. I can't rule anybody out. It wouldn't be fair, would it? But nothing's set in stone. Come to dinner, have some fun, and you can decide afterwards. You don't have to join, but you'll get a free meal. Okay?'

Hannah relaxed and smiled. 'You won't take what I said about Alicia, you know, too … too…'

'Don't worry.' Franky put a hand on Hannah's shoulder. 'Everything will be fine. Oh, do you know where Craig is?'

'I think he's in the lounge.'

'Thanks.'

'See you tonight. Can't wait.' Hannah gave an apologetic grimace. 'I'm sorry. It's just me.'

'I know. Now off.' Franky chuckled. '*Off.*'

Hannah, shaking her head and grinning, went into the Reading Room.

'Hmm.' Franky stared after her and then mounted the stairs slowly, in deep thought. Was Hannah scared of Alicia, or scared of what she might do, herself, if Craig became the piggy in the middle? It occurred to her that Alicia's rudeness was bound to surface at some juncture and Hannah's reaction could be interesting from a dramatic viewpoint. But was the risk worth taking?

Her mind was going round in circles. This, in turn posed the question: wasn't she, herself, similar to Hannah, deep down in the subconscious, always searching for emotional security?

As she made her way to the lounge, she remembered the time when she was eight, outside the house and playing a solitary game of hopscotch.

Through an open window she heard *him* say, *I still don't know how that redhead came to jump out of you. You know that red hair isn't in my family or yours, don't you?*

Yvette had said something like, *Now, don't start that again.*

Franky had puzzled over it for a long time but couldn't remember jumping out of anything. It was only when she grew up that she realised the significance of what her father had said.

Then there was the time she returned home from a summer camp in North Carolina and proudly told her father of her success in a field-hockey competition. He said, '*Well done*,' at the same time sticking out an arm in an instinctive move to embrace her, but had rapidly withdrawn it, pretending his attention had been caught by an item in his newspaper.

It was a small thing in itself, but a sickening blow to a kid who'd dearly wanted that arm to hook round her, just once would have done, she'd wanted it that badly. At the time it was the most painful disappointment of her young life, and you didn't have to be a sensitive soul to feel upset about your father showing that he didn't love you – *did* you?

She'd first felt a need for love when she was six years old, but it manifested itself in an odd way. She'd fantasised about kidnapping a loveable circus dwarf, but then dropped the idea — she couldn't remember why — and replaced him with an imaginary Grandpa who would arrive a week before Christmas, dressed as Santa Claus with a white beard and red cheeks. He always made a large bonfire that they sat around, singing joyous carols between eating doughnuts or cookies. As her childhood misery increased so did the number of Grandpa's visits. She kept receiving those visits even into her teens. Turned thirteen, her love for him was matched by an increasing hatred for the man supposed to be her father.

She was about to enter the lounge when a door creaked nearby. She quickly turned to look, but there was no one to be seen. What was equally odd was the silence, something she'd not noticed before. Was it the ghost that Corelli's visitor had seen? There it was again. A door creaked, but with no movement of a human being accompanying it.

About to turn the door handle, a memory flashback struck. It was an unforgettable nightmare she'd had. She was outside the cottage in a snow-covered landscape with prowlers about, but only half-human. It was imperative to get into the cottage for safety. Once inside, she was in a room covered with blood and guts, and she, on her knees with a bucket and brush, trying to clean up while being watched by others. Then more blood splashed down.

She saw it came from her own wrists.

She found Craig in the oak-panelled lounge, a notepad on his knee, his work illuminated by a standard-lamp with a floral shade. The room and its decor belonged to almost a century ago, reminding her of an aged aunt's living room where she was once forced to sit dutifully while family conversation droned on and on.

On seeing her enter, Craig gave a little sigh.

She misread it. 'Oh, sorry.' She turned to leave.

'No, don't go. Just making a few notes.' He put down his pen. 'How's your dissertation? You said you were seeing Annabelle.'

'Oh, yes, I did.' She put her bag down and sat on the front edge of an armchair to show she wouldn't bother him for long. 'I'm doing Shylock now, how the character affected the actors who played him.'

'You don't sound very thrilled.'

'No, it's okay. It's based on a character written over four centuries ago and how he's mirrored in the theatre today. That's the general idea. I haven't developed it yet, not in terms of originality,' that is if there's anything left in Shakespeare's canon that hasn't been done already.' She put on a smile. 'What are you submitting, do you know yet?'

'Yes. A tragic hero's sense of loss. Not sure which one though.'

'Oh.' She paused. 'Is it your idea?' she said casually. 'Or did Annabelle suggest it?'

'Mine Well we sort of arrived at it together. She was asking how I was getting along, and it came up.'

'Uh-huh. Did Annabelle tell you that my topic was the same as yours?'

'No?' Craig looked surprised. 'I'd no idea.'

'You told me you were going for Shakespeare in Asia?'

'Yes. Peter Brook's production.'

'Annabelle not like it? Is that the reason why she —'

'No, no. We talked about it, but then sense of loss came up., talking about my own loss. It kind of fitted.'

'I wasn't prying. I just wondered, that's all.'

'Don't worry. We're expected to discuss these things. No problem.'

'So long as it works for you…' she tailed off, looking round the room. 'You know, I can't work in here. I tried but I had to go. Don't you feel it's a bit oppressive?'

'No. I find it relaxing. I can concentrate in here.'

'Have you heard of *genius loci*?'

'Erm … yes. Something like feng shui, isn't it, a spiritual thing?'

'Yes. About your spiritual connection with a place.' She looked round again. 'Well, must let you get on.' She got up to go. 'Will it be awful for you at the break?' she said suddenly. 'I mean, going home at Christmas?'

'I won't be. I'm staying in London.'

She bit her lip. 'Erm, actually I came for something else. To put something to you.' She gestured at his notebook. 'I can leave it if you want, talk later?'

'No, it's okay. Shoot.'

He placed the notebook on the floor beside him and then leaned back, locking both hands behind his head, smiling leisurely at her. 'I had the feeling you were angling for something.' He'd never been alone with Franky before and felt a shade uncomfortable. She was generally too sharp and edgy for his liking. 'So, to what, and to whom, do I owe the pleasure?'

'You.' She sat down again. 'I've come for you, mister hunk.'

'Get outta here.'

'No, I'm serious. I have plans for you.'

'Oh yes? You're gonna make my day. How?'

He listened to her cottage pitch in growing incredulity. 'You're going to cough up all that money, why?'

'Because it's the only way I can get four people to live with me. I need company. A pity you're all paupers, but there we go. That's life. Gotta do what you gotta do. I've been left a lump sum. I can afford it.'

'Okay.' He looked serious. 'Five. You, me – who else?'

'Hannah and Tom, that's all at the moment. I'm taking you all out for a meal tonight, and we can talk about it. That okay?'

'Sure. Sounds fun. But I'm buying.'

'No, you're not.'

'At least my own meal.'

'No.'

'The drinks then.'

'No way.'

'Come on.'

'Get thee behind me Satan.'

Craig chuckled. 'Okay. You win.' He leaned down to pick up his pen that had fallen on the floor. When he straightened up she noted that his grin had faded and his eyes had a lost look – but only for a moment. She frowned to herself. He'd not stolen her dissertation, her instincts told her that. She hadn't lost it through *his* doing. That left her with only one conclusion … and that she couldn't face. Not now.

It couldn't even be entertained as a notion.

It was never a possibility.

It was stupid even thinking about it.

Chapter Six

From her garden seat Franky watched a yellow leaf float down, like a parachute, to land in her lap. She thought about her meeting with Craig. Yes, she could easily imagine Annabelle being overwhelmed by his tragic tale, robbed of both his wife and son in the same year. She would be shocked and then overflow with sympathy and sadness. By her own admission she was studying *sadness* in the cultural history of the emotions, wasn't she? And was not melancholia part of the corpus of romantic tragedy?

Whatever had passed, or happened between them, and whichever way Franky thought about it, she concluded that she'd been cheated. It was nothing short of daylight robbery, so iniquitous and brazen that it had her grimacing, digging fingernails into the soft flesh of her palm, one moment disbelieving it, the next plunged into utter confusion.

Surely, she asked herself, scholars had to bring their sensibilities, as well as intellect, to the study of human nature in all its guises. And who, dealing with great literature, would *even think* of stealing a student's idea? Scholars were not given to being duplicitous. The majesty of Shakespeare demanded honesty in every respect, didn't it?

Was it her own fault? In showing the hatred she had for her father, had it given Annabelle the ideal opportunity to cast doubt as to her intentions regarding him, this giving her an excuse to pass her dissertation on to Craig?

She regretted not pressing her case hard enough. If she'd insisted that her sense of loss had been magnified by a consequential loss of happiness, respect and self-worth, as had Hamlet whose flaw of indecisiveness mirrored her own, maybe then she would have won the day! How stupid she'd been! She'd already planned to present herself as a latter-day Hamlet, hopeless in her agonising, embattled with herself, seeking revenge but getting nowhere. And now she'd thrown it all away.

Enough. She swept the leaves from her lap, irritated by her bitterness, so pointless and so demeaning. Her whole life seemed full of it.

And then came an idea like a thunderbolt. Forget Annabelle and Craig. They could be laid to one side as an exciting notion took precedence.

She went into the conservatory, empty at this hour and sat down breathing excitedly. Her novel could be a means of getting revenge on *him*, her father!

Was it a crazy idea?

No, because a theme had jumped into her mind: a girl exiled to a foreign land by her father. It had happened to her, hadn't it, as it had to Cordelia in *King Lear*? Her father rapes a child. Knowing she's a witness, he engineers her exile to England. There she plots her revenge.

Feverishly she began to make notes, but eventually slowed down, retaining enough objectivity to remind herself that, if the book were to be successful, she wouldn't get revenge by damning her father from day one. She had to build a situation in which the protagonist, based on herself, became so ensnared in an impossible situation that she had no alternative but to defeat him.

She went over the structure. It was as sound and commanding as it was simple. From that conflict of father and daughter she would fashion a plot-line – oh, how happy she was in her choice of housemates. The characters would be based on the rather exotic and intellectual Tom, Craig the laid-back cowboy and the selfish, extrovert Alicia who was already feared and disliked by the well-meaning and innocent Hannah.

Now the nature of her revenge. If it were to be morally acceptable, it would have to be proportionate to the degree of injury inflicted. She would write it, of course, in the first person.

She let out a sigh and sat back to glance at her watch. An hour and a half had passed as if it were ten minutes. She read quickly through her notes, ensuring that she'd not made a fatal error. It all seemed to hang together.

With that out of the way she was able to get on with her course work. The novel, she would return to, whenever the urge took her.

She closed her eyes, stretching out her arms in great satisfaction. And then suddenly she sat up straight in the realisation that she was doing exactly what the therapist had recommended, thinking of herself objectively in a therapeutic attempt to exorcise her demons!

Enough. Shylock called. She went unhappily into the library. There, waiting, were copies of magazine and newspaper articles that the librarian had reserved for her. Furnished with these, she sat down, stuck her elbows on the table, pressed her fists against her cheeks and, with brows furrowed, ordered herself to grapple with Shylock's need for revenge.

Would he have settled for something less than bloody? She'd written an essay at college in which she'd quoted Marcus Aurelius; he'd said that the most satisfying revenge was *to be unlike him who causes the injury*. She'd found it noble but self-demeaning. It could be argued that, in taking her father's money, she was being more than vengeful. But, wasn't it justified if there was no other kind of justice to be found, with only herself as witness to his crime?

A sudden gust tore into the garden, sending yellow leaves swirling in a circle outside her window. Her feelings hardened as she watched them flutter down. There was no doubt that she'd been robbed of her symbiotic relationship with Hamlet and consigned to study a less than heroic figure in Shylock. She loved Hamlet; she felt for him. But not Shylock. She may have professed a horror of anti-Semitism, but what lay underneath was the picture of the stooping archetypal Jew, spurned and embittered. She thought that, in some ways, he was a mirror-image of herself. And how could she love that kind of figure? It was a depressing thought.

Another gust rattled the windows with a host of dry leaves. Frustrated, she gave up thinking about Shylock and turned back to her novel. There was no doubt that the cottage was ideal for her purpose. Where better to watch and learn about character than inside her new dominion? She had a ready-made stage on which to watch the players around the clock, looking for trigger points that revealed their strengths and weaknesses. And in what better setting would tension come to the breaking point than in a remote cottage in the countryside – winter, darkening afternoons and isolation, with the possibility of adding a little spice here and there, aided by an occasional, gentle stir of the pot? She'd be extremely careful not to overdo it. She still wanted the idyllic existence that the cottage offered – didn't she?

So, there she had it. Five American students living in a country cottage near Stratford. Writing in the first person would give it a sense of immediacy along a timeline of events leading up to the child rape, after which came murder.

She spent the next half hour feverishly scribbling down note after note and, by the end of it, sat back in satisfaction. Not only would she be following the therapist's advice in keeping her days and nights busy but, by the careful balancing of ambition and hope, it would provide her with such self-esteem as to shrug off her chains of self-doubt—forever?

She sat back smiling. It was set to become what was needed. Was it a case, not of art imitating life, but the converse? Was that called Aristotelian or Wildean?

She left the library to march towards the conservatory, with leaves swirling, skittering and dancing on the path before her. There was the cottage to celebrate and a dinner to look forward to in The White Swan, one of the historic restaurants in town where, it was said, Shakespeare purchased a tipple or two.

She no longer felt gloomy. She felt good. Really confident and really good.

She drew in a deep breath of the leaf-rotting smell of autumn.

She found Alicia in the kitchen washing up a pile of dishes.

'Alicia' she said, 'Tell me what's your bedsit like?'

'My bedsit, why?'

'Nothing, just wondered.'

'Oh, well, mine's square. It's got a bed, central heating, an armchair, TV and a radio. A tiny kitchen, and a shower I squeeze into.' Alicia tossed her hair back. 'I sleep there. Period.'

'Manky.'

'Excuse me?' Alicia gave her a puzzled smile.

'Manky. I got it from my landlord. He was in the British army. He said it's a word they used for being dirty and untidy. Sounds right, don't you think?'

'Now I come to think of it, yeah, it's okay.' She pointed a finger. 'Manky Franky!'

Franky was a fraction late laughing along with her, which was the time it took to realise she'd meant it as a jokey exercise in alliteration, rather than a slight. 'Okay,' she said. 'I've got a proposition for you. An offer you can't refuse.'

Intrigued, Alicia listened, allowing Franky to finish the pitch. 'Wow. You've knocked my socks off! But why us trailer trash? There must be people around here who're not dirt-poor. What's behind it?'

'Nothing. It's because I want to.'

Alicia grinned at her. 'C'mon. There's gotta be something.'

'Are you turning it down?'

'God, no. No way. I just find it *amazing*.'

'And so do I. I just came into a trust fund, that's all.'

'Really? Hey, you're the first student I've met who isn't broke.' Alicia gave a laugh.

'So, are you in?'

'Am I in? I'll say so. And thanks.' Alicia looked at her watch. 'Yikes, I'm due at the dentists.' She tossed the dishcloth on the worktop. 'Franky, do me a favour, finish these few?'

'Sure. But before you go, are you free tonight because I'm taking you all out for a meal.'

'Really? Holly shit. Where?'

'The White Swan, six thirty. Know it?'

'Yes, I do … fantastic.' Alicia grinned in bewilderment. 'You are something else. Six-thirty and thanks a million, *millionaire!*'

Franky watched her lithe figure stride into the narrow passage leading into the conservatory and then set about the dishes.

When finished she went back outside. The wind had dropped and with it the sun, now breaking into a myriad of sparkles through the branches of the copper beech. She removed her hat as she sat down, now having no need for covering up.

Her thoughts strayed back to the therapist's warning, relayed to her by Yvette. She had to take care that her struggle for domination didn't get in the way of her relationships, as well as her work, creativity and ability to evolve as a mature adult. In trying to climb above others she could not only hurt herself, but also others on the way down. The warning, she remembered, had been embodied in a printed document full of recommendations, ready for her to read when she was old enough to understand.

Well, Yvette had produced it on her nineteenth birthday, but it was hardly a present. She'd read it and thought it garbage. If what she was doing made her feel better, what did it matter if she convinced herself that she was more talented and more deserving of recognition than those around her? When all was said and done, if life was to be at all worthwhile, there had to be some risks taken — hadn't there?

A humorous image came to mind, that of herself as a puppeteer towering over the cottage while manipulating Hannah's strings, along with that of the other marionettes below. Hannah was so warm-hearted and forgiving that a little tug here and a tweak there would see her right again, that was for sure.

Shivering a little in the cooling air, she stood up to go back inside, feeling rather smug.

A chattering and laughing crowd greeted her as she entered the conservatory. She thought it strange. She sensed that some of them were amused by her late appearance, but couldn't think why.

Suddenly she stopped dead. There, surrounded by a group of students, was Alicia, regaling them with a story that had them laughing and she the centre of their admiring attention. No more than twenty minutes had elapsed, surely, since she left the kitchen in a hurry? She must have cancelled her dental appointment. But *if* she'd cancelled it, she would have returned to finish the dishes. Except she hadn't.

Franky entered the Great Hall and sat down. Scrabbling inside her bag, she took out a notebook and pen. With her mind at fever pitch and riding a wave of excitement, she wrote *cottage … student dies – apparently – or disappears and then reappears*. It reminded her of the classic 1970s film, *Don't Look Now*.

She continued making notes until she stopped, realising that the idea had skidded away from the plot designed to wreak revenge on her enemy. On the heels of that thought, came another. Why not get on with the novel immediately and quit the course! She had the money. If it failed to get published, she could restart the MA and then —she stood up, her mind spinning out of control. She put a hand to her face and sank down again, her excitement dying in the realisation that it was time to be rational, time to untie her emotional and mental knot, time to take just one thing at a time, otherwise she was in danger of—

'Sorry Franky.'

She looked up.

Alicia approached her. 'I had a call from the dentists. He's ill. Thought I'd better tell you as you'll think I skived off, okay?' She went back into the conservatory, with a wave of her hand. 'Thanks for the invite!'

She watched her go, back to her admirers. Her initial reaction was one of relief. She hadn't been a witness to psychic phenomena, or a sudden, unexplained, time-jump. And Alicia had come to apologise, hadn't she?

Her relief was cut short by an unpleasant thought. Alicia had left her to finish the dishes in order to spend time with her cronies, *of course* she had. What a bird-brain she was in finding an excuse for her.

She went back into the conservatory to see Alicia and Annabelle, deep in a lively discussion. As she passed by, their voice levels seemed to drop.

About to turn into the kitchen she stopped and glanced back to see them, once more immersed in animated conversation. Her blood temperature, already high, was now boiling. Fast swinging a long-handled axe, she decapitated Alicia with one blow.

Chapter Seven

'Franky says we've only got this afternoon to visit the cottage,' said Hannah, having found Tom fiddling with a DVD player in the Reading Room. 'The estate agency called. Apparently, there's others want to rent it, so we have to move fast.'

'I'll be with you in five minutes,' said Tom, absorbed in his task.

Hannah rejoined Franky in reception. 'So, you got Alicia.' She looked unsettled.

'Yes. Now I want to get rid of her.'

'What!' Hannah's jaw dropped.

'I made a mistake,' said Franky grimly. 'You were right.'

'But you've invited her, you can't do that. She'll go bananas—' she sucked in her breath— 'hey, you didn't say I was worried about her, did you?' Hannah looked scared.

'No, of course I didn't.'

They moved into the conservatory to see Craig and Alicia waiting in the car park.

'Franky,' said Hannah. 'Have you thought what you're going to say when you tell her she's been fired? Just think about it. She's accepted your invitation. I don't like her but—I'm worried for you, what she might do or say. '

'Don't. I thought you'd be pleased.'

'I would have been *if* she hadn't been invited. Honestly, Franky, I wouldn't be able to look her in the eye. And both Craig and Tom know she's been invited. I don't think you've got a leg to stand on, I really don't. I'm saying that as a friend.' Hannah grimaced in her appeal.

Franky sat down, sighed and put a hand to her forehead.

Hannah sat beside her. 'Look. I promise I won't argue with her, or do anything to upset her. Does that help?'

Franky looked at her with a sudden smile. 'Yes, it does. I'm sorry Hannah. Look. I'm drawing up rules of behaviour for all of us and then she'll have to toe the line. Is that the way we should go?'

'Yes. Absolutely. That sure is the way to go. Don't worry. It will be fine.'

Franky stood up. 'Good, all sorted.'

They left the conservatory.

'Franky.' Hannah stopped walking. 'I am worried about one thing.'

'Like?' It brought Franky to a halt.

'Erm …' Hannah frowned. 'I don't think I can share a room with her. Is that possible, I mean, to have my own room? I know it's a lot to ask but I'm being honest. I just —'

'Don't worry. You've got it. It was in the plan anyway.'

Hannah breathed a deep sigh of relief. 'Oh, that's good. Thanks Franky.' They resumed walking. 'And I'm really pleased you've got Craig.'

'No need to tell me that. 'It's obvious to everybody you're madly in love.'

'Oh.' Hannah sighed. '*That* obvious?'

'You know it is. It's no big deal. It's called hormones.' Franky put a consoling arm around her shoulders. 'C'mon.'

Hannah came to another stop, looking forlorn. 'I honestly don't think I can, not if …'

'Of course, you can. Let's talk later.'

'No. This is wrong. I embarrass him. Yesterday he suggested I drop my dissertation about insanity in the tragedies and do something else. He'd even got a title for me: *Patterns and Themes in Shakespeare's early Comedies.* Trying to lighten me up, I guess. I must seem pathetic. Am I?'

'No. You? You're the best. Now stop feeling sorry for yourself.'

'But I feel terrible now that …'

'Okay.' Franky said tersely, glancing ahead at the others chatting in the car-park. 'Okay,' she repeated. I'll put you out of your misery. I've seen them together. Alicia and Craig.'

'What!' She stared at Franky.

'I overheard them. They were standing outside the library hidden by the bushes. I heard him say she's had a hard time.'

'Who—who has?'

'He said he was waiting to sort himself out.'

'Who did he mean!'

'*You*, of course! Waiting to sort himself out since his wife and kid died. He said it wasn't Alicia's fault. He didn't intend to lead her on. He said if he was going to go with anybody it would be you.'

Hannah stopped to stare at Franky. 'He said that?' she said, awestruck. 'He really said that?'

'Sure did.'

'It sounds a bit too pat for me, Franky. Be honest, are you telling me the truth? Swear to it.'

'Absolutely.'

'Really?'

'Yes. Okay? Now stop—look—' She broke off as a sob escaped Hannah and was about to embrace Franky but, glancing at the others now watching, checked herself. Instead, she took out a tissue, pretending to blow her nose.

'Hannah, listen. Remember this. If it gets too much you can leave the cottage at any time, without owing any money. Okay now?'

'Oh, Franky. You're far too good for me. Thanks.' They continued walking. 'But promise what you've just said about Craig is true?'

'Oh, for God's sake, what do I have to do, cut my heart out? C'mon.'

She took Hannah's arm. 'And no need to worry about Alicia anymore. Now, no more emotes, okay?'

On the drive out of town, questions were asked about the proposed rental. It was decided that Craig, being the oldest of the group and the only one with experience of owning a property, would help Franky liaise with the landlord over any problems that might arise.

Franky, in the front passenger seat, grimaced to herself at what she'd done. She'd lied to ease Hannah's fears, but now, looking back, wished she hadn't. What if it rebounded on her? She could think of ways in which it could happen.

Her gaze lowered from the windscreen to the footwell. Acting without thinking— *again*. Should she confess, admit her failings and throw herself on Hannah's mercy? No. Too late. She'd be devastated and probably wouldn't talk to her again. What an idiot she was. She slipped a hand down to lever the back of the seat.

As it jolted back Franky heard a slight exclamation from behind.

'Oh, so sorry, Hannah!' Franky half turned in apology.

'It's okay, Franky. I'm fine. No worries. Craig? Can you stop outside Anne Hathaway's cottage? I know we're going on a group visit but it would be good to take a look, wouldn't it?

They gazed at the large white cottage. It stood at the end of a line of modern houses with pasture land beyond.

'This can't be a single cottage,' said Alicia. 'It's three put together, isn't it? How many rooms has it got, anyone know?'

Hannah brought out a tourist leaflet. 'Okay,' she said, reading. 'It's got twelve. Extensions were made to it in the seventeenth century. It's got wattle and daub wall-panels set in oak frames cut from trees growing in the twelfth to thirteenth centuries.'

Hannah, having examined the house from all angles, shook her head in disbelief. 'It's not chocolate box, it's real. Shakespeare came courting here! Here, *just here*!'

They resumed their journey, Hannah, staring excitedly through the windscreen. 'How far now?'

'Nearly a mile,' said Franky.

Eventually they turned left into Tithebarn Lane. Its surface consisted of two concrete tracks running parallel, each two and a half feet wide, the space between them riddled with grass and weeds.

Craig suddenly stopped the car at a spot that enabled them to see into the field below. 'See that sheep, the nearest? That's a Lincoln Longwool. And the one to its left? That's a Southdown. My Grandpa had them. Most sheep in America are British in origin.'

Alicia smirked at Tom. 'There. Don't tell me that's something you didn't know, Tom?'

'I confess,' he said. 'But I'll tell you about the wool trade if you like?'

'No, Tom,' said Franky. 'You start on that and the day will be gone. Coming up now, people. Get ready …. for your first sight of…'

A white cottage appeared, about a hundred yards ahead.

'More Tudor England!'

They peered forward. The cottage was smaller than Anne Hathaway's but, with a modern extension at the rear, it still occupied a substantial piece of land.

Craig stopped the car outside the white five-barred gate, inset from the lane by a few yards. Even before he'd switched off the engine, Hannah was out of the car to gaze at their new home. On the left-hand side of the cottage, was an open-fronted woodshed.

She was joined by the others.

'Isn't it great?' she breathed. 'Love the log store.'

'Do the logs come with it?' said Tom.

'They do,' said Franky. 'And the garden.'

They looked to their left. The garden was narrow and elongated, stretching about eighty yards down a slope, a thick hedgerow separating it from the lane. Nearest to the cottage was a large vegetable patch with rows of upright canes for runner beans and, at the bottom of the garden, some rough ground on which a compost pile stood, contained by a three-sided wooden frame made from old railway sleepers. Everything looked neat and tidy.

'Who does the gardening?' said Craig.

'Not us, I hope,' said Alicia dryly.

'No,' said Franky. 'In early spring the gardener comes once a week through summer. And then we're away.'

'Any chance of looking round, Franky?' said Hannah, straining at the leash.

'Of course,' Franky opened the gate for them to go round the cottage and peer through the small-paned windows. Unfortunately, it was one of those days when low, thick cloud kept light from the glass, so revealing little of the cottage interior.

At first expressing her disappointment, Hannah exclaimed in making out the shape of a huge fireplace. 'That's it – the inglenook! Oh, what a shame we can't go in!'

There came a jingling, metallic sound. Hannah turned round to find Franky with her arm raised, a clutch of keys dangling from a bent finger.

'Oh!' exclaimed Hannah, realising. 'They let you borrow the keys!'

Franky remained in teasing mode, her chin tilted and eyebrows raised.

'You've paid,' said Tom suddenly. 'You've paid the deposit.'

Franky, grinning, went to unlock the front door.

'What? Ugh!' Hannah suddenly exclaimed and pulled a face. 'That *smell*, where's it coming from!'

Then the others caught it as the wind veered slightly: the unmistakable reek of human waste.

Craig grinned. 'It's okay. That'll be the septic tank. My Grandpa had one.' He set off, trotting past the woodshed and continued down the garden.

At the bottom he stopped to stare at something on the ground, then bent down to take a closer look.

'What's he doing?' said Hannah nervously.

Craig jogged back and stopped, slightly out of breath. 'It's full. That's the reason.'

'What's full?' said Hannah in trepidation.

'The septic tank.'

'It's okay, Hannah,' said Craig. 'The local council will collect it. Right, Franky?'

'Yes. It's obviously due. I'll give them a call.'

'What are you talking about?' Hannah looked nervously from one to the other.

'Pumping out,' said Craig. 'They come round with a truck. In Shakespeare's time they called them gong farmers. My Grandpa called it "the honey wagon."

'Well,' said Alicia airily. 'If we're going to live the Elizabethan life, we've gotta get used to it.'

'Don't worry,' said Tom. 'It only smells when it's full to overflowing. Today it's an easterly, and they mainly get westerlies coming off the Atlantic. We'll be mostly free of the stink and when it's emptied there'll be nothing.'

'Tom,' said Alicia wryly. 'I didn't think your thoughts ever stooped that low.'

Hannah, who had listened to all this in growing horror exclaimed, her voice high-pitched. 'Are you telling me we have to go down there *to do it? And there's not even a shed?*'

It was met with roars of laughter.

'What?' Hannah looked bewildered, scanned their faces.

Franky put an arm around her shoulders. 'No, Hannah,' she said, grinning. 'We do it in the laundry room. There's a hole in the floor.'

'She's shitting you,' said Alicia, to more laughter.

'We're not connected to the main sewer system,' explained Craig. He pointed down the garden. 'There's a big tank sunk in the ground. The waste pipe from the cottage goes into that. The sewage, with nature, forms a thick crust, trapping in the smell. That only happens when it overflows into a drainage ditch.'

'Oh, for a moment…' Hannah clapped a hand to her chest, her shoulders sagging in relief.

'Don't worry, Hannah, I'll call the council today,' said Franky.

'There you go, no worries.' Alicia gave Hannah a comforting tap on the arm. 'Okay now?'

'Oh my God. *Who* is stupid?' Hannah started laughing, shaking her head.

'Folks, note the five-lever lock for security.' Franky unlocked the front door. 'Soyez les bienvenus, mes camarades Américains, à notre chaumière anglaise.' With a gracious smile, she ushered them inside.

Hannah was first in, followed by Alicia.

'Franky,' said Tom, 'where did you learn to speak fluent French?'

'My Mom's French. I was brought up speaking it, along with English.'

Hannah stood on limestone floor tiles, staring up at the ancient beams.

'This is great,' she murmured, lowering her gaze to take in the hallway with its single narrow window set almost two feet deep in the thick white wall. 'Simply great.'

Franky led the way up the richly carpeted stairs and into the first bedroom off the landing.

They could smell the expensive built-in furniture and white woollen carpet. The curtains and fittings were also of the highest quality. The décor, in cream and lavender, suggested that the room had been planned by an interior designer. A computer desk stood against one wall. The white sliding-door wardrobes were split by a matching dressing table with concealed down-lighting.

'Must have cost them an arm and a leg,' said Alicia.

'It must have,' said Hannah.

'Awesome. Franky, is the whole place like this?'

'It's for you to see.' Franky, thrilled, took them to the window from where the view stretched over hedgerows and fields into the far distance.

'Franky,' said Tom, 'are you sure we're paying a peppercorn rent?'

'*You* are. I'm not.' Smiling, she took them out onto the landing and into a bathroom where they found a roll-top bath, shower unit and washbasin all fitted with gold taps.

Next door along was a second toilet and washbasin, also with gold taps. It elicited a hushed murmur from Hannah and a rumble of appreciation from Craig.

The second bedroom was as luxurious as the first, but smaller. Next door to that was a third bedroom, similarly fitted out with a computer desk and the same expensive brand of wardrobes.

'This place is quite something,' said Alicia quietly.

'I can't believe it,' said Hannah.

'Oh dear,' said Tom, in a show of grave disappointment. He paused as they stared at him.

'What?' said Franky with a look of alarm.

'We shall have to pay in kind, I fear. Cleaning, scrubbing and polishing on our hands and knees, no gold tap with a blemish.'

'No,' Franky chuckled. 'I've got your number, Mr Tom. It so happens there's a cleaning company that comes in every two months and blasts everything. Two of them, four hours each and no cost to us. No worries. Okay?'

She led them downstairs into the hallway, where a door opened to reveal a toilet-with-washbasin. It had a row of clothes pegs on the wall. 'They call this the cloakroom.'

Then came the kitchen. A glistening black marble worktop ran around three walls. Franky tapped part of it. 'I was told the slabs came from Italy.'

'Hah,' said Tom. 'In that case it's likely they came from quarries in the Carrara region.'

'Oh, shut up, know-all,' said Alicia, mock bashing him on the head with her fist.

Tom went round the kitchen, peering at manufacturer's names. 'Sub-Zero refrigeration, Gaggenau oven, Miele coffee maker, very nice indeed.'

He slipped into the adjacent laundry room. 'Fisher and Paykel fridge-freezer, Bosch washing machine and dryer and a Worcester Bosch central heating boiler. Hmm, doubly nice indeed.'

'Expensive,' said Franky, picking up a note from the letting agency. 'It says the dishwasher's out of order.'

She waited for Alicia's laughter to cease. 'They're fixing it soon. Hurrah.'

'What a dump,' said Alicia, ironically. 'Let's go. It's all a con, Franky.'

'Well, come and be conned by this.' Franky, still smiling, led them from the laundry room into a small vestibule, the start of the recently built modern extension.

Off one side was the fourth bedroom, and on the other a large second bathroom, similar to the one upstairs with a toilet, a sink with gold mixer taps, a large roll-top bath and another, expensive shower.

'And with a whirlpool, look!' exclaimed Hannah. 'Great!'

'Seriously impressive,' said Tom.

'Franky,' said Craig. 'I gotta hand it to you. This place is stunning.'

Alicia looked at Franky. 'You sure we haven't been conned? Next month we get a bill for five grand each?'

'Franky, how much is the year rental?' asked Tom. 'Did you say £20,000?'

'No. It's more than that. I'm not telling you because I don't want any sympathy, okay?'

Alicia looked at her dubiously. 'You sure you didn't win the lottery?'

'Positive.'

Franky led them into the fourth bedroom. It was fitted out with the same brand of fittings as those upstairs, complete with a computer desk and sliding wardrobe doors. The room itself was decorated in a subtle shade of grey and heated by two oil filled, plug-in radiators.

Hannah went to the window and stared out at the rear garden that was mainly grass. A hedgerow separated it from the field beyond. 'Is that gap in the hedge so we can walk into the field?'

Franky went to look. 'I don't know. I didn't ask.'

'It's probably where a tree stood,' said Craig, joining them.

'And what's that?' said Hannah, pointing through a side window. 'That big black thing at the back of the woodshed?'

'That's the heating-oil tank,' said Franky. 'It gets filled from a gas truck that comes when needed. The landlord deals with all that.' She turned to lead the way out. 'C'mon. Now for the *pièce de résistance*.'

'Hah! The inglenook!' Hannah clapped her hands. 'I can't wait.'

Grinning in her excitement, she allowed Franky to lead them back through the laundry room and kitchen, then down the hallway to the living room, its entrance close to the front door.

Inside, they stopped to gaze at the huge inglenook fireplace that dominated the heavily beamed room. It was crossed overhead by a massive beam, part of an oak tree, its central section blackened by the smoke of centuries of fires.

'Oh, just look at that,' said Hannah, slack-jawed. 'Those narrow bricks are genuine Tudor. Pity about the canopy, but I guess it's there to stop smoke coming into the room.'

'That is certain,' said Craig, 'probably put in during the Industrial Revolution when they were making lots of steel.'

'The fire-basket's the crème de la crème,' said Alicia.

'Yes,' said Tom. 'In Tudor times they had fires on the brick floor.'

'I love the knights,' said Hannah.

At each side of the large fire-basket was the casting of a medieval armoured figure with shield. At the base of the inglenook's side walls – and facing each other across the fire basket – were two low redbrick seats, crested in oak and topped with royal-blue cushions. A set of hefty fire-irons hung on the right-hand wall.

'Oh, I've just got to sit in there,' said Hannah, 'waiting for my Tudor knight to come home.'

She ducked down under the beam to sit down. 'Franky,' she said suddenly, 'can we turn off the radiators in here and have the fire instead?'

'Yes, if we all agree. If it's freezing outside, we could have both.'

'Wonderful.'

'Anybody object?'

'No. Hannah's our firelighter, I guess,' said Alicia. 'Hannah, I bet you can't wait to get the logs in. Go on, on the double.'

'You've got it. Will do. That is, if Craig will give me a hand?'

'Yeah, I'll be your fire buddy.' Craig gave her a smile.

Hannah suddenly pointed to the centre of the room. 'Wow, look at that table! And the patina! It's got to be centuries old. We're going to eat in here with the fire going! Franky, that is just fantastic —' Ow!' In getting up she bumped the beam, clutching her head.

She waved the others away. 'I'm okay, I'm okay. It's only stupid Hannah who thought the toilet was down the garden!'

They laughed with her.

Franky took them back upstairs to re-enter the first visited. At the outset she rejected their insistence that it had to be hers, given all the work and money she'd put into the project.

'No. We draw lots.' She sounded - and looked - adamant. 'We're all equal here.'

'Come on,' said Craig. He glanced at the others. '*Who* is it, gets this room?'

'Franky,' said Alicia, folding her arms. 'We wouldn't dare.'

'Yours, I'm afraid,' said Tom, raising his eyebrows.

Hannah put up her hands in a blocking gesture. 'Franky, we couldn't. What are you thinking of!' She started to sing 'For She's a Jolly Good Fellow' but stopped, a shade embarrassed when no one else joined in.

Franky shook her head. 'No. I still think we should draw lots. We don't need any bad feeling.'

'Franky,' said Craig. 'If you don't take it, I'm quitting. I couldn't live in this room. I just couldn't. It's yours, okay?'

'I'd quit as well,' said Hannah, nodding firmly.

'C'est une affaire faite,' said Tom, with a shrug.

'Franky, it's yours.' Alicia shook her head. 'No argument.'

Franky sighed. 'Well, okay, if you insist.' She looked the picture of sadness, while hiding her delight. 'Okay. Now two of us must share a room. Who are the heroic volunteers?'

Alicia and Hannah automatically looked at Tom and Craig.

'I think I could play the Elizabethan gallant,' said Tom. 'How about you, Craig?'

'Do you snore, Tom?'

'Only in the mating season.'

Amid the laughter, Franky relaxed. 'Okay folks. We're nearly done. Alicia and Hannah, you both have a choice. Upstairs or downstairs? Where would you like to be, Alicia?'

'I like being small and cosy, 'I'm okay with the smallest up here, but I bet Hannah won't like the downstairs. No beams.'

'You're wrong,' said Hannah. 'You don't see beams when you're asleep. And downstairs I can dash out any time and run in our meadow! I'm okay with that.'

'Now the bathrooms,' said Franky. 'I'm happy to share the bathroom up here with the boys so long as I also get the toilet next to it as well. Any objections?'

Craig and Tom murmured their agreement.

'I'm very happy,' said Alicia, 'because Hannah and I have got *the whirlpool!*' She gave Hannah a quick hug.

'Well, yes, but shouldn't we all share it' said Hannah. 'To be fair?' I —'

'Aaagh!' Alicia let out a screech, putting her hands at Hannah's throat, pretending to strangle her. Then she relaxed with a rueful smile. 'Yeah, I guess. Fair's fair.'

'I'll draw up a rota for the whirlpool,' said Franky, 'hence no argument.'

They went downstairs to file outside, Tom taking Franky's hand to administer an Elizabethan kiss. 'Françoise, vous êtes une dame extraordinaire.'

'Merci, monsieur. Pas de problem.' Franky locked the front door.

'Oh, I forgot to tell you,' she said, as they went to the car. 'If Craig for any reason can't take us any morning, there's a community bus. It stops just down from the end of the lane. And we all share the gas when he does take us. Craig? You okay with that?'

'Yes, but the chauffeur has a problem. At home the tip is twenty per cent; in England it's only ten. Any contributions will be gratefully received.'

Grinning, he unlocked the car doors to a few chuckles.

Chapter Eight

It was 6.50 p.m. in the warmth and cosiness of The White Swan.

Franky, in dark wash jeans and a white frilly top, stood at the bar. A visit to a hairdresser that afternoon had resulted in her tresses taking on a richer hue. She thought that Tom, standing alongside her, looked the part of a lawyer in his grey suit, tie, blue-striped shirt and protruding cuffs.

A minute later Craig entered. He'd ditched his baggy jacket for a smart blue one. 'Hi, what are you two having?' he said, taking out his wallet.

Tom shook his head, holding up a craft beer.

'Craig,' said Franky. 'I'm buying. I told you.'

Ignoring her, he gestured at the drink by her side. 'What's the cocktail?'

'Hey!' Franky laughed as, in one swoop, Craig lifted her off her feet, swung her around and placed her back on the floor, kissing her cheek.

A flash of fluorescent yellow caught Franky's eye. It was Hannah, in the entrance, hanging up her anorak.

Seeing Franky look her way, she tripped rapidly towards her, like *une danseuse de ballet*.

'Hi.' She ended in the third position, giggling a little.

'Hannah, what's yours?' said Franky, turning to the bar.

'Erm ... a lime and lemon, if that's okay.' She joined Tom who was staring at a poster advertising the forthcoming production of *A Christmas Carol*, by the RSC.

'I played Mole at school,' she said. 'I've just gotta see that.'

As Tom and Hannah went back to join Craig, Franky waited to be served at the bar.

At that moment Alicia arrived, a vision of strength and beauty wearing dark blue pants and a white Rhode Island sweater.

She made straight for the group of Hannah, Tom and Craig, while giving a cursory wave to Franky. 'Hi, Franky.'

Franky watched as she rested a hand on Tom's chest and burst out laughing at something he said. 'Yes, Tom, and many more of them!' She turned to Franky at the bar.

'If you're buying, Franky, mine's a gin and tonic, thanks!' She turned her back to address the others. 'Has anybody eaten here? What's the food like?'

'It's good,' breathed Franky to herself, trying to focus hard on a line of illuminated spirit bottles lining the back of the bar. Unable to stop the heat racing into her head, she grabbed her long-handled axe and, swinging round, cleaved Alicia's head wide open

Breathing harshly, she went to the cloakroom, poured water into the cup of her hand, wet her forehead, then patted it dry with a paper towel. Suddenly she became motionless, staring at herself with an intense self-loathing.

She walked back, the four of them watching her approach. It reminded her of the devil-worshippers greeting the mother of Satan, in the movie *Rosemary's Baby*.

She went straight to the bar.

She was joined by the others gathering round her.

'Hey, Franky,' said Alicia. 'We're paying for our own. You've done enough.'

'We've decided,' said Tom.

'You're not to be a martyr.' Hannah hooked her arm round Franky's. 'No argument.'

'Okay.' She picked up her cocktail. 'If you all insist.'

'We do.'

As soon as they all had drinks, Franky, smiling prettily, led them into the heavily beamed dining room.

She stopped at a long oak table, close to a large fireplace where logs burned merrily.

'Oh,' said Hannah. 'Another inglenook. But not as good as ours—I mean *yours* Franky,' she added quickly.

'Of course. We don't do things by halves.' Franky spread out her hands in open invitation. 'So, look round, everybody. What do you see?'

Turning round, their gaze was caught by a large glass or Perspex screen covering most of the plastered wall opposite. It protected a wall fresco in faded red, obviously of historic value. Hannah went straight to a plaque next to the painting and, with the others crowding round, read aloud the story of Tobias and the Angel, a work commonly believed to have celebrated the opening of the tavern in 1560.

'And get this,' added Hannah. 'The granddaughter of the owner here, married Shakespeare's best friend in 1588.' She suddenly turned to them. 'If that's so, the wedding reception could have been here!'

'Could easily have been,' said Franky.

'And if it's Shakespeare's best friend getting married,' said Craig, 'he could have been best man.'

'Did they have a best man in those days?' Alicia posed the question.

'They did,' said Tom.

'How do you know that?'

'They had to, because the best man had to be strong.'

'Strong? Did the wedding ring weigh a ton?' Alicia said, with a chuckle.

'No, but—'

'Look,' interrupted Franky, 'why don't we all sit down, and let Tom tell his tale?'

To murmurs of agreement, they sat down at the dining table, Franky ensuring that she was at the end nearest the inglenook, a position from where she could see all their faces.

'Now, Tom, finish your story.'

'Well.' Tom shuffled his chair forward and placed his elbows on the table. 'It started in Anglo-Saxon England when men captured women, forcing them into marriage. Now the groom needed a tough guy to deter any of the bride's family who might beat him up in trying to rescue her. So, being the strongest, he was the best man to pick as bodyguard.'

'Wait,' said Alicia. 'You're suggesting that Shakespeare was strong. Who said? Where's the proof?'

'Well, didn't he poach a deer and was wanted by the landowner? There's evidence that he did.' Tom lowered his head to stare at her, over the rim of his glasses. 'In those days you would have had to drag or carry it away. Imagine lifting and carrying a deer on your shoulders, with all that blood, muscle and fat. It would have been two hundred weight at least.'

'How do you know he wasn't on a horse, dragging it?'

'Well, with a horse he'd be seen more easily, wouldn't he? He's stealing, don't forget.'

'Maybe he had his cronies helping him,' Alicia pointed out. 'Maybe the groom?'

'Hah,' said Hannah. 'That's why the marrying guy is called the groom because he looked after Shakespeare's horse while he's out poaching!'

'Hah.' Tom, smiling, pointed a finger.

'Good one Hannah,' said Craig, with a chuckle.

'Well,' said Alicia, seeming to miss the joke, 'is there evidence that Shakespeare was a poacher? I read there's none.'

'Okay,' said Franky, relieved to see the waiter approach with a bunch of menus in his hand. 'I think we'll all agree to disagree. Let's order, shall we?'

'Tom,' said Alicia, ignoring her. 'There's another problem with your story.'

'Oh?'

'You said the custom started in "Anglo-Saxon" times. That ended in 1066. That's five hundred years *before* Shakespeare's time.'

'Alicia,' said Tom, 'there is such a thing as tradition.'

'Okay,' said Alicia. 'I accept women could still be forced into marriage, but not by Fred Flintstone. Remember, both sides fixed a marriage for their own financial benefit.'

'You may be right,' said Hannah. 'But Shakespeare could still have been best man. No?' She looked to Craig for support. 'What do you think, Craig?'

'Who knows?' Craig broke the ice by mixing his Okie dialect with a Southern twang. 'Say, y'all, why don't we talk about our own interests?' He dropped the twang. 'What's yours, Tom?'

'Hah.' Tom adjusted his glasses. 'I don't know what those interests are until I'm interested. I've no hobbies, but I do occasionally indulge in a spot of hash from Himachal Pradesh, simply the best in Asia.'

There was a momentary silence and then they were all talking at once.

'Well, that's fine if that's all it is.'

'I ate the cake once, and my face felt so big I couldn't get my hands round to wash it.'

'I used to smoke the odd joint, but when I heard you could become schizoid from it, I junked the junk.'

'Anybody tried heroin?' Craig's deep voice silenced the chat. 'No?' He looked from face to face. It appeared that none had. 'Okay, I had a close friend at seventeen. His first fix was like your first drink of alcohol. It never seemed a problem because he used it for weeks, stopping and starting with no cold turkey. Then one day down the line a switch flipped in his head. We lost him four years later, on his twenty-first birthday.'

'Oh, how terrible,' said Hannah. 'That's awful.' She stared at him until her face crumpled. 'Oh, Craig. Your wife and son as well. Too much.' With a quick 'Sorry, sorry' and a fluttering of hands, she hastily produced a tissue and dabbed her eyes.

Craig put up the palms of his hands. 'I'm sorry, Franky. Back to the party. How about *Quotes*? We go round the table, ask the person next to you?'

There were nods of agreement.

'Shall I start?' Franky looked at Tom, sat on her left. "Say from whence you owe this strange intelligence." Character, please?'

'Macbeth,' said Tom. 'To the three witches.'

'Correct.'

'Easy,' said Hannah, then found Tom at her elbow about to address her. She averted her face, arms raised with a grimace. 'Go on then, do your worst, mastermind.'

Tom stared at the ceiling. 'Yes … erm … "The valiant never taste of death but once."'

'Oh.' Hannah gave it some thought. '*Henry V?*'

'No.'

'*Caesar?*' said Craig.'

Tom bowed his head.

'Your turn, Hannah,' said Franky.

Hannah screwed up her face, staring at Alicia. 'Erm. "Madame. I would challenge you to a battle of wits, but I see you're unarmed."'

'I would have said Beatrice in *Much Ado*, except it isn't.' Alicia's smile widened.

'How do you know that?' said Hannah. 'Tom? Come on, back me up.'

Tom gave a sigh, 'Alicia's right. Shakespeare may have said it, but he didn't write it, I'm afraid. There was a lot of hoo-hah over it, years ago.'

'We fear it's you, Hannah,' said Alicia. 'You're the one unarmed. Hey, why aren't we ordering?' She turned to face Franky. C'mon, action stations! We've gotta eat, chop-chop.' Grinning, she picked up her menu card.

Franky closed her eyes, before smacking Alicia in the teeth with a right hook. 'And now, ladies and gentlemen,' she announced, her face flushed. 'Here comes something truly Elizabethan.'

The waiter approached the table with a tray bearing five large glasses, each containing a golden coloured liquid.

'Hey,' said Craig with interest. 'This isn't wine, is it?'

'No. It's mead,' said Franky, still smarting. 'It's what they probably drank at the wedding. Tom? Want to taste?'

In the event Tom made no pretence of a ritual tasting, merely holding it in his mouth for a moment and then swallowing it. 'Hmm. Nice.' He waited while their glasses were filled, then raised his. 'Franky, on behalf of your brothers and sisters, I humbly thank you for your beneficence and wish you good health and happiness.'

'My thanks to you all.' She raised her glass. 'And because I move into the cottage tomorrow you can all move in with me.' She kept a straight face.

The four, glasses raised, suddenly became motionless.

'What?' said Alicia, lowering hers. 'What do you mean, "we can all move in?" She cast a quick look at the others.

'I mean that we can all move in tomorrow.' Franky flickered a little smile.

They continued to stare.

'*Tomorrow?*' said Tom, his brows knitted.

'It's Saturday, no seminars or tutorials. Why not?'

'That can't be done, Franky,' said Craig. 'We have to give a month's notice to our landlords.'

'That's right.' They nodded at each other in confirmation.

'No worries. I'll compensate you for it. I'll pay for all of you for the month. So, we'll be in by tomorrow night.'

More exchanged glances.

'Erm…' said Tom, frowning. 'Far be it for me to look a gift horse in the mouth but the practicalities here rather escape me. Are you actually saying that you will pay each of us the amount we need to—'

'Exactly,' said Franky. 'I will pay every penny you need to compensate the landlords for breaking your contracts. Don't worry, any of you,' she continued, 'I'll keep my promise. And from tomorrow, we're insured, okay? Oh, one more thing. I took the liberty of switching on the hot water and central heating before we left, except for the living room.' She glanced at Hannah. 'I thought you'd like a log fire on our first night.'

'Oh yes!' exclaimed Hannah. 'Franky, you are *amazing*!' She looked around. 'Isn't she?' She laughed excitedly.

'Well,' said Alicia, 'here's to Franky, our champion. Long may she reign.'

'Eternally', said Tom, who couldn't help but look at Franky with a puzzled smile.

Franky gave a royal wave of the hand, basking in their adulation. Never in her whole life had she felt so good. If it hadn't been for Alicia's slights…

It was 9.55 p.m. Franky stood with Hannah on the windswept pavement outside The White Swan, both watching Tom stalk away, his long coat flapping crow-like in the northerly wind, while clutching his floppy hat. Suddenly he stopped and turned to see them staring. Standing with his back to the wind, he buttoned up his coat. Then, lifting his collar, he gave a short wave, turned and was gone.

Franky raised her eyebrows at Hannah, the last to leave. 'You okay?'

'Oh yes, but … Franky, I'm going to pay you back one day … no, I mean it.' On impulse she put out her arms to give her a tense hug. 'I can't tell you how happy I am about Craig.'

'What about Alicia? You happy with her?' Franky, holding her with both hands, pushed her gently away, looking into her eyes.

'Erm, I don't know. What I do know is that I'll do everything I can to keep the peace. And I'll be friendly with her. That okay?'

An icy gust had her trying to pull forward her anorak hood, but unable to find its hard edging.

'Just a moment.' Franky calmly unrolled the hood, drawing it forward over her head. She patted it with the palm of her hand. 'That's it. You can go home now and be good.'

Hannah smiled back. 'Thanks. I will.'

'Tomorrow Craig might have to take us there in relays, because of baggage and stuff. Now, stop worrying. Go to and mark the day.'

'I will hasten to do your bidding.' Hannah grinned, waving her arm in departure.

Franky walked towards the centre of town, just as it started to sleet. She stopped and turned to see Hannah struggling towards Greenhill Street, huddled against the wind, her luminescent yellow anorak bright under the sodium street lamps.

She resumed her walk. Poor kid, she thought, going to her bedsit for the last time and all manufactured by her largesse, not to mention the time spent finding the cottage, then researching and costing it. But Hannah was still a friend, the first real one in her life and money couldn't buy one.

She strode down Wood Street unbothered by the cold. She could have been immersed in an ice-bath for all it mattered as, within a few minutes, she'd be in her warm and comfortable apartment.

She examined her feelings. Yes, she'd been elated at the gratitude she'd invoked in them, not dissimilar to the feelings her teenage acolytes had aroused in her, but it would have been a heck of a lot more gratifying without Alicia. By inviting her had she made the biggest mistake of her life? Getting angrier and angrier, she relived each of the two slights that Alicia had inflicted on her that evening.

As her blood came to the boil the contents of a shop window caught her eye. On a central stand was an electric saw surrounded by orange and black tools. She grabbed it fiercely with both hands. In the space of a few seconds she sliced through Alicia's neck, arterial blood spurting.

Ecstasy smashed by despair. Dear God, would it never end?

A short distance past the shop frontage was her apartment, accessed by entering through an oak door. She climbed upstairs, stopping on the landing to check the electricity meter.

She was getting ready for bed when she suddenly remembered the parcel that had arrived that day from America. There had been no time to open it, a present to herself costing $325 with value-added tax and import duty paid.

Inside the parcel was a Pratesi pillow made of pure linen and full of the finest Canada goose-down. Back home it could only have been found on Madison Avenue. She pressed her face into it, luxuriating in its smell and feel.

She got into bed, switched off the bedside light and sank down into her gorgeous new pillow.

Chapter Nine

That I did love the Moor to live with him,
My downright violence and storm of fortunes
May trumpet to the world
Othello, Act I, sc. iii

Franky got out of bed to pull the curtain drawstrings, then lay back relishing the thought of the day to come. What could surpass this moment, with so much to anticipate and enjoy! She smiled at the thought of Hannah racing around the cottage in innocent delight.

After breakfast she sent the meter reading to the power company, after which she began packing.

And paused. Slowly, she picked up the framed photograph of herself as a young teenager, sitting alongside her dog, a spaniel.

She studied her image. There was something she'd not noticed before, the expression on her face. It was one of anxious appeal, as if saying, "Yes, my dog's loveable, but can't you love me too?"

She sat down on the bed clutching the photograph. The boy, Jason, had appealed too, hadn't he, in his distress? She'd read *Heart of Darkness*, the Conrad novel, a searching exploration of good and evil, sanity and insanity. It had prompted her to ask the question: is the killer present in everyone, and is savagery just beneath the surface?

Her father *was* a savage. Just the act of *thinking* about him sent her pulse racing. So why had she never attacked him in fantasy, she wondered, his crime way beyond that of a slight? When thinking of him, why was it that rising body heat hadn't pushed her core into critical mass, followed by a knife to his guts? Was it something embedded in her DNA, some hereditary allegiance that prevented it?

In that moment she settled into despondency, bereft of her early optimism. She sat there for some time, thinking and questioning herself. In that sombre mood she suddenly dismissed all thoughts of quitting the course to become an author. The risk, she realised in a moment of cold logic, was far too great.

After washing, dressing and cleaning her teeth, she switched on her tablet to search "Hypersensitivity to Slight." Had there been a development in the study of the mind to show a link between that and other kinds of mental disorders? She wondered why she'd not contemplated the possibility before. She hurriedly scanned two websites, but neither revealed anything new, just the same old information. She was about to switch off when she spotted a few lines taken from the American magazine *Psychology Today*:

Slighting. The Dangers of Being Disrespected
Martin Daly and Margo Wilson, Professors of Psychology at McMaster University, Hamilton, Canada, estimate that two thirds of all murders in north America are committed by men hypersensitive to slight. In recent years in the US there has been a disturbing rise in the number of "flashpoint killings" triggered by trivial confrontations.

Her breathing quickened. She read it again. Her only consolation, or hope, was that the murderers were all men. But hadn't she been known as a tomboy in childhood? Suddenly she needed air, more than that which filled her lungs.

Panicking, she stood up and raced downstairs, wrenching open the front door to stare up at the cold and cloudless sky. She watched aircraft vapour trails lengthening and widening in the pale blue expanse. Forcing herself to breathe slowly, her panic gradually subsided.

She looked carefully down the street, both ways, a luminous and wide passage full of shadows from the autumnal sun.

Slowly, she went back upstairs to continue packing. When finished she struggled downstairs with the luggage, parking it neatly in the hallway. She studied her reflection in the hall mirror. A face stared back that smiled when she smiled. She pushed a strand of hair away from her eyes and looked again. Her expression held no fears.

Leaving her luggage behind, she strode through the town in growing optimism. She was going to meet Annabelle, having given her the benefit of the doubt over her dissertation. She made a vow to herself: she was determined to be more prosaic and would cast off all negativity.

She was buoyed by another thought. Not only was the cottage firmly in her sights but also *Othello*, an Institute Players production that Annabelle was to direct. She'd sent her an email with an attached copy of a Boston theatre review from two years ago. It described her Desdemona in a college production of *Othello* as "moving."

Smiling to herself, she walked down Church Street, imagining the evening meal that was to come, vowing to act the part of the perfect host. Should Alicia slight her again she would ignore it and keep an icy control over her emotions to ensure there would be no repeat of yesterday. This was *her* day and she wasn't going to ruin it. She'd make sure of that.

It was going to be a good day, a great day.

It just had to be.

She waited outside Annabelle's door, silently rehearsing Desdemona's speech, line by line, remembering the nuances, stresses and inflections that she would bring to the part.

The door opened, letting out a student. Annabelle stood there, smiling as ever. There was that aroma again, of a Tuscan vineyard, perfumed by sage and rosemary.

'Franky. How are you today?'

'Very well, thank you, Annabelle. And you?'

'Wonderfully well. No, don't sit there. Here.' She motioned her into the leather armchair. 'More comfortable, easier to chat.'

Franky sat down. 'Thanks.'

'So, how is everything?' Annabelle sat at her desk, smiling benignly.

'Good, so far. Erm…' She hesitated. 'I know this is about welfare but may I ask about *Othello*? Did you manage to read my email?'

'Yes, I did. Your Desdemona. Very impressive.'

'Oh, good.'

'Yes, in one way it's a pity. We were thinking of doing *Antony and Cleopatra*. You look just like the Herculaneum portrait of Cleopatra – have you seen it?'

Franky shook her head. 'No, I haven't.'

'She had red hair. Here…' She clicked a few keys and then swivelled the screen in Franky's direction.

'Wow.' Franky shook her head, smiling. 'She's prettier than me.'

Annabelle laughed a little. 'Don't you think she looks alarmed?'

'Yes, and she had cause to be.'

'Without a doubt.' "O wad some power the giftie gie us".

'Scottish floors me,' said Franky. 'It sounds like Burns. Is it?'

'It is indeed. "Oh, would we have the power to see ourselves as others see us." Yes, I could imagine you with *very* imaginative hair extensions. You would have looked fabulous.'

Franky took in Annabelle's pale features and dark, soulful eyes, her smooth forehead merging into the lustrous black hair. Just *being* with her was dreamlike …

'Back to Othello.' Annabelle's voice cut into her reverie. 'We'll be doing auditions in about a fortnight. Now, that's that. We're here to talk about you. Have you—'

'Annabelle.' Franky cut in, clamping her hands on the sides of the armchair, ready to lever herself up. 'To save you time, I can do the "I did love the Moor" speech now, if you like?'

'No, no need,' she said. 'We have to do auditions to be proper, but I'm sure you'll be the front runner for Desdemona. Happy with that?'

'Oh yes, of course.' Franky, her face flushed, hesitated before easing herself back into the armchair.

Annabelle frowned. 'Are you all right? You look disturbed.'

'Do I? No, no, I'm not. I'm fine.'

'Sure? Let's wait a moment, shall we? I suggest you close your eyes and breathe in and out slowly – you know the drill. Relax. That's it. Breathe slowly … in … and out. That's it.'

She obeyed, but a feeling of uncertainty had forced her to pretend. When she opened her eyes, she caught Annabelle switching from a thoughtful gaze to a quick smile.

'All right now?'

'Yes.'

'Good. So, how are things?'

'Okay. No problems. Well … erm.'

'We were talking last time about your father.'

'Yes.' Franky frowned a little. 'It's actually finding a place to start.'

Annabelle stretched out an arm. 'Take your time,' she said in a measured voice. 'Pretend I'm not here.'

As Franky took a deep breath, Annabelle suddenly changed her mind. 'No, you're not ready. I think I'm putting you under too much pressure. Maybe we should—'

'No, Annabelle, honestly, I'm fine.'

'No Franky. I think you should have a session with a professional counsellor. We can arrange it. This thing goes very deep, doesn't it?'

'Yes, but I'd rather it be you. It's that, well sometimes I get stressed, because all my life, well, for most of it, I've suffered from slights. I'm hypersensitive to them. I can't help it,' she said rapidly and then inhaled deeply, holding her breath for a moment.

Annabelle leaned forward, her eyes large and tender. 'Oh, you poor thing. I've heard of it, but that's awful. It must torment.'

'It does. I saw a psychotherapist when I was sixteen. I had a number of sessions, but it didn't end it completely.' She shrugged. 'I'm sorry to be so awkward.'

'Oh no! You're not. Look, I've got an email to send. While I'm doing that why don't you ignore me and just think about what worries you most, then we'll go to it. I promise you won't shock me.'

While Annabelle tapped her keyboard, Franky looked down at the floor, gathering her thoughts.

With the email sent, Annabelle turned to her, putting out a calming hand across the table, speaking softly, 'Are you all right?'

Franky nodded, steeling herself.

'Begin when you're ready.'

Franky settled herself in the armchair, trying to find the words, trying to make a start.

Annabelle waited …

The silence was broken by the sound of a heavy truck in the street outside, rumbling louder until it began to fade.

'Franky.' Annabelle spoke softly. 'It's not a slight, is it.' She paused. 'Something awful happened. You can tell me. Don't be afraid.'

Franky took a deep breath.

'Relax. Why don't you tell me about the slights first? How and when did they start?'

'Yes.' Franky's voice was taut. She licked her lips and began to explain the slights that had affected her since childhood, going through the teenage years of anger and resentment, together with her visits to the psychotherapist.

'Was there any common factor in all this, something or *somebody* that linked it together in your mind?' Annabelle's voice was almost a whisper.

'Yes, my father.'

'Do remember, this is only between the two of us. I promise never to repeat it to anyone.'

Franky hesitated. 'It's …'

'Franky.' Annabelle rolled her wheeled chair closer, stretching out a hand to hold hers. 'I won't be shocked, and you'll feel better if you tell me.' She paused on seeing Franky's pursed lips begin to tremble. 'Did he do anything to you?'

Frankly shook her head.

'If you feel the need to cry, then cry.'

Franky took another breath and began slowly. 'I … I think it began when

I was playing hopscotch on the patio. The window was open and my father was in the kitchen with my mother. Suddenly I heard him say, "How did that redhead come to jump out of you?"

Annabelle instinctively put a hand to her mouth. Then quickly recovering, 'Franky.' She paused a moment. 'Tell me. Were those his actual words? Or were they something that—'

'No. It's exactly what he said. I've never forgotten them. I was about ten. I didn't understand at the time, him saying "come to jump out of you." I didn't think it was me. I was far too young. But later…' She swallowed hard and winced.

'Go on,' Annabelle whispered, 'Don't stop.'

'Yes.' Franky's eyes sparkled in the low sunlight piercing the window. A tear emerged, dribbling down her cheek. She brushed it away with the back of her hand.

Annabelle got up to kneel at her side, placing a hand on her arm. 'What happened after that?' she whispered.

Franky bit her lip.

'Franky. You have my complete confidence. It won't go any further. I promise.'

Franky's chest rose and fell.

'I'm your friend. Let it out. You've been humping this baggage around far too long. What happened?'

'I…'

'Where were you?'

'At home.' Franky swallowed hard.

'When?' Annabelle stretched out to grab a box of tissues, handing her one.

'My last year. At college.' She dabbed her eyes. 'I came home a day early and…'

'And?'

Annabelle's hand grew firmer on Franky's arm as she listened to her story that was interspersed with sobs and difficult silences. Franky left nothing out, describing the shock that still persisted. 'I can't think of home without *him* being there, like some lurking animal. That's what he is.'

Annabelle said nothing for a while. She withdrew to sit on her chair. 'How do you feel now?'

'Better.' She tried to smile. 'Thank you.'

'Did you tell your mother?'

Franky shook her head. 'Oh no. I couldn't.'

'Do you want to tell the police now?'

'Yes, but…'

'Scared of him?'

'Yes. Except—'

'Except what?'

'I was escaping, from myself, but now, I want revenge. The therapist told my mother I might one day. Not on people who slighted me. But him. He's responsible for that boy and for what I am now.'

'Franky?' Annabelle's voice remained soft, but her tone was cautious. 'Tell me. Do you think you will – or could, turn violent?'

'No.' She grimaced. 'But if I found him again with a boy, I don't know what I'd do. Scream probably, as I did the first time. And then I'd … yes, I would. I'd attack him with everything I could lay my hands on. Wouldn't anyone, at that moment?'

There was a silence. 'I'm going to help you with this baggage. You've carried it around on your own, far too long, haven't you?'

'Yes.' Her face crumbled, and she began to sob.

Annabelle grabbed another tissue. 'Franky, we're going to sort this out. Remember, it stays between the two of us. I promise.'

Franky returned to her apartment to make her final checks and then, finding she had time, left her luggage in the hallway to go outside. She locked the door before crossing the road to the half-timbered cafe opposite.

She sat next to the quaint bay window and looked around. There was Maggie, the elderly student, on the far side of the room, sitting with her back to her. She was in conversation with a man of about the same age, presumably her husband. He looked the very image of a well-to-do professional with his neat silvery hair, club tie and blue blazer.

When the coffee arrived, she took in the calm way they talked together, her tilt-back of the head, their light, restrained chuckles. *Insiders*. While many lived on the rocky shores of life – she counted herself one of them – they were well inland, burrowed comfortably in a world surrounded by friends of their own class, with its own standards and common code.

She took a call. It was Craig, saying he was running early and could she be ready in ten minutes.

She finished her coffee, paid the bill and left, pausing to allow traffic to pass by. Meanwhile, Japanese tourists crowded together on the pavement outside her apartment, one of whom was snapping the cafe with her in the foreground.

Having crossed the road, the plump, smiling photographer offered his camera so she might take a shot of himself with the group. Franky was only too happy to oblige.

The picture taken, she handed the camera back with a laugh that, for some reason, prompted him to laugh, and then the others joined in while parting their jolly ranks to let her through to the front door.

The day had started well. She was smiling to herself when she deposited her luggage out on the pavement, then posted the keys back through the letter box.

As she waited, the clear blue sky of early morning vanished as a cold wet wind swept down the street, forcing her to stand in the shelter of the doorway. It did nothing to dull the spirits of the animated Japanese who wandered away, putting up umbrellas, chatting amiably.

She amused herself by imagining a spring day full of birdsong, while walking between white-blossomed hedgerows with bucolic lambs frolicking about until they caught sight of her and scurried towards their mothers. Wood smoke lazily drifted from the chimney, its scent sharp and welcoming, the cottage redolent with the smell of coffee and the malty aroma of baking bread. Hannah was there, cheerfully wiping her hands on a white apron. Together they cut hot scones in two, lathering them with butter and jam. The kettle whistling…

Her reverie was cut short by Craig's arrival, his car towing a small box-trailer. He parked by the pavement kerb, then got out to help stow away her luggage.

'You rented this?' said Franky, passing him the second of her bags.

'Had to.'

'How much?'

'Forty-five pounds for the day.'

'I'll pay you back.'

'No, you won't.'

'Craig, it's my party.'

'No,' he said firmly, closing and locking the box lid. 'You've shelled out enough. C'mon.'

He got back in the car.

Franky was a little irritated to find Alicia occupying the front passenger seat, but it quickly dissipated as she opened the rear door to a chorus of 'Hi, Franky!'

'Hi, gang.' She squeezed herself alongside Hannah and Tom. Crammed in, she struggled with her seat belt until it clicked into place. 'Okay, Craig. Go, man.'

As they set off, Hannah grinned at her. 'I was really down when I heard it was going to rain,' she said, 'but who cares?'

'Time travellers,' said Alicia, 'have no weather.'

"Travellers never did lie",' said Franky, "though fools at home condemn them." Play, please?'

'No idea,' said Hannah happily. 'And I couldn't care less,' she said, with a giggle.

'Is it *Hamlet*?' said Alicia.

'No.'

'No idea,' said Craig. 'I'm with Hannah. Who cares?'

'Yes, who cares?' said Tom. 'But I'll have a guess. *The Dream*?'

'No.'

'Hurray,' said Alicia, clapping her hands. 'Tom doesn't know everything, after all. That's amazing.'

'Is it *The Tempest*?' said Craig.

'Correct. Who is it?'

'Haven't a clue.'

'Could it be…' Hannah paused. '*Antonio?*'

'Correct,' said Franky. 'He's commenting on how time travellers see things clearer, being in a fantasy world. It's the fools in the real world at home who are so blinded by reality that they can't see beyond their narrow confines.'

'This is what we're going to do,' said Hannah, 'in fantasy, go back to the Tudors. I can see that inglenook, the fire blazing and little ole me inside. I can't wait.'

'Okay. When we arrive,' said Alicia, tossing a grin back at Hannah, 'your duty is to make the fire.'

'I still can't wait. I've got one,' she said. "Let every man be master of his time".

'*Hamlet?*' said Craig.

'No.'

'The *Dream?*' said Alicia.

'Nope.'

'One of the Henry plays?' Franky looked at Hannah.

'No.'

'It's *Macbeth*,' said Tom. 'Macbeth to Banquo.'

'Correct,' said Hannah.

Alicia groaned. 'Tom's at it again.'

'I think he deserves a free Prosecco when we get there,' said Franky. 'Shall we allow him that?'

'I think we should,' said Alicia. 'And we'll join him!'

'The problem is I only drink Moët & Chandon," said Tom firmly.

'Get outta here. It's Prosecco from Tesco.'

They all laughed, including Tom.

Hannah saw Anne Hathaway's cottage coming up on their left.

'Hey, Anne?' she called out as they passed by. 'Eat your heart out. Our cottage may be small but it's big in heart.'

'Hear! Hear,' rumbled Craig.

'Does anyone know how "Hear, Hear," started?' said Tom.

'No! And we couldn't care less,' said a grinning Alicia, amidst laughter.

'It was in Parliament in the late seventeenth century. The phrase used was "Hear him, hear him."'

'Oh, belt up Tom.'

'By the late eighteenth century, it was reduced to 'Hear, hear' It was also used in the King James Bible when—'

He broke off at Hannah starting to giggle, followed by Alicia.

Tom looked around in mock bewilderment. 'What?' And then he raised a hand in royal acknowledgement. 'Forgive me, I'm just a snapper-up of unconsidered trifles.'

Franky felt an enormous relief, almost as much as that following her confession to Annabelle. It was matched by a deep excitement, the like of which she had never before experienced. She was at the head of good company, heralding a new life. The future looked as good as it could possibly be.

She felt epic.

Chapter Ten

On arrival at the cottage, Craig backed the car and trailer as near to the front door as possible.

'Thanks, Craig,' said Hannah, getting out.

When the front door was unlocked, she and Alicia carried the shopping bags straight to the kitchen where they distributed bread, frozen food, milk, vegetables, meat and fruit between fridge, freezer and pantry.

Meanwhile, Tom and Craig began to fill the hallway with pieces of luggage.

'What's in that, Tom?' Hannah pointed to a long black case that he'd propped up against a corner by the door. 'A machine-gun?'

'No, my rocket launcher.'

'I know what that is,' said Alicia. 'It's a keyboard. My brother has one.'

'Tom, did you bring it from home?' said a surprised Hannah.

'No, I rented it.'

'Oh, okay,' said Alicia. 'You're now a musician. Is there anything this man isn't?'

'What are you going to serenade us with, Tom?' said Franky. 'Rock, pop or classical?'

'Oh, I love romantic melancholy,' said Hannah. 'Give me Rachmaninoff's Second Piano Concerto. I get tingles — oh it's raining!' She dashed outside to gather her last few pieces.

'I think Bach is Tom's thing,' said Alicia. 'Master of counterpoint. Right, Tom?'

'What's that?'

'I said Bach's your thing because it's arithmetical.'

'No, not arithmetical— mathematical.'

'Oh, because arithmetical doesn't add up?'

Tom chuckled. 'No, Bach plotted the math of line against line. Mozart's music was applied math.'

Outside, Hannah yelped as the rainfall turned into a thick downpour sluicing down the roof and bonnet of the car. She grabbed her final item and hurried back inside.

Craig went out with a coat over his head, scouring the car for anything left behind. Satisfied, he zapped the car locks and headed back so quickly that he stumbled over bags and cases, crashing into Tom, to a spontaneous outburst of laughter.

Craig put out a hand to help Tom to his feet. 'Sorry, Tom.'

Tom smoothed himself down. 'If this is how it's going to be,' he said in his gravest of tones, 'I shall be speaking to my lawyer.'

'Craig?' Hannah suddenly spoke in alarm. 'The car keys – do you mind? There's something missing.'

'There's nothing left in the trunk. I've checked.'

'No! I must look.'

'Or in the car. There's nothing left.'

'I know,' she said rapidly. 'But I must look. Thanks.' Taking the keys, she hurried out into the downpour.

A minute later she was back, her forehead plastered with strings of tangled hair dripping water, her mouth open, eyes staring. 'I can't find Bernard, I put him in a bag but he's gone.' She clutched her head staring around her. 'Oh my God!'

'You sure you brought it?'

'Yes!' She hurried down the hallway into the kitchen.

Alicia exchanged glances with Tom and Franky. 'Bernard? Who's Bernard? Have we got ourselves a stowaway?'

'It's her teddy bear,' said Craig.

Alicia rolled her eyes around. 'Teddy bear? Jeez.'

'Hah.' Tom's voice attracted their attention. He'd moved his keyboard case, revealing a paper bag. He bent down to produce a brown and worn-looking bear.

'Got it, Hannah!' Craig's voice thundered down the hallway.

A pause and then 'Aaagh!' Hannah, crying out, came hurrying back, hands raised, her relief turning to sobs as she clutched the bear to her chest. 'Oh, thanks, Tom. Sorry, everybody. What a bird-brain. I'm putting him in my room. He'll never be allowed out.' She set off back to her room.

'Hannah?' said Alicia.

'What?' Hannah stopped and turned.

'What's with our sixth resident that makes him so special?'

'Oh, lots.' Hannah came back, still breathing hard. 'Craig knows this story. He was Grandpa's mascot. He flew bombing raids over Germany in World War II. Then, when Grandpa died, my mother had him. She believed it brought good luck because he'd survived the war as a bomber pilot when most didn't.' Hannah drew a breath. 'She gave him to me when I first went to college. I know it seems stupid and infantile but—'

'Hey,' said Craig, interrupting her. 'Hannah, we all have things we treasure. It has your Grandpa's life in it. Huge sentimental value.' He glanced at Alicia. 'Nobody's knocking it — *are* they?' he added, as a mild threat.

'No,' said Alicia. 'I didn't know. Sorry, Hannah.'

'Thanks, but it's not you, it's me.' Hannah waved a hand. 'Oh God, I am, aren't I, a dimwit?'

With Bernard tucked firmly under her arm, she picked up the bag and went down to her room where she placed Bernard on the window ledge.

She took a shower, telling herself there would be no more panic stations and no more shows of emotion. Instead she would commit to a grown-up level of hard work, helpfulness and lack of self-pity. She would stop giggling. She would no longer react to anything on impulse, but would show restraint.

Showered and warmly dressed, she went into the kitchen where Franky and Alicia were sorting out the meal.

'Hi, I'm on fire duty with Craig. Tell him I'll be in the woodshed.'

'He's still in the bathroom,' said Franky.

Hannah went to the bottom of the stairs. 'Craig?' she called out. 'I'm getting some logs in. When you're ready can you give me a hand?'

'Yeah, coupla minutes' came the voice from above.

Hannah put on her anorak and went outside. It had stopped raining.

She found the wheelbarrow inside the woodshed and took out the red fire-gloves lying there. She put them on, then climbed to the top of the woodpile.

As soon as Craig appeared, she began to drop logs on to the concrete floor, close to the wheelbarrow.

'Shall we take enough for a week,' said Craig. 'Save us doing it day by day?'

'Great idea, Craig.'

Hannah watched him make five journeys from the woodshed to the side of the cottage, each time tipping the load close to the kitchen door. For the final journey a bag of kindling sticks was added.

Their next task was to dump the logs into a huge wicker basket until it was a quarter full and then haul it into the living room. There, the logs were stacked neatly at the side of the inglenook. Four more journeys resulted in a neat and attractive looking stockpile.

'Great job, Hannah.' He raised his hand to give her a high-five.

She reciprocated. 'Yes, don't log piles look nice.'

'They do.'

She was conscious of Craig standing next to her. No one was watching. But nothing came from him, no movement, no sign, nothing.

She turned to a pile of newspapers that she'd pulled out of litter bins in the town. 'Were you ever a boy scout, Craig?' She slipped out a double page from one of them.

'No, I wasn't. But I know how to light a fire. Though I may be watching an expert. Show me how you do it.'

Hannah crouched down in front of the fire grate. 'Well, this is the domestic version Girl Scouts taught me.'

Feeling tearful, she folded the double page twice, twisted it into a stick and laid it pointing to the back of the fire-basket. Screwing up more paper sticks, she placed them in the same direction as the first and soon covered the basket bottom. Another layer was placed on top, at right angles to the first layer. Then came the kindling sticks, stacked with plenty of space between them, allowing the air to circulate.

During her assembly work Franky, Tom and Alicia, having lived with central heating all their lives, gravitated into the room to watch the delicate construction of the pyre. When it was finished Craig produced a matchbox.

'Hannah, you have the honours.'

'Thank you.' Hannah took the matchbox and read the label: '"Bryant and May." Well, you two, whoever you are and wherever you are, thank you.' She struck a match and held the small yellow flame to a number of paper twists that protruded through the bars of the fire-basket.

'Arden Cottage alight,' said Alicia.

'I hope not. I think you mean warm,' said Tom with a wry smile.

'*Soon*,' said Craig.

It didn't take long for the curly little flames to spread along the front of the grille. Within a few minutes the kindling caught fire, at which point Hannah selected two logs, smaller and lighter than the others. She bent down to place them carefully across the flames, ensuring that their outer ends rested on the edges of the basket. As soon as they began to burn, she carefully placed a thicker log, bridging both of them.

'That will get it going,' she whispered and, keeping her eyes fixed on the fire, took off her gloves and sat slowly down on the inglenook seat.

Franky entered with a tray bearing five glasses of Prosecco, handing them out, before raising her own. 'To Arden Cottage,' she proposed.

'Arden Cottage,' was the toast.

With the meal seemingly held in abeyance and no one minding, they settled down, the fire beginning to burn brightly, warm air drawing the flames into the chimney.

Tom rose to leave the room and returned with a CD player.

'Oh,' said Franky suddenly. 'Forgot to tell you all. The dishwasher. I called yesterday and they've fixed it.'

'Good omen,' said Hannah. 'Tom? Why aren't we listening to your keyboard?'

'Because,' said Tom, inserting a disc. 'Pachelbel's Canon in D Major's best heard played by the best musicians.'

It wasn't long before they became captivated by the music's repetitive melodic phrases and harmonic variations. Hannah shook her head slowly, her lips parted, her senses on full alert.

When the cello and three violins drew out the final chord, it was received in silence, no one wanting to speak, lest they be accused of breaking the magic of the moment. Instead, with cheeks reddened in the firelight glow, they watched the flickering shadows on the walls and beams.

'It's remarkable,' said Tom slowly, 'that people who sat here would have known Anne Hathaway. We're the only cottage next to it. She and her parents would have been our neighbours. They'd meet riding, or walking through the woods, to the market in Stratford.'

'Yes,' said Franky, 'You were right Hannah. We *are*, aren't we, truly back in time.'

'We certainly are!' Hannah grinned, her luminous eyes shining in joy as a sudden woosh of flames, like a flock of trapped birds, rushed up the chimney.

Franky lay back, marvelling how, in the space of one day, she'd been transported between two worlds, one filled with doubt and anxiety, to another, filled with friendship and in surroundings she'd never dreamt possible. Had she really intended to stimulate conflict as fodder for a book when she was as full of pleasure as she could possibly be? Wasn't harmony, that which she really sought?

Craig stood up, breaking the silence. 'Sorry, folks, it's time for me to take the trailer back, else it's another £25 tomorrow.'

'Do you want anyone to go with you?' said Franky, sitting up.

'No, I'm fine.'

'You sure?' Hannah sat upright, ready to stand.

'No, I'm okay – thanks.'

'We'll have the meal ready for when you get back,' Franky called out. 'And thanks a million.'

'Okay!' Craig's voice echoed from the hallway.

Franky lay back in her armchair.

Once again there was silence, apart from the crackle of burning wood.

'I think,' said Alicia, 'if the family were in dispute, they'd come in here. I think they'd sit by the fire and come to an agreement. And, of course, talk about the weather. The Brits talk about it constantly, everywhere you go.'

'It's because they're more reticent than we are,' said Franky. 'It gives them the cue to start a conversation.'

'Wash day,' continued Alicia. 'All the windows would be open to get rid of the steam. Even when it was freezing. Think about it. We have the best of their legacy, this cottage, this atmosphere. But it was just a place to eat and sleep for them. How lucky are we?'

'But,' said Tom, 'if Polonius hadn't been behind the arras he wouldn't have been pierced through. Time for the main event.' He left the room.

'Isn't he a hoot?' said Alicia, chuckling.

Tom returned with his keyboard.

'What are you going to play Tom?'

'My music, to start with. I presume I'm allowed that privilege?' He placed the keyboard at the side of the inglenook.

'Tom,' said Alicia, 'you're allowed whatever you want. Hit those keys.'

Tom took a chair from under the dining table and placed it in front of the keyboard, then plugged the cable into a nearby power point. He sat down. Making himself comfortable, he raised his hands and – as if about to bang them down at the start of a Tchaikovsky concerto — began to play, *White Christmas*.

It brought instant laughter.

Tom stopped to peer at them in tutorial fashion. 'It was President Roosevelt who refused to kill a bear he'd captured,' he said in a monotone. 'It was on a hunting expedition and that's how teddy bear came into parlance. It was Michtom who later actually…'

'Oh, belt up and play, Tom,' said Alicia, laughing.

Tom, his dark eyes glittering, settled down to his task, playing Chopin's smooth and gentle Nocturne, Op. 9, No. 2. He sat erect, his long fingers delicately tickling the keys from the low octaves to the high.

As the final tinkle died away there was no applause, again no one wanting to break the spell. Instead, they rose to join Tom at the keyboard.

'Oh my,' breathed Hannah, wiping a tear from her eye. She kissed his cheek. 'So sad, so beautiful.' Her tears were not for the music. It was Craig.

With Craig's return, they sat at the dining table, their faces lit by fire and candlelight. A Mozart CD played quietly in the background. Tom and Alicia were praised on the arrival of a chicken salad, to which had been added croutons and a Caesar dressing.

'Don't congratulate me too soon,' said Tom. 'You've not eaten it yet.'

At that point Franky went out to return with a bottle of champagne. She handed it to Craig, along with a corkscrew. 'You can do the extraction big feller.'

'Hang on.' Tom wanted to study the label. 'Hah, Dom Perignon 2002. Should anyone be doubtful, I must let it be known that I have never tasted this vintage. But I know of it. And it is extremely expensive.'

The bottle opened and the contents distributed, Franky pointed her glass at Hannah. 'To our fire chief.'

'Our fire chief,' was the response.

'And Tom, our musician extraordinaire,' said Hannah.

As they toasted each other, Franky remembered a day at college spent on the river, lying on a cushioned barge and hearing only the swish of oars and the occasional quack of a duck. It had evoked the same sensation that she felt now, one of sheer tranquillity.

After the salad came an orange pudding.

'From a sixteenth-century recipe,' Alicia said proudly, placing it in the centre of the table.

Hannah looked at the pudding. 'Did you use sugar?' she said hesitantly.

'No, you're okay. It's a sugar substitute.'

'Oh, good. Thanks,' said Hannah. 'Sorry to ask.'

'That's okay,' said Alicia brightly. 'What I did was take orange rind, pare it thin, boil it, then add four ounces of butter, the yolks of six eggs, four ounces of sucralose and a pinch of salt. Then I beat it and baked it in the oven.'

'Nice,' said Hannah. 'I bought a diabetic cake from Waitrose, should last me a week or two.'

'Oh,' said Alicia, pausing. 'You should have said. Everybody's got the sucralose. I wasn't going to cook two lots, was I?'

'Oh no!' Hannah said, in dismay. 'I thought you'd done this for me specially.' She looked round forlornly. 'I'm sorry, everybody.'

'No need, Hannah,' said Franky. 'I told Alicia to do it. My mistake.' Having lied, she smiled to herself. Judging by Alicia's expression, it seemed evident that she knew she'd lied. That's the way to handle her, she thought. Be good to her and make her feel indebted.

'What a change from my bedsit,' said Hannah.

It was an hour later, the five sitting in an arc in front of the inglenook. The table had been cleared and they could hear the dishwasher rumbling away in the kitchen. The candles had been left alight at Hannah's request.

Hannah stood up to make a flowing movement with one arm while raising her glass in the other.

'To our host. On behalf of us all, and with apologies to our Bard, my kind Franky, I can no other answer make but thanks.' She bowed her head. 'And thanks. And ever … thanks.'

'Hear! Hear!' said Craig, standing up with his glass. 'To Franky.'

It brought the others standing. 'Franky,' was the chant.

'Franky,' said Tom. 'Long may she reign.'

They sipped wine and sat down again.

At a signal from Tom, Franky rose to her feet. 'Thank you. And it's my pleasure.' Raising the palms of her hands she intoned:

'If we shadows have offended,

Think but this, and all is mended

That you have but slumbered here

While these visions did appear'

'Hurrah!' Hannah clapped.

'The play, please?' Franky looked round the table.

'The *Dream*,' the four said, almost in unison.

'Which act?'

'Four?' asked Hannah.

Franky shook her head. 'No.'

'At a guess five?' said Alicia.

Franky bowed to her.

Tom stood up and likewise raised his hands.

'First, rehearse your song by rote,

To each word a warbling note,

Hand in hand, with fairy grace,

Will we sing, and bless this place.'

Franky, still standing with hands raised, continued:

'Not a mouse

Shall disturb this hallowed house.

I am sent with broom before,

To sweep the dust behind the door'

Amid laughter, Tom and Franky turned to stiffly bow to each other and then sat down to enthusiastic clapping from Craig, Alicia and Hannah.

'Hey,' said Alicia. 'You two have been rehearsing.' She took a sip of wine. 'I can't remember a thing. As my British grandma used to say, "I'm puggled."'

'Puggled,' said Hannah. 'What a great word Alicia.'

In response, Alicia raised her glass with a smile.

Gradually they began to settle down, luminous faces lowered as they watched and listened to the burning wood, accompanied by the patter of rain on the windows.

'If I wasn't rather inebriated,' conjectured Tom, 'at a rough guess I reckon they've had about 190,000 fires here in five hundred years.'

No one made a comment, too passive and too sleepy.

After dozing for ten minutes, Craig slowly dragged himself to his feet. 'Well, don't know about you folks, but I'm tuckered out.'

Before leaving, he bent down to give Franky a kiss on the cheek. 'Thanks for inviting me.' He withdrew, patting her arm. On his way out, he turned. 'Hey, who's emptying the dishwasher?'

'Tonight, it's Hannah and me,' said Franky. 'You're on tomorrow night with Alicia. The roster 's on the kitchen board.'

'Okay, night everybody.'

After the others had gone to bed, Hannah and Franky began tidying up the kitchen, ready for the morning.

With the jobs half-done Franky tapped Hannah's arm. 'You get to bed. I'll finish.'

'Sure?'

'Yes. Go.'

'Franky, I can't believe it. What you've done for us … it's just…' She flapped her arms. 'You're incredible.'

'Glad you came, huh?'

'What – how dare you!' Hannah gave her a quick hug. 'I wouldn't have missed it for the world. Night!'

With Hannah gone, Franky went back to the living room and doused the candles. She took great care to ensure the fireguard was fixed in the correct position. Then she paused to gaze at the shadows that the firelight magnified, flickering high upon the walls, its reflection orange in the small window panes.

She straightened the chairs at the table and, before leaving, stood in the doorway to picture the room as it would be on their final evening before the Christmas break. She would organise a celebration to remember.

For a moment she stood motionless, more sensing than listening. Then she went out, closing the door softly, before going upstairs.

It was strangely quiet as she reached the top. At the first creak of the landing came a communal shout: 'Thanks, Franky!'

She stood for a moment, thrilled. 'And thank you all for coming,' she replied and went into her room.

While they waited for Craig to return, she'd disappeared to leave a manila envelope on each bed, containing rules of behaviour, a protocol for settling disputes, emergency phone numbers and the location of the nearest shops and other facilities. A card read, 'With love and welcome'. She'd added a chocolate truffle from Harrods, wrapped in cellophane and tied with a red ribbon. The printed label read: 'Good welcome can make good people,' a line from *Henry VIII*.

She thought it the happiest moment of her life.

THE FALL

Chapter Eleven

Franky, rounding a bend, stopped dead in her tracks. Ahead was a tunnel, formed by arched tree branches, meeting from both sides of the lane. It looked dark inside and, given her black mood, a depressing prospect. And —dare she admit it to herself— rather frightening? She decided she'd walked far enough and turned round to go back.

She grimly relived the events of 25 minutes ago. Following a spat with Alicia, she'd plunged out of the cottage into a cold north-westerly. She'd covered well over a mile before she became calm enough to take in her surroundings.

She retraced her steps, walking between crimson-leafed hedgerows, bedecked with shiny necklaces of red berries. The English countryside reminded her of Massachusetts. Then, as a teenager, she would welcome glorious days in the fall that she would hold in her memory, emotions stirred by the discovery of wildflowers in a sheltered dell, yellow and brown leaves blown into swirling masses, the wind rippling across the lake, and then, on cold evenings, to sit in front of the fire to watch caves and animals, monsters and grotesques form in its glowing depths.

Suddenly, she stopped walking as her blood began to boil. What had taken place that morning had ended with her taking hold of a fantasy lump hammer and smashing Alicia's head with it.

Sweating, despite the cold wind, she found herself gripping the top bar of a gate, dwelling on the mistake she'd made in taking her into the fold. She had to accept that she'd put ego and inflated ambition before common sense.

Since arrival at the cottage some weeks ago, she'd ignored the little annoyances that stemmed from communal living, allowing Alicia's pinpricks to pass without challenge, discounting them beforehand, knowing that in any new 'family' there were bound to be petty annoyances. She'd pledged herself to retain her dignity as leader of the household, not to stoop to retaliation, but to dismiss them as transient and not worth the bother.

She had succeeded. Until now. The incident that sent her storming out began with her pinning a note to the kitchen noticeboard, appealing to whoever it was who had left hairs in the washbasin of the downstairs bathroom. Hannah and Alicia were its sole users. Alicia's hair was dark whereas Hannah's was blonde. The loathsome hairs were dark.

Maybe matters would have righted themselves if she hadn't pinned up an accompanying note printed in large, red capital letters: 'IT MAKES ME SICK!'

The altercation started after Tom, Craig and Hannah had left to go shopping, leaving her and Alicia alone in the cottage. Franky had been standing in the hallway, broom in hand and was about to bend down to use the dustpan when she looked up. There was Alicia standing at the head of the stairs, looking down.

'Franky, why did you print it in red block capitals and with an exclamation mark?'

Franky rested the broom against the newel post. 'You know why. To make sure it's noted. I've asked everyone before and nothing changed.'

'You only mention the downstairs bathroom. Why not upstairs? I'll tell you why, you were getting at me, not Hannah. Admit it.'

Franky folded her arms. 'Sorry Alicia but her hair isn't that colour and you're the only one to share the bathroom with her. Who else could it be? I'm sorry, but it has to be you, doesn't it?'

'So why didn't you tell me privately? Why blazon it on the board when you could have texted me? Why tell the world in capital letters that I make you sick? No, you wanted to humiliate me, vent your anger on me. Okay, I'll now tell you what makes *me* sick. Whenever things go wrong, or you tell us about not leaving lights on and stuff, you always look at me when you say it. Why haven't you ticked off Craig for leaving things lying around, or Hannah, forgetting her turn to clean the oven? We're not perfect. I'm sorry I didn't clean the washbasin. But I'd ease off, if I were you.' She turned to go back upstairs.

'And if I don't?' Franky's tone was ice-cold.

Alicia stopped on the penultimate step before the landing. 'No!' She turned, making a cutting gesture with her hand. 'Let's not do this.'

'No. I want to know what you meant by "If I were you".'

'Right.' Alicia walked down a couple of steps. 'If you want to know, I'll tell you. We hear you muttering about this and that. You complain all the time. We're getting cheesed off with it.'

'We? Who's we?' Franky sucked in her top lip.

'Us. Us four. Your housemates. Who do you think?'

'You don't get it, do you,' she said, breathing heavily. 'I just happen to be paying for all of us, and you talk about *we?*'

'You chose to do it Franky— Oh I don't need this.' Alicia waved a dismissive hand and turned to climb back upstairs, at which Franky flung the broom clattering down the hallway.

'Yes, you do, Alicia!' she shouted. 'You do need it because you make me FUCKING SICK!'

It was then she seized the lump hammer.

Franky returned to the cottage at 1.10 p.m. and nipped up to her room. After much reflection she'd decided not to confront Alicia anymore. There was no alternative. It was important to keep the ship afloat.

She ate lunch in the living room and then, joined by Tom, watched CNN's early morning news. Afterwards she went up to her room to work on her dissertation.

Around 4.15 p.m. she went downstairs. Looking down the hallway she saw Alicia at the kitchen worktop.

'You okay?' she said, entering.

Alicia turned to glance at her. 'I guess,' turning back, 'you?'

'Yes. Want a coffee?' She went to pick up the kettle.

'No, I'm good — thanks,' Alicia added quickly.

'Alicia…' Franky stared at the kettle for a while and then spoke quietly and calmly. 'I know how difficult it is for you. But we did agree to keep washbasins, baths and showers clean and tidy? I wasn't getting at you. I didn't know it was you at first. I –'

'Yes, but stuff happens. We're not robots. You can't cover everything.' She went to empty the dishwasher.

'You're right.' Franky waited until she was handed a few warm plates for stacking in a cupboard. 'Just thought I'd mention it.' She summoned up a smile. 'We can only do our best, can't we?'

'Yes,' said Alicia — before turning her back on her.

Fuck! As soon as Franky entered her bedroom, she flung open the window to take a deep breath of cold air, disgusted with her cowardice. She'd capitulated and got nowhere. She'd conned herself into thinking she could control Alicia, when it was her very presence that irritated her.

Yes, she'd admit that the strengthening undercurrent of tension in the cottage wasn't due to anything that Alicia actually *did*. It was her general demeanour, an amalgam of bits of body language, like an arch of an eyebrow or a curl of the lips suggesting she wanted to be elsewhere, rather than cooped up with someone she'd rather not know.

It had led to a general increase in tension, with Hannah, Craig and Tom doing their best to lower it. As a result, the cottage was a less than happy place, with no one wanting to say, or do anything, that risked disruption to their otherwise, well-organised, life.

Franky, trying to remain calm, had tried to manage their communal living, making it as comfortable and agreeable as possible. Well, for God's sake, hadn't she made every effort to keep up the conviviality and camaraderie? Hadn't she persuaded Tom to play his mood music on alternative evenings to Shakespearean quotes, so creating some fun between the inevitable crises with essays, the demands of dissertations and the disruption caused by evening and weekend jobs, not to mention the stuffy lingering cold that was passed round ever since Hannah first brought it there? And was she thanked for her efforts? No, she was not – except, of course, by Hannah who was clearly trying hard to maintain a balance, being as nice to everyone as she could.

Franky was well aware that battle lines had been drawn. From now on, the slightest dispute could pitch them into open warfare in which Alicia would finally quit, leaving her to pay out rental compensation to the landlord as per agreement and how stupid and overgenerous had she been with that!

It was like walking on eggshells. It might take just one small incident to tear apart the fabric of their hitherto, mainly peaceful, existence. It would be Alicia who would trigger it. Of course, she would. It seemed as inevitable as night follows day.

"Alisseeur." Spoken slowly, the name sounded like a snake hissing.

It threatened to come to a head one evening, just after dinner. Franky was alone in the living room, working from notes when she heard raised voices coming from the kitchen.

It sounded like Hannah arguing with Alicia. She stood up and went to enquire, but by the time she got there the voices had fallen silent and Hannah was nowhere to be seen.

'What's with Hannah?' she asked Alicia, who was tidying up the kitchen.

'Have a guess,' said Alicia ironically. 'It's the water, would you believe.'

'Water - in what way?'

'Better ask her yourself.'

Just then Hannah came in from outside, carrying an empty bucket.

'Tell Franky about it, Hannah,' said Alicia.

Hannah shook her head. 'I'm sorry, Franky. I'm trying to explain why I need the water checked out.' She put down the bucket. 'I don't think Alicia believes me.'

'Pardon me?' Alicia stared at her. 'I believe you *want* the water checked out, okay?' She turned to Franky. 'The issue is, *why*.'

'Yes, why, Hannah?' said Franky. 'Is it dirty?'

'No. It's not dirty. It's—'

'Apparently it's got the wrong ingredients,' said Alicia, smiling and shaking her head.

'No, Alicia. That's not it. I told you why.' Hannah looked hurt.

'I know you told me, but you have to admit it's a touch weird. All this time saying nothing and then wham, it's a big deal. I mean it's a goofball bunch of malarkeys, if we're honest.'

'All right. You've told me. I won't mention it again.'

Hannah grabbed hold of the bucket and took it into the laundry room, put it into the broom cupboard and came back sighing.

'Franky, I get an allergy from water.' She held out the backs of both hands. 'Look, see how red they're getting? That's what happened last year. It could be the start of dermatitis. Back home a dermatologist tested the water and said it was removing protective fats and lipids from my skin and might have minerals that weren't good for me. He said it could be a mild form of aquagenic urticaria. It damages the lipids—'

'Aquagenic what?'

'Urticaria.'

'It hurt to carry her!' Alicia laughed out loud. 'Oh Hannah, he said it *could* be. He didn't say it was. You didn't have a diagnosis, did you?'

Hannah, red-faced and stiff-backed, stared at her. 'Alicia, I'm saying that it didn't show as he thought, so he wanted to make certain, that was all.'

'So, have you got it?' Alicia gave a short laugh of bewilderment. 'What's the problem? You're saying you get it just by being in contact with water, right? You'd have got it by now. It's the weather. Your hands are chapped. Look at mine. I've got the same as you. Mine's from getting hands wet and going out in the cold, not properly dried, yours the same.'

'No, Alicia, I'm sorry.' Hannah stretched out the flat of her hands, fingers displayed. 'Look, I had proper tests back home. My hands were looking just like this. Then I got hives, itchy red skin. I tell you in all honesty Alicia, that it drove me crazy—'

'Hannah.' Franky interrupted her gently. 'Alicia's got a point. We've been here two months, so why hasn't it already happened?'

'I don't know, Franky. The dermatologist told me to look up the water supply. I forgot. All I want is to check it out before it happens. All I need is the water tested so I can sleep nights. That's all.'

'Haven't you looked online, searched the water supplier?' Alicia raised her eyebrows.

No, I haven't. I don't know how.'

'What's all this about water?' Craig, having entered the kitchen to make coffee, gave a grin. 'Have we got the wrong kind?'

'No. Hannah thinks it could be bad for her skin,' said Alicia.

'I have an allergy,' said Hannah. 'I was told to check it out. That's all.'

'Give her a cuddle, Craig,' said Alicia. 'She's looking for a Daddy figure.'

'I do not need a cuddle. I just want to arrange a test.' Hannah splayed out her hands. 'I'm sorry if I sound awkward. I don't want to upset anyone. I really don't.'

'Test the water by drowning her in it,' said Alicia, then ruffled Hannah's hair a little, chuckling as she did so.

'Hear that, Craig? They want to kill me. So, big fella, what do I do?'

Craig touched her elbow. 'Let's sort this water thing, shall we? C'mon.'

Alicia watched Craig escort Hannah out to the hallway. 'So, who'd have thought a drop of water…'

"I to the world am like a drop of water," quoted Franky, "that in the ocean seeks another drop."

'What's that from?'

'Can't remember. I looked up lovesickness, by the way.'

'Lovesickness— Hannah?'

'I don't mean the romantic swooning and stuff. It's a proper illness, loss of appetite, nausea, tears. She's got it all now. Haven't you noticed?'

'Yes. But what did the Bard say?' Alicia put milk into her coffee. "Love is merely a madness?"

'Yes, and isn't there also something about "curing it by counsel?"'

'I think there is. Do you think Shakespeare meant counselling as done today? Hey, I may have discovered something.' Alicia gave a short laugh.

Franky hesitated, thought about saying, 'No, I discovered it,' but decided against it.

She took her coffee down to the living room and found Craig sat in an armchair, looking at his tablet. Hannah sat on the armrest looking down.

She glanced at Franky. 'He's fixing it,' she said.

'Okay, got the water company, *Severn Trent*. Here we go.' Craig made a single key stroke. 'Allergies. None known. None reported.'

'Oh, Craig.' There was a moment of hesitation and then her arms went around his neck. 'Thank you so much.'

'That's okay,' he said gently. 'Glad to have helped. Now I've got work to do.'

As he went out Hannah and Franky looked at each other.

'You okay Hannah?'

'Yes. I am.' She winced a little. 'I'm sorry, Franky. You've been great. Thank you.'

Franky went back to her room in relief. The bust-up that she dreaded had not happened. There was hope yet.

Then, just as she was beginning to feel comfortable …

Came the spider of unease …

Chapter Twelve

Franky stood at her window watching a full moon emerge from behind a strip of cloud. It cast a light blue sheen over the darkened landscape, transforming it into a ghostly panorama, fit for the melding of reality with fantasy. There was no doubt in her mind that the dynamic within the cottage had changed, strengthening her suspicion that Alicia was bent on cutting her off from the rest. Something that happened the day before had confirmed those suspicions.

The power had suddenly failed. She'd gone into the living room on a hunt for a flashlight when she discovered Alicia and Tom in quiet conversation at the fireside. As soon as she entered, they had broken off to watch her open the sideboard drawers and cupboards.

'Looking for the flashlight. Where – oh, I know.' And there it was, to her relief, nestling in a drawer.

Having left the room, she'd paused in the hallway to hear Alicia say, 'It's all in the lap of the gods.'

Then came Tom's reply, 'Who can tell?'

That was followed by a silence, suggesting they might suspect she was listening. On its own the incident would have raised a frown, little else. *Except* it was an echo of that moment in the Institute when she'd come across Annabelle and Alicia in conversation and they, also, had broken off until she was out of earshot.

Alicia, ominously, had featured in *both* incidents.

She went to her desk and sat down, staring at her screen. Into the search box she typed the word "Paranoia." Up came the following:

A part of the brain called the Endocannabinoid System works in controlling the fear-safety circuit linked to the amygdalah, the organ in the brain that stores emotional memory. If it becomes switched off, rather like an electrical circuit sparking and spluttering to its death then, in the psychotic range of mental disorders, the patient may become delusional. Victims of this disorder should still be able to function normally at work and in the daily round, providing they do not hear voices inside their head, strange noises or have hallucinations.

She sat back comforted by the final sentence. She'd never heard voices in her head or strange noises, nor had she hallucinated. Clearly, the fact that she feared paranoia was surely a sign that she *wasn't* paranoid. It was obvious that no one of sound mind could be so afflicted if being capable of studying and understanding the symptoms of paranoia, could they? There again, wasn't she being objective, exactly as the psychotherapist had advised?

But, as she continued reading, she came to a description of a full-blown behavioural disorder that gave her more cause for alarm, the symptoms being unstable emotions, *quick changes of mind* and, above all, fear of abandonment. She'd never thought of herself as fearful of being alone, but now began to consider it as a possibility. And look at the times she'd changed her mind over the novel, one day high as a kite over it, the next full of gloom.

Her pulse racing, she made a quick link to a *New York Times* article in which she read that this problem could be treated. It said that Marsha Linehan, the creator of "dialectical behaviour therapy" had suffered from the disorder herself. Franky wrote down the address of the Society, just in case she needed to contact them.

There came a knock at the door. It was Hannah.

'Just had another email from the NEA.' She had a printout in her hand.

'Good news?'

'Yes! Well, there's a small no.'

'Come in, tell me about it and we'll celebrate. Is Bouchard Pere et Fils Fleurie ok ?'

'You kidding?' Hannah entered the room, closing the door.

Franky began to pour out two glasses of wine. 'Go on, good news first.'

'The NEA have asked me to submit my proposal, but the bad news is they want it by the end of January.'

'Oh.' Franky turned to her. 'End of January?' Frowning, she handed her the drink. 'That's impossible, isn't it?'

'Yes. That's the problem. But it's what the theatre director says that's good. Here, read it.'

She handed the printout to Franky who read it aloud: "Dear Hannah, I'm retiring soon and I would love to go out with a grant for your putative organisation. What you propose is a wonderful idea. However, we may only have a window of opportunity given that the President looks like demolishing us in the presidential budget."

Franky grimaced at Hannah, sighing in sympathy.

'Read the last sentence.' Hannah's face was flushed with pleasure.

Franky read on. "But this, for me, is the bravest and most worthwhile of ideas that I've looked at in my term of office." 'Wow,' she said quietly.

Hannah, smiling, put up her hand.

Franky smacked it. 'Hey, that's great! Did you email back?'

'Yes, I did. I said if I can't do it in time could he work something out while I make an abbreviated proposal that gets a holding tick. Now here's the really good news.' She paused to tease Franky a little.

'Go on.' Franky's smile widened.

'He called me just now and said he'd do his darndest.'

'That's amazing. You're a star!' She hesitated. 'Hannah, if you got going, you could take in *all* the states. Thought of that?'

'All the states?'

'Sure. They all give grants to the arts, some far more than others. And there are poor communities everywhere, aren't there? Every state has them, including the richest. Added together, their grants might total more than you'd get from the NEA. It would be insurance in case it folds.'

'Yes! You're right!' Hannah's eyes lit up. 'Franky, that's a brilliant idea!'

'Then you'll be touring the whole of America. It's what you want, isn't it, to spread the word?'

'Absolutely. I'm a gypsy at heart.' Hannah giggled, but cut it short on remembering her self- imposed vow.

'Well.' Franky raised her glass. 'Here's looking at you, kid.'

'And to you. You're a genius.'

'Not quite.' Franky narrowed her eyes, opening her mouth to say something. 'Hannah,' she said hesitantly, 'has Alicia said anything to you— about me?'

'How do you mean?'

'I get the feeling she's up to something. She's not buttonholed you, got you on your own or anything? I know it sounds cuckoo but—'

'Alicia? Up to what? I'm sorry, I don't understand.'

'I don't know, that's the problem. If she hasn't, that's fine. No worries.'

'No, she hasn't.' Hannah wrinkled her forehead. 'But why should she? I don't know what you're getting at.'

'It's okay, you've answered the question.'

'Franky…' Hannah hesitated. 'You've got me worried now. What exactly do you mean?'

Franky took a deep breath. 'Okay. It's just that twice I've seen her talking to people but she stops as soon as she sees me, then starts again as soon as I've gone. Isn't that suspicious to you?'

Hannah, staring at her, swallowed hard. 'I guess. Yes, of course, but …'

'Could you, I mean, if you're alone with her, could you – would you - kind of, well, put it to her in some way?'

'I'm sorry, I don't get it. You mean ask her why she's suspicious about you?' I don't—'

'No. Forget it,' Franky cut in quickly. 'I'll leave it to you. But if there's any way of finding out, would you do it?'

'Of course.'

'Great. Thanks. I know it sounds stupid. Guess it's just me. Stir-crazy.' She attempted a chuckle, then stopped to point a finger at Hannah. 'You've forgotten something.'

'Forgotten what?'

'You've not asked me to join you in Hannah's Troupe.'

'Would you? Would you really!'

'Of course. I would. You need somebody to keep you in check — stop you eating too many cookies in those clapboard communities.'

Hannah burst out laughing in delight.

Franky forced a big smile.

Two weeks later, on the Friday night, two more incidents occurred that rocked further the, already, unstable boat.

It began in the living room before dinner. It was Alicia's turn to choose the mood for Tom at the keyboard. She went through a pile of music scores kept in a drawer and found one that brought a grin to her face. Tom raised his eyebrows on seeing it proffered him.

'I bet you haven't even heard it,' she said, giving Franky a smirk.

Then, to everyone's surprise, Tom went straight into the locomotive rhythm of *The Rolling Stones* number, 'Honky Tonk Women,' then added percussion to strengthen the beat.

Hannah, making up the fire, paused on seeing Alicia slip off her track top and begin to rock out, jerking her head back and forth while gesturing at Craig to join her. After an initial show of reluctance, he smiled in surrender, rising to his feet.

Franky, sipping wine, happened to look at Hannah who was attending to the fire. With a fresh log in her hands she'd paused to watch the dancers.

As Alicia got raunchier, Franky noted Hannah's chest rise and fall, her breathing rate increasing by the second.

Suddenly, Hannah put down the log and walked quickly out of the room.

Franky waited a moment before going down to Hannah's room. She tapped lightly on her door. It's me,' she said gently.

There was no response.

She knocked again.

The door opened. Hannah stood there, holding a tissue.

'Nothing's happening,' said Franky. 'They're only having fun.'

Hannah dabbed her eyes. "Fun." It's okay, I'll be down in a minute.'

As the music ended, Franky returned to the living room, her eyes raking Alicia with contempt. She picked up some notes she'd been working on and stalked out.

Alicia grinned at Craig. 'Well, it's your turn for the music tomorrow night. What will we get? It's country and western for you Okies, isn't it?'

'No. That was last time. Maybe nostalgia?'

'Hah, but nostalgia ain't what it used to be.'

She slung the track top over her shoulder and strolled out of the room, with a laconic smile.

Franky, back in her room, attacked Alicia, first by smashing in her front teeth, after which she beheaded her with a meat cleaver. She fell immediately into misery and frustration out of which she decided on a change of tactics. She went down to the pantry, intending to select her most expensive wine for the evening. It would be one of *her own* bottles, the idea being to demonstrate her magnanimity once more, so making Alicia feel bad enough to behave less provocatively.

She found herself staring at six bottles in the wine-rack, when there should have been seven. She re-counted slowly to make sure and then searched the pantry. The last time she'd opened one of her high-end bottles was on Tom's birthday, but that was a month ago when there were eight in a row. There was no doubt about it. One had been taken without her permission.

She gritted her teeth and went to the living room, stopping inside the doorway, arms folded, waiting to draw their attention. However, not being able to imagine Tom or Craig as a thief, she instinctively looked at Alicia.

Alicia glanced up from the magazine she was reading. 'What?' she said with a frown.

'There's a bottle of Pinot Noir missing. I just thought you might know what's happened to it.'

'Me? You talking to me?' Alicia sat up straight.

'No, it's just that Tom's birthday was the last time I brought one out. It was the Châteauneuf-du-Pape. Now the Pinot's gone, and we've celebrated nothing since. That's all.'

'So why look at me, Franky?'

'Have you looked everywhere?' said Craig.

'It was in the pantry, in my wine rack,' said Franky, patiently. 'I keep the high-enders there. There were seven left after Tom's birthday. Now it's just six. I want to know what happened to it.'

'You mean did I purloin it?' Alicia laughed a little, her eyebrows raised. 'Franky, you know something? I'm getting a wee bit pissed off here. Why don't you—'

'Alicia, just …' Craig put up his arm, silencing her, keen to forestall a bust-up. 'Franky, I'm lost. Are you really saying there's a wine thief among us, you sure of that?'

'Craig, she was looking at me when she said it, not you!' Alicia stared hard at Franky, before returning to her magazine. 'Jesus wept …'

'I'm not accusing anybody. I'm —'

'No Franky.' She pointed her finger. 'You came in here and looked at me when you said it. You're accusing me of stealing one of your bottles. Are you serious?'

'I'm not accusing you of anything. I just want to find out what's happened to it.'

'Well, don't dare look at me again.' Alicia glared hard at her magazine.

'What if we had a sneak-thief,' said Craig, 'or someone broke in?' He stood up. 'I'll go check the windows—'

'No, Craig,' said Franky. 'They'd only get in on the ground floor and I check doors and windows every night. I know that Hannah's window is always locked. Can we get this straight: I'm not saying anyone stole it, I just want to know what might have happened to it.'

'Have you asked Hannah?' Alicia shot Franky a hard glance.

At that moment Hannah came in and sat down, staring rigidly ahead.

'Hannah?' Alicia stemmed the sudden urge to laugh. 'You look like a Brontë tragedy. What's happened?'

'Nothing.' Hannah kept her head erect.

'Franky's on a mission. She reckons someone's knocked off one of her high-end bottles.'

'I know, I heard, and I didn't.'

'Franky,' said Tom. 'You sure you've not made a mistake?'

'No, Tom. The bottle's missing. I know everything alcohol-wise in that pantry.'

Alicia stood up. 'Tom?' she said abruptly. 'We're the cooks. Time to go.'

Franky shook her head. 'This is crazy.'

'It is,' said Alicia. 'Look. How about all of us club together and we'll buy you a new bottle? You happy with that, Craig?'

'No, that won't do. I'm sorry.' Franky turned to go. 'I'm going to my room. I'll wait ten minutes. Then whoever took it can tell me. And whoever it is must pay for it. And we'll forget all about it and say no more.' She went out.

She stopped at the top of the stairs as she heard Alicia mimicking a British upper-class voice.

'Oh darling, these peasants are so troubling. I shall take to my bed, and do pass the smelling salts.' Her voice turned into a weary drawl. 'Come on, Tom, dinner time, let's do it.'

Franky's grip on the banister-railing tightened. She was about to step back on to the landing when she heard Hannah shoot down the hallway through the kitchen and then into her room, slamming the door behind her.

Alicia's voice echoed from the kitchen. 'Wow, who's the startled rabbit?' She opened the freezer to draw out a pack of frozen vegetables. 'There's little love around tonight.' She set the oven temperature. 'Lord give us strength, hey, Tom?'

He made no reply at first. 'Forgive me if I'm wrong,' he said, 'but wasn't the landlord coming here this week?'

Alicia hesitated, her mouth open, awareness coming to her face until she jabbed a finger, her eyes flashing. 'Yes, you're right! I was with Franky when she got his text message. She actually mentioned it, that he was coming yesterday afternoon. We were all at the Institute for the visiting lecturer. He said he had to do an inventory. It was in the contract. That's it.' She snapped her fingers. 'Must have been him. Tom, will you tell her? I don't want to bring her the good news.'

She switched on the oven. 'She'll only accuse me of making it up. She is such a...'

Turning, she found that Tom had already left the kitchen.

Franky rushed back into her room as he appeared on the stairs.

He came up to knock on her door.

After a pause, she opened it. Before he could speak, she gestured for him to enter. 'I've just remembered,' she said. 'The landlord came yesterday afternoon to check out the domestic inventory. It must be him.'

'Yes. I was about to tell you that.'

'Tom — look. I can't come down at the moment. Will you tell them I'm sorry, and we'll forget about it?'

'Oh, I think it's sackcloth and ashes, I'm afraid. Don't you think?'

She stared at him. 'Okay.' Her voice was almost a whisper. 'I'll be down.'

'What are you proposing to do about the landlord?'

'Lock up the bottles from now on, I guess. If I accuse him without evidence, he could kick us out.'

On hearing Tom's news Alicia gave a loud laugh in triumph and, in a singsong voice chanted, 'We are due a big *a–pol–o–gee.*'

Five minutes later, Franky went down to the living room, to find Craig there.

'I made a mistake,' she said quietly. 'I'm sorry Craig. I mean it.'

'That's okay. Don't worry about it.'

Alicia was looking inside the fridge when Franky entered the kitchen. She opened the pantry door and went inside. She came out, holding a Brauneberger Riesling and offered it Tom. 'Je suis désolée. J'espère que ce sera acceptable?'

Tom looked at Alicia over the rim of his spectacles, showing her the bottle. 'Alicia, est-ce acceptable?'

'I don't speak French. What did she say?' Alicia looked at him airily.

'I said I'm sorry.'

'Now we have it.' She turned her back on Franky to open a cupboard door. 'Good. Next time wait before you accuse people.'

Franky hesitated, then swung round and left the kitchen.

Alicia gave a shrug. *'Absolument pathétique.'*

Hannah entered the living room and found Franky, alone, sitting by the fire. She sat next to her, saying nothing for a moment or two.

'I'm sorry,' said Franky, 'putting you through that.'

'That's okay. No worries.' Hannah, twisted her hands, frowning anxiously.

'What is it Hannah?'

'What?'

'Something is bothering you.'

'Erm ... yes.' Hannah turned to face Franky full on. 'It's Craig.'

'What about him?' Franky felt her stomach turn over.

Hannah swept her hair back, sighed and shook her head. 'Franky, what you told me, before we all came here for the first time, remember? You said that if Craig was going to go with anybody it would be me. Right?'

'Yes.'

'No. You must have missed something because we've been here long enough and it makes no sense.'

'He said that — he said exactly that.'

Hannah looked miserably into the fire.

'He meant it. I could tell.' Franky felt her stomach shrink.

'Well, it takes some believing. Not a flicker, not a sign, not even a glance. And then all that with Alicia ...'

Franky sighed. 'Yes. I wish I hadn't said anything now. I'm sorry Hannah, but I don't know any more than you do.' She got to her feet. 'Can you tell them I don't feel well and I won't be joining them for dinner?'

'Oh no. No Franky. No, please not that. I'll feel even worse!'

Franky studied her face. 'Okay.' She nodded slightly and drew in a short breath. 'I'll be there.'

The meal was eaten in relative silence with Franky keeping her head down, leaving Hannah looking embarrassed, doing her best to prompt her into conversation.

After the beef stew, potatoes and kale, Alicia presented the table with a genuine Elizabethan sweet, a syllabub.

'Whipped cream, lemon juice, brandy and half a teaspoon of sugar. I didn't make any for you, Hannah. Instead I got you a surprise.'

'A surprise?'

Alicia went out to bring back another dish. 'As we're coming up to

Christmas, I got you a veggie plum pudding.' She placed it in front of her.

'Oh, thank you so much.' Hannah looked at Franky, hesitantly. 'Isn't that nice of Alicia, Franky?'

'Yes.' Franky, glancing across the table, continued to chew doggedly.

Hannah put on a smile. 'Tom, last week you were telling us about your college thesis. Anthropology. All about bonding. It was fascinating, wasn't it, everybody?'

'You sure you don't mean bondage?' Alicia laughed briefly.

Hannah frowned. 'No, Alicia, no, I don't. I was interested because we talked about groups bonding as a shared blood tie. And I loved all that stuff about immersion in icy water and walking through flames to get social cohesion. So, when did human language start, do we know?' She glanced at Franky, but her head was still bent over her plate.

'No, not precisely,' said Tom. 'There's a shortage of empirical evidence. My guess is that, at first, hunters made animal-like guttural and then bi-labial sounds with gestures to each other, meaning "where", or "bring back", simple instructions. Then they had to extend their vocabulary as abstract ideas and concepts out of sight and hearing, had to be communicated. The start of language.'

'And was it their imagination that developed abstract conceptual thinking?' said Craig.

'Yes. And those concepts,' said Tom, 'made it possible to communicate and forge links with the wider world. So, more and more, abstract ideas were exchanged without any reference to the five senses. Then much later, sat around the fire, more than eighty per cent of group conversation was storytelling, often about people living far away or in the spirit world. Humans were unique in that they made ties with others outside their immediate group or tribe. They talked about them. So, getting round the fire expanded the listener's sense and knowledge of language, I'd imagine.'

'And then came Facebook,' said Alicia. A pause. 'Why don't we play the game?' she said suddenly.

'Oh yes,' said Hannah. 'Let's do that. Okay, Franky?'

'If you want,' came the desultory reply.

Hannah thought hard. 'Okay. I've got one. "But we have reason to cool our raging motions, our carnal stings." Anybody?'

'Sounds like *Othello*,' said Craig.

'You're right,' said Hannah. 'Anyone know the character?'

'Is it Iago?' said Alicia.

'It is. Who's he talking to?'

No one had an answer.

'It's Iago with Roderigo.'

All four heads turned to Franky who sat staring at her plate, speaking in a flat voice. 'It's when Othello takes Desdemona offstage, and Iago asks what is virtue. He ends by saying that man has the virtue of reason to cool his carnal lusts.'

'Oh,' said Alicia, 'you've reminded me, I must get on with the lines.'

After a pause Franky turned her head sharply towards her. 'What lines?'

'Desdemona's. Annabelle asked me to read the speech. "Farewell, for I must leave you."'

Franky stared. 'She told me she wasn't auditioning yet.'

'Didn't you get her email?'

'No.' Franky held her spoon motionless.

After a pause she scraped back her chair and went up to her room. Her tablet was already switched on. She went straight to emails.

Minutes later, she returned to the living room.

Alicia watched her all the way to the table. 'You okay?'

'Yes.' Franky sat down stiffly.

'Seemed like you had one hell of a shock. Was it something I said?' Alicia looked around innocently for support.

Franky stared at her, biting her lip, then stood up suddenly. 'Got a headache,' she muttered. 'I'm sorry but I must go to bed.'

They watched her leave the room.

'Yikes,' said Alicia quietly. 'What did I do?'

'She'd set her heart on Desdemona,' said Hannah, shaking her head slowly. 'Annabelle told her she was the front runner.'

Alicia groaned. 'Oh, yikes and double yikes. Why didn't someone tell me?'

Franky lay on her bed, staring at the ceiling. There came a light tapping at the door. She knew whose door-knocking signature it was. The tapping – a little louder this time – resumed.

She slipped off the bed and opened the door.

'Yeah?'

Hannah offered her a strip of Paracetamol tablets. 'In case you haven't any.'

'Oh,' she said, taking them, 'thanks Hannah.'

'Did you check your junk mail? It just occurred to me …'

'Yes, I have. Thanks.'

'I know how much you want Desdemona. I just thought—'

'I know. Thanks Hannah.' She put a hand on the door.

'Well.' Hannah, getting the hint, produced a quick smile.

'Much appreciated. But I mean it, I'm going to bed.'

'Oh, okay. You sleep tight now.' Hannah stepped back.

'I will.' She inched the door forward with her hand.

Hannah was still lingering. 'If you need anything, call me. Promise?'

'Sure. Thanks, Hannah.'

She slowly closed the door and remained still, listening to the lashing of wind-driven rain on the window.

Chapter Thirteen

The housemates sat in Craig's car bound for the Institute, but on a different route than normal, owing to roadworks.

It was a cold, wet Monday morning, the start of the working week, and traffic was heavier than usual. It was enough to dampen their spirits, but had no effect on Franky, as hers were already flatlined. She'd gone to bed the previous night in the hope that Annabelle had forgotten to tell her about the auditions and there would be a text message, or email, awaiting her in the morning. But there was nothing.

She decided that if her pigeon hole at the Institute was empty, she would just have to confront her. It was a terrible prospect, but it had to be done.

A forced detour for road-works had them stopping in traffic alongside New Place, the garden where Shakespeare's house once stood, their gaze taking in the slatted timber entrance through which they caught glimpses of modern sculptures.

'I don't like the bronze tree,' said Alicia. 'And what's the big globe doing there?'

'The globe's meant to be the world as it was in Shakespeare's day,' said Hannah.

'And the sphere,' said Tom, 'shows Shakespeare's understanding of the world around him.'

'But why was the house pulled down?'

'It was a parson,' said Craig. 'He got fed up with people knocking on his door wanting to look inside what was Master Shakespeare's house. That's what I read.'

'Cutting off his nose to spite his face,' said Alicia. 'What an idiot. When was it pulled down, anyone know?'

'Middle of the eighteenth century,' said Tom.

'Well,' said Hannah. 'I heard it was because he wanted revenge on the local council for having to pay too much poor tax.'

'I heard something quite different,' said Tom. 'He was being pilloried for chopping down a mulberry tree in the garden. So, he thought fine – have at you. I'll chop the house down as well. So, stuff that in your pipe and smoke it.'

'I like Greg Wyatt's sculptures around the garden,' said Craig.

Franky fidgeted with her fingers, having no inclination to join the debate. She wasn't even listening, weighed down as she was by anxiety. She prayed that she had got it wrong, that Desdemona would be hers as promised, with Annabelle explaining there had been a mix-up and all would be well.

Halfway down Chestnut Way, the car turned slowly through the open gates and into the small car park.

Franky stared into an empty pigeon hole, lowered her head for a moment, then walked up the stairs to Annabelle's office. After drawing a deep breath, she knocked lightly on the door.

After a pause it opened and Annabelle stood there, eyebrows raised. 'Franky,' she said in surprise. Then, after a hesitation, 'Come in. I think I know why you're here.'

Franky caught her cautious expression as she entered.

'I should have contacted you.' Annabelle closed the door, leaving her hand on the knob for a moment, before going to her desk. 'But something happened to stop me. Do sit down.' She motioned Franky into the armchair.

'I'd rather stand, if you don't mind?'

'Oh…' Annabelle sighed. 'I'm sorry you're upset, and it's all my fault. Please sit because I need to apologise and explain what happened.'

Franky sat down on the edge of the chair.

'I've just got back from seeing my father. He'd fallen ill on Friday, and I had to go and deal with it. I made a note to call you but then I completely forgot. I'm so sorry.'

'Oh no. It's me who's sorry.' Franky perked up, her hopes quickly rising. 'How is he now?'

'He's fine. No problem. He thought he'd had a stroke, but they found it was an inner ear thing that's being treated as we speak. So, all's well that ends well!' She laughed a little, then paused a moment. 'So, there it is.'

'Oh, I see.' Franky, in her relief, missed Annabelle's hesitation. 'I thought you were going to drop me … when you'd…' She tailed away at Annabelle's expression, one of painful sympathy.

'Franky.' Annabelle grimaced at the news she had to impart. 'I've decided not to cast you, I'm afraid.'

As Franky gasped, she put out a hand. 'I'm afraid for you. I wanted you to play Desdemona. You're a fine actor, but I discussed it with the Director and he agrees with me. I know I said you were favourite and would be still if—' She broke off as Franky's chest began to heave. 'Oh, you're hyperventilating again.'

She quickly opened a desk drawer and brought out a brown paper bag. She twisted the edges of the bag into a funnel, then poked her finger through to widen it.

'Here.' She handed it to Franky. 'Breathe into the bag and then breathe in. Keep doing it. Your carbon dioxide lowers the oxygen. You've taken in too much, saturated with it. Keep going until you feel better.'

Franky, the bag at her mouth, stared into Annabelle's face before following her instructions. After half a minute she was able to lower it.

'Feel better now?'

Franky nodded and offered the bag back.

Annabelle gestured. 'No, keep it. You may need it again.' She paused. 'We did it for your sake, Franky, please believe me.'

'But why! There's nothing the matter with me.'

'Oh. Oh dear, this is so difficult. I don't think that's true. You see, when you were here last, if you remember, you were very agitated. You're a very good actor, Franky, you would have been my choice. But I can't now. I'd be worried for you as well as for the production. I could see you having a breakdown.'

'But—I can't believe this. I'm perfectly all right. I—'

'Please listen. We have a duty of care. As your welfare advisor I can't let you do something that I don't think is safe. All this weekend I've been hating this moment but I have to do it. I just—'

'But none of it's true! I am. I'm perfectly safe. You have to believe me!'

Annabelle shook her head. 'No. I could get into trouble if I allowed you to slip into panic attacks— no, *please* listen. You could have one during the production that could ruin it. So, you see, we do have a real problem. I hate this. I know how much you wanted the part and I wanted you but—'

'I'm sorry.' Franky stood up, wrenched open the door and left quickly in mounting tears.

'Franky—'

Annabelle went out of the office, only to hear Franky's footsteps clattering down the steps to the hallway below.

Out into the street, marching, focusing on the ground, a pounding in her ears, shops and lights blurring by, cars moving, but nothing real, distance and time meaningless, no intention other than escape.

You were going to say something about your father.

Slowing down, standing on the pavement edge. Traffic crossing slowly.

The pounding in her ears gone.

At a red light she crossed the road to enter the coffee shop.

She sat in a window seat, watching people and traffic moving normally, her thoughts frozen in the realisation that she'd been robbed, not once but twice. She'd come to terms with the first, giving Annabelle the benefit of the doubt, iniquitous an act though it was – but *twice*?

From out of the street came a ragged burst of laughter from a group of uniformed schoolboys passing by.

'Hi, Franky.'

She looked up. It was Maggie.

'Hi.'

'I saw you come in. Want a coffee? No, stay there. You're an impoverished student.' She hesitated and frowned. 'Are you okay, you look rather pale?'

Franky exhaled and hesitated. 'As a matter of fact, no, I'm not okay.'

'Oh dear' Maggie sat down next to her. 'What's happened?'

She listened to Franky's story. 'Just a minute,' she said. 'I don't understand. "Not fit for it." How do you mean?'

'Annabelle says I might be having a breakdown and so can't risk me in the production.' Franky glanced at two customers about to sit near them.

'But why should she say that? Have you had a breakdown of any sort?'

'No. Never.'

'So, what's it all about?'

'Can you keep a secret?'

'Of course. Go on.'

'I saw my father rape a schoolboy.'

'Oh my God.' Maggie stared with her mouth wide open.

'Yes. I know this sounds crazy but he sent me here, not for Shakespeare, but to stop me telling the Boston police. Now I find he's got Annabelle involved. Don't ask me how. I just know it. And now she's given my dissertation to Craig and stopped me auditioning for Desdemona, after telling me I was the front runner. That's twice she's done it. It's not a coincidence.'

Maggie screwed up her face. 'But… I … I'm sorry Franky. I mean how does Annabelle come into it? I mean —-'

'I don't know. That's what I'm trying to find out.'

'Franky. I— I just can't take it in. *Annabelle*? You *really* think she's helping your father … against you?'

'Yes. I know she is.'

'*How* do you know?'

'Things that have happened, apart from what I've told you.'

'What exactly?'

Franky shook her head. 'I can't talk about it. There are things … you know? All I —'

'Franky. Listen to me. If you're that worried you must talk to your welfare, straightaway, before this thing gets out of hand. Who is it?'

'Annabelle.'

Maggie stared and then sat back suddenly, letting out a quiet 'Oh.'

Franky walked back to the Institute, deep in contemplation. There was no doubt that she'd been victimised by someone in whom she'd placed all her trust, someone who'd promised to be her rock, her refuge, her friend, someone who'd given her warmth and comfort for the first time in her life, as well as the prospect of a future life without torment, and now she had taken it all away. She saw it all so clearly, Annabelle, with her oily and unctuous posturing, the honey-tongued murmurings, the smile on the face of a soft-talking and beguiling witch!

She charged into her office wielding an axe and feverishly hacked off her head.

In the self-hating aftermath, the word 'sukha' came back to mind, the Sanskrit word meaning happiness and contentment.

Now, sounding the word inside her head, its meaning was turned upside down.

She had, indeed, been *suckered*.

Chapter Fourteen

It was 7.45 a.m. with the cottage under siege. The shrieking, hissing gale rattled the woodshed and hammered the cottage doors and windows. Somewhere a shutter banged. Above the howl a drainpipe rattled furiously.

Franky entered the kitchen to find Alicia at the stove and Tom and Craig at the table, poring over an Ordnance Survey map.

'Just heard,' said Tom. 'The Shottery road into Stratford's blocked by a fallen tree. We need a detour.'

'Some poor guy's trapped in his car,' added Craig. 'Looking for another route.'

'I thought the UK didn't get storms like this,' said Franky.

'They do,' said Tom. 'It's coming in from the Atlantic, a massive depression colliding with a high-pressure system.'

Franky put a slice of bread in the toaster.

'And then there's snow coming,' said Craig. 'That could be a real problem, stuck out here.'

Just then Hannah entered, her arm raised in triumph. 'Da-dah!' she cried with the panache of the pantomime heroine proclaiming the hero's rescue from the bad guys. 'I am she!'

'Hey,' said Alicia, turning round from the stove. 'What side of bed did you get out of?'

Hannah kept her big grin. 'Don't you know what the storm's called?'

'Bloody awful?' said Franky.

'No! I've been waiting for years to find my name given to one. It's the remnants of *Hannah*! Up from the Caribbean. Yippee!'

'So,' said Tom. With his head back, he pointed at her in the exaggerated and dramatic pose of a silent-screen actor. 'You can be no other *than…?*'

'*Hurricane Hannah*!' Hannah crooked back her forearm to produce a tiny bump for a bicep and stomped around a little. 'Hannah is here, folks. Watch your cotton socks.'

'Cripes,' said Alicia. 'Hannah, you're giving me a headache.'

'Oh. Sorry, Alicia.' Hannah sighed and joined Craig and Tom at the table. 'I heard the news. Finding an escape route?'

'Yeah,' murmured Craig. 'We're trying to navigate a way into Stratford after the storm's gone, forecast around one. The other day I had a chat with the farmer round here and he said living in Tithebarn Lane could be great in summer but a nightmare in winter. The lane is never gritted so if your car spins off, you need a tractor to haul it back to the main road.'

'Now he tells me.' Alicia remained with her back to them. 'A bit late for that, Franky? We should have known before we came here, shouldn't we?'

Franky glared at her back.

'Didn't he also say a blizzard could pile up snowdrifts?' Alicia continued. 'Three to five feet high in the lane? Why didn't you check it out?'

'Because I didn't think about it,' she said shortly. 'The sun was shining. It was idyllic.'

Franky sat on the bed. Having decapitated Alicia in the bloodiest fashion possible, she wallowed in the usual stew of loathing, self-disgust and despair.

She picked up an opened paperback that she'd bought online, *How to Stop Self-Torment – Rewire your Brain*. It told you to summon up a thought, something unpleasant that made you feel depressed. You had to do it a number of times each day until the amygdalah, inside the lower brain, got fed up and replaced bad chemicals with those that made you feel good, endorphins and dopamine.

She'd tried to follow the instructions, but had become quickly frustrated. 'Yes, maybe when you've done it a million times!' She tossed the book aside. It didn't even tell you *how* to do it, lying down, standing on your head, or what!

She took a deep breath and allowed her unwired brain to settle once more on the matter of achieving revenge, through her novel.

Then, suddenly, she had it, its driving force. Her main protagonist, aged *23, plots to kill her father before he kills her!*

The ideas continued to come. It would be good to relate the story from her own perspective, that of an American student at the Institute, thoroughly immersed in Shakespeare. It would centre in and around the pressure cooker of a remote cottage. She, calling herself Alison, would be the protagonist, the one narrating the story in first person, a voice hushed in fear as the tension builds. She witnesses her father rape a child, so he exiles her to the Shakespeare Institute. There, she plots her revenge while, unknowingly, he recruits "Annabelle" the tutor, to induce fear in her, setting her up for the hitman. In England, or America? Whichever, the murder would echo that of Claudius inciting Laertes to murder Hamlet and —!

Steady. She was allowing herself to get carried away. Don't stretch the reader too far, she told herself. Get the basics right, the foundations and from that allow it to grow. Nevertheless, the plot, as it was, had to be compelling. It would be a fast-paced thriller with plenty of character and lots of imaginative detail.

She lay back on the bed and smiled. Her father surely couldn't fail to miss the connection. In being proportionate to the degree of pain he'd caused, it would make a clean and neat kind of revenge, as well as a potential best-seller.

Her excitement was suddenly cut short as a thin branch thrashed the window, startling her. Relieved that it hadn't broken the glass, she returned to her task. Over the next two hours, to the accompaniment of the maelstrom, the ideas came like pulses, one after the other.

Tired and satisfied that she'd milked her brain until it was dry, she was about to shut down when she thought of a title. *Murder by Proxy.* Or how about *Remote Control*? She then recalled Hannah seizing on a line from Hamlet for her dissertation. What was it?

She went to the *Shakespeare.mit.edu* website and scanned Hamlet's longer speeches. She found what she was looking for, in Act V, scene ii, Horatio with Fortinbras:

And let me speak to the yet unknowing world

How these things came about. So shall you hear
Of carnal, bloody, and unnatural acts;
Of accidental judgments, casual slaughters,
Of deaths put on by cunning and forced cause
"Casual Slaughters."

What a great oxymoron! Slaughtering casually. Wasn't that exactly what she did in fantasy, her loops so transient and meaningless that, in the scheme of things, were hardly worth a mention? How many had she 'killed' at random in that manner, sometimes on a daily basis? There could be no argument over the title.

She poured out another glass of wine, thinking how thrilling it would be to have her father and Annabelle electrocuted in Florida or gassed in California, perhaps hanged in Washington, each state still with its own brand of execution. She could see Annabelle's face as she read the book. Oh, the satisfaction that would bring!

Suddenly, her excitement quickly waned. She clapped a hand to her forehead, sighing and groaning, plunged into depression. *Why, oh why,* did she allow her emotions to transport her into cul-de-sacs? It was a great idea as a literary thriller, but it was the wrong time and the wrong place in which to commence the long road to a successful novel. It would not be published for ages. She had to remind herself, yet again, that authors often took years to write a bestseller. She decided that she would continue with it, but drop it as a means of revenge.

She wanted satisfaction *now*. The wound in her psyche demanded it.

And she'd changed her mind – yet again!

Her head was full of pressure.

She let out a sob of frustration.

'*Kill her. Kill her!*'

Wide awake, in a sweat, she sat up quickly. Was it voices in a dream? She went to the window. The wild landscape had not a human or animal in sight. How would she feel when the snow came as forecast and she was stuck with Alicia?

It reminded her of the Overlook Hotel in *The Shining*. She'd watched the movie twice and always sympathised with the marooned Jack Nicholson having to put up with a simpering wimp of a wife who was horrified at seeing his manuscript packed with nothing but the line: *All work and no play makes Jack a dull boy.* She should have made her call to the emergency services before he'd time to smash the radio transmitter, their sole communication with the outside world. She should have had more get-up-and-go, the silly bitch.

Her mind drifted to brood on the iniquity of Annabelle. She would not assist the production in any way whatsoever. She could not possibly stand by, watching Alicia wreck the part that she'd played to perfection at college. She would clear off into Stratford on the day of the performance. She would not help backstage. She'd feign sickness.

A quick rush of heat to her chest and head, sweaty hands at the ready, the pressure intense. At boiling point, she rammed a red-hot poker straight up Alicia's ass. That made your eyes pop, eh, me hearty?

The creak of floorboards on the landing, was followed by a single knock at the door.

'Franky, it's me.'

'Yes?'

'About the book?'

'Oh ... yes.' She remembered. 'Just a minute.' Franky hastily scribbled down a memo in her notebook against a list of names. *Red-hot poker up ass, eyes popped, great laugh, wet rag.* 'Yeah, come in.' She sighed and swung herself slowly off the bed.

Hannah entered. 'What a storm. It's never-ending.'

'It's you, my dear.' Franky looked around for the book. 'Oh, I know where it is.' She put up a finger. 'Stay there, hurricane Hannah.' She went downstairs.

Hannah, alone, gazed around the room, her eye eventually falling on the open notebook lying on the bed.

She stepped forward to stare down at the open pages, her mouth opening wide in shock.

Hearing Franky come up the stairs, she stepped back, breathing hard.

Franky entered with the book, handing it to her. 'Here, hope it helps.'

'Thanks,' Hannah said and went out quickly, closing the door behind her but then swivelled round, mouth wide open, eyes staring at the closed door, rooted to the spot.

Franky was about to sit on the bed, when the door suddenly opened.

'Franky?' Hannah entered, gesturing at the notebook. 'You've said I need a red-hot poker up my ass? I'm a wet rag, what's all that about!'

Franky bounded off the bed with a finger at her mouth. '*Ssh*! It's not you.'

'But, Franky, it's — it's next to my name! A red-hot poker up my ass. I'm a great laugh. I'm a wet rag.' Her face crumpling, she dug a tissue from under her sleeve. 'I can't believe it.'

'Hannah.' Franky put a hand on her shoulder. 'Hey, angel, I swear, cross my heart, it's not you.' She went to the door, opening it cautiously to check the landing was clear, then closed it and came back. 'Let me explain. C'mon, sit.' She grabbed hold of the chair and dragged it towards the bed.

'That's ... horrible, Franky.' Hannah, sitting down, dabbed her eyes. '*Why?*'

'It's not meant for you. I wrote it about Alicia. I'm going to write a novel and—'

'But you've got all our names listed, and the red-hot poker is against my name!'

'Mistake. I wrote it down quickly, not looking at names. They were already down. I'm going to explain. But first, do you believe me when I say it's not you?' Franky sat down on the bed, facing her. 'Why should I do that?'

Hannah looked at her, frowning.

'Hey.' Franky got up to put her arms around her in a soothing embrace. 'Okay. I'm going to tell you something now. Something I've never told anyone. I hate telling you this but, well, I'm hypersensitive to slight.' She sat down again.

'You're *what?*'

'To slight. I'm hypersensitive to it.'

'Well, I'm hypersensitive to what people say or write about me.' Hannah tried to chuckle, while drying her tears.

'When I was sixteen Mom took me to a psychotherapist. If anyone upset me, slighted me, I fantasised about killing them. I've been doing it for years.'

'With a red-hot poker?'

'Yes, anything. It's called a personality disorder. Alicia slighted me a number of times, the first time was on induction day. I was telling her something and she just broke off, turned away to talk to Craig. Then she did it during that first dinner and then when you had the water problem and now this morning when she asked why didn't I check out the lane in winter before we came here – remember? Blaming *me* for the snow? After all I've spent! I just freaked out at that.'

'Yes, but what happens? I mean, inside your head?'

'I explode, imagining the attacks. Then I go into self-immolation mode. I want to die.'

'That's awful. How do you stop it — I mean—'

'You don't. Will power's useless. That's' why it's called a personality disorder.'

'But. there must be something. Do you go for psychoanalysis, or what?'

'No, it's not psychoanalysis.' Franky took out a chocolate truffle from the bedside cabinet. 'It's psychotherapy. My therapist's solution was for me to write things down, how I felt, try and get as objective as possible, make myself another person who I write about. I should create "distance". So, I came up with the idea of writing a novel in the first person. I only seriously thought about it when I got here. There's the cottage, five of us, so I got the notion to use you guys as kind of templates for the characters I devise. I need faces to look at while writing. You're just pegs for me to hang my characters on. I wrote down your names. My first idea was to base it on your own characters. Then I thought about libel. So now you're just pegs.' She touched the notebook. 'Alicia happens to be my bête noir right now so I'll see her in my mind's eye when I write, as she'll represent the baddie.'

Hannah shook her head in wonderment. 'I had no idea.'

'You were at the door knocking when I scribbled it down so as not to forget. I promise I did it without looking at your four names. It happened to land next to yours. It could have been anybody's.'

'Okay. So, Alicia gets the red-hot poker, not me! I like that.' Hannah laughed a little in relief. 'Oh, Franky, I had such a shock.'

'Here.' Franky offered her the chocolate truffle. 'Help you get over it.'

Hannah accepted it. 'Thanks. It was a real shock. I mean that, Franky. Heck of a shock.'

'I know. Forgive me?'

'No.' Hannah paused long enough to get a reaction. 'Because I believe you. There's nothing to forgive.'

She unpicked the chocolate ribbon. 'Stupid. I'm way over my calorie limit. I'm a bit worried about Alicia. I'm so glad it's not me who gets the red-hot poker. Oh!' She nearly choked with laughter. 'This is crazy, isn't it? Enough to make you crack up – it's a bit like *The Connors*.'

'No, more like *Roseanne*.'

'Who else have you killed, Franky?'

'Who else have I slaughtered recently? Oh, Professor Woodbridge.'

'No! Get outta here!'

'I was in the theatre bookshop. I caught his elbow by accident and he looked at my hair and said, "red sky in the morning is the shepherd's warning." I've killed him loads of times.'

'So that's why you went for him. We all wondered why you did it.'

'What?' Franky's smile suddenly froze on her face.

Hannah frowned a little. 'Sorry?'

'You said we – *we* all wondered.'

'Yes.' Hannah lost her smile completely. 'Why?'

Franky stared at her for a moment. 'Nothing. I was thinking of something else.'

'Well,' said Hannah. She bit into the truffle, nibbling it. 'It's not your fault you can't stop it. Is there a cure?'

'Supposed to be. "Objectivise," I was told. I did all of that. I read my notes out loud, like she said. Okay, it has a bit of an effect. It spaces out the loops, that's what they call the attacks, like video recordings in my head. Maybe one day I'll stop them.' She gave a shrug.

'Can I say something?' Hannah stopped talking, to digest the truffle. 'I saw you had Craig as a con man, Tom a psycho and Alicia a part-time hooker?

She'll explode if she finds out, Franky.'

'Well, she won't. *Our secret.* Yes?'

'Yes, absolutely. But what you've told me … it's scary.'

'Roll up, roll up, see the freak show, folks.'

Hannah fell silent for a moment. 'That's quite something, you know, you telling me something you've never told anyone else.' She suddenly looked dewy-eyed. 'I mean that.'

'Hey, now don't go all mushy on me.'

'I'm not.' Hannah dabbed her eye with her finger. 'It's just that when something happens to suddenly change you … I mean you think you know someone and then you don't, you know, it comes as a surprise.'

'Looking at me in a new light, huh?'

'Yes. It's like when I went to Poland last year with a tour group. We had a day in Warsaw. It's all concrete now, nothing left of the original town destroyed by the Nazis. We found an old red-brick wall about twenty yards long. It was part of the Jewish ghetto wall. Five relatives of mine were put inside. It had a memorial plaque on it. A big guy in one of the apartments saw us looking and came out to tell us about it. He spoke English. He said five bricks had been taken out of the wall, sending two to the Holocaust Museum, Washington and one each to museums in Yad Vashem, Houston and Melbourne. I saw him as a kind of, well, a heroic figure, you know, almost saint-like in spending his time with us. He then insisted we went into his apartment. It was surreal. He'd got weapons, guns, a sniper rifle, machine gun, a mortar weapon, all kinds of World War II ammunition, shells, bullets and stuff. All on show with cards written in English telling you how they were used. It was his personal museum. He wanted us to give him money, which we had to with all those weapons. I was scared. How we see people and think we know them…'

'I didn't know you were Jewish.'

'Half Jewish.'

'Okay, so what? I'm with you, any outsider, Jewish, black, poor, Aborigine – whatever. I know how it feels to be picked on. Tell me more.'

'Nothing much, except Dad's family came from Warsaw. They came with

Grandpa to America to escape the Nazis. But he wanted to fight them, so he came here to fly bombers. I told you all this.' She frowned and shook her head. 'And still I behave like an idiot.' She paused, looking serious. 'And I've never told anyone I don't want to appear Jewish. I'm a real coward, Franky.'

Franky waited on her look of dejection. 'Hannah,' she said softly. 'You're no coward. Look at what you want to do. That's brave in my book. Fuck your silly conscience. I'll tell you something. 'I wished you'd lived near me when I was a kid. My life would have been different.'

'Do you really mean that?'

'I do. We'd have had fun.'

'No red-hot pokers.' Hannah giggled a little.

'No, yeah … it's that I did have a bad time. My dad raped me when I was thirteen.'

Hannah clapped both hands to her cheeks— '*What*!'

'Once, but it was enough.' Franky stood up and went to stand at the window, gazing out, cutting a tragic figure. 'Now,' She turned round, making a show of looking business-like, 'no more of this, what matters is you.'

'Oh, no! I can't believe it! Your father did *that* – to *you*?'

'Cross my heart and hope to die, stick a needle in my eye.' Franky put on a brave face and sat down on the bed.

'Did he go to prison? Did you tell the police!'

'No. I couldn't do it —I just couldn't. That's something I couldn't tell anyone, certainly not my mother.'

'Oh that's … Hannah remained awestruck. 'Franky. That's terrible.'

Franky shrugged.

Hannah blinked rapidly. 'I can't imagine what you've gone through. It's unbelievable. My God.'

She remained silent for a moment or two, then hesitated. 'Franky, you've told me things you've kept a secret, and now I'll confess something to prove I *am* a coward. I was at high school with this little Jewish boy. One day he got kicked around really hard for being just that, Jewish. I was the only one to see it. I said nothing, did nothing. I thought I was lucky to have blonde hair.'

Hannah hesitated, glancing at her watch. 'Look, I've got work to do. This storm.' She looked out of the window. 'It's not as noisy. I think it's going.'

She went to the door. 'Well.' She opened it. 'I ought to say Shalom Aleichem.'

'I know the shalom, but what's the rest?'

'Peace be unto you.'

'Nice.'

'Oh, forgot to ask.' She closed the door again. 'You didn't tell me what my character does in your book. You told me Tom and Craig were in, but not me.'

'I don't know yet. I think your face will belong to an ordinary student who finds herself living with an intellectual, like Tom the con man.'

'Tom? You've got Craig as the con man.'

'Have I?'

'In the notes you have.'

'Oh, hell.' Franky grimaced. 'It's … it's this wind. You heard of the mistral in France? It drives everybody mad. Look, forget me. What matters is you. Do you feel better now?'

'Yes, I do, in a way.' Hannah opened the door. 'I'm glad we talked.' She was half out of the room when she stopped. 'Oh, Craig wants to go to the Institute at one o'clock, if that's okay?'

'Fine by me. Now buzz off.'

'Okay.' Hannah smiled, closed the door and went.

Franky lay back on the bed in contemplation. In the normal course of events, she'd be punching the air. She'd turned Hannah from furious accuser into a compliant soul. But why did she lie to her, the one person she really liked? The therapist would have said it was to buttress her ego, reminding her that, in the face of her father's cold-heartedness and mother's indifference, she'd been doing it all her life.

She rolled on to her side, wrinkling her nose and tightening her brows. Why had she lied to Hannah about Craig in the first place? There had been no need, except her own need to feel good, be thanked, to receive praise and acceptance. The therapist had hit the right button with *that* warning.

Lying there, something else stirred in her mind. *Him*. Why had Annabelle continued to talk about her father at their follow-up meeting? *It points him out in a very unpleasant light. If he's as bad as you imply, won't it land you in trouble with him?*

It seemed to Franky that she was more concerned for her father than she was for *her*. What was the connection linking him with Annabelle? There had to be some form of pre-existing bond, hadn't there?

It was two hours later and the five cottagers, while waiting for Touch FM's latest weather forecast, were having a 'ploughman's lunch' of bread, cheese and pickle, basic fare since the pantry was short of anything more appetising. Craig and Alicia were on rota that evening to do the weekly shop.

Franky's thoughts, as she chewed a lump of cheese, were increasingly bitter. She only had to think of what she'd done *for them,* the huge expense she'd incurred in heavily subsidising them for the cottage rental; the lavish meal at The White Swan; her guarantee that everyone could opt out at any time free of charge; the compensation for the early move; the expensive wine and Harrods truffles even. And what had they done for her in return? Zilch.

Tired with jet lag she'd dragged herself around estate agencies for *their* benefit. Had any of them bought her anything? Had they taken her out for a surprise meal, or even handed her a box of chocolates? Had they bought flowers for the table, made the bed for her, taken over her rota duty for a week? She'd put herself on it to keep goodwill and earn respect, yet she should have been freed from all tasks, not even having to put a mug in the dishwasher for the whole year. She'd been crazy to think that the warm feeling she'd enjoyed was due to how they felt towards her. The bottom line – and the only conclusion she could draw – was that she'd demeaned herself.

She went back to her room and sat motionless, eyes lowered, hands loose upon her lap, mulling over the undeniable fact that she'd spent her whole life harbouring the vague notion that others were out to get her, in some way or other. Now the likes of Helen Bookbinder and John Black had been replaced by Alicia and Annabelle, offspring of a darker god.

She suddenly perked up, aware that something had changed in the room. It was the silence. The shutter and the drainpipe were no longer banging and rattling in protest. She watched a pale shaft of sunlight light up part of the windowsill.

She relaxed and sipped a glass of water.

Once more she saw Alicia tousle Hannah's hair in a show of affection. Not in character. Was she making a statement, putting out a warning? Well, many things had happened to leave her suspicions confirmed. There *was* a conspiracy and it was led by Annabelle. And her father was behind it. But how and why did it come about?

Chapter Fifteen

With the wind now no more than 'middling to strong', they drove through town, passing men with chainsaws, cutting through fallen branches. Other workmen were up on rooftops, struggling to fix pale-green waterproof covers over missing tiles.

The scenes of damage added to Franky's depression.

As flies to wanton boys,
are we to th' gods.
They kill us for their sport.

The lines from *King Lear* crossed her mind. She'd written an essay on Greek Tragedy at College, asking the question whether there was justice in the world. and the answer was no, only the sport of vicious gods. The only certainty in life was a disturbing uncertainty about everything, because, although the wicked died, so did the good. Aeschylus, the father of Greek tragedy, made it clear that only a divine power could resolve conflict, in that the concepts of earthly justice were prey to transient values and notions which were destroyed by human conflict. She felt a victim of such wantonness and so went with Shylock in hoping to achieve some form of justice by causing pain to his oppressors.

She became aware of Alicia sitting behind her, an uncomfortable presence. She turned and caught her eye. Alicia gave her a smile.

She suddenly asked herself the question: Who, beside her father, were her oppressors? Certainly not Craig, far too decent a guy to get involved in any sort of conspiracy. But was Annabelle bisexual and having an affair with him and Alicia separately?

And then there was Tom. Where was he in all this? She envied him his aplomb. How she wished that she could shrug off a slight as he had when the schoolboy made fun of him. Was he really part of the conspiracy? One day he was. But then the next? Difficult to tell.

No, it wasn't a persecution complex that she suffered from. She felt persecuted because she *was* persecuted.

Then, in the midst of her misery, came fear. Had she revealed too much to Hannah, exposing her weaknesses? Had she told her of the conspiracy as she had to Maggie? She couldn't remember, having talked freely with them both, so many emotional episodes. Well, she had to be careful from now on. No longer would she take risks with so much at stake.

She fell into bitter reflection, from which brought a faint smile to her lips.

I am not in the giving vein today

It was Hannah, talking about Richard the Third, that had drawn her to him. She loved that line, one of the most amusing in the whole of Shakespeare. King Richard was fascinating and so thrillingly bad. Why couldn't she act in a similar manner and get some payback for all the effort and trouble she'd taken in making her housemates' lives so comfortable? Why be always good? Cause a little pain today. Why not take away a little of their comfort, instead of continually *giving*?

The afternoon went quickly, busy with a seminar and a lecture on "Early Modern English". She would be late home. Time to enjoy some payback for all her generosity and big-heartedness. Instead of catching the bus she decided to ask Craig to pick her up in town – at her convenience, of course. It was *her* cottage. They were there at *her* pleasure, not the other way round. Well, an outsider doesn't go along with the majority's love of the hero; it's much more fun identifying with the baddie. When you're on the outside, whether with a Jew's nose, hunched back, or red hair, you're justified in having different aims and values.

Aren't you?

While waiting for Craig to arrive, she stood alone in the floodlit garden at New Place, the site where Shakespeare lived and died.

She'd met the gardener, a woman who told her that she'd sacrificed wealth as a banker in exchange for a stress-free life, drawing peace from the soil. Looking into her fresh face and twinkling eyes, how Franky had envied her. The gardener had taken a pay cut of £100,000 a year to achieve it. Franky thought that gardeners' wages were shocking and said as much. How was it that they, the literal salt of the earth, could be treated so poorly!

But then, look at what the gardener had in return: working with nature, a Wordsworthian idyll, content in a safe and secure life, surrounded by family and friends. As Franky listened to her calm and warm voice, she'd felt like an alien.

She walked slowly around the garden, its sweeping lawn flanked by a footpath lined with exquisite topiary of yew and, at ground level, flower beds. She came to behold an Elizabethan 'Knot Garden', a floral piece of perfect symmetry, reflecting the over and under threads used in a needlework pattern. It was so exquisite that it brought a lump to her throat. So much devotion.

Further on, she came to a tall, bronze figure, drawn by its strange and twisted treelike appearance. It was one of eight sculptures dotted around the garden, each celebrating one of Shakespeare's plays, this one discreetly labelled *The Tempest*.

The sculpture's air of mysterious command, and the knowledge that Shakespeare would have sat scribing the play not more than twenty yards away, had her slowly circling around the sculpture, her lips parted, a trailing hand feeling its twists and turns, her breathing half suspended … until she came to a sudden stop.

There, from out of the gnarled bronze trunk, a man's head protruded, his eyes closed. It reminded her of an old wooden ship's figurehead. Was he drowned at sea – no, not drowned, a*sleep? And dreaming*? Was the streamlined protrusion meant to be Prospero, the sorcerer, suggesting that life itself could be a dream, nothing but a mere interval between the sleep before birth and the sleep after death?

She allowed her fingers to drift over the sleeping head. Was he tempting her to escape the forthcoming pain and distress that was surely her fate if the persecution continued? When it was over, when good overcame evil, would she then find peace, or would she always be plagued with doubt and fear?

The blare of a car horn shocked her into sudden awareness. Looking back down the garden she could just make out Craig's car. She knew it was parked on double-yellow lines, risking a penalty fine.

With a gasp she set off running towards it, waved to the gardener and shot through the modern artworks and out through the gate on to the pavement.

'Sorry, Craig,' she said, scrambling into the car.

'No worries.'

She glanced at him as she fastened her seatbelt. He looked, as usual, calm and solid when she'd expected him to look irritable at being ordered out late. She'd lost her bitterness and the desire for payback. The sleeping head had flowed into her, morphing into something warm and comforting.

'So, what have you been up to?' he said, pulling away into light traffic.

'Stuff. Library. Looking round here. You know the sculpture *The Tempest*?'

'Sure. One of Gregg Wyatt's – I met him once, comes from New York.'

'It's Prospero, isn't it? Suggesting life itself could be a dream?'

'I think it is,' said Craig. 'What did he say? Something about sleep before birth and sleep after death?'

'That's right.'

'Doesn't it mean why bother, stay asleep? It negates life but then you don't worry, you don't fret, no pain.'

'Well…' She relaxed in her seat. 'It could be for me, for all the anxious times I've had.'

'Really?' He flicked his eyes towards her in surprise.

'Yes. Why should everyone be expected to enjoy life? For millions it's shit. Now we're worrying about the end of the world through climate change and rising oceans full of plastic.'

She raked her seat back, to rest her head.

Craig glanced at her with a smile. 'So, what led you into the garden?'

'Erm, I like gardens. I really felt calm there, next to the sculpture. I felt good. I really did.'

'The sculpture did that?' Craig glanced at her.

'It felt like it.' She paused before rolling her head towards him with a smile.

'You never seem to get upset. Don't you ever get pissed off by people?'

'Now why do you ask that?' He shot her a grin.

'What do you think of Alicia?'

Craig hesitated before answering. 'She's okay. Don't really know her.'

'What about Hannah?'

'Hannah? She's a great kid. Why?'

'Just wondered. What about Tom?'

'Hey, what *is* this, an interrogation?'

'No, I'm really interested. Go on. Tell me.'

'Tom? You know what he's like – austere, scholastic, an aesthete, a dry, ironic sense of humour.'

'I meant what you *thought* of him.'

'Oh. What I *like* about him is … I guess his brain. What I'd give for that. But he's also quiet. Half the time I think he's not there.'

'Not there? You think he's insane?' She almost laughed.

He chuckled. 'No. I mean he's like the invisible man – until he speaks and then he can be riveting. For me a guy who doesn't snore, is okay,' he added with a louder chuckle.

'Hannah. You know she's nuts about you? You do know that?'

'What?' He attempted a frown but produced more of a smile.

'I was told she stalked you round town.'

He knitted his forehead and sighed. 'Yeah, so she did. I'm sorry for her, I really am. I mean that.'

They listened to the traffic swish past.

'Craig?' she said suddenly. 'Do you ever talk about your loss?' She put the question in a calm and sympathetic voice.

It was some time before he spoke. 'No. Why do you ask?'

'I'm interested. I mean, dear God, what you've been through. I see you always relaxed and I just can't make it out. I think what if it was me—oh, I'm sorry!' She put up a hand. 'I shouldn't be doing this!' She raised her head. 'I'm really sorry.'

'It's okay.' He blinked as main headlights swept across his eyes. 'I guess the denial phase has gone now, helped by coming here. Facts have returned to being facts. You get to accept reality.'

She waited a moment. 'So, does it get better in time — oh, stupid question!' She wriggled impatiently in her seat. 'You just said it, facts become facts. You learn to live with it. That it?'

Craig hesitated. 'Yes. The pain becomes an ache that's always there to some degree. It's the best I can do.' He stopped at a red light and turned to her with a smile. 'But thanks, Franky, appreciated.'

She looked at him in surprise and then gave a frown. 'Look, I'm sorry I called you out. I should have caught the bus.'

'No way. Think how much I owe you. C'mon.' He paused. 'I think what you've done for us is incredible.'

'Yeah? I think so too.' She rested her head back, closed her eyes momentarily and then found him glancing at her, at which she burst out laughing. He laughed too.

When they arrived at the cottage there was a car in front of the woodshed.

'Whose is that?' she said, getting out.

'Alicia's got a couple of friends in. They're celebrating.'

'*Two* friends?' As he zapped the car doors, she stopped to stare at him. 'Celebrating -celebrating what?'

'Alicia thinks she's got Desdemona. I don't get it. You'd think it was an Oscar. It's only an amateur production.'

As they stepped into the hallway a burst of female laughter from the living room was followed by an unintelligible comment that brought more laughter. She waited while Craig climbed the stairs to his room, then hesitated at the living room door. It was ajar. She pushed it open and entered cautiously.

The laughter died away on her entrance.

'Hi, Franky,' said Alicia.

She and her two guests were sitting around the inglenook, bathed in the red glow of firelight. Lit candles surrounded them. An opened bottle of wine was warming by the fire. All three had a filled glass in their hands. Franky recognised the 'friends': Brooklyn, a tall and willowy girl with glasses perched on a mop of mousy hair and wearing a roll-neck brown sweater and jeans;

Julia, a small black girl wearing green pants and a grey top.

Alicia picked up the bottle. 'Franky. Have a drink with us.'

'No, I'm good.' She paused. 'Thanks. Could I have a word Alicia?'

'Sure.' Alicia followed her out of the room.

Franky marched into the kitchen, holding the door open. As soon as Alicia entered, she closed it. 'Okay,' she said. 'The rule is one visitor. You know that.'

'Yes.' Alicia took up a stance with legs apart and arms folded. 'Julia was with Brooklyn when I called, so I felt socially bound to invite her as well. May I go now?' She made a move to open the door.

Franky blocked her. 'Who was smoking? Somebody's been smoking in there. It's banned in the rental agreement. Who was it?'

'Brooklyn. I went to my room to get the drinks, and when I came back, she'd lit up. I told her she couldn't, so she stopped. And, just in case you noticed, we were drinking Merlot – which *I bought*. We both know what this is about, don't we?'

Franky stared back at her under lowered eyelids, swaying slightly. 'No. You tell me.'

'I didn't know you were in line for Desdemona until you dashed out during the meal to look at your emails and that's when Hannah told me. I don't mind you getting the part, I really don't, so don't hold it against me if I do, okay? It's only a one-nighter and there's no money involved, so who cares?'

'So why celebrate?'

'We're not. If I said it, I was joking. It's just a social evening. Oh, just for the record – Annabelle didn't tell me anything about you, regarding the production. You have a serious problem, Franky. *Now* may I go?'

'I've not finished. I had an email from the power company. They're doing work around here and it said we might get a power outage – we've already had one. So, I bought candles and put them all around the place, each with a box of matches, reason being all five of us wouldn't have to stumble around too much in the dark looking for them. I told you all that. If I were upstairs now and we lost power you'd be fine, but I could break my neck coming downstairs to get one of them. Get it now?'

Alicia nodded. 'Yes. I'm sorry. I'll go now, switch on the lights, and blow out the candles. Now, please, do you mind?'

Franky opened the door and stood aside.

Alicia stopped halfway and turned to Franky, giving a fair imitation of her voice. "Oh, Alicia, you'll love it there. We'll have a great time."

With a faint smile she turned and went back to the living room.

Franky lay on the bed, engulfed in misery. She'd just ripped, stabbed and hacked Alicia in a succession of fantasy attacks and was now at her lowest.

A spasm of laughter came from the living room. She slipped off the bed and crept downstairs to sit on a step that was level with the top of the closed door, ready to dash upstairs should it open.

She heard murmurings at first, but then came a chuckle from Alicia.

'I reckon more than odd,' she said. 'I think there's a screw loose somewhere.'

Franky heard a creak of floorboards from the landing and quickly went down into the hallway, pretending to be searching her anorak pockets.

Tom stepped downstairs.

Her eyes dropped to the half-bottle of whisky clutched in his hand.

He noticed and gestured with it. 'It's mine. I'm looking for a glass. Fancy a drop?'

'Erm…' She glanced at the closed living-room door, paused for a second and then decided. 'Yes, okay.'

She followed him into the kitchen.

'Why does alcohol taste better from a glass?' he said. 'What's your theory?'

'It's psychological, isn't it? You can see the colour. If it were the colour of water, I don't think we'd drink half as much.'

He poured out two half-fingers of whisky. 'I think you're right.'

'Thanks.' She took the glass.

'If it were blue the association would be poison. Brown is fire and maturing leaf. And whoever likes drinking wine from a mug or cup must be an alcoholic.'

She took a sip as she watched him roll the whisky around the glass, before raising it to his nose.

'And the shape of the glass also affects taste,' he said, before sniffing. 'It dictates how vapour rises.'

'But isn't alcohol supposed to be man's worst enemy?'

'Hah, but the Bible says love your enemy.'

Grinning, she poked a finger at him.

'Do you believe in life after death?' He took a sip. 'Hmm?'

'Do I believe…' She felt suddenly shocked. *Prospero … the eternal dream. Again.*

'Yes. One comes up against the imponderable. A fellow asked me that and I said no, because I believe that death is a misnomer in that it suggests a state of some kind of existence, whereas I believe that you are how you were before you were born. Not even part of nothingness.' He raised his eyebrows slightly. 'What do you think?'

'Well, it's an invalid question, isn't it?'

'Why invalid?'

'Because it has no answer. It contains an assumption that's not applicable. But you're right because at the time, you weren't born to *be* you, were you? Oh, I don't know. I'm not into philosophy. It's playing with words, isn't it?' She licked her lips and cast a glance back down the hallway.

'Hah.' He rolled his glass around, regarding her with a kind of intimate amusement. Then his smile turned into a frown, observing her like a head teacher, wondering what to do with an errant child for whom he had sympathy. 'Tell me. Are you pleased we came here?'

'How do you mean?'

'I've seen you rather … worried recently? You're worried now, aren't you?'

He's probing.

'No, why do you say that?' She took a lingering sip of whisky. 'Well, maybe things have been getting at me. And I don't know why.'

'What things?'

He bent down to pick up a scrap of paper from the floor and place it in the waste bin, then stood upright, resuming his stare at her. 'Do you mean people?'

'Yes, I think so. I think it started when Alicia told us she was being auditioned for Desdemona.'

'You were pretty shaken by that.' There was a thin smile on his lips as he spun the glass slowly before raising it to his lips. 'No?' He took a sip, his eyes flicking sideways at her.

'No. I was just surprised. Annabelle told me I was the front runner and then says the same thing to her. I found it strange. That's all.'

'Hmm. So, what are you doing for the production?'

'Me? Oh, I don't know. Having been let down I don't feel like doing anything, if I'm honest.'

'Hmm. You feel betrayed.'

The spider was back, crawling up her spine.

'Well, I do in a way. Don't you think it's weird that I'm virtually promised the part and then find out someone else has got it? How would you feel?'

'What's your explanation?'

'I don't know. I—' She broke off, irritated. 'Tom?' She spoke accusatively, dropping her caution. 'May I ask you something? Why do you find everything so amusing?'

'Do I? If you'd asked me about life, I'd admit I do – in the sense of the theatre of the absurd. Did you see *Rosencrantz and Guildenstern Are Dead*?'

'No, I didn't.'

'Two minor characters transported back to Elsinore. Wandering around trying to catch up on the action. Wonderful concept, the two of them trying to find out what's wrong with Hamlet. I found it highly amusing, their cogitations about the futile hazards of daily life while he considers suicide. It reminded me of Dr Strangelove, fitting perfectly into the internal logic of a nuclear war, ending with the cowboy riding the atomic bomb, waving his hat into eternity. Gloriously absurd.'

'Oh. Yes. Well, I'm glad you're easily entertained. I wish I were. Sorry, Tom but I'm tired, I must go. But thanks for the drink.'

She went back up to her room and stood waiting to hear Tom climb the stairs, enter his room and close the door. She waited for another minute and then went down to resume her vigil.

After a burst of laughter, she heard Hannah's voice.

'She's misunderstood. If you talk to her long enough, you'd find out.'

'No, it's *actions* that matter,' said Alicia, 'not what goes on in her head. There's the constant chivvying, do this, do that, don't do that, be careful, who had the bath last, it's not been cleaned properly. It goes on day by day, there's no end to it. You say *we* misunderstand her? She got us here for her own benefit. She's the owner, we're the servants.'

'Oh, that's not true, Alicia,' said Hannah. 'We're all on a fixed rota of jobs. Including her, don't forget.'

'Okay. Let me give you an example. I'm doing the weekly shop with Tom, okay? We get through the list – it's taken us an hour and a half and we're loaded with stuff. We call Craig to come down as per usual to pick us up, but he can't make it. Why? Because Franky has commandeered him to take her to the hairdresser *knowing* we need the car. That's meant to be cruel – don't you think?'

'I don't think she means to be cruel. Franky's had a hard life.'

'Okay, how about this? Next time there we are, carrying these bags with stuff that weigh half a ton, all the way from the supermarket to the bus stop, all of ten minutes waddling like pregnant ducks – and guess what? It's suddenly raining and we didn't take umbrellas because our hands would be full. So, she calls saying there's something she forgot and would we go back to the supermarket for it. Are you making excuses for that? It's the pits, isn't it?'

'Yes,' said Hannah. 'But look what happened about the bottle of wine. She did say she was sorry.'

'Did she? Not to me. Anyway, saying sorry is the easy bit. *Showing* it is a whole new ball game.' Alicia drank from her glass.

'Yes, of course it's frustrating but you have to remember —'

'I was more than frustrated, Hannah, I was spitting feathers. I know she's paid thousands to get us here, but not for us to be slaves at her beck and call.'

'I know and I understand. But let me tell you something. She came up with the idea of writing a novel – she told me this. To see the characters in her mind's eye she decided to use our faces for the characters. We'd just be pegs to hang them on. If you didn't know that and you heard about it, you could think it was libellous. She does get misunderstood sometimes.'

'We're pegs for her book?' Alicia let out a short laugh. 'You gotta be kidding.'

'No,' insisted Hannah. 'She just needs faces to look at, that's all. You see, you're drawing false conclusions already. And I was the same when she left her notebook open while she was out of the room. I happened to see what was written. She had some names down. You, Alicia, me, Craig and Tom. Against my name was 'wet rag'. She said it wasn't me. I won't bore you but she explained and I believed her. Some wouldn't.'

'So, who was it? Did she say?' Was it me who was labelled?'

'She didn't say.'

'I bet it was. So, what was on my peg? What does my character do in the great novel?'

There was a pause, during which Franky, eyes hooded, sat with her head lowered to her chest, her mouth open, listening intently.

'Well, go on. What does my character do?'

'Well. Erm …' Hannah stifled a giggle.

'Hey, c'mon. What am I?'

'A hooker.'

Brooklyn and Julia laughed out loud, Hannah giggling with them.

'A hooker.' Alicia nodded. 'A hooker hanging on a peg.'

'Yes.'

'Uh-huh. Just that – a hooker.'

'Part-time.'

Brooklyn and Julia, howling with laughter, were both forced to put down their wine glasses fearing a spillage.

'Oh. Only part-time? That's not work, that's pleasure.'

'Alicia,' Julia pointed to her, spluttering, 'two nights a week patrolling the sidewalk. Mister Institute Director, how you doing? A short time down by the river, only thirty bucks!'

'Jesus,' said Alicia. 'What else did you read about me?'

'Nothing.'

'How disappointing. Just a hooker, uh-huh.' Alicia took another drink. 'Will you swear to that?'

'I swear.'

'Hey,' said Brooklyn suddenly. 'What about Julia and me—are we named?'

'No. Look, I'm sorry,' said Hannah. 'I shouldn't have told you that. I've had too much to drink. But she does worry me rather.'

'Why?'

'She gets ideas that — no, I don't want to get it wrong, but I do think she worries a lot about what people think about her.'

'She has reason. Look at what she causes with all that nagging. I tell you this, Hannah. If her book ever gets published, which I doubt, and I see myself, I'll sue the hide off her.'

'I wouldn't worry, Alicia,' said Julia. 'It won't be published. She's daydreaming, that's all.'

'I know why we're here!' exclaimed Alicia suddenly. She had to put her glass down, she was that excited. 'You've explained it, Hannah. I wondered why she picked me to come here, knowing I don't like her much. Have you noticed, she's always gazing at people, studying them? If she *is* writing this novel about us, I reckon she invited us here to do just that. That's why she's shelled out all this money. I wondered what she was getting out of it. She's spent loads subsidising us, hasn't she? We give her *added value*. Who gives all that money away unless they're crazy, *or* they're up to something like this?'

Julia turned to grin at Hannah. 'You sure we're not in the book, Brooklyn and me?'

'I didn't see your names.'

'What's Craig down for? Do you know?'

'A con man. And Tom's a crazy psycho.'

'Oh, superb!' Alicia joined Brooklyn and Julia in laughter. 'At least I've got my marbles. That changes everything. Why should I grouch? I'm in great company!' She raised her glass at the ceiling. 'Cheers, Franky.'

'Erm… 'Hannah hesitated. 'She told me something that might, well, explain everything.'

'What, she's just one weird cookie?' Alicia shook her head and took a drink.

'No. She told me her father raped her.'

Alicia blinked and raised her eyebrows. 'Pardon me? Her father— *raped* her?'

'Yes.'

'And you believed her?'

'Yes, because it's not the kind of thing you expect anyone to tell you, is it?'

'No.' Alicia shook her head contemptuously. 'No, c'mon. She did it to get *sympathy*. Maybe she's got a grudge against him, and it makes her feel better. She's a drama queen, she'll say anything to be the star.'

Franky suddenly dragged Alicia into the kitchen, seized a carving knife and cut off her head with a final wrench.

Hating and despairing, she went back upstairs.

She switched on the bedside lamp and downed two Diazepam tablets without thinking. It wasn't long before the fire that drove her mind began to cool. She reached the borders of sleep when thinking what a pity it was that Hannah had been with Alicia and that it was best not to talk about her problems anymore and that it was also best not to lie to her anymore …

Suddenly, she was awake with a mental jolt. Disorientated, she fumbled for her watch and saw that she'd been asleep for nearly forty minutes.

Slipping out of bed, she put on her dressing gown, picked up her notebook and pen, then carefully opened the door. She could still hear voices from down in the living room. Leaving the door open, she crept downstairs, back to her listening post.

She sat down, touched her forehead with the tips of her fingers and rubbed them lightly together. Damp. She wiped her forehead with a sleeve of her dressing gown.

After hearing them chat about the role of *Lady Macbeth*, in the latest production at the RSC, there was a silence, broken by Julia commenting on the late hour and suggesting that she and Brooklyn should think about getting back.

'Just one thing, Hannah,' said Alicia. 'She said she'd been raped by her father. What happened after that? Did she go to the police?'

'I don't know. She didn't say.'

'Well, there you go. You should have asked her that.'

'Maybe I should.' A pause. 'I don't know. She's had a hard life. I feel sorry for her.'

'I told you she's a drama queen. Look at all the lording she does over us. We're not her pegs, we're her *targets*. All she wanted was to get us here and manipulate us for her fucking book.'

'I know. But just think how much money she's spent on us.'

'I keep telling you *why* Hannah. To get added value! We're just objects on a chess board, to move around. Look. It doesn't matter what *she* says, it's how she *looks* at you. It's in her eyes, the way she reacts to things. She's nuts. Hannah, keep me informed about this book. I want to know how I end up in it, okay?'

'If it gets published, you'll know.'

After a pause Julia chuckled a little. 'If she does put you in her book, Alicia, I guess you'd say that Redsinfrit.'

Franky had to speak the word inside her head to realise it wasn't one, but four, words.

Red's in for it.

Later, when the stillness of the night was punctuated by the occasional hoot of a barn owl, Franky lay on her bed. By her side lay the notebook in which she'd written: *By day the beguiling witch had soft, luminous eyes that signalled kindness and compassion. By night her closed eyelids were furnace doors that, when opened, revealed the glow of hellfire.*

She curled up, tight in misery and, like Lear, burning with a sense of injustice. There was no doubt that she'd been robbed of Hamlet and now, Desdemona, for her the most attractive female character in Shakespeare's canon. Contemporary audiences could still be moved by her.

She would have made them cry – it tore at her heart strings. How she mourned and, now, how she hated.

Chapter Sixteen

I am disgraced, impeached, and baffled here
Pierced to the soul with slander's venomed spear
Richard II, Act I, sc. 1

Hark. The owl again.
   It was the owl that shriek'd, the fatal bellman,
Which gives the stern'st good-night.
   Suddenly, in her mind's eye flashed a light in a dark garden. With eyes closed, she reached once more for the sleeping head in New Place. She felt nothing; it was no longer there. There was no relief from the pressure, no escaping her embittered thoughts.
   She dwelt on Tom, the cool-headed intellectual who hid his darker side through wit. *How are your father's robots getting on*? she'd put to him, after a recent seminar. What was his answer? *The train now standing on platform one will soon be put back on the rails.* At that he'd drifted away, his chin raised with that teasing flicker of a smile.
   Then there was the other day when she'd found him in the Shakespeare Centre, perusing books in the shop. *Tom, what are you doing? Everything worth reading about Shakespeare is in the Institute library, isn't it?* He'd cocked his little smile at her. *I know that. I need a present for someone.*
   They went to drink coffee in the Birthplace cafe, discussing dissertations.
   'Mine will begin,' he said, 'with an acceptance that the emerging Gothic writers of the eighteenth century used Shakespeare. They were trying to create

a new sub-genre of the novel that flowered later in the nineteenth century.'

'Used Shakespeare? Do you mean copying or borrowing?'

'Well, I think "borrowing" is apt. I think those novelists tried to persuade readers that rather than undermine the Gothic novel as a literary genre, they were paying homage to the great man, himself.'

'His imaginative vision?'

'Yes. I'm going to explore *Macbeth*, its wild landscapes, grotesque buildings and the supernatural.'

'Witchcraft and Banquo's ghost?'

'Exactly. The blurring of distinctions between sanity and insanity.'

'I'm sure you'll enjoy it.'

'Hmm.' He studied her. 'You said that as if you—' He stopped himself.

'What? As if what?'

'I just thought you said it with familiarity – a kind of knowledge.' His dark eyes twinkled.

'Did I?' She looked round as if looking for a means of escape. 'What do you mean?'

'Don't be alarmed. Maybe I'm wrong, but I think most people feel a sense of evil, either inside or outside, at some time in their lives. But we separate thought and action, don't we, those of us who are normal?'

'"Normal" – you said evil. Oh … look, I'm sorry … I'm confused.' She tried to hide her fear with a grin.

'Rest assured. We know little of the dark side of the moon. We can but speculate. You said it was all a game.'

That teasing smile.

Up until now she'd doubted his involvement in the conspiracy. He was an individualist, too egocentric to get involved in anything so sordid. But, what had he said? *The blurring of distinctions between sanity and insanity.* Was he conditioning her mind on behalf of Annabelle and her father? When she heard that he was being auditioned to play Iago, she thought how right it was. How fitting that he should play the schemer who sought the shadows, a character who would observe, but not *be* observed, a man like Tom, of supreme intelligence with dazzling linguistic skills, given to making tongue-in-cheek remarks, sometimes garnished with a timely pinch of malice?

Had Annabelle detected in Tom a fellow spirit, recruiting him to find out about people, to probe their minds, so revealing their indiscretions? In that investigative role he needn't take part in any plotting, need he? It would be beneath him.

Could he be … the *conspirator's muse*, as well as i*nformant*?

Again, the owl called across the cold night air.

She was forced to quell her rising anger. Wasn't she Franky O'Tierney, of fighting Irish stock – her father discounted – fused with Gallic cunning? She vowed to take on the lot of them, Annabelle included. It was outrageous to find herself betrayed and at the same time condemned to the ignominy of having her ambition destroyed.

She recalled her first meeting with Annabelle, who was quick to pose the question: *You were going to say something. About your father*? She'd probed further at their next meeting. Why was she so concerned about him?

And why had she kept pursuing it *if she didn't know him*?

The next morning Franky went to Boots, the store and pharmacy in Bridge Street, where she bought a tube of antibiotic ointment for a painful stye in her right eye. While she was there, she noticed Hannah walk into the store, with Alicia.

She noted that they both wore something red, Alicia a jacket and Hannah a scarf.

She quickly moved out of their field of vision and disappeared behind a cosmetics counter stacked high with boxes of perfume.

From there she observed them approach the dispensary, where Alicia paid for a white package.

Franky left the store as quickly as she could, her heart thumping.

It was 2 p.m. and it was raining.

Thirty-eight students, the whole student body, sat on the red chairs around the periphery of the Great Hall. Annabelle stood in the centre, smiling.

'Good afternoon everybody. Are we all present, anyone missing?'

There was a pause while the students looked around.

'Yes. Franky,' said Craig.

'Oh. Any idea why?'

Annabelle was met with shrugs and silence. She glanced at her watch.

'Well, we've got a lot to get through today. You all have a copy of the notes. I need volunteers for stage manager, set designer, costume, lighting, sound, make-up, props manager and front-of-house manager. Anyone here acted as stage manager before?'

'Yes, I have.' The raised hand belonged to a slim and small Chinese student. She'd told Franky that she was educated at Cobham Hall, a girls' boarding school in Kent, a favourite among wealthy Chinese parents.

In the library, not more than sixty yards from the Great Hall, sat Franky, a solitary figure next to a window. She watched the silvery, staggering paths that raindrops made as they blew across the glass. The Boots incident was at the forefront of her mind. How was it that Hannah went shopping with Alicia, when she'd said how much she disliked her? And was it a coincidence that they both wore red?

Alicia was grooming her

Some kind of action had to be taken – and soon.

And then came the answer. How had she not thought of it before? Why bother with the enormity of grappling with a novel that may be published – or not – in two to three years' time? She had the perfect means with which to deter Alicia from recruiting Hannah into the conspiracy and, at the same time, point the finger at Annabelle.

Her *dissertation*.

A germ of an idea had been implanted in a recent lecture. Part of it had dealt with Elizabethan coding and cipher. What if she planted a coded accusation in her Shylock dissertation, something that both Alicia and Annabelle would easily detect and then decipher, something that would allude to their chicanery and abort the conspiracy? At the very least it would give them pause, wouldn't it?

A further idea gave it momentum. Students were actively encouraged to discuss dissertations with each other. She would ensure that Annabelle and Alicia were both present when she read aloud her poisonous barbs! Oh, to see their faces! Oh, the warmth that true revenge would bring.

She looked around the library. She was alone, apart from the librarian. She searched her tablet and found the notes that she'd taken during the lecture. She was reminded that there were three types of coding used in Elizabethan England, the first involving the replacement of sensitive names with numbers. Hopeless. The second related to a play on words that were allusive or involved the use of puns. Much too obvious. The third type used a code of aliases and the use of mythical narrative.

With a sigh of exasperation, she gave up on the whole idea.

Another change of mind.

From her window seat she looked dispiritedly beyond the dripping laurel bushes, towards the patio and conservatory. Her gaze foreshortened to settle on a plump raindrop tracking down the window. Frowning, she sank her head into her hands. Hamlet, with his sense of loss, tore at her heartstrings – even Macduff would have been more appealing than Shylock, he the selfless, honest and just man, whose revenge on Macbeth was in keeping with the moral code. She would have shared his ease of conscience if, like him, she was forced to take revenge in the name of justice, his by the sword, hers by power of the word.

Despondently she returned to Shylock, her job initially to find the associations, links and parallels that she shared with him. It was a painful exercise. Where was the joy, the pleasure, in dealing with such a character? She glanced round to catch the librarian rise from her desk and disappear behind rows of bookcases.

She turned back to rest her elbows on the table and watch another raindrop on its trickling, downward path. Was all lost? Wasn't it better to sleep the sleep of death, all fears and worries gone in a continuum of nothing?

Her eyes flicked sideways to see the librarian's hand put before her a magazine, as well as copies of newsprint.

'Thanks.' She picked up the magazine, with an inward sigh. Casually, she noted the date, 15 July 2010. A slip of paper inside, took her to an article that dealt with those actors who had been adversely affected, when playing Shylock on stage. She scanned through the introduction and came across a passage dealing with a performance of *The Merchant of Venice,* in Central Park, New York. It dealt with the Shylock of Al Pacino.

She started to read in a desultory fashion when, suddenly, her stomach tightened. In rising excitement, she read Pacino's answer to a question from the press: *Every actor tries to make a character their own. I'm playing Shylock as a pragmatic sufferer of slights.*

Her breath taken away, she stared at the phrase. As far as she knew – she would check – nowhere had she read about hypersensitivity to slight as a topic! She had even found it difficult to track down as a recognised personality disorder.

But there it was, unbelievable and mind blowing. Pacino's Shylock, faced with her own dilemma, had the same need to find a suitable form of revenge according to the degree of slight experienced!

Breathless, her fingers scrabbled at the keyboard, making mistake after mistake. Closing her eyes, she took a deep breath and began again. She searched for *Jews in Venice.* Their history revealed that they had been persecuted as early as 1516, when the Republic of Venice enacted a decree to formally isolate them. Following Nazi persecution post-1940, most of those arrested had their lives ended in Auschwitz. Of a total of 246 Venetian Jews deported to the death camps only eight of them survived.

Franky found that Pacino's Shylock had been categorised in stage reviews as "a histrionic Jew", "a Hebraic Jew", a "stage Jew" and "a bearded, lisping, guttural Jew". She took note of the unifying racial categorisation.

Poor Shylock. He would have suffered slight after slight without a murmur – and did he seek revenge, as she did, in fantasy? It was more than probable, she thought, almost certain.

So, in the end, despairing of ever getting justice from the state, he decided to take it into his own hands, to *watch a man have a pound of flesh cut from his body.*

Shakespeare understood. Rather than have to laboriously explain Shylock's anguish wrought by the multitude of slights committed against him, when questioned as to his motive, Shakespeare gave him the simple reply: '*Because it pleases me.*' Oh, how wonderful, how fitting. He had no cause or duty to explain, as nor had she.

She had mourned Hamlet and his "sense of loss," but now she had a new and true kinsman. She would fight Shylock's corner. Slighted they both were, he by the sneering, contemptuous call of "dog", she by the turn of a person's back against her. How many fantasy attacks had he gone through before it became too much to bear? Pacino would have shown Shylock's broken bond as the final straw, the point at which he sought to inflict real pain upon his oppressor.

What choice had Shylock? Where were his tools of justice? He had none, as neither had she.

In rising elation, she would have stood up and cheered had she not been in a quiet library. She needed to go outside and inhale fresh air, so she could fill her lungs and punch the sky.

But wait. She sat down, her heart palpitating. She needed to get her developing thoughts down, lest she forget. First, she needed to know if other actors had suffered abuse playing Shylock. It was not just a feeling of alienation she looked for, but of rejection because of the character they were playing.

And there it was. An article in *The Guardian,* May 2011, reported that a number of actors playing Shylock had felt oppressed, including Patrick Stewart and Anthony Sher. Not only were they treated with reserve by the other actors, but had even been victimised, even off stage, during rest periods.

And now the dark forces of the far-right had re-emerged all over Europe, reminiscent of the rising Nazi party of the early 1930s.

Franky quickly scribbled down a note: "Hadn't the Nazis forced all the Jews in Germany to wear a yellow star, and didn't her red hair also serve as a symbol of being an outcast?"

She hesitated. Was it an odious and ridiculous comparison? She decided not. Professor Woodbridge had pointed to her hair— her label— as exactly that, hadn't he? And wasn't anti-Semitism spreading throughout the US as well as Europe, even embroiling the British Labour Party in an internal conflict - how much more synchronistic could it get?

She continued making notes for some time, leading to the decision that her dissertation would not be an appeal for sympathy, either for herself or Shylock, but for *understanding*. It would carefully and logically examine the nature of fantasy revenge and how it related, empirically, to what had taken place, both before and after the deed.

But then, as she looked at earlier reviews of *The Merchant of Venice,* she found one from 1984 that had come in for extraordinary criticism. Ian McDiarmid, the actor playing *Shylock* with the RSC that year, was lambasted for "failing to protect himself from linguistic forays into "bastardised German" as well as "dubious historical deduction."

From the critics' perspective he was *the* Jew, framing him as one of a race of predatory individuals, but each behaving in an identical fashion and possessed of the same characteristics, stripped of their own personality and virtues. Racism disguised as stage reviews.

Thankfully there were critics, she discovered, who mollified her outrage. Of those who loved McDiarmid's performance, Michael Billington, drama critic of *The Guardian*, made no mention of 'the Jew' in declaring his Shylock "the greatest ever". John Barber admired his "intensity and passion," also without touching on race, and Jack Tinker simply called his performance "dazzling". Nick Baker went one better in judging it as nothing short of "magnificent".

A strip light overhead began to flicker. It brought to mind something that happened when she was nine years old. She saw her father inside an outhouse on a dark day in summer with dense black clouds above. The door was open, and he was bent over his mini-tractor. Suddenly, a strip-light had clicked into a constant flashing.

She heard him snap out 'Fuck', a word she'd never heard before. He'd glanced up at that point and caught her staring at him. His scowl in the intermittent lighting turned into a false, flashing smile showing his teeth. That image had stayed with her.

Her initial notes finished, she left the library to stand hidden behind the copper beech, arms outstretched and head raised. In the watery half-light, surrounded by falling leaves, she breathed deeply of the cold, dank air.

She turned round and gazed at a tall wooden building that was reached by a flight of steps. She'd been told by a member of staff that it was called The Watchtower, an eighteenth-century folly. She could imagine herself up there as a child, playing in a make-believe world that held no threat, and in which no sinister father skulked.

Suddenly a fierce gust of wind thrust a cloud of leaves, like birds into the air, throwing them around in all directions.

She went back to the library.

Sitting down, she typed:

"Shylock's sadness brought yearning, as he sought a greater good, as so do I. He wanted to *belong*, as do I. His fatal flaw was hubris. Mine is being a redhead. For both of us the law holds no redress, totally uninterested in both our plights."

She sat back and closed her eyes. No longer need she worry about her dissertation. Annabelle would find it hard to deny her this time. If she did, then the Director would soon know of it, she'd make certain of that. There would be an enquiry. Annabelle could even be fired. That would also amount to true revenge.

She gazed out of the window, the November darkness all enveloping. A glance at her watch told her that the meeting in the Great Hall was due to end shortly, after which many students would gravitate to the conservatory to chat and drink coffee.

She decided to join them and bent down to pick up her bag – but suddenly froze, aware of someone standing at the other side of the table. Strange. She'd heard no clicking of the turnstile.

Came that musky-sweet fragrance.

She stood up slowly.

'Franky.'

She stared into her large and luminous eyes.

'I've been looking for you, said Annabelle with a smile, her head inclined to one side. 'Had you forgotten the meeting?'

Franky cast a swift glance towards the librarian's desk. She was missing.

Her breathing quickened. 'I'm sorry. Yes, I did, I forgot,' she said in a taut voice. 'I've been working on Shylock. It's exciting, and I'm afraid I got caught up.' She stared at an iridescent silver eye hanging from a chain around Annabelle's neck. Her mother, she remembered, had an eye like that. She called it the '*mauvais oeil*' that was meant in legend to harm whoever looked at it.

'Well...' Annabelle sat down. 'Shall we?'

'Oh, of course.' Frankly quickly sat back in her chair, thinking desperately. 'I really am sorry. I'm also sorry about, you know, rushing out on you.'

'You already apologised.' Annabelle smiled, raising her eyebrows. 'You sent me a text and I replied remember?'

'Yes, I do, but I mean it.'

'Good. Forgotten.' Annabelle studied her for a moment, caught in a dilemma. 'Franky, do you feel alright?' She spoke hesitantly. 'I mean in yourself?'

'Yes, why?'

'Well... we are still worried about you, Franky. You look upset, even now.'

Franky blinked quickly with a frown. 'I'm sorry?'

'I said we're still worried about you.'

'Yes, but if you remember, you said it would remain between the two of us. You promised to keep it to yourself.'

'Oh, no – no. I had to tell the Director. We're both part responsible for your welfare, and it would be remiss of me if anything happened and I hadn't reported it.'

'Oh, I see.' She glanced towards the entrance to see the librarian back at her desk.

'Franky.' Annabelle chose her words carefully. 'You're very tense. Almost as if you want to get away from me again. Is that how you feel?'

'No. Maybe I'm worried for missing the meeting. I don't want to find that it—'

'Oh no.' Annabelle was quick to interrupt. 'You won't get a black mark or anything silly like that.' She paused. 'Now then, we're in luck. Nancy just called me. She's the head costumier at The Other Place. I asked, on your behalf, if she needed another volunteer apart from Brooklyn. She said that you could assist in selecting costume that reinforces the mood of a scene and maintains the style of production. Would you like to do that?'

'Of course. I'd enjoy that.'

Annabelle stretched out a hand. 'So, no more worries. Relax.'

'Yes. It's just I don't like upsetting people.'

'I know. It's settled and forgotten.' Annabelle smiled brightly and nodded at the research material on the table. 'How's it going, Shylock?'

'Amazing.'

'Really?'

'Yes. I've discovered something. Al Pacino played Shylock in Central Park as a man suffering from slights. The same as me. Hypersensitive. It's generated a whole new dynamic. I'm going to—'

'That's excellent. Hang on.' Annabelle glanced at her watch. 'I've a tutorial.' She got up, nodding at her tablet. 'That is wonderful. Really wonderful and I do mean that. I'm so pleased for you. I'll look forward to your notes, when you're ready. Do let me know if you need anything. Text is the best way. It's quicker.' She paused. 'Take care,' she said softly.

'I will.' Franky got to her feet. 'And thanks, Annabelle.' Bitch.

Franky, angered and deeply suspicious. watched her pause briefly to exchange words with the librarian, before exiting.

She watched her through the window, a figure illuminated on and off by the errant strip light, but soon lost to the darkness of the shrubbery.

Franky approached the conservatory, only to become aware of a figure standing outside. She could see the glow of his cigarette. It was Tom.

Seeing her, he gestured with it. 'Caught again.'

'Don't worry,' she said. 'I haven't told anyone.'

'I am trying.' He bent down to crush the cigarette under a stone and followed her inside.

They sat down, just as a strip-light began to blink. She stared upwards with a frown.

'No joy with the anti-smoking drug then,' she said, looking at him.

'No. I've stopped taking them. They make me angry. It's a side effect of Varenicline, the drug. We missed you at the meeting. Where were you?'

'In the library. I forgot.'

'Hmm.' He shot her a quizzical look.

'I'm sorry I cut you dead. I was suddenly very tired. Tell me, how's the dissertation?' Grinning, she poked a finger. 'And don't give me the 2.30 to Birmingham.'

'Hah.' He chuckled a little and pointed his finger. 'I see you've caught my wavelength.'

'How's *Macbeth* and the dark Gothic?'

'The usual. Castles, darkness, violence and the devil. Quite ominous, thankfully.'

'It's rather weird,' she said, 'don't you think?'

'What is?'

'The serendipity. Do you realise that we're all marching over the same kind of ground?'

'Are we?' He lowered his head to peer at her over his glasses. 'How?'

'Well, aren't we all pursuing bleak paths? Hannah's insanity, Craig's sense of loss. You're doing the Gothic bit. And there's Alicia doing psychoanalytical criticism.'

'And you are?'

'Shylock, wanting his pound of flesh. Where's comedy? Where's joy?'

'Well, Shakespeare does show a rather negative view of the human condition.' He studied her for a moment. 'It seems to have got you down.' He raised his eyebrows. 'Has it?'

'No, not really. Just anxious.' She shielded her eyes at the sweep of headlights from the car park. 'I want to deal with Hamlet as well. I'm now hoping to join him with Shylock.'

'Well, if you have Hamlet as well as Shylock, you three would have made good company, wouldn't you?'

'Oh, why?'

'The three of you. Seeking revenge?'

'What!' She stared at his face, flickering in the on-off strip lighting. 'Who told you that?'

'Oh, I thought that since both Shylock and Hamlet can't get the revenge *they* want, I naturally thought you chose them to mirror you, that you were also seeking revenge, for some reason?'

'No. That's not it.' She felt a stab of fear.

'Not in some way?'

'No.' She looked at her watch, urging the others to arrive.

'So, what is the link?'

'It's still in the gestation process. I'd rather not talk about it. I'm at sixes and sevens, to be honest. I wish they'd come. I'm getting cold.'

Another blast of wind threw leaves at the windows with a rattling sound.

She heard Craig's bass voice rumble out from the depths of the passageway.

'They're coming.' She picked up her bag in relief. 'Good.'

As Alicia, Craig and Hannah entered, Tom opened the conservatory door to lead the way down the garden to the car park.

Craig zapped the car doors from yards away.

They clambered inside, Franky beating Alicia into her rightful place, the front passenger seat.

'It's going to snow,' said Alicia, as she slammed shut her rear door. 'That'll be fun – Franky ordering us all out to clear the driveway.'

'I wouldn't order you to do anything, Alicia.' Franky's face was a mask.

The ride home was a tense affair, the four passengers sitting trance-like, listening to vehicles swishing past.

They entered the darkened countryside.

'See it!' Craig jabbed a finger. A small white ghost flapped across the headlights before being swallowed in the darkness.

'A barn owl,' he said.

'Hark the "fatal bellman,"' said Alicia.

"It was the owl that shrieked", intoned Hannah.

Franky closed her eyes. Tom's remark about her seeking revenge had come as a shock. Even so, he'd remained in character with that teasing twinkle of the eyes. It was alarming. He'd either read her thoughts or was it yet another coincidence?

Unlikely.

On arrival at the cottage she went straight upstairs to sit at her desk, determined to clear her mind, to think clearly and positively, to determine what was safe and what was not.

As she typed, she recalled Tom's eyes caught in headlights, glittering and charged.

It was then she felt that her fears were justified. It was not proof that he was a conspirator, but the synchronicity of events involving them both, could not be dismissed as such, for— what was the saying— *Once is happenstance, twice coincidence, the third time enemy action?*

She thought about her father's part in the conspiracy. There had to be a material linkage with Annabelle, despite the fact that he'd never been to England and, from a chance remark she'd heard Annabelle make, it appeared that she'd never visited America, either.

But, even if she found a link, informing the police would be a waste of time. No crime had been committed. They would never believe that both her father and tutor were involved in a conspiracy, he directing it from America.

But look at it from her father's viewpoint: There was no doubt that he'd be worried. He would fear her going to the police, the main reason, of course, why he'd sent her abroad. She had searched the topic and learnt that the British police would only act if an extradition order was made against her. But, wouldn't he be scared she might go to the Boston PD on her arrival home? Accepting that this was her intention, wouldn't he want to stop her *before* she got home?

Wouldn't he want her ... *dead?*

She caught her breath. It led to another thought, another reason why he would seek her death. She was screwing him for money and, for *him, money* was as important as life itself. That alone would suffice as a motive. She wasn't dealing with a novel any longer. He had real contacts who also had contacts. What was a hitman worth on a job? Whatever it was, he could afford it. He—

Suddenly she stood up. She was living her book. She was Alison, forced to kill her father before he killed her. She shivered in fear. She needed to escape, but not outside, but from *inside herself.* Breathing hard, she sat down to begin an 'Autogenic' exercise, a meditation technique that she'd recently learnt online, the art of total relaxation and training of the mind, an escape from stress by casting off all thoughts of everyday existence through a systematic act of mindfulness.

It was impossible. There was no escape, not given her deeply rooted fears.

Chapter Seventeen

During the meal, prepared by Alicia and Craig, there was no small talk, apart from the occasional request along the lines of 'Would you pass the gravy, please?'

Afterwards, Craig settled down in the living room to watch a recording of a baseball game while Hannah, Alicia and Tom went to their rooms.

Franky, feeling claustrophobic, put on a sweater, donned her anorak and stepped outside.

She had a hand on the gate-latch, then paused to stare at a sliver of moon, framed like the white crescent of a fingernail. It grew bigger until the darkness lifted and the landscape appeared in a pale blue light suffused with a sense of eeriness, a night for witches and nightmares.

She opened the gate and closed it behind her, before setting off down the lane. She'd gone no more than fifty yards when she heard the chugging of a tractor. It was strange for one to be out after dark.

Turning round, she saw its headlights illuminate the whiteness of the cottage and then swing round to dazzle her. As if angered by her presence, the tractor's roar intensified.

She shielded her eyes as the machine bucked, bumped and rumbled towards her. There was hardly any space to stand aside. She clung to the hedgerow.

'You bastard!' she screamed at the driver, as he thundered past. She thought he shouted something back.

The tractor's lights lit up a distant field, then dipped downhill and were gone. She sagged in relief.

She hurried back to the cottage and up to her room, where she poured out a glass of wine and sat down at the dressing table to stare at her face, now bearing a scratch mark. Had Alicia recruited a farmer into the conspiracy? But how would he have known she was there, outside the cottage?

She realised that she'd drunk the whole glass of wine and poured out another.

Gradually, sedated by alcohol, her thoughts drifted back to where it all began. The house called home. The glimpse into the bedroom to see her father with the boy. He'd named him Jason, a name she would never forget.

Dear God! It suddenly occurred to her – it was like a blow to the heart – that she'd never thought of the boy himself, his feelings, his need for guidance, the aftermath. How had he coped! She'd completely ignored him in preoccupation with herself. Not once had she thought – no – *considered* how he felt. She'd read of abused children being devastated by wide-ranging psychological effects of abuse that could affect them into adulthood, but thought little of it. Had her father threatened him to keep his mouth shut? Thank God she had not heard, or read, of a boy being murdered in or around Boston, nor anything about his disappearance.

She gulped down more wine. Why hadn't she gone to the police? It was because she'd made money out of it, entirely out of greed. Even worse, in not reporting his crime, she'd given him time in which to rape other boys! How many more might there have been since she left home? Or even before? Maybe he'd been doing it for years, and she was merely allowing him to continue his assaults! She drew in a lungful of air, but found she needed more.

She stumbled towards the bedside cabinet to draw out the paper bag that Annabelle had given her, rapidly screwing it into a funnel into which she began to breathe and inhale. Gradually her panic subsided, but she remained standing, the paper bag in her hand. She began to shake and sob.

Collapsing on the bed in tears, she wept not just for what she had done, but also for what she had not done.

She wept for a long time.

When her tears ceased, she went to the desk and searched for *Failure to report a crime*. She found that, in Massachusetts, where a child was the victim, it was the adult's duty to report it. If not, they could be arrested for committing a crime called *Moral Turpitude*. It allowed a judge to impose a sentence from a wide-ranging choice of punishments. In the case of covering up a serious crime, then imprisonment was likely, usually between one and five years. She could be incarcerated. She had enabled a criminal to escape justice.

She rapidly went to the website of the Boston PD and their *Report a Crime* page. She moved the cursor to the beginning and started tapping out her name, but then stopped on realising the futility of it all. She ran another search and her fears were confirmed. In making a formal statement the witness had to be there in person, an officer present to observe her signature. She had no option other than to wait until she landed in Boston.

She sat back, closing her eyes in despair. How could she cope with the demands of scholarship and at the same time keep safe? More to the point, how could she look Annabelle in the eye while working with her, exchanging ideas – all this *before* the Christmas break?

Later, having cleaned her teeth she took a Temazepam tablet and selected a CD, a sixteenth-century choral work, *Spem in Alium* by Thomas Tallis.

Soon, tucked up in bed and with the cool and pure sound of the trebles soaring over the harmonies of forty choristers, her thoughts were no longer tumbling over one another. Calm and drugged, she closed her eyes and snuggled down to sleep.

But something niggled her.

She tried to dismiss her anguish but finally had to get out of bed, grab the chair and wedge it under the door handle.

As a consequence, some time passed before she managed to find sleep.

The next morning, she awoke at 7.35 a.m. feeling dull and listless, her grim mood reinforced by staring outside at a drab landscape, under a thick, dark-grey sky. If ever the weather was suitable for a hanging, murder or suicide, this was it.

Since the itinerary of the day was crowded, she went downstairs, earlier than usual, to find Hannah and Alicia in the kitchen.

Hannah smiled as Franky entered.

'Hi,' she said.

Her smile, hesitant and wary.

'Hi,' she replied and set about making coffee.

'You okay?' said Hannah.

'What?'

'I said are you okay? You said you had a headache last night.'

'Oh, yes. Yes, I did. I'm fine.'

She moved aside to allow Alicia to place a bowl of porridge in front of Hannah.

'Thanks.'

'Want some honey – honey?' said Alicia lightly and held out the bottle.

'Thanks, I will.' Hannah took the bottle and began to squeeze out trails of golden liquid around the surface of the porridge and then suddenly stopped — aware that Franky was staring down at her.

She looked up. 'What?'

Franky opened her mouth to speak, but stopped at the sudden roaring in her ears. She stared at Hannah's moving lips.

'Are you okay?' It was Hannah's voice, the roar dying as suddenly as it began.

'Yes.'

Then a tinny voice emanated from the recesses of her mind.

Can't you understand? I've got nobody. Someone, somewhere, can't you love me a little?

She was nine years old, and Yvette was standing outside the house admonishing her for doing something she couldn't recall, the world getting darker and darker with each sharp word that she spoke. She wondered why her mother couldn't understand her pleading.

'Morning, everybody.'

She spun round as Craig entered the kitchen, sounding a shade breathless. He was wearing a brilliant-white track jacket with jet-black bottoms clad with heart-shaped silver traffic-reflectors.

Amid the greetings Alicia glanced at his tracksuit. 'Hey, Elvis, eat your heart out.'

'Where've you been, Craig?' said Hannah.

'Just a jog. Coupla miles.' He went to the worktop and plucked a banana away from its bunch. 'Get my weight down a bit.'

'Great. I'll go with you tomorrow, if you like,' said Alicia. 'I need to get back in training.'

'Okay. The more the merrier. Is the water hot, anybody? It wasn't, late last night.'

'It's okay,' said Hannah. 'I took a shower.'

'Good.' Craig went out, munching his banana.

'It wasn't hot, last night,' said Franky, 'because somebody pushed the clothes basket against the wall. It just so happens the hot water control-panel's there and the basket gets pressed against the off-button. I always look to see. It would help if others did. There's a note about it on the board.'

Alicia, about to insert a spoon into a marmalade jar, opened her mouth to retort but then stopped herself.

'I've got bad news,' announced Hannah. 'The NEA think it's going to be shut down. I may have to get the organisation's grant through as quick as I can, but how do I do that when I haven't got an organisation? I'm still just an individual.'

'Hannah,' said Alicia. 'You kid them you've got one and by the time they consider it you will have. Don't be put out. Just do as you planned. Put in the individual application first, follow the guidelines and you'll be okay.'

'I'm doing that. I'm sending it today.'

'You'll get there. Keep trying.'

'But beware Greeks bearing gifts,' said Franky in a thin, taut voice. She selected an apple from a wicker basket, rinsed it under the cold water tap and then polished it with a sheet of kitchen paper. After placing it on the chopping board, she picked up a long, sharp knife.

'Greetings.' It came from Tom entering. 'Rather chilly this morning.'

'Cold,' said Franky through gritted teeth, chopping the apple into pieces.

Tom opened the freezer door and prised from its bondage, two slices of brown bread. "To-morrow and to-morrow, and to-morrow," he intoned, popping them into the toaster, "creeps in this petty pace from day to day, to the last syllable of recorded time."

"And all our yesterdays have lighted fools the way to dusty death", said Alicia.

'Just a moment.' Franky ceased chopping. 'I don't get it. I suggest a quote competition. You all get fed up with it, but now you're back doing it.'

She threw a forced smile first at Hannah, then Alicia. 'You'd have been ten points up on that. You wouldn't have had to clean the windows.'

No one laughed or even chuckled.

'Franky,' said Alicia, with her back to her, 'where's your mojo? We're only trying to get you back in the mood.'

Was that a sly smile she exchanged with Hannah?

'What mood – what for?'

Alicia turned to Franky with a grin. 'To lighten up a little!' Franky was forgetting their row in the hallway. She was again issuing reprimands, telling them to draw the curtains, put the spare key back in its place, look at the daily rota, make less noise, switch off unwanted lights – her complaints were frequent and irritating. It had been a steadily increasing habit of hers over the latter part of the semester.

Alicia suddenly froze, her gaze fixed on something around Franky's right hip.

'Franky,' she whispered in horror, 'what the fuck!'

'What?' Franky looked down to see her right hand tightly gripping the knife, the blade pointed at Alicia's stomach. She quickly withdrew it to sweep the remaining bits of apple into a bowl.

'Alicia, you okay?' said Tom, seeing Alicia's face turn pale.

'It's nothing,' she said quickly.

Franky, using a large spoon, ladled yoghurt over the apple, picked up her mug and went out, in her haste spilling coffee on the floor.

Alicia waited until she'd climbed the stairs. 'Did any of you see that?' she said, breathing heavily.

'See what?' said Hannah.

'Her knife pointed at my stomach. *Didn't you see it*? My God!'

'No. How, what—'

'Tom? Did you?'

'No, I didn't.'

'Jesus.' Alicia clapped a hand to her forehead. 'Her knuckles were white. She was going to stab me! I swear to God she was going to kill me!'

Tom bent down to wipe up coffee that Franky had splashed on the floor tiles.

'She's under great stress,' he said. 'She gave me a ghastly look yesterday over something. But she calmed down. We have to try and talk calmly to her.' He washed the rag in the sink.

'Tom.' Alicia fought for breath. 'I don't think you're listening to me. I'm telling you she meant to *stab me*! I'm not staying here, I'm going —'

'No, wait.' Hannah put out a hand. 'Let me talk to Franky first, okay? I know her better than anyone and—'

'I wouldn't go up there Hannah. You might never come down.'

'But I know her, Alicia. I won't do anything that—'

'Hannah, she meant to kill me. If I'd been on my own, I think she would have. She needs a shrink. Okay, yes, you go up there, go talk to her and then come down and tell us what she said and then we'll agree that she's dangerous. As soon as I can I'm out of here.'

She sat down with a shake of the head.

Two slices of toast popped up with a metallic click. Tom placed them on a dish decorated with poor representations of Princess Diana and a uniformed Prince Charles.

'Yes. She needs help,' he said.

'What? It's me who needs help. Save me from a crazy woman. Tom, I am not joking. I could now be lying here in a pool of blood, you know that?'

'I'm going to talk to her,' Hannah said and went out before anyone could stop her.

Franky stood in her room, staring blankly at the floor, having left the door partly open. She heard the creak of the stairs and turned to see Hannah looking cautiously at her through the aperture.

'You okay?' she said tentatively.

'Come in. Shut the door.'

Hannah did as she was bid.

'Did Alicia send you?'

'No, she didn't. It's just … well, we're very worried about you and want to help if there's a problem. What is it Franky? You can tell me.'

'*We.*'

'Pardon me?'

'You said *we're* worried. I'm getting it all the time. Who are "we", Hannah? *Name* them.'

'Erm, sorry. The four of us. And I'm worried the most. Are you all right, Franky? Please tell me what's wrong?'

'"The two of us." Then it's the four of us. And you're full of Alicia who happens to be getting your breakfast, taking you into town, buying stuff, backing you for the NEA application, ordering you to do this, do that and—'

'What?' Hanna shook her head rapidly in confusion. 'I don't know what you're talking about, honestly.'

Franky pulled up the chair. 'Sit down. Go on.'

Hannah, keeping her eye on Franky, sat down slowly.

'Right. What is she up to, your friend and mentor, Alicia?'

'What do you mean?'

'Be honest. Don't tell me *you don't know?*'

'Franky, I don't. In all honesty, I don't.' Hannah nervously twisted her hands together.

'You haven't noticed. That's her way. That's how she does it. You're spending more and more time with her and you don't realise what's happening.'

Franky sat on the edge of the bed. 'And there's the two of them, Annabelle and Alicia. Haven't you noticed? Nothing stirring in the grey matter?'

'No. I'm sorry—'

'Can't you guess—isn't it obvious?'

'I don't know. Guess what?'

'No? Oh, come on, Hannah.'

'No.' Hannah shook her head and swallowed hard. 'I'm sorry Franky, but I don't know what you mean and I'm so worried.'

'All right. Okay. Let's just say she's been brainwashing you. No, let's call it grooming. You don't know it because they're clever. That's how it works.'

Hannah licked her lips. 'Franky,' she said hesitantly. 'I really—'

'Hannah, *listen*! I told you what my father did to me, He's scared I'll go to the police. He's so scared he's given me loads of money to stay silent. How do you think I could afford this place, the thousands I subsidise you guys with? How do you think I paid for that meal and everything? He's worried while I'm over here. You only have to think about it. He sent me here. He *meant* me to come here. Why? Isn't it obvious? Didn't you see Alicia just now, making you porridge with honey and comforting you about your application when she'd done none of these things before? Not until the signal came from Annabelle, who got it from my father? I'm a danger to him, Hannah. Whatever they say or do, don't let them persuade you otherwise. Promise me—*promise*.'

'I promise.' Hannah said hoarsely.

Franky went to her, arms outstretched to circle around her neck while looking solemnly into her eyes. 'Matters are coming to a head,' she said quietly. 'So be careful. Okay?'

'Yes, I will.' Hannah stood up and went to open the door. She hesitated, was about to say something, but changed her mind.

'Hannah.'

She turned in the doorway. 'What?'

'Don't tell them anything. Just say I'm fine. I don't want them worrying you. Say I've been worried about my mother. She's not well. Will you do that?'

'Yes.'

She left the room and went downstairs.

Alicia and Tom looked up from the kitchen table as Hannah came in, tearful.

Alicia got to her feet. 'What's happened?'

'She's… she's paranoid. I think we —'

'Yes, exactly. Who's her welfare, do you know?'

'Yes, it's Annabelle.'

'Okay. I think we should all see her together. To show we're all of the same opinion. Do you agree Tom?'

'No, I don't.' He paused as he digested a piece of toast. 'Four reasons. One, it will be disruptive for all of us. She'll have a psychiatric assessment. Chances are she won't come back. Two of us, at least, can't afford the rent to make up for her gone. The landlord will say we'd broken our contract in any case. Out we'd go, but to where? Bed-sits and apartments are in short supply at this time of year. And there's one more thing. She's probably going through a psychotic episode. It's known for many young people to have them. A lot are kept secret because of social stigma, with the loss of job and parents not wanting it being known. Now many of them recover. We don't want to ruin her. I think we should keep watch, observe and play it by ear. Any of you disagree?'

Chapter Eighteen

The next morning, Craig dropped off Franky near the riverside, close to The Swan Theatre. Averting her face from the skimming sleet, she pulled forward her anorak hood, lowered her head and crossed the road to approach The Other Place, the RSC's theatre and creative hub for rehearsal, learning and research. It stood back from the road by fifty yards, its protruding Tudor-style frontage happily painted in a warm orange and duck-egg blue. Attached, at its side, was the RSC costume store, coloured in a tasty looking chocolate-brown.

Franky hurried through the double doors into Susie's Café Bar that doubled as reception. She found Brooklyn seated at a table, clad in a sweater and clasping a mug of coffee.

'Hi, Franky.' Brooklyn sounded – and looked – friendly. 'Want a cup?'

'No, I'm good, thanks.'

'Did Annabelle tell you what it's about?' Brooklyn bit into a biscuit.

'Yes. I'm going to help the designer draw up the costume plot and see how we can reinforce the mood of a scene as well as the production style. 'Erm, before we start, may I look in the theatre? I've got an idea for something.'

'Sure. Let's do it.' Brooklyn drained the remainder of her coffee, set down the mug and stood up. 'Come on,' she said, 'let's go see.'

She escorted Franky through double doors into a wide corridor. 'This could be my future, working in costume. I simply love it.'

They passed one of the well-equipped rehearsal rooms and spaces for experimentation, before entering the 200-seat flexible theatre.

Brooklyn took her backstage. 'Here's the tiring room, for quick costume changes.'

Franky, putting her head inside, noted the tall mirror facing the entrance. Next, she was taken into the attached building, the costume store.

'How many costumes are there?'

'Over 60,000.' Brooklyn grinned at Franky's reaction.

'*Sixty* thousand?' Franky thought she hadn't heard correctly.

'And the rest. But we're selling half of them. We're having a jumble sale. Should raise quite a bit, and with the money we're planning to update the costume workshop.'

'You hire out costumes?' said Franky casually, as they strolled around.

'We certainly do,' said Brooklyn. 'Historical docs, dramas, films, amateur groups, all sorts.'

'How much does it cost to hire a costume, say, just for a day?'

'No.' Brooklyn shook her head. 'It has to be for a week. A full costume is £90. Here, let me show you something.'

She took Franky past innumerable racks hung with costumes in a wide variety of colours, predominantly made of either silk, velvet, damask, wool or cotton-lawn fabric. Silver buckles, belts, and other ornamentation added to the rich display, glistening in the pale light.

'It smells of leather and cinnamon,' remarked Franky.

'Yes, other people have said the same. I don't smell it now, too used to it.'

Franky walked along a row of costumes with her mouth open. 'Amazing,' she breathed. 'You could get a paying public to come in, just to look around.'

'We do that for groups. They have the whole experience, the costume store, rehearsal rooms, flexible theatre, café bar, everywhere.'

'Great. Are the rows coded so you know exactly where a costume is at any given time?'

'No. They're grouped by type, history and age, that's all.'

'Uh-huh.' Franky stood surveying a run of costumes along the "Tragedy" racks. 'The RSC did *Othello* two or three years ago. Is Desdemona's costume still here?'

'Yes, it is. It was out recently. Want to hire it?' she said half-jokingly.

'I'm thinking about it.'

'Oh?' Brooklyn showed her surprise. 'For what?'

'A photo.'

'Oh. Okay. I don't know what the discount is for students. C'mon. You're in luck. It's only half a mile away.'

Brooklyn, chuckling, led Franky on a relatively short walk to a row featuring costumes in sober colours. They arrived at two that, in terms of design as well as colour, were almost identical, both made of sumptuous cream-coloured silk and dotted with a deep-red floral pattern, the only difference being that one had an off-the-shoulder wide band across the chest.

'Yes, they're the ones,' said Franky. 'I saw them online. I guess one was worn to match the mood and style and then changed to the other for another scene, a different mood?'

'Yes. I guess you're right.'

'I like this one.' Franky pointed to the one without the band. 'I'd like to have a shot of me outside the cottage. I want to send it Mom. It's her birthday soon.'

'Okay. The costumes aren't on the work-list at the moment. I can't swear you'll get as big a discount as for theatre tickets, but I'll ask Nancy and let you know.'

'Thanks, Brooklyn. That's really kind. They were actually made for Joanna Vanderham. Hugh Quarshie played Othello. Really beautiful.' She trailed her fingertips down the silken material.

'Yes, it goes with your red hair.'

Franky glanced sharply at her.

'Could have been made for you,' Brooklyn said, without a trace of guile.

'Brooklyn, erm, is there any chance of me putting it on for a selfie now, just for five or ten minutes, enough for a photo? I still want to hire it.'

Brooklyn glanced around, but no one seemed to be around or within earshot. 'Okay. But don't let Nancy see us. Gotta be quick.'

'Oh, thanks, Brooklyn. You're a star.'

'Let's take it to the tiring room. There's a full-length mirror there.'

She took the costume off the rail and led Franky back-stage.

Brooklyn helped put it on. She'd just started the back fastenings when she stopped to check her watch. 'Oh, just remembered. I've got to make an urgent phone call. Back in a minute. You okay?'

'Fine.'

When Brooklyn returned, she helped Franky with the back fastenings. When completed, she stood back. 'It fits. Fabulous.' She allowed Franky space in which to admire herself in the mirror. 'That looks *really* good,' she said with enthusiasm. She went round the dress, titivating it here and there, then spoke in a lowered voice. 'I hear Alicia's auditioning for Desdemona. Don't tell anybody but, whatever she wears, Alicia won't look half as good as you. I hear you're auditioning for it?'

'I was, but not now.'

'Oh. Hang on.'

Brooklyn adjusted the costume a little around the waist, then stood back, scanning Franky up and down. 'Hey, Desdemona. Perfect. Got your cell?'

Franky set it to "camera" before handing it over.

Brooklyn lined up the shot. 'Nice smile now.'

'No. I want to *be* Desdemona. Give me a few seconds. Do you mind?'

'No. But don't take long.'

Franky, taking in slow and deep breaths, thought and felt herself into the part, ending with a rather fragile and vulnerable look.

The photo taken, Franky studied it 'Thanks, Brooklyn. It's pretty good.'

'Now, you promise you won't show it to anybody but your Mom?'

'You've got it, don't worry.'

Brooklyn helped her out of the costume. 'So, what changed your mind about the part?'

'Nothing. I didn't want it that much. It's okay.'

'Oh, it's not what I heard. Now, if it were me, I'd be inclined to—' Brooklyn broke off, swallowing the rest of what she intended to say. She ran the tip of her tongue over her lips.

Franky spoke to Brooklyn's reflection in the mirror. 'You'd be inclined to what?'

'Oh, nothing.'

Three days later, the five housemates arrived at the Institute in Craig's car. It had snowed for a short time in the night, leaving a white covering over the car park.

They walked down the footpath beside the white and green mottled lawn, then stepped onto the red-brick patio, where the snow had already melted. Before entering the conservatory, they brushed their feet on the large bristled mat.

Franky had said very little on the journey. She faced a meeting with Annabelle to be given the 'verdict' on her new dissertation topic. It felt like she'd be sitting down with the enemy before battle.

She sat, waiting, in the conservatory, continually glancing at her watch. Her cell phone buzzed and moved in her pocket. It was Annabelle, letting her know that she was available.

As she climbed upstairs, she could hear her talking with someone on the staircase, a flight above. Then the conversation went dead, and she heard footsteps descend.

Franky stood back on the first landing to allow the Director to pass down. He gave her a big smile. 'Morning Franky.'

'Morning.'

Then Annabelle came downstairs. 'Sorry Franky, I've been terribly busy.'

Franky allowed her into the office, entered and closed the door.

She sat stiffly on the upright chair in front of Annabelle's desk, a notepad on her lap. She noted that, on this occasion, Annabelle hadn't insisted she sat in the armchair.

Annabelle tapped her keyboard, made a few entries and then turned to her with a smile. 'Are you all right? I do hope you haven't had any more panic attacks. Have you?'

'No, I haven't.'

'Oh, good. That's really good. Always have a paper bag with you, remember?'

'I do, always.'

She's still wearing the evil eye

'That's good. Right.' Annabelle looked at her screen. 'You now want to deal with Hamlet, as well as Shylock.' She grimaced in sympathy. 'I'm afraid it's going to be a character too far, Franky.'

'Oh?'

'Yes. You'd need a max of 30,000 words to cover both characters, and you're only allowed 15,000 for a dissertation. A pity.'

'Yes,' said Franky. She looked at the evil eye. 'It is.'

'I'm sorry. But it's the rules I'm afraid. Please take it from me that you'd run out of space very quickly, in attempting both characters.'

'I suppose so.'

'But what we can do, is discuss Hamlet, as you proposed to deal with him. It could be a useful exercise, don't you think?'

'Yes.'

Annabelle hesitated at Franky's automatic responses. 'Look. Don't be too disappointed because I don't think it would have worked as you imagined it. You'd be even more disappointed if you'd written it only to be told to cut it by half, wouldn't you?'

'Yes.' Franky flickered a semblance of a smile. 'That's one consolation.'

'Yes.' Annabelle scrolled down her screen. 'Now, take the scene with Gertrude and Hamlet that you refer to. You say that he sees the ghost. Are you sure of that? Gertrude can't see it. So, is Hamlet hallucinating, or is he pretending to see it? He's either doing one or the other.' Annabelle read some more. 'Now, you say you've found evidence to show that he's sane, but what you're ignoring is plenty of evidence that points to him as being insane. Would you accept that?'

'Yes. But I wasn't dealing with insanity. It was his need for revenge.'

'Hah, but aren't you deciding Hamlet's sane because you want him to be? Because, if he's insane, then his reason for revenge becomes irrelevant as the audience would see insanity as clouding his mind. He wouldn't be taken seriously. He could be taking revenge on *anyone*, and you'd be just examining the effects of insanity itself as your topic. There'd be no connection to him in terms of motive, morality or justice. Would you agree with that?'

'I would, yes.'

Annabelle put out a gentle hand. 'All I'm really saying is that you can't cherry-pick the evidence, can you?'

'No, of course you can't.'

'Actually, what you propose was put forward by the British Council. They sponsored "Living Shakespeare" two or three years ago, calling upon authors to write about their emotions, as well as their social and political experiences, while relating it to Shakespeare. But you've addressed Hamlet downplaying questions of law and justice in terms of moral equivalence, because that's good, as it's important.'

Franky felt anger arising. Here she was, stuck with the enemy playing around with academic notions when all the time she was planning something against her that was morally unacceptable, *in any shape or form!*

'Yes,' she said. 'Hamlet asks the question, is justice only attainable at the expense of morals and ethics, and if so, is it then still justice? And if not, what is there left but revenge?'

Annabelle's eyes flickered. 'You say that as if challenging me, Franky,' she said softly with a smile. 'Just tell me, erm, am I right in thinking that you were associating yourself with Hamlet's dilemma? You are, aren't you—it *is* about your father, isn't it? Are you still feeling the need for revenge?'

'Yes. Wanting but, like Hamlet, unable to take it.' Franky found it difficult not to stare at the evil eye.

Annabelle drew a deep breath. 'There's one thing that still worries me greatly. I have to ask you once more. I hope you don't mind.' She splayed out her hands. 'I didn't want to speak of it again, but I feel I must. She drew in another deep breath. 'I don't know quite how to put this. Erm ...'

'Have I harmed anyone, is that what you mean?' Franky remained expressionless.

'Yes.' For a moment she looked surprised. 'It is. Have you?'

'No. If I did, it would only be in self-defence, like anyone would do.'

Annabelle nodded slowly. 'Good.' She looked at her screen, continuing in a level voice, 'You then admit to having suicidal thoughts, as did Hamlet.' She hesitated. 'You're being honest admitting that. But you say nothing about yourself when it comes to Hamlet being fearful of losing his mind. Is it because you're fearful ...' she turned her head slowly back to Franky and spoke in a scary voice, dropping almost to a whisper, 'of losing your mind?'

Franky stared at her. 'No. Never.'

Insanity and suicide. Planting the seeds.

'Thank goodness.' Annabelle exhaled in relief. 'Yes. We can't ever know what real torment of the mind is like, can we, unless we experience it ourselves?' She gave a sigh. 'Well, I hope I've not given you any more stress. Have I? I do hope not.'

'No. You've not,' she said, her head full of heat. 'Actually, I feel much better, talking about it.'

'Well, thank goodness for that. I'm so pleased.' Let's end on that feeling, shall we? You're going to go away feeling better, positive, not negative.' She spoke gently, putting out a hand of friendship.

'Yes.' She summoned up a big smile for the black-cloaked monstrosity. 'Thank you, Annabelle.' On fire, she gripped her long-handled axe, lifted it high and set about her with abandon, chopping her into pieces, turning the office into a blood-filled shambles.

With the back of her hand she wiped beads of sweat from her forehead and walked downstairs in tears. Hamlet had been denied her a second time. It was like losing a brother. He was her salvation and *she, the bastard,* had killed him. They had lived together in a world of doubt, uncertainty and fear. Both, lurching around the moral maze, had taking themselves to task for being ineffectual, both incapable of taking any form of decisive action. And hadn't they both lost their innocence through trauma, he shocked by his father's murder and she by witnessing her father rape a child and wasn't she doing exactly what Hamlet did in questioning the world's lack of righteousness and justice to such an extent that she, also, contemplated suicide? And didn't she also share, with him, a nostalgic yearning for lost love, he for his murdered father and loveable court-jester Yorick, she for her loveable Grandpa of make-believe? It could not be coincidence. The synchronicity was overwhelming, its psychic drive undeniable, out of time and space.

She paused on her way downstairs and turned to look upwards. Annabelle was standing outside her office, watching her. At Franky's anguished and hostile stare, she quickly stepped back inside.

Franky left the Institute knowing that Annabelle would now be emailing her father, giving him every detail of what had passed between them.

She recalled what Brooklyn had said to her: *Don't tell anybody but, whatever she wears, Alicia won't look half as good as you.*

She trusted no one and cursed herself for telling Hannah all that stuff about her father. Now that Alicia was luring her into the conspiracy, she felt the need for action.

It was even more pressing that she made a pre-emptive strike.

And not in the fantasy of the imagination.

Chapter Nineteen

It was a morning when Stratford lay blanketed in snow. It was still snowing a little but, with near blizzard conditions expected within a few hours, the AA and RAC traffic monitors were warning of travel disruption.

Most of the student body, including Franky, Hannah and Alicia, stood huddled outside The Other Place. With road noise muted by the downfall, Franky watched tiny snowflakes whirl across the blue, orange and chocolate-brown frontage.

The three colours aroused the memory of something she'd read, following a study of 150 hospitalised mental patients. Blue was their favourite colour, she recalled, followed by orange. None of them liked brown. But what did that prove, other than blue was their favourite colour? It was worrying because she liked blue, herself.

At 9.45 a.m. the doors were opened 15 minutes early, allowing the students to thaw out in Susie's cafe-bar. After being outside in arctic conditions, they found the place hugely inviting and warm, smelling of coffee and toasted teacakes lathered in hot butter and sprinkled with cinnamon or jam.

Franky and Hannah dumped their bags at an empty table. As they sat down, Franky noted Alicia sit down with Brooklyn to be immediately engrossed in conversation.

'Coffee?' said Franky, anxious to get in line at the counter.

'Yes. … hey.' Hannah opened her wallet to dig out money. 'Here.' She held out a £5 note, expecting Franky to ignore it with her usual friendly, gesture.

Franky took the note.

Hannah watched her go to the counter, hoping against hope that the paranoia she'd shown yesterday, was short-lived. She'd been to a medical website to check out Tom's comment on the frequency of psychotic episodes amongst the young. She had found it correct as well as the motive for parents not reporting it, prompted by a familial fear of attracting a social stigma, leading to loss of friends or jobs. It gave Hannah relief. There was hope yet.

Franky had just been served when she caught sight of a bulky, well-wrapped figure approaching the glass doors. It was Dr Ainscough, their first lecturer of the day.

Before entering he tapped his briar pipe on a raised heel.

Franky liked him. He reminded her of the imaginary Grandpa of her childhood, a bear-like man wearing a full-length sheepskin coat and a Fair Isle woollen bobble-hat pulled well down over the ears. Anyone standing close to him might smell the fragrant toffee-like aroma of Dutch pipe tobacco.

Hannah looked up with a smile as Franky came back with two coffees.

'Thanks, Franky. I love this place, don't you?'

'Yes, nice.' She dragged something out of her pocket.

'Oh, you've bought me a cookie. Great, thanks. Then, realising. 'Aren't you having one?'

'No.' Franky sipped her coffee. 'I saw you in town yesterday with Alicia. You promised to tell me anything she said.'

'She didn't. She said nothing about you.' Hannah unwrapped the cookie. 'She was only showing me something to buy.' She closed her eyes and opened her mouth, fearful of where it might lead.

Franky raised the cup to her lips and peered at a thin necklace around Hannah's neck. The pendant was exactly like Annabelle's.

She closed her eyes, counted to six and opened them. She was wrong. It was not an *'evil eye'* but a silver fish. She nestled the cup carefully back into its saucer.

A burst of laughter drew her attention towards Ainscough and Nancy, head of costume at the RSC, chatting nearby. They were not laughing at her so she could relax.

'I like Dr Ainscough,' said Hannah, smiling brightly. 'He's fun, isn't he?'

'He is,' Franky replied. 'But there's no one you don't like, is there?' Franky managed to pick up her coffee with a steady hand.

'There is. I don't like the President. I need that grant.'

'Fingers crossed.' Franky's eyelids drooped as she ruminated. There seemed little doubt that, if anyone was likely to let something slip or drop a clue about the conspiracy, it would be Hannah, so often impetuous and uninhibited in conversation and especially now that Alicia was friendly with her. Maybe it was just a case of waiting and picking the right moment?

'Hannah.' Franky drew in a deep breath. 'If Alicia or anybody puts it to you that I'm paranoid, I'm telling you something now that you must keep secret. I'll know if you don't. Promise?'

Hannah raised three fingers in the Girl Scouts sign. 'Scout's honour.' She shuffled her chair nearer Franky, holding her breath.

'Three years ago, I showed signs of being a tad paranoid. The medic said it was a psychotic episode, not permanent. He put me on an antipsychotic drug, and I've been fine ever since. So, if anybody says anything about me, don't worry, okay? Else I'll stuff you in the malmsey-butt.'

Hannah laughed and gave up a silent prayer, believing her lie. 'Thanks be to God.'

The general drift out of the cafe-bar began with Ainscough shepherding his flock into the studio theatre. Franky and Hannah followed, joining students in the first few rows. Their chatter subsided as Ainscough went to stand before them, hands raised.

'Good morning, everybody.' His strong baritone resonance in the lower ranges was stimulating. 'Doctor Lloyd, just to remind you, is holding auditions after this session, so those aspiring to be Othello, or any of his gang, should remain behind.'

He paused in a theatrical pose, hands raised and his stubbly chin tilted upwards. 'We are innocent. We know nothing,' he proclaimed. 'We have arrived to perform a play. We know not what it is. We've not read it. We've got our dialogue, bits of parts, but that's all. Who are we?'

Franky, for whom the day was critical, spoke up before anyone else, anxious to make her presence felt. 'Shakespeare's actors, the "King's Men."'

'Yes. It's 1604. The writer, the eminent Master William Shakespeare, has been summoned to court by King James the First and ordered to perform his new play, to be staged while he dines at supper. His Majesty asks him what play he will be writing next.'

Ainscough acted Shakespeare: 'Methinks it will be about an ageing king sire, one who decides to retire from the throne and divide his kingdom evenly among his three daughters.'

'Hmm,' murmurs the King. 'I trust it is not about my good self in any degree, shape or form?'

'Oh, of course not sire. I would not be so disloyal.'

'I'm not enamoured of kingship retiring. But, in that respect, I have something even better. I have the history of a Scottish lord that pleases me, that which I could see you perform, his wife spurring him on to murder the King and suffers from conscience thereafter. A very bleak, very riveting story, I hope you'll agree. And for me, as a King, a little bit worrying.'

Ainscough paused for a few chuckles. 'And what is the play you have just finished scribing, Master Shakespeare?'

'Sire, it is a play about a blackamoor.'

'A *blackamoor*? Gadzooks and Beelzebub!' Ainscough waved his arms. 'Well, if you must, I suppose I would have you stage it for me, in return for my history of the Scottish lord? Shakespeare agrees to the deal.'

'But make sure you're well-rehearsed, Master Shakespeare.'

'Indeed, sire'.

'Would a week of rehearsal suffice?'

'Hah, that might be awkward, Your Majesty. 'If 'twere two weeks from this night I could be here at your pleasure sire?'

'Then two weeks of tonight, it shall be. Goodnight Master Shakespeare.'

Ainscough paused to address his audience. '*So*, by sheer coincidence, the play that he's just written is now yours, for you are the King's Men. You have not long in rehearsal. It's a play about a black man living in Venice. And that is all you know.' He clapped his hands, speaking quickly. 'Right. What's the image that we generally conjure up at the mention of the name Othello?'

'A black tormented face on stage.' It was Hannah who spoke. She sat next to Franky in the front row.

'Yes. But fifty-two years ago, you wouldn't. You would have seen a large poster on a billboard featuring the face of Laurence Olivier as Othello, a film made in the sixties. A white actor, blacked-up. Unthinkable now for the RSC, or any production, to do that. A different time, different codes and values. Let us go back four hundred years *before* Olivier. How was it then for *you*, my King's Men?'

He paused once more.

'It is first rehearsal. What do you possess when you turn up? There's only one manuscript or book with the full play in it. Before first rehearsal, this "book" will have been passed round from the actor Othello, down to stop at the spear-carriers. From this manuscript each of you will have written down your lines on a roll of paper as well as the cue lines for each speech. That's it. All the rest, the story, the entrances, exits, moves and interpretation of the text will be explained to you by me, Shakespeare himself. And you may make suggestions. But, can you imagine the confusion, the ruckus, that could occur with all these bits of paper, Shakespeare getting one set mixed up with another? Romeo and Juliet with Hamlet and possibly Macbeth?'

Ainscough began to stomp back and forth, rapidly spouting one-liners, one moment being Juliet, the next Mercutio or Macbeth and vice-versa.

'Romeo, Romeo! wherefore art thou Romeo?'

'Where the devil should this Romeo be?'

'Who are you?'

'Mercutio. I'm searching for him also.'

'No, Mercutio, it is I who *needs* him. I'm Juliet.'

'The lady doth protest too much'.

'Hey, that's from *Hamlet*. I'm not in that!'

'My lady, we know not what we are in.'

'Misquote! This above all – to thine own self be true. I'm off. I have lived long enough. My way of life is fallen into the sere, the yellow leaf...'

He broke off amidst laughter.

'*So*,' said Ainscough, grinning, 'there comes the day when Shakespeare stages *Othello*, before the King in the Banqueting House in Whitehall. Is it a big risk that Shakespeare takes? Or was he that famous he could get away with almost anything?'

He paused to draw papers from his briefcase.

'So, my trusty King's Men, these are the cue scripts for Act One. We'll see how far we can get in the time available. Now, who'd like to play Othello?'

'May I volunteer?' They looked to a smiling student from London, the only black face there. He was beaming, to laughter.

'David. You're playing him in the production, I believe.'

'I am. Pure coincidence.'

More laughter.

'Desdemona?'

Franky stuck up her hand, but Ainscough was looking over her head.

'Hah, yes, Alicia. I believe you're being auditioned. Is that another coincidence?'

He handed Franky a clipped sheaf of papers. 'Please pass them back.'

Franky twisted round to hand them to Alicia then turned back quickly, her face reddening.

Ainscough, having cast the play, furnished the actors with their individual cue scripts.

'I am William Shakespeare,' he declared. 'I am a product of my time. I do not exist in a vacuum but am tied to a theatre company. I work according to current theatre and acting practices and I'm also affected by the social circumstances of my time. I am liberal in the presentation of my work. I encourage anyone to make suggestions. If you feel the need to explore the text, either to experiment, or innovate, then interrupt and make your point, then be my guest. Remember the play within the play? Hamlet gives the players advice. "Speak the speech trippingly on the tongue."'

Ainscough adopted a Cockney accent: 'If you just mouth it, I'd as rather get the bleeding town crier, for gawd's sake.'

They were still laughing when he turned round to address the audience. 'Audience, you are all delighted with the play. Nobody ever asks for their money back. If the actors are speaking well, and with good gesture, it registers with you. And don't just sit there. If you feel like moving about, then do so. You paid for an area to sit or stand in. There are no fixed seats. Comments so far?'

'Yes,' said Hannah. 'If the interaction between audience and players was so fluid, how could they concentrate enough to understand the play?'

'Good question. And, from what we know, audiences are reported as saying that the plays were good, and we must take their word for it. And do remember, this is compelling entertainment for a mass audience. One seventh of the population of London went to a theatre *each week*!'

He turned back to the cast. 'If someone in the audience yells out something, take it in your stride. Do as William Kent or Robert Armen do, actors known as the company clowns. You don't develop a reputation just by sticking to your lines. Play off the audience, if you feel like it. Do as they do - extemporise. As you read my plays, you'll find that I have certain written instructions such as "Go and stand by the window and look out", or "stab Polonius through the curtain," "strangle her", or simply "drop dead."

He paused for more laughter. 'We need this to be a lively session. There may be experimentation and role-swapping, all overseen by my good self, Master Shakespeare.'

The two hours went well, with much humour and a certain excitement at their "discoveries".

At midday the session ended, with Ainscough announcing that the play had been launched, he thought, successfully.

'In the spring term,' he continued, 'we will work our way through the centuries, concerning ourselves with experimentation conducted by modernist and postmodernist directors of Shakespeare. We shall take into account changes in language and culture as time goes on.' A "diachronic exercise", was the term he used.

Ainscough waved his arm and bowed in a royal flourish. 'Okay, thank you all. And keep warm!'

He received sudden, standing applause, an unusual occurrence, but showing the students had enjoyed it that much. During the general noise, Franky slipped quickly out of the theatre before anyone else and entered reception. There was a parcel waiting for her on the desk.

As she waited for her Mastercard to be processed, she glanced outside to see Annabelle turn the corner into the theatre forefront, her umbrella pointing into a blizzard that had been forecast and had now arrived.

Franky watched the receipt crawl from the machine and whipped it out at the last moment, just as Annabelle entered, black-booted up to her knees and wearing a padded grey jacket littered with snowflakes.

'Franky,' said Annabelle. 'What a day.' She brushed her feet on the mat. 'How are you?'

'I'm fine, thanks,' said Franky moving sideways to cover up the parcel lying behind her on the counter.

Annabelle came up with a sympathetic smile, laid a hand on her arm and squeezed it. 'Are you happy working with costume? I do hope so.'

'Oh, yes. Absolutely. Thanks.'

'Oh, good,' she said, conveying, once again, that musky-sweet scent of sage, rosemary and lavender. 'Wonderful.' Annabelle released the grip on her arm and gently patted it before heading for the studio theatre.

As soon as she went through the swing doors, Franky followed, clutching the parcel, but instead of following Annabelle into the theatre auditorium, she went round the back, to enter by the stage door.

Inside the tiring room, Franky scrutinised herself in the tall mirror. It had taken her nearly half an hour to dress herself as Desdemona, having spent a frustrating fifteen minutes trying to insert the topmost back hook into its eye. She gave up on remembering that she would spend the time looking downstage, the slight sag at the shoulders hopefully not noticed by the audience.

She switched now to the business of preparing herself. She began to mouth words while practising regular breathing, as taught by her vocal coach at college, the aim being to reduce tension in the neck, shoulders, jaw, back and stomach. The best projected voice, she knew, came when one's posture was erect, yet relaxed.

After stretching out her tongue – point up, point down – she braced it behind the lower row of teeth, pushing at its centre, while massaging the muscles of her jaw and face. She then stretched her neck a little by leaning it from side to side and then rolling it front to back. She made different sounds quietly while sticking out her tongue, then panting to open up her breathing.

The exercises concluded with her emitting a prolonged and faint '*bee*' sound.

The lunch hour was over. Auditions were about to begin. Franky stood behind a 'flat', a piece of scenery held upright by a rear-strut, brace and weight, currently in use for a new play, one of a number commissioned by The Other Place each year. It was separated from another flat, by an angled space between them, enabling her to see a large part of the stage, without being seen by the audience.

She watched Annabelle call out Marie, an Irish student.

Marie left her seat on the front row and joined Annabelle on stage.

It brought Franky to attention, while breathing steadily.

'Remember,' said Annabelle, 'you're Amelia. You started all the turmoil by giving the handkerchief to your husband, Iago. You have a bitter relationship with him while being devoted to your lady, Desdemona. She's frightened now, so needs comforting. I'll give you a moment to think yourself into it. Start when you're ready.'

Franky watched Marie come into view, centre stage.

After a pause, she began. 'A halter pardon him!' She continued to the last line of the speech … 'even from the east to the west!'

Franky drew in a deep breath, exhaling slowly.

Annabelle (reading Iago's lines): 'Speak within door.'

Marie: 'Oh, fie upon them! Some such squire he was, that turned your wit the seamy side without and made you to suspect me with the Moor.'

Franky's lips parted.

Annabelle: 'You are a fool; go to.'

Franky stepped out on stage.

Annabelle, looking up as the audience gasped, clapped a hand to her mouth.

Franky, head erect, the figure-hugging dress setting off the colour of her hair, looked a lady of distinction, her face bearing the pain of the wrongly accused:

'O God! Iago, what shall I do to win my lord again?
Good friend, go to him; for, by this light of heaven,
I know not how I lost him. Here I kneel.
'If e'er my will did trespass 'gainst his love,
Either in discourse of thought or actual deed,
Or that mine eyes, mine ears, or any sense,
Delighted them in any other form,
Or that I do not yet, and ever did,
And ever will – though he'd shake me off
To beggarly divorcement – love him dearly,
Comfort forswear me! Unkindness may do much;
And his unkindness may defeat my life,
But never taint my love. I cannot say 'whore';
It does abhor me now I speak the word;
To do the act that might the addition earn,
Not the world's mass of vanity could make me.'

At the end of the speech – as at the beginning – there was a stunned silence. The hiatus was caused not just by audience bewilderment and apprehension, but also by a performance that was flawless.

After the opening lines, Franky had paused before 'Here I kneel', at which her mouth had frozen in a sudden catch of fear. Then, timing it to perfection, her voice sank down to declare herself innocent, protesting a purity of spirit and lack of bitterness that was neither pompous nor defiant. It was a statement laid out in all honesty, giving her a semblance of majesty. And on 'Comfort forswear me!' there was a hesitation, followed by a crack in her voice demonstrating that her brave attempt to remain steadfast had wavered and that she was, indeed, in fear of her life. The line "I cannot say whore" was spoken with a wince of pain, emphasising her purity. Her pause on the final line, ending in rising determination, was compelling. Her emotional delivery had used the full range of her voice and her projection, articulation and phrasing were impeccable.

The shocked reaction to Franky's sudden appearance on stage was less significant than the one that followed her speech. It had not been – nor could it have been – a performance that precedes an outburst of rapturous and standing applause. No, it was in recognition by everyone there that the delivery of the speech was not one to be expected from an amateur actor and that Françoise O'Tierney had made the character her very own. Her performance had been nothing less than the portrayal of an entirely believable and impressive Desdemona.

Franky relaxing out of character, flicked her eyes to Annabelle, who still had her hand to her mouth, then turned quickly to head back into the tiring room.

Annabelle swung round to stare at the students who, animated in their whispers, made a scratchy sound, like dry leaves blown over hard paving.

There was one who failed to join them in their cloistered excitement.

Alicia, in the midst of them, her head bent forward, stared straight ahead under lowered eyelids.

And with the curl of a smile on her lips.

Chapter Twenty

I will do such things,
What they are, I know not;
But they shall be
The terrors of the earth.
King Lear, Act II, sc. iv

Franky spent some time in the tiring room, packing away the costume. Any minute she expected Annabelle or Brooklyn to enter, but neither did.

Hannah stood waiting in reception. She summoned up a quick smile on seeing Franky come through the swing doors carrying the costume bag.

'How did you get on?' said Franky.

'Me?' Hannah looked uncertain.

'Yes, as Amelia.'

'Oh no, I didn't. I think Marie got it. She was really good.'

Franky smiled. 'Well, how did I do?'

'Well, it was great, but...'

Franky put an arm around Hannah's shoulder. 'It's okay,' she whispered in her ear. 'If Alicia asks, what will you say?'

'Asks?' Hannah looked bewildered. 'I don't—' She broke off as Brooklyn entered.

'May I?' With a grimace of a smile, Brooklyn relieved Franky of the costume bag and took it to the desk.

'Oh,' said Hannah, remembering. 'Craig won't be going yet. And Tom and Alicia are staying. They've got tutorials.'

'No problem. I'll get the bus. What did you really think?'

'What?' Hannah faltered. 'You mean, your…?'

'Performance.'

'Well, it was brilliant, amazing. I just worry that…'

'No. Don't worry. Everything will be fine. It was fun. See you back there.'

'Yes … okay.' Hannah watched Franky go out into the blizzard.

'*Well.*'

Hannah turned at the familiar voice. Joined by Brooklyn, Annabelle stood watching Franky halt before the pavement to allow a woman, towing an empty sledge, to cross her path.

Franky stood at the bus stop, stamping her feet while swinging her arms. Then she stopped, staring at clouds of snow whipping through arcs of street lighting.

It took her back to when she was eight years old, a snowy day when she discovered that she had the power to switch the outside lighting both on and off. It was amazingly simple. All she had to do was stand fifty yards from the house, take a step forward and then one straight back. She had wished she could make the house, as well as her father, disappear, so she could go and live in an ordinary house with other kids playing outside, one of them with red hair, somebody who was kind and tough, somebody she'd stand alongside ready to challenge anybody calling them names and, if they did, punch them on the nose.

Franky resumed stamping her feet, imagining what was taking place on campus, her peers excitedly discussing her stunt – *Have you heard? What did she think she was playing at? Is she crazy?*

She wasn't scared by what she'd done. Yes, it was partly an act of revenge, but the main reason was to show she would not be cowed by Annabelle, or any of the conspirators. Nor was she scared of higher authority. If summoned to the director's office to give an explanation for her behaviour, she'd give a very good account of herself. For days now she had worked on her rebuttals, memorising them, so they would flow out of her, with impact.

She looked at her watch and decided it was time to make a call, one that took a little courage. She took out her cell phone.

'Hi, Marie, it's Franky.'

'Oh … hi. Are you okay?'

'Yes. Look, I'm really sorry for butting in like that but Annabelle told me I was right for Desdemona, virtually promised it me when all the time it was going to Alicia. I can't tell you what I know, but when we meet up, I'll explain everything. I'm just sorry I couldn't tell you before. I hope you'll understand.'

'No, don't worry. I got Amelia. It was great what you did,' she said, laughing. 'What high drama!' Her laughter died. 'I don't know how Annabelle will take it, but there's Alicia. I saw how she looked. Not pretty.'

'Did she get Desdemona?'

'I think so. Alicia wasn't bad actually but you were better by far. And I *mean* far. So, I guess I'll watch this space.'

'Yeah, okay. Thanks, Marie. See you soon.'

She ended the call just as the bus approached, its headlights whitening the blizzard.

She got inside and took an aisle seat, glad of the warmth. But then she frowned, as a miniature schnauzer, sitting on the lap of a woman behind, stretched forward to take an interest in her hair.

'Sammy, naughty!' the woman said, pulling the dog back.

It was too late. Franky had already taken evasive action by transferring to an empty seat across the aisle, where she began to 'rehearse her scene' with the Director. Yes, she did understand why Annabelle had decided not to give her a part in the production. She would agree that Annabelle had shown a concern for her welfare that was genuine. She would admit to everything.

When she turned to her defence she would not, dare not, refer to the conspiracy that had dictated Annabelle's decision to rob her of Desdemona and Hamlet. Instead she would pose questions and challenges, while being unafraid to emphasise her points: Was it not a breach of contract to deny her participation in any single part of the course? And, regarding the *Othello* production, wasn't it expected that every effort would be made to ensure that students took part in coursework suited to their natural talents and ambitions? Wasn't it all there, authoritatively printed-out in the course prospectus? Then there was the matter of her father paying a small fortune to send her to the Institute. Was he getting his money's worth with his daughter banned from part of the course?

On the other hand, she would apologise, sincerely, to Annabelle for the covert manner in which her "audition" had been conducted. Yes, it was true that she'd broken down in her tutorial, but that was entirely due to Annabelle's show of concern and sympathy, her words of comfort making it easier to weep than not. Even so, wasn't it the case that the best actors were close to their emotions, something that the Lee Strasberg schools taught? And how was it that she was banned from performing on stage, but at the same time allowed to take part in experimental exercises in drama, on the lawn, in the Great Hall or at The Other Place? Wasn't it all a touch hypocritical? Based on this, she would insist that she'd felt compelled to show that her talents were unaffected by any emotional problem and that the only means by which this could be achieved was by performing her skills on stage, before an audience. What other option did she have?

The whole thing was crazy, right from the start. Annabelle's assumption that performing on stage would be dangerous for her mental health was utterly ridiculous. Acting, for her, was always a release, a cathartic event that literally took her out of herself. Take the famous actors who'd suffered emotionally, the likes of Vivien Leigh and Marlon Brando, through to Christian Bale and Alec Baldwin, a few among many who'd suffered for their art. In fact, Vivien Leigh, one of the greatest performers of the twentieth century, had managed to win two Academy Awards for best actress, while undergoing psychiatric care in hospital.

She'd also point out that Annabelle was not trained as a counsellor, she'd said so herself, hadn't she? Shouldn't she have suggested that a psychotherapist be consulted to decide if a student was safe enough to go on stage, rather than make a unilateral decision based on her own, non–professional, assessment?

She would go on to stress that she was the victim of UK "health and safety laws", or "elf and safety paws" as it was often mocked by the elderly, showing they were generally held in contempt and joked about among their generation.

Yes, of course she would accept that The Shakespeare Institute was different from commercial theatre in that it had a 'duty of care' for its students. However, she would point to a recent doctoral thesis that dealt with that very subject, concluding that young people of today were badly advised. Rather than take measures to avoid risky situations, shouldn't every effort be made to encourage them to take risks? And wasn't there a growing belief that the increasing rate of mental disorder among the Western world's younger generation was due to their media-induced fear of impending doom, whereas previous generations had shown a resilience and mental toughness, at no time better demonstrated than during World War II, when suicide rates in the UK, as well as Europe, were at their lowest?

Finally, she would suggest that her action had not harmed anyone. Yes, she'd broken protocol and caused embarrassment, and for this was deeply apologetic. But what she'd done had been the only way left in which to stake her claim as the best actor competing for the much-coveted role of Desdemona.

She would end with an appeal in Latin: "*Et prostraverunt non petito vernia*" – "I lie before you begging forgiveness."

The bus slowed down and stopped. Through the opening door came a sudden gust of freezing air, bringing snowflakes fluttering into the compartment. As a passenger alighted Franky observed the schnauzer, its head to one side, staring at her with soft, appealing eyes. She stretched out an arm across the aisle and ruffled its bushy eyebrows.

The dog's owner gave back a relieved smile that prompted her own smile in return. She couldn't remember the last time anyone - other than Hannah - had actually smiled at her with *feeling*.

Her smile faded as she recalled those moments with Brooklyn. Why, on her first visit, had she suddenly left her in the tiring room to make a phone call? Was she calling Annabelle to report what was happening and *she*, the cunning one, had instructed her to go back and encourage her with flattery, telling her how wonderful she looked in costume, the sub-text meaning: *Let her get on stage to show off her talents. She'll make a hash of it and that will be the end of her.*

Then there was Brooklyn's sly comment. *You must be pissed off, not getting the part*? And then another, as she was leaving. *Now if it were me, I'd be inclined to...*

Inclined to what? Hadn't Brooklyn deliberately provoked her with the first remark and then left the second hanging in mid-air, so as to seed the idea that she staged her own audition in the most dramatic way possible and then see what a fool she would make of herself?

Who were the fools now!

Tactically she could not have played it better. She'd defeated them, at least for the time being, a successful holding operation, giving her time in which to work out her next move.

But first, consider the enemy. Annabelle had taken a severe blow. How would she retaliate? Try to get her dismissed from the course, stating that she'd broken her signed contract that included a clause relating to *Student Discipline Regulations?* Or, could it happen that Annabelle would brief her father on her unscheduled performance, so that he would discipline her in stricter ways than any university would devise?

Well, she would see about that. She was ahead of the game. She knew who her enemies were: Annabelle, Tom, Alicia and— Brooklyn? Hannah was also at risk. How she wished that she'd confided in her earlier, maybe then she would not have been chosen as a target by Annabelle and Alicia.

So, knowing her enemy, she would start digging in, while making plans for attack. She was now convinced that she had no option, other than to see out the last days of the semester by launching a deterrent. And it wouldn't be by acting on stage.

After that she would go home to deal with *him*.

She put her head back and drifted into reverie as the bus rumbled on. She romanced her childhood, remembering the times when she used to wake up on a winter's morning and listen to the dead silence that a snowfall always brought. Then, how delightful it was to peel back the curtains and stare over a sunshine-flooded expanse that twinkled into the distance. After breakfast she would hurry outside and crunch through the virgin snow, with only her footprints marring the pristine landscape.

As the bus approached her stop, she took out her satellite phone and checked the forecast. Snowflakes appeared on the screen. However, it promised relief in the form of an Atlantic depression bringing rain and milder weather within the next forty-eight hours.

She stood up to make her way to the exit, while thinking about Hannah. It would be interesting to note her body language when she arrived home that night.

Home? What was home? She had no home, no real home … anywhere.

She stepped on to the snow-covered pavement, lowering her head against the north-easterly blast. As she did so it pleased her to forget Hannah. Instead she pictured Alicia arriving back, struggling in temperatures forecast to drop as low as minus nine and even lower, in the blizzard. With a tough smile she pulled tight the drawstrings of her hood, drew up the anorak zip and clamped its collar against her mouth.

As the bus growled away, she staggered forward to gain traction and suddenly slipped.

'Christ!' She just managed to stay upright.

She thought of what lay ahead, long dark hours hemmed inside a remote cottage with her enemies. Would she – *could* she – get through the night to come?

After twenty minutes she thankfully turned into Tithebarn Lane, when came the mechanical chugging noise of an approaching tractor. Horrors, the same as before? This time it was towing a heavy cartload of logs that swayed from side to side.

Gasping in fear, she flattened herself against the hedge. With seconds to go, it suddenly braked and slowed down to trundle past. She looked up at the driver.

He put up a hand, giving her a grin.

She launched herself at him, stabbing and ripping his neck until an artery split, propelling a glorious red spray, carried over her head to settle behind on the snow. She saw it briefly as a floral display of red petals, spread over an enormous white dress.

She picked her way over the last hundred yards, aware that snowdrifts were starting to build against the north-facing hedgerow. She guessed that an hour would pass at the most, before the lane became impassable.

She let herself into the cottage. It was empty, quiet and cold. Why had she put the central heating on low? Habit.

She took off her anorak and boots, then went into the living room to find the fire reduced mainly to ash. Only the middle portion was glowing.

She set aside the fireguard and put on a handful of kindling before adding two thin logs. She then switched on the two room radiators before going into the laundry room to turn up the heating.

Later, as she stood under the hot spray of a shower, she harboured the hope that the others might not make it back, that she would be alone and not have to jam her chair under the door handle that night.

While drying herself, she remembered something that was vital to her plan. She put on her dressing gown and went quickly into Craig and Tom's room and found what she was looking for, two blue and white medication packs. She took out a silver strip from the one already opened and then replaced both in the drawer, exactly as she'd found them.

She took the strip into the bathroom where, using a spoon, she crushed five tablets into a white powder, carefully sweeping it into an empty pill box.

Once back in her room she began to 'dress' herself as yet another Shakespearean character. It was relatively easy this time.

It didn't require costume.

Craig, Tom and Hannah arrived at the cottage at 5.55 p.m. after a laborious journey, Craig having negotiated the main roads successfully in the four-wheel drive BMW, but slowed down by nervous drivers ahead.

Tithebarn Lane was a different matter but, with a few slalom manoeuvres, he was able to deliver his passengers safely at the cottage.

'Well done, Craig,' said Hannah in relief.

'Heartily seconded,' said Tom.

Hannah was first inside, going into the living room to find Franky sitting in front of a brightly burning fire. She slipped into the inglenook and sat down, clasping both arms around her chest.

She gave Franky a nervous glance. 'Has anyone called you?'

'No. Should they have?' Franky's eyes gleamed in the firelight. She watched Hannah fidgeting with her fingers. 'Well, go on. Tell me what you want to say.'

'I'm just thinking. Erm, wouldn't it be better if you call Annabelle before she calls you?'

'Why?'

'We all think you should.'

"*We*" Franky stared hard into the fire.

'What?'

'Has Alicia talked to you?'

'No. I saw her afterwards. She was so tight-lipped, that I didn't dare speak—'

Hannah broke off as Craig entered the room.

'Diesel engines,' he said disparagingly. 'The heater kicks in just as you get here.' He came to lean against the inglenook beam, rubbing his hands together, then holding them out to the fire. His face, lit up by the flames, was ruddy and luminous. 'You must have got one of the last buses, Franky. They've stopped running beyond Shottery.'

'I'm worried about Alicia,' said Hannah. 'She had that late lecture.'

'They could have cancelled it,' said Craig. 'She'll call anyway, if she's in trouble.'

Franky, her gaze lowered into the fire, smiled faintly to herself.

'Not much we can do, unless she calls.' He turned to leave. 'I'm going for a real hot shower. I hope we've got enough food in.'

'No need to worry,' said Hannah. 'We've got a few scraps.'

'Pigswill? Great.' His chuckle echoed in the hallway.

'A thaw's forecast for tomorrow afternoon,' she called out.

There was no reply. Hannah drew in a deep breath and looked at Franky, framing words on her lips. 'Yes, it was a great performance Franky. It was. But, erm …'

'But what?' Franky stared intently into the fire.

'I don't know why you did it. I mean, I can't see what you hoped to get from it. I'm not criticising you,' she added quickly, then broke off again, this time as Tom entered the room.

He came to sit in front of the fire, opposite Franky, stretching out his legs to luxuriate in the warmth. 'What a relief,' he murmured.

'I think I'll grab a shower as well,' said Hannah, suddenly getting up and going out.

Tom, waiting a moment, closed his eyes. 'I thought your Desdemona was superb.'

'Oh.' Franky looked at him. 'Thanks.'

'Albeit unexpected.' He looked at her with a curious half-smile. 'How are you feeling now?'

'How do you mean?'

'In retrospect.'

'Good. I was getting a bit of revenge, *if* you want to know.' Suddenly she turned her head to him in an impetuous challenge. 'For Annabelle not letting me audition.'

'Oh? And why was that?'

'I'd rather not talk about it.'

'Hmm.' He sank his chin into his chest, put both hands on his stomach and steepled his fingers together. After a pause he looked at his watch. 'Methinks I may need a substitute cook partner.'

'You mean Alicia.' She shot him a reluctant glance.

'Yes. Our turn feeding the five. And marooned. Marooned, like Lear, on a wild island with his daughter.'

She stared at him, seeing his eyes masked by the reflection of firelight in his glasses.

The spider ran up her spine.

She remembered a dream of the previous night that had her father ranging around the house, searching for something, Jason watching him fearfully. What was he looking for, salvation? There seemed to have been no outcome to it, nothing gained, either for *him* or the boy.

Suddenly, either through divine inspiration or the subconscious, she felt closer to the answer she'd been seeking for weeks.

She stared hard into the flames and set her mind to picture the sequence of events following the boy's rape: her flight into the woods, the return to the house, her father and his victim no longer there, then going up to her room to find the blood-stained note that she knew by heart.

The Shakespeare Institute, England, has a one-year course for an MA or PhD. One of my students went there—

She stopped.

One of my students went there …

The blizzard having ceased, she lay down on her bed, contemplating her discovery. The answer had been there, all the time, in the bloodstained note her father had left her. One of his students obviously had Annabelle as tutor. As a Bostonian judge in the national Shakespeare competition he'd have Skyped, emailed or texted Annabelle to ask how his ex-student was getting on, at the same time flattering her and praising the Institute for its excellent work and splendid tradition. He'd have lathered it on, his head swelling vaingloriously by simply talking to a premier scholar at the home of Shakespeare, he not having got beyond a Bachelor of Arts degree.

Yes. *There* lay the connection. She saw him in his study, acting the part of the concerned father: *How's my daughter doing, as I'm a shade worried about her.* He'd add something else like *How I wish I hadn't sent her to England.* He would tell Annabelle that she was dangerous, repeating the psychotherapist's warning. *She's also concocted a crazy story that I've committed child abuse, so she can blackmail me for lots of money. She's threatening to call the police, telling them her father's a paedophile and rapist. She's got me over a barrel. I've no choice but to pay up.*

Franky stretched out an arm to pick up her wine glass, took a sip, then lay back, staring at the ceiling. She could see him at his six-screen desk equipped with light bulbs that changed colour from white to yellow and blue to red, all designed, he would say smugly, *to suit my circadian rhythms.*

Franky sat upright and drank more wine. Her hand shook a little. It was okay plotting her course of action but wasn't it obvious that her father would do the same out of self-preservation? Wouldn't he need a pre-emptive strike of his own? Clearly, he'd primed Annabelle to scare her into silence. Was she now planning to scare the wits out of her, so giving *him* a psychological advantage on her arrival home at Christmas, the idea being to upset her mind, to confuse, draw her sting, laying herself open to murder?

He would wait until she flew home. He would have her killed then. Less worry, less chance of the unforeseen happening. The local mafia, the Patriarca. Ten — fifteen thousand dollars a hit?

Paranoia? Purely for the birds.

She lay curled up on the bed, her palms sweaty. The tips of her fingers felt numb and her heart was thumping so hard and fast that she could even hear it. She could see *him* walking the red history-line that ran along the sidewalks through Boston, an invitation to trace its historic roots and cultural history.

He'd have two men with him, both well dressed and smoking cigars, "men of respect" working out a plan to extinguish her life during the Christmas break, facilitated by knife or bullet. There would be a cab driver at Logan arrivals holding up a placard printed 'O'Tierney'. He would ask her to sit beside him in the front passenger seat, saying the rear seats were damp from a clean-up after a child had been sick. He would quickly divert to a lonely stretch of scrubby road, when someone would rise from behind her seat, holding a sliding wire loop.

She was sweating again. Her troubles at the Institute, her dissertation, the loss of Desdemona and Hamlet, all faded into nothing in the frightening realisation that her life was in real danger.

The bedside lamp was on, but why was the light fading? She flicked her eyes to the far corners of the room where, to her mounting horror, curls and wreaths of smoke curled upwards to rapidly merge into two black curtains that began to race around the walls in opposite directions.

With a gasp, she slipped under the duvet, rammed it tightly over her head, eyes tightly shut. After a minute or two, she gathered courage to raise it a little and was rewarded by a rim of light. She eased it higher, and then higher still, until all the mundane and familiar boundaries of the bedroom came back — bedside lighting: cabinet: computer desk and normal curtains. Was it possible to be awake during a nightmare?

Time for resolution and determination. It was even more imperative that she struck first. She would get a registered airport cab to make sure she was safe on her journey to the Boston PD where she would make her witnessed statement, but get home before they came to arrest him, by which time he would be dead. Yvette would not feature. She would be in France with her relations, as always, in the few days before Christmas. She would discover his body and how satisfying that would be.

She concentrated on her carefully constructed and memorised plan. After visiting Boston PD she arrives home around mid-day. Before entering the house, she collects one of her childhood climbing ropes left in the outside shed. From it she fashions a noose with a running "*Figure 8 follow-through*" knot, a simple and dependable type that she'd learnt with Canopy Climbers, one capable of taking heavy weights. Silently, she enters the house by the back door, then goes into the large hallway where she might hear music coming from *his* study, as it often did. If not, she would either hide in her room until his return or check in at a local hotel. At some point, with him back in his study – his Saturdays were nearly always spent in money-making activities - she would regain entry to the house, flit up the left of the two curved staircases on to the wide spacious landing, tie the rope to the main post of the balustrade and then lean over to shout "Dad?"

He emerges from his study, a slim, lightweight figure. He looks up to see her place the noose around her neck. She says "Goodbye."

He races up the stairs to prevent her suicide. It would be instinct that prompts it, not wanting her to die in his presence for all manner of reasons. As he lunges forward to grab her, she whips the noose from around her neck and slips it over his, yanking it tight, then grabs his thin legs to tilt and slip his lightweight body over the polished roll-top of the balustrade. Maybe the fall fails to break his neck, in which case it leaves him swinging and thrashing about, gurgling desperately. Maybe he tries to haul himself up on the rope, his eyes bulging red with the effort. She could picture him grunting, trying to get a hand on the bottom of the railing but, suddenly exhausted, falls to an abrupt stop, his body swinging, head tilted.

She went over the details that would leave the police in no doubt that he'd committed suicide. Her witness statement, would say that she found him hanging from the rope, had raced upstairs to slide down and untie the noose, but was too late. His motive for suicide? The fear of being arrested for a crime that carried with it a lifetime in prison. Simple.

But was it? Breathing hard, she closed her eyes. Had she the willpower and courage to carry it out?

And, like Hamlet, could she actually see herself *doing* the deed?

Franky, carrying a manila folder, knocked on Hannah's door. 'It's me,' she said.

Hannah opened it with a hesitant expression. 'Franky.' She let her in and closed the door.

'I've got something to tell you.' She quickly searched Hannah's eyes. 'He sent me here instead of Harvard or Ashland. I wondered why, because he's tight with money. I soon realised. He wanted me out of the way for the year while he works out what to do with me.'

'How do you mean, "do with"?

'Kill me.'

Hannah stared at her with shallow breathing. 'But why would he … do that?' she said in a slight, tremulous voice.

'Because he's worried about me.'

'Why?' Hannah's eyes darted around before settling on her fearfully. 'You mean the rape?'

'Yes, reporting him. And because dear Annabelle told him about my dissertation that she stole from me because it was anti *him*, my father. He's been paying her to keep an eye on me. I'm telling you this because you might have been hearing the opposite, that I'm a danger to everyone, that I'm—'

'Just…' Hannah raised the palms of her hands. 'Franky, can we just stop a moment and—'

'No, *listen*. I'm the only witness. He's hiring somebody to kill me. He knows he'll go to prison for life if I stay alive. Kind of puts things into perspective, doesn't it?'

'Oh, Franky.' Hannah's face crumbled.

'Yes. My own father.'

'But…' Hannah's voice had weakened almost to a whisper.

'Annabelle's recruited Alicia and Tom. I also think they're trying to recruit you. It's a conspiracy and it's real.'

Hannah mouth open, shook her head. 'But they're not, Franky. Nobody's out to get you in any way. I promise … I …'

She tailed off as Franky opened the manila folder and took out a bloodstained note.

'Read it aloud,' she said in a commanding voice. 'Go on. Aloud.'

Hannah took it.

'Go on. Read it!'

Franky watched Hannah's face as she read the note, her voice shaky.

'The Shakespeare Institute, England, has a one-year course for an MA or PhD. One of my students went there. You love Shakespeare. It's made for you. If you go, I'll give you $25,000 plus the course fee.' Hannah's voice faded again to a whisper, 'but this is between the two of us. No one else must know.'

Stunned, Hannah slowly looked up to stare at Franky.

'He made up the bribe to $35,000, Doesn't that prove he has something to hide?' Franky pointed to the bloodstain. 'See that? He fell flat on his face, trying to pull his pants up after the rape.' She took the note from Hannah's hand and replaced it in the folder. 'This is the evidence. The police won't ignore this. Believe me now?' She went quickly to open the door and listen.

Satisfied, she closed it and turned to look at Hannah.

'You're shocked? How do you think I feel? Tell me, how is it that you're suddenly friends with Alicia, after all that's happened?' Her eyes narrowed, watching Hannah's reaction. 'Ask yourself that. And then be honest.'

Hannah looked at her, shaking her head. 'That's not how it is, Franky and I am being honest.'

'What? *After* you seeing them dance together and you in your room, blubbering? Haven't you thought it weird, Alicia making overtures, doing this and that with you, *being nice*?' She jabbed a finger. 'Don't you sense a conspiracy?'

'No, I don't.' Hannah dabbed her eyes with the back of her hand. 'It's actually the other way round.'

'What is?'

'It's me. Alicia hasn't been grooming me. I've been grooming *her*— in a way. You told me to find out what she says about you, remember? I've been doing that, exactly what you wanted me to do. I tried to open a conversation about you, but got nowhere. She's said nothing about you, nothing at all, at least not to me. I've also been trying to find out something else, what was happening between her and Craig. I found nothing. I'm not part of any conspiracy against you. How could you even think that?'

Franky studied her face. She was acting the part well, as taught by Alicia. But her explanation was all too pat, what you'd expect from someone who had been prepped for it. No, it was obvious that battle-lines had been drawn, and Hannah was not on her side.

Not anymore.

Chapter Twenty-One

It was nearly 7.30 p.m. when Alicia came in, announcing her arrival by deliberately banging shut the front door. She'd waited half an hour in the blizzard for a bus that terminated at Shottery, leaving her to struggle through the blizzard for over a mile. Her battle with the elements had left her wet, tired, cold and hungry, serving only to fuel her rising anger.

Wrenching off her anorak and dumping it on the floor, she marched down the hallway into the kitchen, leaving behind clumps of snow on the floor tiles.

Franky, startled by the noise, got up from her computer and came warily downstairs. She stopped at the bottom, leaving a hand on the newel post, while staring into the kitchen.

Alicia spooned coffee into a mug, breathing hard. '*Why?*' She gave a sideways glance towards her. '*What for?* Are you for real?' Alicia tossed the spoon, clattering on the worktop. 'You aren't, are you! Of course not, I'm forgetting. You're Desdemona!' She turned to face Franky. 'Well?'

'Well what?'

'Are you going to just stand there *and say nothing!*'

Franky sauntered towards her with tightened lips. 'What do you want me to say? That I wasn't given the audition as promised, that I was virtually guaranteed the part and then banned from, without any reason?' She stopped in the kitchen doorway and folded her arms.

'Okay. So, you delivered a speech.' Alicia nodded. 'I suppose, little me, I'll have to crawl into my hole and forget I was ever there, that I ever did a fucking audition*!*'

'Well you did have an audition and I didn't. So, I made myself one.'

'But *why*? I'll tell you why.' Alicia pointed a finger. 'You did it to show how much better you were than me and make me an apology for Desdemona!' Suddenly she picked up the mug and raised it with a straight arm. *Didn't you*!' She smashed the mug on the floor.

'Ah!' Franky stepped back, touching her forehead, then looked at the blood on her fingertip.

'It's all over the campus!' Alicia shouted. 'You ruined my audition, making me a laughing stock, as well as Marie!'

'But you got the part.'

'Yes. But no thanks to you!'

Franky turned, going into the hallway, conscious of Tom, Craig and Hannah, grouped at the bottom of the stairs, staring at them.

Franky, ignoring them, went into the cloakroom, leaving the door open.

'What's going on?' said Craig. 'Alicia, let's calm it down, huh? And we'll talk?'

'Alicia,' said Tom. 'We signed an agreement. Remember?'

'No Tom.' Alicia made a cut-off gesture with her hand. 'This is between her and me.'

She walked into the hallway to stare at Franky standing in front of the mirror, about to stick a plaster on her forehead. 'You know I spent time with Annabelle talking about you – you know that?'

Franky froze, her finger on the plaster. After a pause, she smoothed it down. 'Talking about me."

'No, we were talking about the fucking weather!'

Alicia went back through the kitchen into the laundry room, returning with a dustpan and brush.

Franky moved to stand in the kitchen doorway, watching her sweep up bits of broken pottery.

'So, you were talking about me."

'Yes!' Alicia paused in her sweeping. 'Some people said you meant it as a joke. A *joke*! I nearly covered up for you! I nearly said "Franky didn't mean anything by it. Just one of her silly jokes." How magnanimous would that have been? Know something else?' She pointed a finger. 'I nearly said, "forget it", she's spent a lot of money on me to come and live here. You are quite something. I think you're...' She tapped the side of her head.

'Insane?'

'Oh!' Alicia chuckled ironically. 'Let's not put too fine a point on it.'

She bent down with the dustpan when Franky stepped forward to slap her across the face, but slipped.

She thought she heard Craig shout 'No!' before her head struck the edge of a worktop, the light splintering and then going out.

Her unconsciousness was short-lived, a matter of seconds.

She opened her eyes to a circle of faces staring down at her – Hannah, her hands clasped to her cheeks, Craig and Tom just behind.

'You okay?' said Hannah anxiously.

'Yes,' she croaked. 'Help me up.'

'No, hold on.' Hannah gestured. 'Can someone get a cushion?'

'No, I'm okay,' said Franky with a grimace, putting up a hand.

'Sure?' Craig took hold, pulling her gently to her feet.

'Thanks.' She touched her forehead tenderly, aware of Alicia standing in the hallway, watching.

'Stay still,' said Craig, peering and touching her forehead. 'I can feel a swelling already. It's a good sign. It's the one you can't see that's dangerous.'

'Here. Drink this.' Hannah handed Franky a glass of water.

She took hold of it. 'Thanks.'

'You should lie down,' said Tom.

'You need Paracetamol,' said Hannah.

Opening a kitchen drawer, she took out a tablet strip and squeezed out a pill. 'Here. No, best to take two.' She squeezed out another and handed them to Franky.

Franky put the pills in her mouth, one after the other, swallowing each with a sip of water.

'Let me take that.' Hannah took the glass from Franky. 'You must lie down, she said, her other hand on Franky's arm, guiding her towards the stairs. 'Come on.'

Alicia stood out of the way, heaved a deep sigh and made a helpless "what do you expect" gesture at Craig and Tom.

Franky, lying fully dressed on top of the duvet, blinked slowly and frowned. She gently ran two exploratory fingers over the throbbing lump that had grown in the time she'd been asleep. She checked her watch and found that it was about 45 minutes. Laboriously, she slipped her legs from the bed to rest on the floor, reached out to pick up the glass of water, and sipping it, downed another Paracetamol.

She stood up and carefully opened the door to hear muffled voices from the living room.

Then the second bedroom door opened and Craig came out on to the landing, dressed in his pyjamas.

'Franky,' he said. 'How do you feel now?'

'Okay. I'll get over it.'

'That's good.' He hesitated, was about to say something else, but changed his mind. 'I think we should talk about this tomorrow morning before we do anything else. Would you back me on that?'

'Sure.'

'Good.'

She watched him go into the bathroom and waited until she heard the lock applied, at which she went slowly downstairs, gripping the handrail, to sit at her listening post.

'I've changed my mind.' It was Tom's cool voice that she heard. 'This thing has gone too far. We have to talk to her.'

'Yes,' said Hannah. 'Will you tell her, Tom? I'd rather it came from you.'

Tom nodded in agreement. 'The only problem could be getting into Stratford. The thaw's not forecast until tomorrow afternoon.'

'If we are snowed in,' said Alicia, 'can we call her from here - each of us talks to her?'

'No,' said Tom. 'We can't. It's far too delicate. We must be one voice.'

'But what if the thaw doesn't come?' said Hannah. 'We'd have to call her then, wouldn't we?'

'No, it will come. Weather forecasting here is an art form. Don't worry.'

'Okay, I'll text her after breakfast,' said Alicia. 'I'll just say it's important we meet. I'll say it's urgent. My God, I tell you, her knuckles were white, gripping that knife. And her stare. I should have kept my mouth shut.'

Franky shivered. So, they were coming for her, at last, with Annabelle in the know. And Hannah was now, without a shadow of doubt, one of the conspirators. But she was ready, she told herself. All it required was the determination to carry out her plan of attack.

Came the voice of Lady Macbeth:

Hie thee hither,
That I may pour my spirits in thine ear
Come you spirits
That tend on mortal thoughts,
unsex me here

Chapter Twenty-Two

We fail? But screw your courage
to the sticking-place,
And we'll not fail.
Macbeth, Act I, sc. vii

The next morning, Hannah entered the kitchen to find Franky holding a spoon, making desultory hacks at a cereal biscuit.

'Hi,' she said, with an attempt at a smile.

A shaft of winter sunshine illuminated Franky's pale face, revealing smudges under her eyes. She stared at a brown knot on the pine table.

'When I left,' she said carefully, 'after the auditions, what did Annabelle do?'

Hannah retrieved an egg from the fridge, thinking what to say.

Tom made his entrance. 'Have you seen the snow this morning?' he said. 'Someone's been out painting it blue.'

'How big was the brush, Tom?' said Hannah looking at Franky, hoping she'd raise a smile. She'd prayed for her well into the night, hoping for a miracle.

'Extremely large. Quite fascinating.' He took a loaf of brown bread from the freezer, stood it on the worktop and, with a downward pressure of his thumbs, split away two slices. 'It's all to do with the red and yellow lights in the spectrum,' he continued. 'They're absorbed by the snow. So only the blue is reflected.'

He popped the bread into the toaster, set the time and locked down the slider.

'Insomnia,' he announced, 'can be caused by too much light, disrupting the body's circadian rhythm. Blue light from a cell phone or just light from a PC tricks the retina into thinking it's daytime.'

'Can anybody hear that?' said Franky, suddenly.

'Hear what?' said Hannah.

'That noise.'

'What noise?'

It grew louder. She stood up to find Hannah talking to her, her voice lost in a thundering roar, like that of a waterfall.

Franky was about to flee when it stopped, as suddenly as it began.

'You okay?' Hannah, scared, put out a tentative hand.

Franky closed her eyes for a moment and then picked up her glass of orange juice. She took a drink, carefully replacing the glass tumbler on the table. 'Yes. I am. I'm fine.'

Craig walked into the kitchen. 'Franky, how are you this morning? Let me see.' He gently swept her hair upwards to reveal the round lump that had developed overnight.

'Nice one.' He grinned at her. 'A prize winner.'

'Good,' she said blankly, staring through the window. 'Am I right in thinking your car's a four-wheel drive?'

Craig exchanged glances with Hannah.

'Yes,' he said. 'It is.'

'You got through the snow last night.'

'Yes, but not snow drifts like we've got now.'

'I may need to get into town.'

'Sorry, Franky, no go. The ground clearance isn't enough. You'd need a tractor for that.'

'*Tractor?*' She stared at him. 'Who do you know with a tractor?'

'The farmer. I told you. He said he'd help if we got stuck. A caterpillar-dozer's what we really need. We'll probably just have to wait for the thaw.'

'Franky.' The tone was curt.

She looked up to find Alicia in the doorway.

'As soon as I can I'll be going. You can start looking round for a replacement.' She turned and disappeared.

After a pause Hannah followed her out.

Franky looked out of the window to see wedges of thick dark cloud looming up from the north-west. She could imagine Hannah, with Alicia, making that phone call to Annabelle.

Well, she was also ready; there would be no more agonising over the meaning and purpose of revenge, no more worrying over esoteric notions of moral equivalence and no more bothering with juries and courts in which fairness before the law was the main issue. It was all over. It was pathetic, even ludicrous, to think that she'd been thinking about nothing but abstractions. She'd been crazy in bouncing around concepts of 'honour' and 'justice' while, waiting in the wings, had been harsh reality. No more of that garbage.

She lay on the bed, staring upwards, her senses on full alert, the room that had been flooded by the snow's brightness, was now gloomy. The room, the cottage, the freezing wasteland outside, were silent. Everything, time, place and life itself, seemed frozen.

She suddenly sat upright, startled by a loud ringing noise, before it morphed into an alert jingle from her iPhone.

It was a text message, Annabelle asking to see her as soon as possible.

Her eyes narrowed to crinkled slits. After a moment she tapped a reply. *Marooned. Will come asap.*

She sent the message and sniffed the air. The smell of acid was there. She had smelt it overnight and with the windows closed, as was her bedroom door. It was worrying.

She went to sit at the computer. Fearful and slightly breathless, she searched for "a smell of acid where there should be none". All the answers were related to different kinds of acids – butyric, carboxylic, aliphatic.

She was about to click out when she caught the caption, *Scent of Disease*. She searched the subject and read about schizophrenic patients, a scientific piece that was difficult to comprehend, that is until she saw the line: *those with schizophrenia often give out a smell from a component called trans-3-Methyl-2-hexonic acid."* It raised a spike of alarm, until she read that the scent was described as *very sweet, like over-ripened fruit.*

She sat back, closed her eyes and exhaled in relief. Her body had never smelt of anything.

There was a tentative tap at the door.

For a moment she sat still. Then, holding her breath, she got up to answer it.

She opened the door to reveal Hannah.

'Can I come in?'

'Wait.' Franky poked her head outside the room. Satisfied that no one was listening, she ushered her into the room, closing the door. 'What do you want?' Her stare was cold.

'Franky ...' Hannah swallowed hard ... 'Whatever you think, please believe me. We really are worried about you.'

"*We.*"

Yes, Franky because we *are* worried! *I'm* worried. We all are. We're on your side, no one's out to get you. Please believe me?' In anguish, she began to sob.

Franky's sceptical look was lost as she went to the window to look out furtively. 'Where's Alicia?'

'In her room. Franky, please talk to Tom? He knows about psychosis. He thinks—'

Franky wheeled round jabbing a finger, her face malevolent. '*You!*'

Hannah gasped in fear, stepping backwards.

'You told Alicia you'd read my notebook. You said I had Alicia as a hooker. You laughed at me. *Didn't* you!'

Hannah took a step back, trembling.

'I know what's happening.' Franky advanced on her. 'I'm not stupid.'

'Please Franky.' Hannah put up her hands. 'I want to help you. I really—'

'Help?' Her stiff forefinger edged Hannah back towards the wall. 'You spied on me. *Didn't* you!'

'Franky.' Hannah held her breath. 'Please listen You don't realise—'

'You told Alicia you'd read my notebook. *Didn't you!*'

'Please don't!' Hannah, her back to the wall, turned sideways, shielding her face.

Franky poked her shoulder. '*Didn't you?*'

'You're frightening me, Franky!'

'I heard you in the living room. "Red's in for it." And what did you say or do? *Nothing.*'

She turned away to sit on the bed, her back to Hannah, staring grimly out of the window.

Hannah flicked her eyes to the door, then back at Franky. Judging the moment, she edged towards the door—

'*Yes!*' Franky, suddenly stood up, business-like. 'Yes, let's sort it out, shall we? Let's go down to your room. They won't hear us down there.'

Franky stood at Hannah's window, staring out at the hedgerows and trees, stark and black amidst the white expanse. There came the raucous cawing of crows. She watched them fly high above the window, then wheel and flap downwards to encircle and finally decorate the branches of a gnarled tree.

'Murder,' she murmured dreamily.

'What?' said Hannah with a sob. Having removed her shoes, she lay on the bed curled up, the bear clutched to her chest. 'What did you say?'

'When they gather. *Crows.* A murder of crows.'

She turned from the window and went to sit at Hannah's side, saying nothing at first. 'Yes. I told you the truth about Alicia and Craig, as it was then.' She stared at a decorative whirl on the cream bed-head. 'But things *do* change. Don't they?'

Hannah stirred, then cranked her body round to stare up at Franky, her wet cheeks smudged by mascara. 'Why did you tell me a lie, Franky? Why?'

'I didn't want you to be upset. I thought you'd find out yourself because they're so obvious.'

Hannah tucked herself into a tight curl and began to rock back and forth.

'It's my fault. Because you were in such a state, I felt I had to.'

Hannah's breathing quickened, the rocking faster.

'It happened one day last week. I thought I was alone. Then I could hear them upstairs in her room, the bed creaking and they were laughing. Alicia said, "Wouldn't it be funny if Hannah came back and saw us?"'

Hannah let out a shuddering groan.

'I called "Anybody home?" I heard them scrambling about, then Craig hurried out half-dressed and dived into his room.'

Hannah let out a hacking sob.

'I thought of telling you then, but I couldn't.' Franky put a hand on Hannah's shoulder. 'I think you need something. Stay there.'

Franky went upstairs to her room where she opened a drawer and took out a flat-shaped bottle of Rémy Martin brandy and the small pillbox containing the white powder. She unscrewed the bottle and poured brandy into a glass, up to the halfway mark. To this she added the powder, stirring it with the spoon until it was completely dissolved.

When she returned, Hannah was lying on her back, staring listlessly at the ceiling. Her bear lay on the floor, close to the bed.

Franky placed the brandy bottle on the bedside cabinet. 'I know how you feel,' she said. 'And I'm sorry that I lied. But there's always mother's little comforter. Take a peep. You said you liked brandy, yeah …?'

Hannah blinked at the glass held before her eyes. After a pause she struggled to sit partially upright and take hold of it.

'I'm very sorry about Alicia.'

'What?'

'Alicia. It's all my fault.'

'What is?'

'All this.'

As they talked Franky pushed the bear with her foot, to stop halfway under the bed. 'I'll tell you about it later.'

Chapter Twenty-Three

Wouldst thou have that which thou esteem'st the ornament of life. And live a coward in thine own esteem?
Macbeth, Act I, sc. vii

Franky sat upright against the headboard of the bed, head lowered, the room dark enough to warrant the light being on. She felt satisfied with her plan of action. During the last hour she'd gone over it time and time again.

Relaxing, she recalled the time when she was six years old, when her imaginary Grandpa had come to live with them, a large, cheerful man who acted as Father Christmas each year, a flamboyant character who also played hide-and-seek with her in the woods, who made a tree house and taught her about wildlife. He'd been part of a parallel world, one which she'd intended to bring into the body of her now 'stolen' dissertation, in which Hamlet's nostalgic thoughts of friendship would have synergised with hers into a shared melancholia, both realising there could be no return to such warmth, he to Yorick, his loveable court-jester, she to her beneficent and imaginary Grandpa.

Here hung those lips that I have kissed
I know not how oft.
Where be your gibes now? Your gambols?
Your songs? Your flashes of merriment
That were wont to set the table on a roar?

She looked at her watch. It was almost an hour since Hannah had started to take in the drug, Varenicline. She got off the bed, picked up the bottle of brandy and went downstairs.

She put her head around the open door into the living room. Alicia was alone, sitting by the fireside, reading and making notes, unaware of Franky looking in.

Franky quietly made her way to Hannah's room. She found her drowsily sitting up in bed, her fingers clutching the empty glass on her lap.

'Hi. Some more?'

Hannah opened her eyes to stare at the proffered bottle and nodded. With a dull expression, she watched Franky half-fill the glass and replace it carefully in her hands.

As Hannah concentrated on taking the glass without spilling it, Franky, with her back to her, snatched up the bear and went out.

She waited in the vestibule for Hannah's cry for her bear, but there was none.

On her way back to the stairs she peered round the living room door.

Alicia was no longer there.

She went to the inglenook and — with a quick glance towards the door— dropped the bear into the flames. Rapidly placing fresh logs over and around it, she hurried out and up to her room.

She waited for another half hour to pass. During this time, she kept looking at her watch. There was no imaginary Grandpa in her thoughts any longer, not in her state of heightening tension.

At 10.55 she slipped off the bed to go downstairs. Once more she peeped into the living room.

Alicia looked up. 'What?' she said in a hard voice.

'Nothing.' Franky withdrew and went down to Hannah's room.

She opened the door to be met by the raw and sour smell of brandy.

Hannah was sprawled out on the bed, snoring loudly, the uncapped bottle perched precariously on the edge of the bedside table, its contents more than half gone.

Franky picked up the glass. With the other hand she touched Hannah's shoulder. She bent down to speak quietly.

'Hannah?'

There was no reaction. She raised her voice, 'Hannah?' and shook her lightly.

Hannah blinked placidly, her eyes balled and heavy-lidded. 'Wha—?'

'I've got some news. Bad news.'

Hannah raised herself, bleary eyed and dazed-looking.

'Craig and Alicia. They've been laughing about you again.'

Hannah struggled upright. 'Wha—-?' She blinked hard to clear her vision.

'You're sweating.' Franky took a tissue from the cabinet and dabbed her forehead.

'Craig…?' Hannah's voice was crackly. 'What … what did you say?'

'I said Craig and Alicia. It's happened again.'

Hannah put a hand to her forehead.

'They've just had sex again. If you'd been upstairs you couldn't have failed to hear it.'

Hannah's face muscles tightened.

'They were laughing at you. Mocking you. Now look, I don't know how to say this, but something even worse has happened.'

Hannah removed the hand from her forehead, her lips moving.

'It's Bernard. He's gone.'

Hannah was motionless for a few seconds, then frowned. 'Bern…?'

'He's gone. It's Alicia. She put him on the fire.'

Hannah's eyes narrowed.

'I said Alicia has burnt your bear. She put him on the fire.'

It was as if a light had been switched on – Hannah's drunken stupor vanishing in a huge injection of adrenalin. She sat up quickly, whipped the duvet off the bed to look frantically around the room.

'Where is he!'

'Hannah, you're not listening. I said he's gone.'

Hannah stopped and staggered, putting a hand on the bed to remain standing.

'Alicia's burnt your bear. She put him on the fire. I saw her do it. She destroyed him.' Franky went quickly out of the room.

Hannah's eyes scrolled from side to side, slow realisation giving way to a threatening growl, turning into a strangled roar as she stood up and stumbled into the kitchen where Franky stood by the door, the knife block close by, a knife sticking out.

'*ALICIA*!' yelled Franky. 'HANNAH'S GOT A KNIFE!'

Hannah went for the knife.

Alicia shot out into the hallway, saw Hannah racing towards her, knife held aloft. She wrenched open the front door and fled outside but, dressed in heavy clothing and shoes, was forced to stomp through the snow, whereas the small lightweight Hannah—her naked feet giving a firm grip, the freezing air and adrenalin sloughing off dizziness — quickly made up ground.

'ALICIA WATCH OUT!'

At Craig's yell from an upstairs window, Alicia half turned her head, only to lose her footing. Stumbling in her attempt to stand, Hannah fell upon her like a wolf, stabbing her frenziedly again and again. Craig and Tom plodding frantically through the snow, screaming at her to stop. Craig tried to grab hold of her arm, but a spurt of blood from Alicia's neck blinded him, the stabbings so fast that Tom, stepping in, failed initially to grab hold of Hannah's arm. Then he had it in a fierce grip.

Hannah motionless, stared at Tom, then lowered her gaze to watch him unpeel her fingers, one by one, away from the knife.

No one moved.

A crow flapped overhead, cawing its way into the murky distance.

Franky suddenly screamed in terror, scrabbling away from Alicia's fast struggling legs, her death throes lasting only a few seconds.

Silence once more.

Craig, Franky and Tom stared in dread fascination at Alicia, the jetted blood weakening into a trickle. Pause. Then a tiny bubble emerged from her lips, ballooning bigger and bigger before collapsing upon itself. It was replaced by a cloud of pink froth effervescing from her mouth, settling around her face and cheeks, her visage changing to that of a greedy child who had devoured a large amount of candy floss.

'Aaargh!' Franky suddenly vomited at the copper and iron stink from freshly shed blood. On all fours she padded backwards, until she could heave pure cold air into her lungs.

Tom bent down to grasp Alicia by the collar, his breath clouding her body. He tugged hard, suddenly slipping to sit down in the blood-drenched snow.

Craig, slack-jawed, watched Tom's second attempt also fail. He plodded towards him without expression and bent down to help. Together they drew Alicia's body, slow and awkwardly, stopping and starting, towards the rear of the woodshed.

Franky stood up, finding herself in a surreal world in which the white-crested twigs in the hedgerow seemed fixed in vivid detail. She transferred her gaze to Hannah, who was no longer sobbing. Instead, mouth open, she was frowning at the redness of the snow around her.

Franky saw the blood spatter as a pattern of red roses on a large white dress. She had seen it before, but failed to remember where or when.

In that awful silence.

Chapter Twenty-Four

Hannah stood, distraught, under a hot shower. She dug the long sharp fingernails of both hands into the skin at her throat. Screaming in pain and anguish, she dragged them down to the vee of her breasts. Rivulets of blood appeared, slipping down her body.

Franky, expressionless, stood in the adjoining laundry room. On hearing Hannah's scream, she'd reacted with nothing more than a slight turn of the head, for she was in a dreamscape in which sound fell largely upon deaf ears. For the last five minutes she had concentrated on soaping and washing the brandy glass. After towelling it dry, she placed it carefully in the dishwasher. She stared at the machine and then took out the glass to hand-wash it all over again.

Outside, Tom ran a slow-blinking gaze over the tops of the hedgerow that ran down the lane. In the whiteout there was still no sight or sound of anything moving, his paralysed mind failing to grasp the obvious, that no cyclist, pedestrian or motorist would be passing by until the thaw arrived.

Craig stood next to him, guarding Alicia's body that lay on its back. Her eyes, like harebells wet with dew, stared blindly up at the thick grey sky.

Tom sat in the kitchen, his hand on the table edge, staring fixedly at the floor. Craig stood at the worktop, shuddering and shivering as he tried to pour water into the kettle. Failing, he collapsed on a chair, elbows on his knees, head in his hands, racking out gut-wrenching sobs.

It was some time before he managed to speak.

'She … she told me … her Dad died … and Mom … worked herself to death to get her … into college. Jesus …' He screwed up his face in anguish. 'Poor woman … poor people … Jesus Christ.'

He fell into a long bout of weeping.

'I know.' Tom's tone was sombre. 'I know. But we have to think.'

Craig's weeping dried up. After a long pause he took a tissue from the worktop, to dab his eyes and cheeks. 'What did you say?'

'We have to start thinking.'

'How do you mean?' Craig dropped the damp tissue into the bin.

'We have to cover up.'

'What?' Craig stared at Tom. 'Cover what up?'

'We moved the body, we've no option.'

'What are you saying?'

'We moved her. CSI will know. And they'll know it was you and me because—'

'Tom—'

'Because we are the strongest and—'

'But—'

'No.' Tom's voice was sharp. Don't speak until I've finished. Please Craig.'

Craig took a deep breath. 'Okay. Go on.'

'The police will find out through CSI that we moved the body. We dragged her all of twenty to thirty yards. An autopsy doesn't start in the morgue. It begins at the crime scene, the body and how it lies. If it's moved from the original position CSI will find out and want to know why. They won't think that Hannah or Franky, or both of them, pulled the body there. They're nowhere near strong enough. It had to have been the two of us.'

'But we were in shock. I didn't know what was happening.'

'Yes, and I felt exactly the same. It's probably a primitive instinct, family hiding the body or recovering the dead. Nevertheless—'

'So, why don't we tell them that! What else can we do for God's sake?'

'Craig. They're not interested in anthropology. They'll think in hiding her we're hiding our guilt. That is certain.'

Craig continued staring at Tom, but was distracted by Franky entering the kitchen.

'Is Hannah still by the fire?' said Tom.

'Yes,' said Franky.

Tom nodded. He wrote something on a piece of notepaper.

'What are you doing, Tom?' said Craig.

'Making a list. Give me a few minutes.'

Franky went to stare out of the window. There was a robin at the side of the killing ground, its breast a pale-red compared with the bloody snow beneath. Had she really been thinking about an imaginary Grandpa, only minutes before it happened?

She'd only meant to scare Alicia, to deter them from making a move against her; it was perfectly clear in her mind. Alicia was a strong and lithe athlete who would easily overcome a slightly built, physically weak and drunken opponent staggering around waving a knife. It was all *his* fault. Wasn't her father so fearful she'd report his rape to the Boston police that he'd tried to frighten her into silence before the Christmas break and all she wanted to do was give them pause, so forestalling what diabolical plan he had in wait for her? She'd not intended that Hannah would be turned into a murderer. The proof of that was undeniable; she'd shouted out a warning to Alicia more than once and were not Craig and Tom witnesses to her efforts trying to save her? And when all was said and done, Hannah was her friend, wasn't she? Only a monster would have forced her to perform such a dreadful act.

'Franky, can you sit down?' At Tom's quiet, incisive voice she turned her head and slowly went to sit at the table.

'Is your mind clearer now?'

'Yes,' she said in a strained voice.

Suddenly she was back in the field with the dog and the small woman staring up at her. Her parting words: *For your sake it's wise not to take too many risks. Take care, my luvver. You take care in your life.*

'You haven't showered have you,' said Tom, expecting confirmation.

'No.'

'Good. I know Hannah's had a shower but she still needs a forensic scrub. I'll tell you what to do. I—'

'Tom.' said Craig. 'You're asking us to destroy evidence.' He made a gesture. 'What are these notes for?'

'I think we can survive this.'

Craig stared at him in astonishment. 'What – *how?*'

'It will take some planning. But I do have a Masters in forensics.'

'Tom. That was years ago! You can't possibly think you can fool them *today?*'

'I keep abreast with forensics. It's not impossible.'

Craig placed the flat of his hand on the table. 'Tom. I've learnt it's always best to tell the truth because it's the only safe bet in the long run. Especially if you're innocent, don't you think?'

Tom took off his glasses, peering at them. He took out a tissue, breathed on the lenses, gave them a polish and held them up against the ceiling lights. In that little act he seemed to have regained a little of his urbane poise.

'But we moved the body,' he said. 'We've already aided a murderer. The police won't give up on that. At home we'd be sentenced to life in prison. I don't know what it would be here, probably the same. And there's something else.'

He replaced his glasses. 'Remember Amanda Knox?' He raised his eyebrows at Craig. 'The Meredith Kercher murder? It ran for years, made headlines everywhere. And now there's *another* student murder? Can you imagine the headlines? "American Students in Shakespeare Murder Drama", "Tragedy at The Shakespeare Institute." We'll be at the heart of a media frenzy. Even if she's found guilty, we'll all be implicated.'

'Yes, I get all that, Tom,' said Craig, 'but nevertheless we are innocent. We were in shock moving the body. We acted automatically, and that can be explained. We were—'

'Wait.' Tom shook his head. 'You know what the prosecution will say to the jury? They'll say the five of them, living together, were joined by friendship until that friendship broke bad. Isolated, stuck in the snow, tensions rose. All four would be involved somehow. Wasn't it proved by the body being moved *out of sight of the road?*'

'Can't we take her back to where she was?'

'No. Useless.'

'I think Tom's right,' said Franky. Watching Craig's face, she grimaced in her anxiety.

'Look.' Craig paused, deliberately. 'Isn't it better to face publicity than screw ourselves over justice? I'll say now that I'd rather be chased by the paparazzi for ten years than spend that time in prison and probably for the rest of my life.'

'Not if Tom's right,' said Franky. 'Every magazine, every paper, TV news, Twitter, Facebook, the whole caboodle, will be on to it. There'll be books written. A movie. We'll be stalked. We'll be on edge all the time, waiting for the police to arrest us again. Did you know that Amanda Knox had to go into hiding? There'll be a whole industry created. Students, all living together in an Elizabethan cottage out in the Tudor sticks, studying and acting Shakespeare? What drama. Not only will the police see us as suspects, but so will millions the world over.'

'But we're innocent,' said Craig doggedly. 'But we won't be if we shield a murderer. Tom.' He nodded at his tablet lying open on the table. 'Check it out. Put in "obstructing justice in the UK".

Tom hesitated, then pulled the tablet towards him and began tapping keys. As he waited, he looked at Craig. 'You know we're forgetting Hannah in all this?'

'How do you mean?'

'What her defence will be if she goes to trial on her own. We'll definitely be called as prosecution witnesses, then her counsel will cross-examine us to confuse the jury by dragging us into it. They'll say that Hannah, being the weaker character of the five, was chosen by us to take the rap. In the witness box she'll claim we were involved. Mud sticks. And there's one other thing. Juries can't help being drawn to people who look as sweet and innocent as Hannah. There's nothing savage about her. She'll cry in the dock. She'll point us out. There's no doubt some of the jury, if not all, will go with that.'

Tom paused to let it sink in. '*But,* if you both allow me to do it my way, we'll stop that happening. In saving Hannah, we save ourselves.'

He adjusted his spectacles and read from the website. 'Here we are, "obstruction" … yes, here it's called "perverting" justice.'

'And the sentence?'

After another click. 'Same as America.'

'Life? It's life, isn't it?'

'Yes, it is. But let us just—'

'Tom, I don't doubt your knowledge of forensics, but remember we're still in shock. You may think you're on top of things, but consider the wider picture in which there's bound to be things you can't factor in at this moment. And there's justice to consider. Remember, *we did nothing*. Do we really want to risk being supporters of a murderer? I don't think I could live with it, never mind sentence myself to life in prison. And another thing. We owe Alicia's Mom true justice.' His voice wavered with emotion.

'Craig.' Tom held up the palm of his hand, spreading his fingers wide in emphasis. 'I know it's outside all the moral boundaries, but the bottom line has to be self-preservation. We can moralise all we like, but *think*, deep down?'

'But won't the police think it's a crime of passion?' Craig leaned forward to make his point. 'That means only one person did it. So, if the three of us hand in the other, the killer, we're almost certain to be believed, aren't we?'

'No,' said Tom. 'I've told you. The police will know that it took two people to move the body. At least one strong male. The police will want to know *why*. We can't escape that.'

'I agree,' said Franky. 'Craig, can't you see that?'

'Yes. But the bottom line is that Tom's asking us to trust him in beating CSI. Right, Tom?'

'Yes. It is a matter of trust.'

Craig sighed heavily. 'Tom, look. The police have amazing tools now, don't they? Okay, you majored in forensics at Florida State. But a long time ago. What was it called – forensic chemistry?'

'No, that's just one speciality *within* forensic science – I covered the whole field. I got my degree in that. I was also the top GPA and valedictorian at the finish. I still take *Forensic Magazine* to keep current on all the latest developments and techniques. I could get a job in CSI tomorrow. Maybe near the bottom of the ladder but I believe I could work my way quickly up.'

'That's good enough for me,' said Franky. She bit her lip, keeping her gaze at Craig, nodding her head, urging him on …

Craig frowned, clasped his hands tightly together and stared at the table top. 'But there's no guarantee, is there? If we're wrong, what happens? We're in the lap of the gods. It's … it's the enormity of it all. Tom, can't there be *something* you'd miss? Don't they have tests that show invisible blood nowadays?'

'Yes.'

'And you say you can even deal with that?'

'Yes.'

'What with? Won't you need chemicals – and how the devil, do you get them?'

'When the thaw comes – forecast not long now – I'll get them.'

'Oh, jeez.' Craig sat back, blinking hard. They'd never seen him so animated. '*How?*'

Tom looked at his watch. 'Can we … let me explain the forensics to both of you later. I've got to work it out, take measurements and other things. Then we'll take a vote?' He searched their faces. 'It needs all three of us.' He looked at Craig.

Craig shook his head before lowering it to rest on his arms folded on the table.

Franky, anxious to escape the tension, suddenly stood up. 'Coffee, both of you?'

'Yes,' said Tom. 'We could do with some caffeine. Sharpen minds.'

Craig looked up, raised his head and took a deep breath. 'Yes, thanks, but time's short.' He watched Franky put out the mugs.

She saw him looking. 'Craig, there's something I've not told you – either of you.' She switched the kettle on. 'I went into Hannah's room this morning, and she asked if I'd got any brandy. I'd got a half-bottle. I gave her a drop. She said she felt better. But before I left, I was looking in the wardrobe for something warm for her to put on, and guess what I found? The wine bottle, the one that went missing. She'd taken it, not the landlord. She'd drunk the lot. It put the brandy out of my head and when I left her, I was carrying the empty bottle, but at the back of my mind it was the brandy I was taking back.'

She broke off to flick her fingers in a dismissive gesture. 'I thought no more about it. I can't remember exactly how long it was before I went back to see how she was. She was plastered. She woke up and started looking for her bear. It was nowhere. She accused me, saying I'd taken it. She was getting more and more freaked out, so I had to tell her that Alicia had burnt it.'

'What!' exclaimed Craig. 'Why tell her that?'

'Because she had. I saw her do it.'

Tom peered at her. 'Why – why would she do that?'

Franky hesitated.

'Yes, why should she do that, Franky?' said Craig.

She raised her eyebrows. 'Over you? That was the reason for the murder, Hannah's jealousy?'

Craig grimaced. I can believe that.' He shook his head. 'There was nothing between them and me.'

'But it was there. I know. I saw and heard things you didn't. And add to that all the brandy Hannah drank.'

'I'd no idea,' murmured Craig. 'If I'd known … poor kid. Poor Alicia.'

'It's not your fault,' said Franky. 'You know that.' She suddenly clapped a hand to her mouth. 'Oh, my God, I've just realised something. Hannah will say I provoked her into it. She'll tell them about Alicia and me, the spat we had in the kitchen. You were all witnesses to it!'

'Don't worry about that,' said Tom. 'The police always get suspects blaming someone else. And where's her evidence, outside this cottage?'

'But there was the audition. They'll say I did it to show I was a better actor than Alicia. That's another motive for me killing her. 'Oh my God.' She took a deep breath. 'Everyone will think I hated her for taking my part!'

'Maybe. It would give the police a lead, but nothing more. A motive without evidence is useless. The issue is whether you trust me. If you do, we can avoid all this. I need to know.' He looked at Craig. '*Now.*'

Craig ran a hand over his face. 'This is one big screw-up.' He shook his head in dismay.

Eventually, he looked up. 'Tom?' He paused. 'The way I see it now, you've got a self-confidence that's impressive. In all honesty, on a scale of zero to ten, how much do you truly believe we can get away with it? And I mean *believe*.'

'Nine out of ten.' Tom's voice was level. 'I can't go higher because there's never any absolute certainty in anything. Not in this life. You know that. The issue now is, do you trust me?'

'Dear God,' said Craig quietly. 'I—'

He broke off at the sound of a low flying helicopter approaching *Whup-Whup-Whup,* getting louder, *WHUP – WHUP – WHUP – WHUP – WHUP* – He sat upright as the racket filled the kitchen … and then relaxed as it began to fade … *Whup– whup – whup …whup …*

Franky, closed her eyes. 'Oh my God. For one moment …'

Craig, mouth open, tightened his fist on the table as he battled with himself. It seemed a long time before he looked up at Tom. He gave a nod. 'Okay,' he said quietly. 'Let's do it.'

Tom took a deep breath and got to his feet. 'Good. Now we learn how to clean forensically and then dispose of the body. Franky, will you bring the clothes you were wearing?'

'Yes.'

'And yours Craig.'

'Okay.' He got up to go out.

Franky gestured with her raised hand. Thank you, Craig.'

'No, don't thank me. I think we're in for quite a ride.'

'Oh, Franky,' said Tom. 'You need to get Hannah into the shower for a forensic scrub. Craig and I, must do the same. There's a lot to be done. I'll write it down, in detail. You must follow it to the letter.'

For the last hour Hannah had been sitting by the fire, her thumbnail pressing harder and harder against the tip of her index finger, until it produced a thin crescent of blood, to which she seemed oblivious. Her mind, despite the alcohol, was working, driven by fear and the consequent rush of adrenaline. She ran again through her head the fragments of memory that she'd retained of the moments preceding the murder. She remembered Franky encouraging her to drink brandy as she told her about Craig and Alicia's encounters. She recalled Franky telling her about her bear. She could see the brightly lit kitchen — Franky must have had all the lights switched on, the ceiling spots as well. The shining blade was half out of the block by the open door into the hallway, an open and clear invitation.

What followed, she'd tried to blank out but failed. The icy dash consumed with rage; the moment she first drove the knife into Alicia, as if there was no knife in her grip, just the thump of fist against back. After that the horror, the metallic stink of blood, the bubble from the mouth, the pink froth…

Something at the foot of the fire-grate caught her attention. She bent down to stare at a small round ball that had rolled out from the white ash. She touched it gingerly and found it warm. She picked it up, rubbing away the dust.

She stopped rubbing:

It was one of Bernard's eyes.

She now knew, without a shadow of doubt, that her bear had been burnt and she knew who was responsible. It triggered her mind to fly in all directions, consumed by an overwhelming tide of revulsion, plunged back into the nightmare into which Franky had tricked her. But why? Why betray the only friend she had on campus and that, initially out of pity! It was unbelievable, beyond all comprehension. In her daily prayers she always asked God to protect her. In return she observed the commandments. She accepted that the supremacy of Scripture did not consist in conveying infallible propositions from the natural world. For her to live and understand life, it had to be in terms of the sovereignty of God, personal, holy and loving in which forgiveness was a Christian virtue and a natural necessity. But was it God's will that she spend a lifetime in prison while the real murderer went free? Impossible to even think about it. If arrested, she would tell the police of Franky's trick in framing her. She would prove her membership of The Church of Christ, sincere Christians who followed the ten commandments. It would convince them that she was drugged and connived into murder.

She closed her eyes as another surge of fear flushed through her body. She would still be charged with homicide and, whatever happened with regard to Franky, she could still face a life sentence. There was no alternative. On release from custody – Tom and God willing – she would achieve her own form of justice.

Franky sat in her room, avoiding the inevitable, desperately thinking of a way out. How could she possibly ask Hannah *to do anything*? Having to go eyeball to eyeball in the shower was a dreadful prospect, from which there was no escape. She was shocked and incredulous that, as yet, she'd not given any thought as to what Hannah's reaction might be, having been so blatantly connived into murder. She'd manipulated her as a military commander would a weapon, one to be moved around the field of battle and brought into action at the moment of her choosing. It was *she* who had murdered Alicia, not Hannah.

Alarmed by a heart that seemed to limp and hurry alternately, she listened to another downpour of rain. There were only three days left in England. She knew that she would never return. Unless by extradition? Fear sent her heart racing again.

She seized hold of the paper bag.

A few minutes later she stood outside Hannah's room. Holding her breath, she tapped on the door. After waiting, she knocked again.

Hannah opened the door, her face peering round. 'Oh,' she said.

'Tom says I've got to scrub you.' The words came out weak and breathy.

Hannah stared at her mouth. 'Yes. He told me.'

'Oh.' She felt her lips trembling. 'Now?'

'Yes.'

She came out naked, Franky standing back to allow her to cross the vestibule into the bathroom.

Franky remained still for a moment, in cautious relief. There had been no slamming of the door in her face, no sign of bottled up rage, no promise of revenge in her eyes, not even a curl of the lip.

Hannah stood in the shower and winced at the painful scrubbing, but made no sound. Tom had warned her that Franky might even draw blood, but agreed that it was preferable to spending a lifetime in prison.

Franky crouched at her feet. Having cut Hannah's finger and toenails as close to the cuticles as possible, she was now completing the work, using a sanitiser brought from Alicia's room. Her thoughts were preoccupied with Hannah's trial. She could see and hear the prosecutor address the jury, his voice echoing in her head. "Françoise O'Tierney chose Hannah to be her murder weapon. She got her so drunk that she didn't know what she was doing." He was now pointing at her in the dock. "It is she, ladies and gentlemen of the jury, she is the cowardly and calculating villain in this story – she is the one who committed this foul and heinous murder!"

Franky did another rapid mental check, running through the points in her defence. She'd claim that Hannah had drunk the brandy at leisure, as there could be no evidence that she'd forced it down her throat. At the same time Craig and Tom would testify they heard her shout a warning to Alicia, then chase after Hannah to stop her, but too late. Of course, she'd not intended to kill, or even injure Alicia, by proxy. It all went wrong, simply because she'd thought that, after shouting out her warning, Alicia would have escaped upstairs. She would have snatched the duvet from her bed and easily smothered Hannah with it as soon as she entered, would have dumped her on the floor and, at the risk of suffocating her, demanded she let go of the knife. Wouldn't she?

Franky thought of another point in her favour. It wasn't her fault that Alicia had been so stupid as to run outside in deep snow, clad in thick clothing and heavy shoes, was it? All she'd wanted to do was give her a fright, a mental jolt that was bound to be passed on to Annabelle as a warning to leave her alone, to give the conspiracy pause.

She finished the scrubbing and turned up the spray to wash the remaining soapsuds from Hannah's body.

The spider was back, crawling up her spine.

After sanitising Hannah's back and reminding her to shampoo her hair thoroughly, she wrapped a towel around herself and dashed up to her room, the voices of accusation and rebuttal echoing inside her skull to the point that she could scream.

Chapter Twenty-Five

While she was washing her face, Franky began to weep tears. At first, she didn't realise she was crying at all. The sobs were spaced out and delivered without emotion. *What was it all about?* There was no logic or reason behind it. She looked at her reflection in the bathroom mirror and thought she looked appalling. Then she found she was shaking all over and became frightened, simply because she felt nothing, nothing at all. Was it *delayed shock?*

She went to find Tom, as much as to seek calm and reassurance as to report on the state of Hannah. They were busy in the woodshed. Tom was sitting on a dirty green plastic chair and trying on rubber boots, one of two pairs they'd found by the woodpile.

'Amazing,' said Tom, stamping his feet. 'They actually fit.'

'I don't think mine do ... 'panted Craig. Grimacing, he gripped hold of more rubber and gave an almighty tug ... 'Hah!' The boot fitted. 'Rather tight, but beggars can't be choosers. How is she?' he said momentarily out of breath.

'She's already asleep.'

'Good to hear.'

'How much Temazapam did she take?' said Tom.

'Forty mill.'

'How long will she sleep with that - any idea?'

'I don't know. The most I've taken was thirty mill. I'd think she'd be out for at least eight hours.'

'Even better,' said Tom. 'Well done.'

Putting on gloves, Tom and Craig went outside, round to the back of the woodshed. There, they rolled Alicia's body into the middle of a large sheet of plastic, also taken from the woodshed. They folded the rest of the plastic back over the body and weighed it down with bricks left over from the cottage extension. They took immense care not to contaminate themselves.

They drank coffee in the kitchen, allowing Tom to outline his plan of action: items of clothing and footwear, that might be difficult to clean forensically, would be burnt in a fire laid on the killing ground. Nail-polish remover, containing acetone, would make a good fire accelerant. The residue would be burnt on the living-room fire. The rubber boots would be individually cycled in the washing machine at a temperature of 30 degrees centigrade and, when dry, would be caked with mud and put back in the woodshed.

'What about *her*?' said Franky, gesturing towards outside. 'Do we need to - you know?'

'Clean the body? No. The blood is all Alicia's. We're certain to have left our DNA on her but remember, we all lived a close-knit family life, so it would prove nothing.'

'So how do we get rid of Alicia's bloodstains on our shoes and clothes?' said Craig.

'We use oxygen bleach,' said Tom.

'Oxygen bleach?' Craig gave him a frown. 'Are you serious - you do mean the washing powder?'

'I do indeed. We need to buy some. The luminol and phenolphthalein that CSI use won't detect haemoglobin, not if we soak contaminated clothes in the bleach. Stains may still be visible, but it's the haemoglobin that gives blood its identity. Destroy those markers and you're safe.'

Craig blinked, mouth open, giving a little shake of the head.

'What about the bathroom?' said Franky. 'All those little coils in the shower hose, the hinges, the back of the radiator, all those intricate, tiny places?'

'We'll coat them thoroughly in it, using brushes. There's a couple in the shed. Don't worry. The bleach will do the job, but it still requires a long session in the bathroom.' He looked at his watch. 'What time does the supermarket close in Stratford?'

'Tesco doesn't,' said Franky. 'They're 24/7, except Sundays and Mondays.'

'Could the clothes be cut up and put in the septic tank?' asked Craig.

Tom shook his head. 'No, that's the first place CSI would look. No, we decontaminate, bleach, scrub or burn. That's the procedure. Craig, I think you and I should make a start in the bathroom.'

'Tom?' said Craig. 'I owe you an apology. You could sell me anything.'

'Thank me when it's over,' said Tom, tapping his arm with a smile. 'Let's go.'

They began work. Cleaning liquids were brought from the laundry room. Tom had no compunction in taking Alicia's toothbrush for scrubbing the linkage, hinge and nozzle of the shower hose and, in particular, the drain holes of the bath and shower. A mini-screwdriver kit was found in a kitchen drawer, ideal for other delicate work. A large towel cut into pieces would be used for drying any item that required burning. Polishing cloths, judged fluff-free enough to assist the work, would afterwards be burnt, along with the toothbrush.

As an afterthought he added 'magnifying glass' to his shopping list. He remembered coming across a tiny shop in Stratford that specialised in all manner of new and used optical equipment.

Tom suddenly looked outside. Rain was bucketing down. It soon became torrential. 'Thank God for the vagaries of the British weather,' he murmured.

He was joined by Craig and Franky, staring out at the downpour. After a moment they looked at each other in relief.

An hour and a half later, most of the snow had turned into slush, making the lane passable to traffic.

Craig and Franky set off for the supermarket, leaving Tom alone in the cottage. First, he checked in on Hannah. She was still fast asleep.

Outside, he paced out the killing zone, measuring its dimensions for blood splatter, allowing space on all four sides in case of error.

He performed the same task along the route that he and Craig had taken while dragging the body to the rear of the woodshed. He did the same when estimating the "corridors" that the three of them had taken, from the murder scene back to the cottage. He calculated that the overall area to be scrutinised amounted to around fifty square yards. Mentally, he added a further ten, to be on the safe side.

Meanwhile Franky and Craig, on the journey into town, had been discussing the events that had taken place and what was likely to follow.

'Tom knows a lot,' said Craig, 'but does he know everything? That's the problem.'

'I'm scared,' said Franky. 'How about you?'

Craig hesitated. 'Of course. But Tom's the bellwether in all this. Look how he's changed. A different guy, no longer the dilettante. I think he knows what he's doing. At least I hope so.'

'I hope so too. I can't believe we're doing this.'

'The worst part's to come.'

She looked at him sharply, taking in his grim expression as he drove. 'You mean moving her? I feel sick even thinking about it.'

'What we're doing is disgusting. In every way.' He gripped the wheel as he saw a police car approaching, keeping his gaze on the road ahead.

It was something that Franky dreaded: the disposal of the body. It was one thing to picture it hidden from view at the back of the woodshed, but another to imagine herself handling a greasy, bloodstained corpse. The image it conjured up, produced not only feelings of nausea but also a growing and unremitting sense of guilt that no self-justification or argument could shut out.

On the return journey, with a dirty old magnifying glass as one of their purchases, they splashed through slush and pools of black water with Franky shrinking further and further into herself, yearning for a safe place with a drawbridge that she could pull up against the world.

She stared out at the drab hedgerows and lifeless fields and wondered at the idiocy of anyone believing in God. Religions were fashioned out of fear and vanity. Fear of the unknown prompted them to invent gods who could be buttered up due to their powers of mercy and deliverance. Vanity, also, played a big part, with a general reluctance and disinclination to accept that humans were basically mammals, distinguished only by a cognitive thinking brain. The Christian idea of original sin was of no use whatsoever. At college she'd preferred Steinbeck to Graham Greene, thinking that his novel, *The Pearl* placed man on the animal level, a far more comforting position than Greene's forays into morality, amorality and original sin.

What she would give to turn back the clock! She broke down, sobbing for the life that she had, the life she had taken and now, Hannah, the life she had ruined.

Craig glanced at her. 'Yes. Cry now,' he said, in a gentle rumble of a voice. 'It's best.'

Franky looked at him in her tears. If only he knew the truth.

They were back at the cottage within forty-five minutes of setting out, Franky carrying two packs of 'OXY Power', the commercial name for oxygen bleach, the total weight 1,000 grams.

'More than enough,' said Tom. 'Well done.'

He examined the packet. 'While you were out, I had a call from someone on the neighbourhood watch committee.'

'What!' Franky exclaimed, her face draining pale.

'Oh, not that. He wanted to contact the previous tenants. Don't worry.'

Franky was told to change her shoes and put on a fresh pair, after which Tom encased them in plastic bags, tying them around her ankles with knotted string. He and Craig put on the rubber boots. Franky had a pair of cosmetic tweezers and Craig a pair of pliers, while Tom had possession of a clean magnifying glass.

They all wore gloves.

Tom went outside and began marking out the areas to be scrutinised, using bits of wood to define "corridor widths." His final instruction to Franky and Craig was that any material found – other than vegetation and however small – had to be placed in a large jug, taken from the kitchen.

'Any doubt,' he said, 'pick up whatever it is and put it in there. If in doubt as to what it is, I'll use the magnifying glass.'

They began their task, Franky and Tom having rubber mats on which to kneel, both taken from the bathrooms. Craig had the use of a garden kneeler.

Tom knelt at the head of the first "corridor." He insisted they kept in a straight line, with himself as the right-hand marker to judge by. It was cold, awkward and painstaking work, frequently forcing them to stand upright to ease their cold and aching limbs.

They covered the total area in just over three hours, after which Tom emptied the jug's contents on to a baking tray that he slid into the oven, setting a high temperature. Suddenly he spotted Craig heading into the hallway toilet and called out to stop him.

'Craig. If you want to pee can you wait? We need it.'

Craig stared at Tom, as he came up to explain why.

At 3.25 p.m. Tom and Craig went out into the gathering gloom carrying a bucketful of bleach. Tom also took with him a stainless-steel colander. They went to stand opposite each other on both sides of the killing zone, where Tom placed the colander on the ground and unzipped his pants.

Craig followed suit. Between them they urinated over the whole killing area. Tom then picked up the colander and Craig the bucket. Standing side by side Craig poured bleach into the colander that Tom swept sideways, covering a strip of ground at a time. By this means the killing area – and more, as a precaution – was covered.

Craig paused at a sudden thought. 'But won't CSI see or detect we've done this? It won't take a genius to work out why.'

'Possibly, but it can't prove anything. They'll be highly suspicious, but they can't charge without evidence.'

Finally, Tom poured plenty of oxygen bleach along the corridor along which they had dragged the body. 'The rain should have got rid of bloodstains but we're not taking any risks,' he said.

It was completely dark by the time they finished.

Tom went into the kitchen to collect the contents of the jug from the baking tray. Outside, by flashlight, Craig scattered the bits and pieces on to the kindling that lay in the middle of the killing ground.

Suddenly, the darkness lifted.

Tom stopped to gaze up at the sky. 'Oh no,' he groaned, prompting Craig to follow his gaze.

A large full moon had appeared, its pale blue light illuminating the cottage and the field beyond.

'What?' Craig asked, in concern.

'The moon. We can't hide the body in this light.' Tom dribbled nail polish over the pyre and struck a match.

The fire was lit.

Back in the cottage, with the acrid smell of bleach everywhere, they found Franky, a large handkerchief wrapped around her mouth, brushing the wet laundry-room floor.

'Tom.' She stopped what she was doing. 'I'm worried. I can't help it. What about blood in the soil? Won't CSI scrape up all the top soil and grass and sieve it, or whatever?'

'Yes, they will. CSI can detect blood invisible to the eye. But urine shows up in forensic light, exactly as blood does, so it proves nothing and the bleach on the corridors covers more than we needed. I wanted to be absolutely sure.'

Franky wanted to question him further, but Craig got in first. 'Tom. What about the shower curtain? Won't it leave molten stuff that—'

'No,' said Tom. 'The shower curtain isn't plastic. I checked. It's hemp. It leaves only ash.'

'The plastic shoe covers?' asked Franky.

'We'll get rid of the residue. In any case, it wouldn't be used as evidence.'

'Good.' Franky gave a big sigh. She didn't ask further questions and, to her relief, neither did Craig.

The fire on the killing ground was out, leaving only a small pile of charred material. Tom scraped up all of the residue, placed it in the bucket, took it indoors and emptied the bits onto the inglenook fire.

He then relaxed in the kitchen, picking up a hard biscuit that he'd nibbled earlier. 'One day,' he said, 'they might talk about "The curious and unsolved case at the Institute".' He bit into the biscuit. 'Very Sherlockian.'

'And subtitle it "A Shakespearean Tragedy"?' said Franky. 'How I wish.'

'It's a book I'll never read,' said Craig grimly.

Franky let out a soft sigh. Would it always be like this? What was her greater fear, being arrested on a charge of assisting a murderer, or facing some dire fate at the hands of the conspirators?

But, she suddenly realised, there were now only three left, Annabelle, Brooklyn—and *him*, her father. Hannah was out of it, mired in fear. And she could now eliminate Tom. In attempting to save all four of them from arrest, he'd proved, beyond doubt, that he was not a member. If he were involved, he would have planted forensic evidence to secure her arrest, wouldn't he, the expert that he was?

And Alicia … it caused anguish to even think of her … was gone entirely.

They sat at the dining table eating chicken with salad.

'There's a problem along with moonlight. 'Tom paused. 'My forensic site tells me that dead bodies are more likely to be discovered in England than almost any country in the world.'

'Why is that?' said Franky, frowning. So far, she had eaten little in her anxiety.

'It's densely populated and it's a small country. Footpaths connect village to village. There are dog walkers, joggers, hikers, farm workers and mushroom foragers. Bodies are usually found in winter, around now, when there's little ground cover. And we don't know how much CCTV is used.'

He waved his fork. 'Farming methods. Electric fences – we know nothing. Which is the deepest reservoir? Where is it? Are the gates locked? Would we choose a place where they shoot for game? And what would we do if we tried to bury it and hit rock? Noise carries far in the countryside at night.' He dug once more into his chicken.

'But you said we need to move her tonight.' Franky gave him a nervous look.

'I did. And we must.'

'Will CSI use thermal-imaging cameras?' said Craig.

'In this weather, no, too cold. They now have cameras that measure changes in light coming from soil and plants.'

'But, erm,' Franky hesitated. 'If she's likely to be found, why don't we put her where we wouldn't be suspected of doing it?'

'How do you mean?' said Craig.

'Like if we put her somewhere at the Institute, no one would imagine students doing it, would they?'

'At the *Institute*?' Craig stared at her.

'Students who are intelligent, I mean. Okay, anyone with any common sense. They wouldn't do it on their own ground? The police wouldn't suspect. Would they?'

Tom regarded her thoughtfully.

'What I'm saying is, if she'd be found at some point, does it make any difference *when*? That is, if we leave no evidence.'

'Far too dangerous,' Craig said. 'Isn't it?' He looked to Tom.

'I'm thinking we should go up the garden,' said Franky. 'On the right-hand side, the shrubbery's so dense you can't see into it. But there is a way in. Go past the Shakespeare plinth to the wall and look right. Between the brick wall and the shrubbery there's a gap. I know so because the wind blew one of my notes in there and I had to go find it. What do you think, Tom?'

Tom had a finger resting on his chin, still deep in thought. He looked up. 'It would need to be someone who not only knows the place, but also when the car park's open.'

'I think this is crazy.' Craig, having already stopped eating, stared at Tom. 'What if the police think it's a double bluff, that we *are* that intelligent to think of it?'

'They may think of it, yes,' said Tom. 'But they go on evidence. The body should reveal nothing, except the cause and, possibly the time of death and the fact it had been brought there. The drag marks would show it came from the car park, not the Institute.'

'Does it matter if the police know it was brought by car?' said Franky. 'You're happy with the trunk, Tom? You can make sure it will be forensically clean?'

'Yes.' He removed the finger from his chin. 'Of course. But we're bound to be suspect, the four of us. That won't change whatever we do. The police will know it's someone who knows the garden, plus the access and closing times. I doubt they'll think of it as a double bluff. But there's something else, in our favour. The body, closer to us, is less of a worry than one that's miles away. If it's found at the Institute while we're here, then we'll know immediately. The Institute will be in lockdown, and we can prepare ourselves for the questioning. If it's found miles away, we may be arrested without being prepared. A tactic of the police is to encourage suspects to think they know more than they do. If we do this, it's unlikely they'll be able to fool us. We'll prepare a story that we all stick to. That's essential.'

'Are you worried about Hannah?' said Franky. 'Because I am. She could say or do anything.'

'That is our weakness.' Tom drank wine from his glass. 'I'm going to talk to her. She'll need careful handling.'

'So, it all hangs on the forensics then.' Craig hesitated. 'Tom, this is a place where we work. We'll be in the conservatory knowing the …' lowering his head he furrowed his brows… 'knowing she's there,' he added quietly, closing his eyes.

'And there's always the smell,' said Franky.

'Unlikely in winter' said Tom. Gardening is in abeyance and she's by the wall, a long way from the path. But again, we'd be ready.' He hesitated. 'Craig. The answer to your problem is not to look.'

'Even so. We'll constantly think about it. Won't we?'

'Yes. I'll never stop thinking about it,' said Franky.' Nauseated, she suddenly put down her knife and fork. 'Sorry, but I'm not hungry,' she said and went out to the cloakroom.

'Tom.' Craig was trying to formulate some words, searching for them. 'I get your confidence.' He looked at him. 'You're basing it on your knowledge. But I have to ask … what if a new development in forensics isn't reported yet and they're using it, something as fabulously new as DNA was in the early days?'

'No. I told you I keep up with the latest technology. I have a subscription to the periodical. I knew about the hyperspectral camera, the one I just told you about, that shows changes in light. I knew about it before it was even used by a police force. Remember, I still need that trust. Because if I don't have it, I won't be able to work out the pitfalls to come. Not with any certainty.' He raised his eyebrows. 'Do you still trust me?'

There was a drawn-out moment in which Craig remained motionless, until he nodded. 'Yes. We'll do it. At least she'll be found sometime and the family can get decent closure.'

'Good.' Tom, in relief, looked at his watch. 'The car park's open till ten tonight. But it's always empty, by eight. When we get there, I'll go in first and check there's no one around.'

'I'm still worried about Hannah,' said Craig. 'How is she going to stand up to questioning?'

'That's why I'm going to talk to her.' Tom hesitated. 'There's one more thing. Before we do anything, we must call Alicia's number to prove we're missing her tonight. At least two of us should call between eight and eight thirty.'

'What about Alicia's cell? If the police find her GPS and SIM card? Even if they're damaged or missing, it can still be traced to here, can't it?'

'No,' said Tom. 'It's the chip inside that actually locates it. I smashed it, then lost it with the rest.'

'Good,' said Craig in relief. 'But I'm still worried about Hannah. I just can't help it.'

Hannah's dream featured a huge clock staring down at her. It was set in a tower at the junction of many streets. At her feet lay a body in blood-red snow. Time on the clock had stopped, the fingers bent out of shape. Shady, indefinable images thrashed at the walls of her skull, like trapped birds in a panic. She hurried towards the blanket of virgin snow that lay ahead, but the faster she ran, the further off it became. She sped past large store windows full of headless mannequins and shining blades, on and on to an archway, where she saw a filthy sleeping bag, slashed in places, its white cheap-polyester innards exposed. Coils of brown greasy hair poked out, slithering onto layers of damp cardboard like snakes wriggling to escape.

She turned round to find a gigantic truck bearing down on her, the hunched driver squinting through his windscreen at her hands held up in horror, hands dripping blood.

It was 8.06 p.m. when Hannah, wrapped in a dressing gown, left the kitchen with Tom. She'd eaten porridge and honey, while listening to him counsel and instruct her, as he laid out his plan of action.

Franky, sitting on the settee, dreaded her appearance, fearful that she will have told Tom what happened, how she'd been driven by her to commit the foulest of crimes.

She could hear Tom's voice as he and Hannah approached the living room. She moved quickly to an armchair that was furthest away from the fire—Hannah would sit nearer—and out of her eye-line.

She caught her breath as the door opened. Tom entered, leading in Hannah. Her face looked polished, almost as shiny as her hair, a world away from the Hannah whose scream of rage still resonated inside her head.

Hannah took the chair nearest the fire and opposite Tom. Having taken sedatives, her expression was calm. Too calm. Where was her fear of arrest, of being locked up for life? Where was the guilt? Where was the ugly stare at the person who had driven her to murder?

'Warm enough?' said Tom gently. He had a notebook at the ready.

Hannah nodded slightly. 'Yes.' She sounded relaxed.

'Hannah.' Tom spoke carefully. 'We've already called Alicia to show how worried we are that she hasn't arrived back. Will you call,' he looked at his watch, 'say, in twenty minutes?'

'But you said her cell has been destroyed.'

'It has but the phone company still keeps messages and all calls are saved in case of police investigations. Just leave a message asking if she's all right, it being so late. Can you remember to do that?'

'Yes.'

'Hannah. Concentrate. If she's found, it's important our stories are the same. Let's see if you remember. I'm the police, doing the interview. Hannah, when did you last see Alicia?'

'Erm … yesterday afternoon. About four— I think.'

'Where?'

'At the Institute. I saw her going into a lecture.'

'Did you kill Alicia?'

'No.'

'Do you know who did?'

'No, I don't.'

'Did you like Alicia?'

'Erm, I didn't dislike her ...'

'But you didn't like her, *did* you.'

Hannah opened her mouth to reply, but hesitated, blinking slowly.

Tom stared hard at her. It had the effect of averting Hannah's gaze.

'Hannah.' Tom paused, speaking gently. 'I don't think you should answer any questions. Too dangerous. But, at the same time, we don't want you to keep saying "no comment." Because you're at risk— you've been through a horrific nightmare—you can't be certain how you'll react. If she's found we'll be questioned, each of us. Alicia was living with us, so it could happen. The police assess body language, how you sound and how you look. We discussed this. The choice is, that you either keep up an act of being distressed, or catatonic. Whichever you decide, you must maintain it, for hours, maybe days. You do understand that?'

'Yes.'

'So, have you decided? Catatonic or distressed? Which do you choose?'

'Catatonic. I think it's easier.'

'Good. It's a part for which you'll never win an Oscar, but it should be that good. Remember, you must keep it up, even if you don't think you're being watched. It's likely there'll be a video camera in your cell *if* you're arrested. Remember, if she's found we will automatically become suspects and suspects have rights. The police have the need to get answers, but they won't question you if you're in a catatonic state. Why? Because they know that any confession, or anything you say, can be argued by the defence as worthless in court.'

'Yes.' Hannah nodded. 'I'll look up catatonic. I'll get into the part.' She glanced at Craig. 'Will you have to put on an act, Craig?'

Before Craig could reply, she suddenly turned round. 'Will you— Franky?'

A coil of fear wrenched Franky's stomach.

It was an expression that flashed the message:

You face the utmost danger, not me.

An hour later, the car had been turned around to face the lane, its engine idling in a cloud of fumes. The trunk lid was open, acting as a screen should a passerby, or motorist, see a long, large and plastic-covered package being manhandled at the rear of the car. They needn't have bothered. No one came, either by vehicle, cycle or on foot.

Under Tom's direction, wearing gloves, they ensured that the corpse would not contaminate the trunk, nor themselves.

'Hannah? You okay?' Craig looked into the living room before setting off.

'Yes. I'm fine.' Hannah was crouched in the inglenook, her face lit up by the fire.

'Sure?'

'Yes.'

Craig thought of adding something else, but finally nodded. 'See you later.'

Hannah listened to the front door shutting and, after a few moments, the car starting and moving away.

Even before they reached the suburbs, Franky could see colourful lights glowing over the town ahead. She had not seen any before and wondered what it was about, and then remembered: Christmas.

She looked at Craig. He was staring rigidly ahead, both hands on the wheel, driving smoothly and carefully.

She remembered that, whenever a funeral cortège passed her by, there were always pale and sombre looking faces peering out from the long black limousines, purring softly behind the hearse. No one inside would speak. How could they, embarrassed and shaken by death, lost in their own grief and sadness.

The sudden whoop and wail of a police-siren, caught her by the throat, had her struggling for breath. Then came flashing blue lights with the siren changing in pitch, creating the Doppler effect as the marked car overtook them and sped away. She closed her eyes in relief.

They entered Evesham Place and turned slowly into Chestnut Walk where looping rows of Christmas lighting illuminated the houses that ran parallel with the Institute wall.

Craig stopped the car to peer through the windscreen. 'They're open,' he said in relief, seeing the space in the wall, with the gates pulled back.

Tom stepped out of the car and looked around, before starting to walk slowly down the opposite side of the street that was all housing. There was enough seasonal lighting for him to focus on doorway surrounds, as well as the sides of each house. He double-checked by performing the same routine on his way back to the car. Halfway up the street he disappeared inside the Institute car park gates. He was soon back. 'No cameras anywhere,' he said, getting into the passenger seat.

Once parked inside the gates, they checked their improvised shoe covers, before putting on gloves.

Craig and Tom hauled the shrouded body from the trunk, while Franky kept watch at the car park entrance.

They quickly rolled the corpse out of its plastic covers and dragged it towards the shrubbery.

Franky looked up and down the street. Still clear.

Craig and Tom were soon back, packing the plastic sheeting carefully back in the trunk. Their return to the cottage was conducted, as it had been on the outward journey, in complete silence.

On arrival back at the cottage, the plastic sheeting was taken from the car and subjected to a sanitised wash before placing it back where it came from, at the rear of the log pile.

The car trunk was given similar treatment.

Chapter Twenty-Six

It was early morning. Outside the Shakespeare Institute, an elderly man, wearing overalls and with a springer spaniel on a lead, pressed four buttons on a brass plate fixed to the wall. The adjacent front-door clicked open.

Entering, he closed the automatic locking door and bent down to unfasten the springer spaniel's lead, its tail wagging furiously.

On release it raced into the conservatory to stand at the door to the garden, stepping impatiently back and forth like a manic line-dancer.

The caretaker's first task of the day was to unlock the double gates to the car park. As he went out of the conservatory into the garden, the dog left him to pad quickly around the lawn, its nose fast-seeking a trail on the ground. On most mornings it would stop at Shakespeare's bust, lift a leg and pee over his noble head, before trotting towards the copper beech.

Today, however, William Shakespeare escaped that indignity as it picked up a strong line of scent that led all the way to the brick wall bordering the shrubbery. Nosing its way inside, it disappeared within to forage among the greenery.

The caretaker, having pushed each of the two gates wide open, was walking back towards the house when suddenly the dog started barking and kept barking. That was, in itself, a highly unusual occurrence.

So, when he spotted the springer's black and white head bobbing back and forth, naturally he went to investigate.

Tom digested his last portion of breakfast cereal and glanced at Franky, sitting opposite. 'Franky, would you take a look at Hannah, see if she's going in with us?'

Franky stared at him, caught in alarm. 'She's still asleep. I looked in.'

'Yes, but time's vital now. Everything must be done as per normal. Would you mind?'

How could she not mind? How could she refuse?

With a sinking stomach, Franky stood up and went into the vestibule. Would Hannah look at her with the same expression as the night before?

Holding her breath, she raised her hand, swallowed hard, licked her lips and tapped on the door, grimacing in fearful expectation.

After waiting, she knocked again, holding her breath.

Hannah, fully dressed, opened the door, recoiling slightly in sudden surprise, her face set grimly. 'Yes?' She stared at Franky's mouth.

'How are you now?' Franky's voice was taut.

'Tired.' Hannah spoke slowly in a manner that signalled: *How do you expect me to feel?*

'We're going soon. Are you coming?'

'I won't be going in.' Hannah narrowed her eyes, still staring at Franky's mouth.

'Tom thinks you should.'

'No.'

She felt a desperate urge to hug and embrace Hannah, to throw herself on her mercy, but before she could do, or say anything, the door was closed in her face.

After the breakfast crockery had been loaded into the dishwasher, Tom glanced at his watch.

'Franky, could you look in again on Hannah?'

'It's pointless. She's adamant, Tom. She's staying.' She was relieved that he accepted it.

At 8.58 a.m. they set off for the Institute, Tom in the front passenger seat, Franky curled up in the rear, alone. They remained silent.

After a short while, Craig switched on *Touch FM*, the local radio station.

There came two minutes of bright and bubbly commercials ending with an upbeat advertisement for Stratford's Christmas street market. It was followed by a transatlantic male voice sounding punchy and dramatic: 'On air – on line – on Touch FM – local news at 9 UK!'

A female newsreader took over: 'Breaking news. Within the last hour a body has been found at The Shakespeare Institute in Church Street, Stratford. Police are investigating. Nothing more is known at this time. We will keep you informed of any developments throughout the day.' Pause. 'The mayor of Stratford, Councillor Will Maskell, has called for a special inquiry into —'

Craig switched off the radio. A hundred yards ahead was a lay-by.

He pulled into it, stopped and cut the engine. They listened to the spasmodic whoosh and rumble of passing traffic and their own, heavy breathing inside the car.

'Oh God,' said Franky, with a shudder.

'No,' said Tom abruptly. 'Just...' He raised a hand. 'Wait. Think.'

'Tom,' said Craig. 'We need to go in as normal.'

'Yes.' Tom puckered his brow. 'I know.'

'I can't believe it.' Franky's voice was hoarse.

'Stay calm,' said Tom. 'There'll be police outside. The place will be on lockdown, including the garden and car park.' He paused, then continued in a firmer voice. 'We didn't hear the news. We drive down to turn in as usual. There'll be someone there to re-direct us or tell us what to do. We know nothing. You okay with that, Craig?'

'Yes. It's the only thing we can do.'

'Franky?'

'Yes,' she said in a strained voice.

Ten minutes later they turned off Shottery Road into Evesham Place. Tom's face was set, his eyes glittering.

As soon as they turned into Chestnut Walk it was evident that they would be denied entrance to the car park. Outside the open gates stood a uniformed policeman at the side of a white forensics van with blue markings, its rear doors pulled back. Beyond the van were two other uniformed PCs, standing alongside three marked police cars, parked in a zig-zag across the road, allowing dead-slow street access only.

'Stop, Craig,' said Tom. 'I'll talk to him.'

Tom slid down his window as Craig drew up at the kerbside, a few yards short of the van. The PC came to Tom, bending down to him. 'Yes sir?'

'Officer,' said Tom. 'We're students here. What's happened?'

The PC took a quick look inside the car, first glancing at Franky and then Craig, before turning back to Tom. 'Are you all students?'

'Yes.'

'Have you ID?'

Craig took out his university identity card, displaying it.

The PC nodded. 'Okay, turn left to the Institute entrance. Stop the car outside. Someone will talk to you.' He retreated back to his guard position.

A plain-clothes detective appeared from inside the gates, staring at them as they drew away.

Having navigated the zig-zag, they turned left into Church Street.

Thirty yards ahead, two police cars and a blue van were parked outside the Institute. A PC stood on the stone doorstep addressing a group of students. His explanation over, they were shepherded through the front door.

As soon as Craig pulled up in line with the parked vehicles, Tom opened his door to face the approaching PC.

'We're students here, officer. Can you tell us what's happened?'

'There's been a serious incident. Please go inside.' He went round the front of the car to speak to Craig. 'Where do you normally park?'

Craig gestured back. 'The Institute car park.'

'That's out of bounds. Go straight on and pick up the blue carpark sign. Follow it and park there.'

Craig waited for Tom and Franky to get out of the car and then drove away.

The PC turned aside, touching his earpiece as he listened to a message. In reply he spoke animatedly along with a frustrated gesture at Craig's disappearing car.

Then he moved quickly to stop Tom and Franky entering the Institute.

Detective Chief Inspector Rees, as one of the two senior investigating officers in the county of Warwickshire, drove as fast as she dared towards Stratford, her blue lights flashing. The 'shout' she'd received on her mobile had informed her that a corpse had been found at The Shakespeare Institute. The message ended: *Rep. Asap, MIR Roth.* Decoded, it read: "Repeat. Hurry to major incident room at Stratford police station.'

She called Detective Inspector Drake, her deputy SIO. 'On my way,' she said. 'Sorry for being late. I missed the shout.'

'Don't worry,' he replied. 'I've done the golden hour. No lead – *yet*. She was one of five American students living in a cottage, near Shottery. I've nicked two of them on suss. We're picking up one at the cottage, and there's another loose somewhere. A Craig Muirhaven.'

As Rees entered the town, she caught a momentary glimpse of a shrouded leisure boat on water, before the left turn into High Street.

At the junction of Rother Street and Scholars Lane she took another left to be immediately shocked at the sight of a white BMW 7 series heading straight at her. Tyres screeched as both drivers braked hard. Too late. A bang of metal was followed by the tinkling of broken glass, the male driver rocking back in shock and amazement at what he'd done.

She was quick out of the car, the driver putting up a hand in apology as she opened his door.

'Police.' She flashed her warrant card. 'Have you been drinking?'

'Oh, no. I'm really sorry,' said Craig, in his deep bass voice. 'Forgot I'm in England.'

'Get in my car.' She looked at the frontal damage to both cars. It appeared they were drivable.

He got inside to join her. 'I really am sorry. Since I've been here, I've kept telling myself don't turn left into traffic.'

'Right.'

'Pardon me?'

'You don't turn *right* into left-sided traffic. You're sitting on my bag.'

'Oh, yes. I'm sorry.' He dragged the bag from underneath him and shook his head, his face mournful.

'Okay,' she said. 'I'm in a big hurry. Stay here. I'll get someone from the police station to come and take your details. Here's my card. And don't move the car. They'll want to photograph it.'

'Police station? Don't we just exchange insurance details?'

'No! You've just committed a traffic offence. What do you expect?'

'Oh, of course.' He sat back and grimaced. 'I really am sorry.'

She gave him a quick scrutiny. Early thirties she guessed, tweed jacket, brown corduroy trousers, nice open face, intelligent-looking.

'You American?'

'Yes.'

'Doing what?'

'I'm a postgrad student.'

'Where?'

'The Shakespeare Institute.'

Rees stared through the wet windscreen. 'What's your name?'

'Craig Muirhaven.'

Rees consulted her screen, then pressed a button to close all four door-locks.

She looked at him. 'You were in a heck of a hurry. Why the panic? Did something upset you? Something worrying?'

'No. No, honestly. I couldn't park at the Institute. The police said something's happened there.'

She keyed the mike clipped to her front lapel, summarising what had happened, asked for backup and ended with, 'I'm taking him to the station.'

She turned to Craig. 'I'm arresting you on suspicion of murder. You do not have to say anything, but it may harm your defence if you do not mention when questioned, something which you later may rely on in court. Anything you do say may be given in evidence.'

Chapter Twenty-Seven

The four students sat in the custody suite at Rother Street police station. Keeping an eye on them was the custody sergeant. Perched on a raised dais, and protected by a glass screen, he looked rather like a strict teacher, surveying a Victorian classroom.

Tom stared at Hannah, sitting opposite. She seemed to be following his instructions in so far as her face was drawn, the only sign of "life" being an occasional and laborious movement of her arms or legs. With four CCTV cameras in use, it was vital that she stuck to her script. But was it physically and mentally possible to stage the appearance of a catatonic state for the many hours that she would spend there?

'I was determined to give up smoking, coming here,' said Tom, careful to appear relaxed. 'I thought I'd achieved it two days ago. I was congratulating myself and now I find myself in dire need of a cigarette.'

'I need something stronger,' said Franky, with a look at Hannah. Despite her semblance of stupor, was there a ghost of a contemptuous smile as she dolefully stared in her direction?

She looked quickly away to watch the custody sergeant end his phone call. She had the dreadful feeling that, having entered the building through a solid bombproof door, there would be no going back.

'Do you know the vernacular for a cigarette over here?' said Tom, addressing no one in particular. 'Fags. But no sexual connotation. And lawyers are called solicitors. Another odd label, don't you think?'

He broke off as Rees entered and summoned Craig to stand with her in front of the desk.

The sergeant looked down through the security window. 'Okay, Ma'am. Name and reason for arrest?'

'This is Craig Muirhaven,' said Rees. 'I've arrested him on suspicion of murder.'

The sergeant tapped in the facts and then addressed Craig. 'I'm here to make sure you keep fit and well. You're now going in a cell. You'll remain with us for twenty-four hours unless you're released earlier. If it's felt we need to question you further then you may be kept here another twelve hours. Do you understand?'

'Yes.'

'Would you like a drink of anything?'

'Yes, thanks. Coffee, if that's okay. No milk or sugar.'

After Craig was booked in, he submitted to a DNA swab and a blood sample. Finally, his fingerprints were taken.

He was then led to a cell. Shortly afterwards the other three were similarly cautioned and led to their cells.

DI Drake and DCI Rees returned to the police station after visiting the crime scene.

They entered the empty custody suite.

'One thing's certain,' said Rees. 'Whoever brought the body must have done it by car or van while it was dark. And somebody who knew the gap in the shrubbery.'

'Well,' said Drake. 'The only student at the Institute with a car *and* an IDP, is Craig Muirhaven.'

He led her into the cell corridor to slide back the peep-hole cover of the first cell they arrived at and stood back. 'Here he is,' he announced with a grin. 'The guy whose car you took on.'

She smiled. 'It wasn't a bullfight.' She watched Craig who was stretched out on the regulation blue mattress, both hands clasped behind his head and staring at the ceiling. He looked mournful.

She stood back. 'Reminds me of the "Marlboro Cowboy."'

'The what?'

'It was a TV commercial. A guy on horseback wearing jeans and a Stetson with a Marlboro cigarette in his mouth. It ran for nearly fifty years, here as well as America.'

Drake showed her Franky's cell. She was sitting with crossed legs on the mattress, her slim body erect, her blue eyes fixed.

'Looks like she's doing yoga,' she murmured. 'I wonder if she's as fiery as her hair.'

They moved on.

'This guy is Tom Vantusian. Reminds me of a headmaster I once had.'

Rees looked into the cell to see Tom standing, wrapt in deep thought, a forefinger at his chin.

'A deep one,' she said. 'Looks like he's working something out.'

'And Hannah Bron.'

Rees looked into the next cell to see her sitting on the plastic mattress, her head against the wall. Her hangdog expression and slack jaw seemed steady, but then her brows suddenly drew tightly together, as if showing pain. Then, as quickly as it disappeared, her dull expression was back, her mouth drooping once more.

'Hmm,' Rees murmured, standing upright. 'Looks like she's had one heck of a shock, that one.'

Hannah caught a flash of the peephole shutter closing as Rees and Drake left the scene. Lying sideways, she peered at the wall. Inches from her eyes was a faint drawing, scratched into the paintwork. She'd been trying to figure out what it was and now, with the coast clear, took the opportunity. How had it been done? Not by a knife. A sharp fingernail? Possibly. She shifted her position to get a better view. It quickly became the outline of a prehistoric mammoth. She'd seen them in a documentary of the cave at Lascaux in France.

Forgetting the instruction to remain catatonic, she grinned at first and then chuckled, lay on her back and started to laugh and laugh, until the laughter peaked and cracked into a silent sobbing, her stomach heaving in waves, her body rocking from the misery within.

Only then did she remember and, with an aching heart, hurriedly returned to looking brainless and dejected.

The Great Hall was buzzing with sets of interviews being conducted. There were six detectives, each with a student, the rest of them sitting on the red chairs lining the walls, awaiting their turn to be interviewed.

Rees hoped that the pre-set questions would reveal new lines of enquiry through the upgraded HOLMES 2 computer programme, an acronym for the Home Office Large Major Enquiry System, by design named after the Sherlock of fiction. Its beauty, as far as she was concerned, lay in its timeline function, along which it could link any number of pieces of information hitherto unknown. She also had a "ballot box" situated near the doors, available for anyone to anonymously slip in any piece of information that might be of interest.

So far no one in the student body had come forth with evidence, or handed in suggestions that aroused any kind of interest.

After their interviews, students formed groups, talking in low tones in the conservatory. Some went into town to walk about, talking more freely. Some students had abandoned their work altogether. A few others were still trying to work, but finding it difficult.

Laughter no longer punctuated the conversations.

The detectives sat around the monitor screen in the MIR. Pictured was Hannah, sitting in the corner of the interview room, her head lowered, hands in her lap, her fingers slowly intertwining.

'Would you like a drink, Hannah?' The interrogator, Detective Helen Reynolds, was a homely-looking, middle-aged woman.

Hannah shook her head slowly.

'How do you feel?'

Hannah blinked.

'How many fingers am I showing?' Reynolds held up four of them.

Hannah peered at her hand and slowly shook her head.

Rees checked her body language on a form devised at the University of Portsmouth, where she'd recently gained a long-distance degree in behavioural science. According to her list, Hannah was already displaying some classic symptoms arising from a stressful situation: dissociative stupor, blurred vision, slow movements and lack of speech.

But was she acting?

'Hannah, if you can answer a few questions?' Reynolds looked at her in sympathy. 'We don't want to keep you long. Is that okay?'

Hannah frowned suddenly, her lips moving but uttering no sound.

'Hannah? We're here to help. You need to get this out of your system. Can you tell us how you got involved? We know what happened, but it's better coming from you.'

Rees noticed Hannah cross her ankles. She ticked a positive in a behavioural diagnostic box.

'You've had a really hard time, haven't you?' said Reynolds. 'It's been tough. And we do know how you feel about it. It's better to talk, isn't it? Let's sort it out. What happened? Was it an accident?'

Hannah tucked her crossed legs further back and folded her arms.

Rees ticked two more boxes. 'Big defence,' she murmured.

'Tell me,' said Reynolds, 'did you get the knife from the kitchen?'

Hannah remained motionless. She lowered her arms, resting them on her lap.

'I think she's acting,' said Rees, and keyed into her loop-induction mike. 'Leave it for now and go to the brandy.'

Reynolds spoke, after listening to the instruction. 'Hannah? Can you look at me, please?'

Hannah looked up, lethargically.

'How much brandy did you drink yesterday morning?'

Hannah continued to stare.

'You see, we've just been told by the doctor who saw you, that you drank most of the bottle.'

Hannah frowned, shaking her head. 'No,' she drawled. 'It was empt—'

Her sudden check had Rees smiling confidently as she ticked another two boxes. 'Getting somewhere. Go lethargic again, Hannah … that's it, there she goes.'

'All right, Hannah,' said Reynolds. 'Now there's one more thing. We found a note in your room, and it said, quote, "I need a red-hot poker up my ass. I'm a wet rag. Something to wring out and toss in the bin." Why did you write that?'

Hannah frowned again.

Reynolds waited. 'Yes?'

'It's ...' she dropped her gaze to the floor.

Rees turned to the door as it opened. A detective came in to hand her a written message. She glanced at it, placed it to one side but, in a sudden afterthought, picked it up again. It was the name that caught her attention, a "Dr Annabelle Lloyd."

She read it carefully — twice.

> *Françoise O'Tierney came to see me over a problem that had me worried, saying that she'd suffered from violent fantasies since childhood. As her welfare tutor I am not normally allowed to disclose such information. However, given that which has occurred and, after consultation with the University of Birmingham authorities, I am now prepared to be interviewed by the police.*

Rees pulled the interview.

Chapter Twenty-Eight

Darkness had already fallen when Annabelle arrived at the police station, amidst a light flurry of snow. Having been introduced to Rees and Drake she was led into a largish room with a window, unlike the small airless rooms used for suspect interviews. She took off her Burberry down-filled coat and was invited to sit at the table.

Rees had planned it carefully, knowing that tutors were obligated to monitor the welfare of students but, by instinct, tended to be protective of private disclosures, much like priests bound by the privacy of the confessional. But this was murder and Dr Lloyd had volunteered, after all.

After sympathising for Alicia's death and the impact it must have had on staff and students, Rees asked if she minded the interview being recorded, for which Annabelle gave her permission.

'Doctor Lloyd, how did you regard Francoise in terms of her behaviour from the time the two of you first met?'

'Well—' Annabelle broke off as a PC came in with coffee. 'Thank you,' she said, waiting until he went out. 'It was evident to me that she had a deep-seated problem, something that she found hard to deal with. At our next meeting she had a full-blown panic attack in my office. Later, she walked out on me in anger. It stemmed from her not getting a part in a play that she'd set her heart on and something I'd virtually promised her. I was worried for her, how she might behave before or during the performance. She told me that when she was sixteen, her mother took her to see a psychotherapist for emotional problems. Apparently, the therapist had warned her mother that when she grew up, she might become violent.'

Rees nodded slowly. 'And what were these emotional problems, do you know?'

'Yes. Being slighted. We're all hurt by slights for a short while, aren't we? But then we get over them and forget. She doesn't. She's hypersensitive to them. It's as if each one glues itself to her memory. Each slight remains in her head, permanently. It never leaves and is never forgotten. Any thought of it can cause her to relive the slight exactly as it happened. A sneer, just a look, can upset her. They can pop up at any time of day or night. It's like running a loop of film again and again. She feels the anger exactly as she did at the time, even from many years ago. In fact, it gets worse, the longer it goes on, out of the sheer frustration of being unable to get real revenge.'

'How do you mean, "not getting *real* revenge?"'

'She attacks whoever slighted her in fantasy. The result is nothing but that, frustration.'

Rees exchanged a glance with Drake. 'How frequent are these imaginary attacks?'

'Entirely at random. Hardly a week goes by without at least two or three recurring. An initial slight can be relived many times in the first week. Then it can remain dormant, maybe for a few days. It varies. She told me it was like killing the hydra with unlimited heads, because she can never destroy it.'

'You said "frustrated." Do you mean she's angry with herself for not getting what she wants?' said Drake.

'Yes, freedom from what she feels is a curse.'

'Has she ever attacked anyone in reality?' said Rees. 'Did she admit to anything?'

'No. She says not.'

'No payoff,' said Rees, 'no reward and no resolution. Revenge is supposed to bring relief and satisfaction, but with her there's none, because it's unreal. Is that how it goes?'

'Yes, exactly. After each attack she's depressed, simply because she has no control over her feelings and so her frustration continues to build. She's honest. She admits it's all futile, self-damaging and a complete waste of time.'

'And willpower's no use?'

'None. None at all. It just adds to the misery. I did some research. The cognitive part of the brain – the thinking part – can't overrule or control the part that stores emotional memory. It's that organ below the brain, called the amygdalah. It switches on so fast that thinking can't intervene. It hits like lightning. She actually described herself as a nuclear reactor that gets overheated and finally explodes, and I think it's an excellent analogy.'

Rees looked sombrely at Annabelle. 'So that's why you're here,' she said slowly.

'Yes. I'm terrified for her — and sickened by what she might have done.'

Rees was silent for a moment and was about to speak when the loud wail of a police car filled the room. She held back her next question until the car was out of the gates and into the street, the siren fading.

'Do you know if Alicia slighted her?'

Annabelle hesitated. 'In the instance I told you about, it was far more than a slight. I was forced to drop Franky from the production of *Othello* and give the part to Alicia. It was Franky's ambition to play the female lead. Unfortunately, I'd virtually promised it her —that is of course, until I became worried about her behaviour.'

'You're implying that Franky was jealous of Alicia getting the part?'

'It's what I fear happened—' Annabelle broke off suddenly, her composure beginning to crumble. 'Sorry.' She opened her bag to extract a tissue.

Rees waited a moment. 'Do you want to stop— take a break?'

'No. Please go on. We need to do this.'

'So … this frustration may have exploded at Alicia?'

'I can't swear to it, but I think so. She blames her father for her upbringing. Not here,' she added quickly. 'In America. She said she saw him rape a schoolboy.'

Rees exchanged quick glances with Drake.

For a moment there was silence in the room, Annabelle pausing to drink coffee.

'What happened – was he arrested?'

'I don't think so. I think she bottled it in. She blames him for all her emotional problems. She told me that she'd like to harm him physically for what he did. But it was mixed up with thoughts of suicide.'

Another silence, Rees nodding her head slowly. 'Tell me,' she said, 'these loops. Did she describe what happens during a fantasy attack? Did any involve multiple stabbings, do you know—did she tell you of any?'

'Oh, yes. She does everything, chops people up, hacks or stabs them to death. There's always lots of blood.' Shaking her head, Annabelle dabbed her eyes with the tissue. 'I can't help blaming myself, I'm sorry.'

'Dr Lloyd.' Rees leaned forward in emphasis. 'We hear it all the time. If only this or that. "If I'd only been at home Jack would still be alive," that kind of thing.' You are not to blame, not in any way. In fact, you're doing a public duty, that should be an example to others.'

'Yes, I know. But I don't want it to be *her* … you can understand.'

'Of course. It's been hell for you, but you've been a great help. Is there anything else you think we should look into?'

'No. I don't think so. I've told you all I know.'

'Well, thank you, Dr Lloyd,' said Rees. 'What you've told us doesn't prove anything. But it helps. It helps enormously.'

'I hope so…' Annabelle was about to stand up when she hesitated. 'Oh. I'd completely forgotten and it's something else. I'm at sixes and sevens. I'm so sorry.'

'Stop apologising doctor,' Rees said with a smile. 'Relax, take your time.'

Annabelle sat back in her chair. 'Yes. I was told that Craig Muirhaven had an admirer in Alicia, while Hannah was besotted with him. I don't know any more than that.'

Drake scribbled another note.

In the light of Dr Lloyd's statement, it was decided to hold back Hannah's follow-up interview. The longer she was left to stew, the better, Rees thought. Hannah's reaction, referencing the bottle of brandy, had aroused her interest especially as it was evident Hannah knew that her mask had slipped. She decided that when she came back for interview, the motive of jealousy referred to by Dr Lloyd, would be carefully brought up.

In the light of this, DS Jenkins was brought in to handle Franky's interview. Normally sociable and cheerful, he was a big man who could put on an ugly stare. It was unusual for him to play 'Bad Cop' nowadays, as it was an outmoded technique. Intimidation and the bullying of suspects rarely produced worthwhile results. However, on this occasion, Rees gave Jenkins that role to play, as Franky seemed to be the tougher of the two females, one who might retaliate to hard questioning in a way that could bring down her guard.

No sooner had Franky sat down than Jenkins pitched straight in with blunt and rapid questions.

'Franky, it's generally thought that redheads have a temper. Have you?'

'No.'

'I've also heard redheads are promiscuous. Are you?'

'No.'

'What did Alicia Somerstone do to upset you?'

'Nothing,' she said abruptly. 'Who told you that?'

'You get upset, don't you?' Jenkins leaned forward. 'I'm talking about the *real* you. Violent and nasty. That's you.'

'No. It's completely untrue. I'm never harmed anyone in my life. And I object to your personal remarks.'

'You saw a psychotherapist. You had violent thoughts. You wanted to harm whoever slights you. True or false?'

'I know who told you that, and it's not true.'

'And you blame your father for them.'

'Look, I was being joshed by other kids because of my red hair and it made me a bit ratty, back when I was a kid. No big deal.'

On seeing Franky's facial muscles begin to twitch, Rees ticked a box.

'Okay.' Jenkins clasped his hands together on the table, dipping his head to stare at her under lowered brows. 'So, Franky, tell us about Alicia.'

'How do you mean?' she said, with a frown.

'What made you explode at her?'

'Explode?'

'Twenty-one stab wounds. Alicia had a horrible death. How do you feel about it now?'

"How do I feel? "… 'I feel awful, what else can anyone say?'

'Tell me how you helped transport the body to the Institute.'

'I didn't help anybody with anything.'

'Well, somebody had to take the body there. There's Craig, big fellow. He helped with his car, didn't he? Who went with him? Was it Tom, or was it you?'

'I didn't do anything. Because it didn't happen.' Franky, sitting rigidly upright, stared back at him, her mouth firmly set.

The hatch in the cell door banged down, and Franky sat down on the mattress. She knew that she'd given nothing away. Beforehand, she'd heard Hannah being taken out of her cell, presumably for interview. It had led her to the conclusion that she hadn't tried to blame her for the murder, at least not yet. If Hannah had pointed the finger, then Bad Cop's attempt to bully her would have been replaced by questioning that would have taken a completely different turn.

However, it begged the question: *why* hadn't Hannah blamed her for the murder? Franky had a disturbing and growing feeling that Hannah was playing with her, like a cat with a mouse, patting her one moment, grabbing her with its teeth, the next.

The cell suddenly felt colder. It became colder still with another thought. It might be days, months or even years, before Hannah struck. Or, had she arranged it to take place at the cottage, on their release from custody?

Who the hell says "awful" in response to being told your friend's been slaughtered like an animal?' Rees looked around her team in the MIR. 'We say that about someone we *don't* know. But *a friend*?'

'Hang on.' Rees looked at her mobile. 'It's the lab.' She read out the text message:

"No sole impressions at the crime scene. Shoes either bagged or slip overs. One, probably a male and much heavier than the other." Rees looked up at the team members. 'Well, we worked that out just being there. Hannah and Franky are the two lightest and Tom isn't heavy. Got to be Craig, together with Tom, hasn't it? He's also got the only car, remember.'

'I just can't see Craig doing it,' commented Drake. 'Seems like the kind of guy who helps old ladies cross the road.'

'We've still got Hannah.' said Rees. 'I peeped in and she didn't look shocked any more. Fearful, I'd say. So, we keep her stewing and press on with Craig, and then Tom.'

DC Reynolds began Craig's interview with direct questioning, his response to which was immediate, apparently made without signs of stress. He said he'd last seen Alicia at the Institute about 4 p.m. the previous afternoon. He'd tried calling her from home later on, about 8.30 p.m., but without success. These pedestrian questions were posed and answered in a formal, but relaxed manner. It was the next question that was designed to shake him up.

'Was it all jealousy?'

'Jealousy?' Craig frowned. 'Who – of what?'

Reynolds smiled. '*Her* jealousy—Hannah.'

I don't know what you're talking about.'

'Did she suddenly snap at something Alicia did? Was that what happened?'

'I still don't know what you mean.'

'Did Franky help you, or was it Hannah?'

'Doing what?' Craig's voice had risen in the frequency band.

Rees ticked a 'response' box.

'Well, didn't one of them help you drag the body from the car park to the shrubbery?'

'I helped nobody with anything.'

'Was it you who cleaned up the blood in the downstairs bathroom? Or was it Tom?'

'No, because there was no murder. None that I know of.'

Jenkins listened to Rees in his earpiece, before putting the next question. 'Well Craig. It seems you're now rather stressed. Any reason for that?'

Craig sat back, waited a moment and shook his head. 'I don't want to say "no comment", but you're tempting me. If I sound stressed maybe it's because I collided head on with a police vehicle this afternoon and what with being arrested as well for a murder I didn't commit, well, I guess it's just started getting to me.' He shrugged, opening up his hands in a gesture that meant *What do you expect?*

It was now 8.50 p.m. Craig's interview had produced nothing of note and Tom's was looking equally unpromising. Rees had brought back Jenkins as interviewer, for no reason other than being conscious of time slipping away. Time was of the essence and he was the gun-slinger, when it came to effective, rapid fire.

Watching on the monitor, Rees took in Tom's body language. Angular and elegant, he had his legs crossed at the knee, but she couldn't award it a positive tick as that was reserved for ankles crossed. She recalled seeing him in his cell for the first time, his pose similar to that of *The Thinker*, Michelangelo's famous sculpture of Lorenzo de' Medici.

Jenkins looked and sounded sceptical. 'Think a lot of yourself, do you?'

'Excuse me?' Tom uncrossed his legs and sat upright. 'In what way?' he asked sternly.

'Who killed Alicia?'

'I don't know.'

He backed up Craig's and Franky's testimony in stating that he'd last seen Alicia at the Institute, ahead of a lecture that she was to attend around 4 to 4.30 p.m. All the details in his account, corroborated those of the others and so Rees brought the interview to an end.

Early, the following morning, Rees walked towards the police station pointing her umbrella into sleet sweeping down Rother Street. She entered the CID office to find Drake alone, sitting at his desk, brows knitted, staring at his tablet.

'What a day,' she said, shaking out the remaining droplets from her umbrella. When he failed to respond she turned to him.

He was looking at her, but in a way that was unsettling.

'What?' She put the umbrella down, slowly.

'The lab called. They put in an extra shift last night.' He shook his head. 'It's the blood.'

A cold dread seized her. 'They've contaminated it.'

'No, not that. It's no use. Somehow the—'

'How do you mean, "no use!"'

He grimaced. 'Unidentifiable.'

'*Unidentifiable?*' She began to breathe heavily. She'd had a good night's sleep and had come in buoyed by the sure-fire certainty that she'd get positives for Alicia's blood on one of the suspects by the end of the day, after which they would be confronted with the evidence, leaving them with no option but to confess. And now it was hopeless. Was this what he was implying?

She stared at him. 'You've got to be joking.'

He shook his head heavily. 'No. They found blood in the bathroom, but it's been robbed of its haemoglobin and of course —' He broke off as the landline rang out. 'It's probably him. He said he'd call back.'

She picked up the phone. 'MIR? Morning Jack. I've just heard—'

She was forced to listen to the lab manager's lengthy explanation. 'Yes, I understand that but surely, isn't there *some* way?'

'No,' said the tinny voice. 'When the haemoglobin is washed out you lose the markers, including DNA. I'm staggered considering the amount of blood lost, but that's where we are, I'm sorry to say. I've not come across this before but I'll hazard a guess that somebody knows about oxygen bleach.'

Rees groaned. She knew that it was the only domestic product that wiped out the markers for haemoglobin as well as DNA. 'Okay, thanks Jack,' she said heavily and put down the phone.

'Hannah, what did Alicia do to upset you?'

Hannah lifted her head slowly.

Reynolds looked at her in sympathy. 'I don't wish to upset you anymore. I'm just a little confused and I'm hoping we can get it straight. You said that the brandy bottle was almost empty. Can you tell me why you said that?'

Hannah stared at her.

'You looked like you were in shock. Did Craig tell you anything about Alicia?'

Hannah's lips parted and moved silently.

'I'm sorry Hannah, I didn't hear that. Say again?'

Hannah looked slowly at Reynolds, as if trying to focus.

'Are you having trouble seeing me?'

Hannah shook her head slowly.

Reynolds raised three fingers. 'How many fingers?'

Hannah peered at her hand. Then her eyes closed as she sat back.

Rees had the awful feeling that it was all over. Even if Hannah was acting, so what? It wasn't proof of guilt. Hannah had shown a chink in her armour over the amount of brandy in the bottle but, again, so what?

She sighed. 'We need the doc back. I'm not taking any risks.'

She looked at her watch. 'We've got twelve hours left.' She took a deep breath. 'Not good.' She grimaced at Drake.

He shrugged and nodded, grimly.

She knew then, barring the discovery of the murder weapon, or a blood positive from the lab, that she was on course for losing her suspects. A final check on HOLMES 2 showed nothing cross-referenced of any interest and CCTV had come up with nothing of value. She made two quick calls, one to the medical examiner, leaving a request for him to see Hannah again asap, and one requesting a psychiatrist to be put on standby.

An hour later, the medical examiner emerged from the custody examination room to say that he was uncertain as to Hannah's mental state and advised that a psychiatrist should attend to determine if she was faking it or not.

The appointed psychiatrist arrived at 12.05 p.m. He spent thirty minutes with Hannah and came out to admit he had doubts about declaring her fit for interview.

'Doubts,' said Rees, 'meaning that you give her the benefit of the doubt?'

'That's about it, I'm afraid.' He spoke of mafia-boss Louis Gigante, who deceived the most respected minds in forensic psychiatry in the whole of America. Over seven years he convinced them that he was schizophrenic when it had all been an act.

'You're saying your job's not worth the candle then.' Rees immediately regretted the derisive remark. She apologised profusely, blaming her frustration.

An hour later the lab manager called again to say that his team had spent most of the day searching for other vital blood markers that would link the victim to the suspects, but without success. He had failed.

No. *She* had failed, she thought. She decided to make the last throw of the dice and called the CID Surveillance Team leader.

She was lucky. He reported that he was not presently engaged in any covert operation and had plenty of equipment with which to bug the cottage.

'How long have I got' he asked Rees.

'Two and a half hours. Long enough?'

'It's going to be tight. First I've first got to assemble the team and make sure the inventory's complete.'

Rees, nervously glanced at her watch. It was now 9.46 p.m. only fourteen minutes before the suspects' release time. She stood in the CID office looking out of the window. There, in the station car park, stood Craig's replacement car, courtesy of his insurance company. The keys were still in police possession and would not be handed over until 10.p.m, on the dot.

She had just returned from the custody area, covertly watching the suspects' body language. Had they shown signs of suppressed joy at being released with their possessions being returned to them? Was there anyone breathing into another's ear? They had been informed that their freedom was not absolute. They were free, but classified as "still under police investigation". However, since they were free to leave and not out on bail, their passports were being returned to them.

Once more, she looked at her watch. She'd had an 'on track' message from the Surveillance Team an hour earlier, stating that they should be out of the cottage by 9.30. p.m. The deadline had passed and, as yet, no message had arrived to confirm extraction. It left her in a quandary. Surveillance teams resent being told to hurry, as they never slacked in their secret operations, for obvious reasons. She tried hard to think of excuses that would keep the suspects in custody beyond 10.p.m

'What about we do something with Craig's car,' said Drake, sitting next to her.

'How do you mean?'

'It breaks down on route?'

Hey, why didn't I think of that?' She went to pick up the phone and then hesitated. 'No,' she said suddenly. 'I don't like it. Things could go wrong.'

'Okay,' said Drake. 'I've got another idea.'

'Tell me.'

It was 9.59 when the custody sergeant took a call.

'Okay. Yep. Got it.'

He spoke to Craig who was watching the wall-clock tick forwards to 10.p.m.

He turned round. 'Yeah?'

'We've a problem with your IDP, your International Driving Permit. It's not correct. You'll have to wait while it's being sorted.'

'What problem?'

'I don't know.'

'Oh my God,' said Franky, sitting down, clutching her possessions bag.

Rees, still watching them through the one-way window, took a call.

'Yes?'

It was the Surveillance team leader. 'I need another half hour.'

It took 36 minutes, with faked phone calls and procedural checks for Craig's driving permit to be declared valid.

During that time the ST leader sent a text from the cottage. *Will extract 22.35*

Rees stood in the CID office, studying an outdated fax machine spew out its paper. On it was listed 36 items deployed at the cottage, together with a marked-up plan showing the locations of a mixture of miniature cameras and microphones. They were concealed in fourteen wall sockets, eight USB drives, five chargers, four computers, three television sets and two electrical adaptors.

'And a partridge in a pear tree,' Rees murmured, looking at her watch. 'They should have left the cottage by now.'

'Has the team leader cleared?' Drake came into the CID office.

'Not yet.' Rees sounded tense. 'They're just finishing the last job.'

'It's only a ten to fifteen-minute drive there.'

'Yes, he knows.'

They swapped grimaces.

'Come on!' she whispered to herself, staring at her screen. Beads of perspiration glinted on her forehead. 'Get out of there.'

Her desk phone jangled loudly. She grabbed it. 'Yes!'

'We're out now and mobile.'

'Thanks.'

She put down the handset and slumped over the desk, sharing a grin with Drake.

"A damn close-run thing," said Drake. 'That's what the Duke of Wellington said after the Battle of Waterloo.'

She nodded, giving him a tired smile.

At that precise moment the suspects' car turned into Tithebarn Lane. The four took no notice of the blue van approaching them.

Chapter Twenty-Nine

'At last,' murmured Craig as they caught sight of the cottage.

At that moment their headlights picked out a dirty white van, tucked awkwardly against the left-hand hedgerow, not more than a hundred yards from the cottage. It showed two red "Police Aware" stickers, one stuck on the front and another on the rear of the van, the aim being to stop unnecessary complaints and reminders about a broken-down vehicle on a country lane.

Craig pulled into the gateway, stopped the car and was about to get out, when Tom shushed them all, a finger to his lips, before beckoning them outside.

They followed him through the five-barred gate and round the cottage to the back garden, stopping at the hedgerow.

'That van back there …' he kept his voice low … 'it could be a surveillance van. It's used to relay sound and vision from a nearby target.'

'Oh my God,' groaned Franky. 'You mean we could be bugged?'

Tom nodded grimly. 'I'd bet on it.'

'Can we disable it?' asked Craig.

'No. There'll be cameras and microphones, all hidden. If they've done this it's likely they'll have bugged the car as well. It's lucky we didn't talk.'

The moon slipped out from a cloud, casting a sheen on Hannah's pale face.

'Can we go in now?' she said, with a shiver.

'Yes. But first, if anyone needs to talk about it, we do it out here. Just a tap on the arm and a gesture, is all that's needed. Remember, our cell phones are probably bugged, so we don't use text. And watch what we say because they can copy conversations as well. It's possible they might continue to locate where we are, even switched off. So be *very* careful, *all* of us.'

'I think we should ask each other who we think may have done it,' said Craig. 'It would be expected wouldn't it?'

Tom looked at him for a moment. 'Yes. The one thing I'd forgotten.'

Craig smiled and reassuringly tapped Tom on the arm as they went back towards the cottage.

'Oh my God, there's no heating.' On letting herself into the cottage, Franky marched down to the laundry room. 'I bet it's the landlord.'

There was a pause. 'It's not off,' she called out, reading a note. 'He says it's on minimal to stop the pipes bursting.'

She joined the trio in the hallway, looking uncertainly at each other, like a group of tourists who had found themselves in an unfamiliar place without a guide.

With questions on their lips, Tom's attention was caught by a discolouration of the living room door-handle.

He ran a fingertip over its top edge and then studied it.

Craig peered over his shoulder to see the object of his scrutiny: Tom's fingertip was coloured green.

Craig followed him into the living room where more of the coloured powder was found.

'CSI,' said Tom, in explanation. 'They could at least have had the decency to clean up, *especially* if you're innocent,' the stress on the word meant for any nearby microphone.

They went back into the hallway, only to freeze at the sound of an approaching vehicle, its headlights illuminating the hallway, flooding it as the car approached, then fading as it passed by.

'Can we relax now?' said Hannah. 'I'm exhausted, and I'm cold.'

'I'll make the fire,' said Craig and went out.

'I'll give you a hand,' said Franky, anxious to get away from Hannah.

They sat around the fire, each with their own thoughts.

'What I don't understand,' said Craig suddenly, 'is that whoever did it, must have known her really well.'

'I was thinking the same Craig,' said Franky. 'Who can we think of, outside the Institute?'

'Yes,' said Tom, 'I think it's someone outside. What's the name of the restaurant Alicia worked at?' He looked to Franky for an answer.

'*The Tudor,* but she worked flat-out. She never socialised with anyone from there. It's a high-end place. We knew her working hours and she was never late back. You picked her up sometimes, Craig. I told the police all this.'

'Tomorrow,' said Craig, suddenly. 'Do we go back to the Institute as normal?'

Franky and Tom looked at him and nodded their agreement.

'Hannah? What do you want to do?'

'Me?' She seemed to think about it. 'No. I'm exhausted. I'm staying here.'

'Okay,' said Craig. 'Because I'm the oldest, shall I see the director and say we're not on bail, we're free and want to get back to work, but we may need some time and space? Is that what I should do?'

'Yes, I think it's exactly what you should do,' said Tom. 'Speak for all of us.'

'Yes, thanks Craig,' said Franky. 'Do that.'

'Hannah. How about you?'

Hannah shrugged. 'I guess.'

They fell silent once more.

Franky, glancing at Hannah more than once, felt the tension unbearable. 'Anyone want coffee?' she said, standing up.

'Thanks, Franky, but not for me,' said Craig. 'I'm bushed.'

Franky's cell phone bleeped. It was an email message from Yvette. The others looked to her as she read the message.

'It's Mom … been told by the American Embassy that I was under arrest … been trying to get hold of me for two days.'

She quickly texted back: "All well. No problems. Back on course."

She gave Hannah another glance before going out. Was she being presumptuous in thinking she had revenge on her mind when she was a devout Christian and so not given to seeking it? Would she turn the other cheek? Was it possible?

As she went into the kitchen, she was struck by another fear. Could Hannah have agreed to some kind of plea-bargain for a lesser sentence and returned as a plant, trying to trap her into an admission of guilt, hoping it would be caught on the surveillance system? It would account for her amazing placidity, her calm 'knowingness' and the unsettling look that she'd just given her. Wouldn't it?

Would the nightmare never end?

She looked at her watch.

It was 12.35 a.m.

12.35 a.m. in the UK was 7.35 p.m. Eastern Standard Time the previous evening in Massachusetts. At that precise moment Kelsie Maylam, a staff reporter on *The Boston Globe*, had begun working the graveyard shift. She'd picked up a feed from Reuters about four American students at The Shakespeare Institute in Stratford-upon-Avon, England, a further development of her breaking story that hit the front page two days before. It stated the name of the deceased and also the names of students who lived with her. It added that they had all been released without charge, but were still listed as "under police investigation."

One of them, Françoise O'Tierney, was reported as being a Bostonian student. Kelsie seized on this and searched social media to find her only on Facebook— and that sparse in terms of personal detail. No friends were listed and there was little activity on her account. She'd performed well in the nationwide annual Shakespeare Competition, and that was about it.

Kelsie sat in contemplation. She'd been working on a story about "Doomsday Preppers," but now shelved it in favour of the news from Stratford upon Avon. For her it had great potential, above and beyond that of a news splash, both as a headline grabber as well as material for a book. She'd long fancied writing a bestselling non-fiction story. She only had to think of the books spawned by the Meredith Kercher murder, a student scandal that still resonated around the world. It was only recently that Amanda Knox had given an interview in which she said that 'People love monsters', while hiding her tears.

Franky's story, Kelsie thought, could become a favourite with American students at home and abroad. The Shakespeare connection was heaven sent. It would remind the reader of that mega best-selling novel, T*he Secret History*. She hoped that students, specialising in Shakespeare, would prove more attractive to the reader than Donna Tartt's students of Ancient Greek.

She made a note to call Franky's parents, the following morning.

After supper, they sat in a semi-circle, close to the fire. Franky sat in the corner of the leather settee, just out of Hannah's eye-line from her position on an inglenook seat. The silence was broken only by the crackling of burning wood.

It occurred to her that, despite their ordeal and tiredness, not one of them had shown signs of wanting to retire. Was it because they felt the need to remain together, as long as possible? Were the other three like her, worried about raising the subject of their individual police interviews, scared that it could throw up awkward contradictions and suspicions? Or, did they share, with her, an almost palpable need to remain safe, to live in peace, sharing a common desire to put it all behind them?

'Do you remember the first night we were here?' said Tom, out of the blue. 'Quite magical. We listened to *Pachelbel* and then I played Chopin's *Nocturne*.' He stared once more into the fire and fell silent.

After a minute or two Craig surprised everyone by emitting a chuckle and giving a slight shake of the head.

Franky looked at him. 'Don't tell me you've got good news?'

'No, I was thinking that in the normal course of events, this would be one for our welfare tutor.' He gave an involuntary wince that morphed quickly into a picture of sadness.

'*Welfare?*' said Hannah suddenly, in a humourless voice.

More time passed.

'We ought to play the game,' said Craig, thinking it would be a signal of innocence to the watchers and eavesdroppers. 'Anybody got one?'

'Yes,' said Tom, quick with his answer. "Is't possible, sits the wind in that corner?" He made a covert gesture with eyes and thumb, meaning the parked van back down the lane.

'Oh – yes.' Craig was late, picking up the cue. *Twelfth Night?*'

'No.'

'*Midsummer Night's?*'

Tom shook his head. 'Nobody? It's *Much Ado*, Benedick to himself. He's eavesdropping on Don Pedro.' He gave Franky a little smile.

Relieved, she put her head back. His smile clearly signified his belief that he would not be returned to a police cell. Would there soon come his little digs and probes? How she yearned to hear and see them once more. She longed for his quirky humour, the seminar on the sun-warmed lawn, the friendly chatter in the conservatory, the five-pound ticket to see the latest RSC production, bees humming and lavender in the air. She mourned for a life remembered. How rich and wonderful it had been. It seemed years ago.

Her nostalgia gave way to thinking about *him*. Was it three days - or four - when she would come face to face with her father? Her mind refused to function. She clicked into her diary. Three days to go … two if she didn't count the flight day. She buried herself further into the squashy corner of the settee.

Craig had also read Tom's manner and coded speech. Lying back, he reciprocated, with a roll of his head towards him. 'Tom,' he said, 'thanks for helping with the dissertation. I think it's going to be fine.'

'Good. I'm pleased.'

With the room warm, the fire still comforting, it still seemed that no one was likely to turn in.

Ten minutes later, it was Craig who made the first move. He eased himself upright. 'Gotta hit the sack,' he murmured.

He was the first to retire, soon to be followed by Tom. Franky, suddenly aware that she was now alone with Hannah, stood up in panic. She was heading quickly for the door when she stopped. Hannah had not even glanced at her. A sudden pang of remorse overruled her instinct to flee the room. She wanted to go to her now, poor Hannah, crouched in the inglenook. She wanted to rush over and embrace her, pouring tears of pity as well as remorse. She wanted forgiveness.

With mouth wide open and with a terrible ache in her heart, she fled up to her room, leaving Hannah staring into the fire.

It had been an unusual December night. It started with a gale racing down the shallow valley towards the cottage, hitting it head on, then moaning through cracks and crevices and rattling windows. At the apparent peak of its ferocity, however, the storm quickly abated and died, leaving behind freezing, northerly air, with yet another forecast of snow.

Hannah had not gone to bed at all. At 8.36 a.m. Tom found her, in her dressing gown, half asleep on the settee, the fire no more than a smoking pile of white ash.

She opened one eye to look at him.

'Tom,' she said creakily, trying to sit upright.

'You all right?'

'Just about.' She clasped a hand on her forehead. 'You?'

'Yes. Wouldn't you feel better going in with us today?'

'No, Tom. I just couldn't.'

'Well, the semester ends the day after tomorrow. I shall be pleased to see the back of it.'

'So will I.' Hannah stood up and trudged out of the room, following Tom into the kitchen.

They found Franky and Craig, making breakfast.

'Craig,' said Tom. 'I need to orientate myself and I'm still tired. Wouldn't it be better if we went in this afternoon rather than this morning?'

He got instant agreement from Franky and Craig.

'You're right,' said Craig. 'I'm still tuckered out. What about you? Could you make it, Hannah? Rest up this morning, go in later?'

'No. I'm staying here all day.'

Franky took a bowl from a cupboard. 'I've been thinking. About reporters.'

'Like me, said Craig. 'There's bound to be one or two sniffing around.'

'Yes,' said Tom. 'It's important we say nothing. We know how one phrase can become a banner headline.'

Franky glanced at Hannah, who was putting coffee into her mug. She was expressionless, a far cry from the girl who always greeted her each morning with a ready smile and bubbling over with the latest good news.

Suddenly Franky's eyes prickled and she hurried out, lest she burst into tears.

Once in her room she looked wildly about. *They* had taken from her the one individual who had meant something, someone who would have been a friend for life. Raging, she grabbed a light cotton shirt and tore it open, buttons flying. Then, mired in confusion and anguish, she fell face down upon the bed.

Before their departure Hannah found Tom in the hallway, putting on his long, black overcoat. "Thank you" she mouthed and reached up to kiss him on the cheek. He nodded, with an embarrassed smile.

'Well…' he said, slightly flustered. You've got my number. Any problems call me.'

'I will.'

Later, she stood in the doorway to watch them drive away.

She slowly closed the door and stood motionless, staring at the floor.

Chapter Thirty

As they entered the town, Franky gazed at the water beneath the river bridge; it reflected the overhead span of street lighting, consisting of all the colours of the rainbow.

They came towards the junction of High Street and Bridge Street, where stood a forty-foot-high 'tree' of twinkling lights, crowned by a massive red-lit star. In contrast, the Tudor buildings had their own atmospheric lighting, a ghostly blue.

They cruised slowly past the Christmas street market from which emanated alluring smells of cinnamon, hot mulled wine, pine cones, and roasted chestnuts. Choristers, backed by a Salvation Army band, sang carols in the street, and a recording of *God Rest Ye Merry Gentlemen* came from a hairdressing salon. The pubs and cafes were packed with tourists and visitors.

'Look at all this,' Craig said sadly. 'And then look at us. Everyone free. It's like we're on parole out of prison.'

'Don't Craig,' said Franky. 'I'm sick already. How do you feel Tom? Are we going to make it?'

'Stop Craig,' said Tom suddenly, looking at something on the adjacent pavement. 'The newspaper. I'll be seconds.'

'As the car stopped, illegally parked on double yellows, Tom was out, disappearing into the adjacent shop.

It left Franky and Craig staring at a display-stand, near the doorway outside the shop. Clipped to it was the front page of the local newspaper, *The Herald*. Its splash headline had their attention: "*Students Released*"

Tom was quickly back with a copy.

As they moved away, he scanned the report and then read aloud:

'Warwickshire Police are appealing for the public's help in solving the murder of an American student, Alicia Somerstone, 23, who was found dead on Tuesday morning this week at The Shakespeare Institute in Church Street. The police have confirmed that she sustained multiple stab wounds.'

He quickly read through the rest of the report and shook his head. 'Nothing we don't already know.'

After parking the car, they entered the Institute. Not all the lights were switched on, leaving darkened corners in the reception hall. Was it done to pay respects to the deceased?

Franky was hit by how oppressive it felt. There was no longer the sound of feet on the stairs, voices at the reception hatch, nor was there sudden laughter echoing from the conservatory. She wanted to leave – and quickly. Suddenly her cell phone smashed the silence.

It was Yvette, saying she was mightily relieved that she'd answered and asked if she was safe.

'Yes, we're fine.'

'A reporter just called. He said you'd been released by the police. Why didn't you tell us? We had no idea.'

'I couldn't. I've only just got back my cell phone and we're driving into town. I was going to do it when we arrived.'

'We've been trying to get hold of you for two days. We've only heard what's happening through the American Embassy and now the reporter.'

'But you know we've been released.'

'Yes, but you could at least have sent a text message.'

'The police had my cell. I couldn't. I'm sorry. Look, I have to go now.'

'Françoise, we're worried about you.' She only used her full name when irked.

'It sounds like you're more upset that I haven't called than me being locked up. I must go—'

'Wait. I'm going to La Rochelle later today and your father wants a word. He —'

'Can't. I've got a lecture. I'll text later. I'll tell you everything, promise.' She switched off.

Meanwhile, Craig was speaking to one of the administrators, asking if was possible to see the Director.

After a brief call she told him to go to the top floor, the first office, on the right.

Craig spent fifteen minutes upstairs with the Director, then came back down to the conservatory where Tom and Franky sat in the otherwise empty space.

He sat down. 'We're okay. We're still on the course, that's the main thing. Today's lectures and tutorials are cancelled. Everyone's working at home. The Christmas party's still on, but no games, no jokes, just readings, that kind of stuff. There's a collection being organised. And there'll be a memorial service at the start of next term. He's sending emails to everybody, reminding us to reassure our families that we're safe.'

'No questions?' said Franky.

'About being in police custody, no. I don't think he's slept. He looks pretty shook up.'

'Does he know the police can recall us?'

'Yes, he's okay with it.'

'He *has* to be. I'll get coffee,' said Franky, grimly, standing up.

Craig got up to join her. 'I'll give you a hand. Want a cookie, Tom?'

'Erm. . . yes, we've everything to celebrate,' he said with a note of irony.

'Craig,' said Franky, after placing mugs on the kitchen worktop. 'I'm worried. Hannah spread it around that I was pretty cheesed off at Alicia getting Desdemona. Did you know that?'

'Yes, you told us.'

'Oh — did I? Well, if so, it's because I'm worried. Yes, Tom's plan worked out – well, *so far* but, if Hannah ever confesses, I'm pretty sure she'll go for me. She'll say I forced her into it. I got her drunk. I egged her on to kill Alicia.'

'Hang on. She can't have done that because you're free. If she had the police would have kept and questioned you about it, wouldn't they?'

'I'm saying she might, if we get called back.'

'Hey. You've gone through enough. Now you're making things up to worry you even more. Worry about things when they happen — yeah?'

'Yes, you're right.' She put coffee into the mugs. 'It's just that I'm scared. Haven't you seen the looks she gives me? She's been like it since we got back. It's like she's saying "I've got you lined up". Then she won't look at me, cutting me dead. I think she's got something planned. And I don't think it's good news.'

'What do you mean, "something planned?" I don't get this. Why should she—'

'She'll spread it around that I told her that Alicia had burnt her bear. I told you all that. Then there's the brandy. I left it with her by mistake, but she could say I did it deliberately – to get her drunk enough.'

'Franky, just a minute. This is crazy. You've got to take a step back and think about what you're saying.'

'I know. But I read her face before we left. I know how she thinks.'

She switched on the kettle.

'Franky.' Craig spoke gently. 'This is dangerous talk. You could say something that lands us back in a police cell when all it does is torment yourself.' He put an arm around her shoulder. 'It's over.' He gave her a squeeze. 'C'mon Let sleeping dogs lie, huh?'

'I wish I had your optimism, Craig. I'm positive she's going to try and get me in some way.'

'Look. The real question is what Alicia did to upset Hannah, not you.' He paused. 'I think we should say no more. *Ever*. It's over. We're free. Tom did his job well. That's all that matters, isn't it?'

'I guess,' she said and shrugged. 'It's me. I can't stop thinking about it.'

'I know. He squeezed her shoulder once more. 'I know. We've been through something really bad. We have to let things cool down. When you get home, it will all go away. Okay?'

'Yes. Thanks, Craig.' Franky nodded, giving him a quick smile.

'I'm going to suggest that *Othello* be dedicated to Alicia. Would you support that?'

'Yes. Of course, I would.'

'Let me tell you something.' Craig took out his tin from a cupboard. 'It's December 1941 and my Grandpa was worried about not having enough money for Christmas. Then came news about the attack on Pearl Harbour by the Japanese. He forgot his worries. Within a week he was in the army, facing death. It's all relative.'

He opened the tin to take out three cookies.

'Yes, I know. But if it *did* go to trial...' Franky closed her eyes. 'If she accuses me in court, you know?'

'Hey, stop. We're still in shock. It's best we go easy on ourselves. Things will sort themselves out. Tom's got us out. Let's stick with that. One thing at a time. If we start losing our heads, imagining what *might* happen, it could be dangerous. For all of us.'

'Okay,' she whispered. She took a deep breath. 'You're right. It's me panicking. Let's forget it.'

Half an hour later, with three empty coffee mugs sat on the conservatory table, the conversation between the trio had turned to their hopes and dreams.

'I think,' said Tom, 'I should first teach at home. But I do like England. And I like Stratford. Would I make a lecturer at the Institute? I'd like to think that. How about you, Craig?'

'Well, I guess teaching, but I haven't made up my mind where. It would be great to get a PhD, but come back here, like you? I don't think so. Too many memories.' He swept crumbs from his knees, then fell silent for a moment. 'Of course, we might have to come back in handcuffs. What's your guess?'

'I don't think we will. But, of course, nothing is certain.' Tom took out his pocket book and did a check. 'Yes, I've got both of your emails and cell numbers. We must stay in touch with each other. Franky, have you got ours?'

'Yes. I have.'

'Same here,' said Craig.

Satisfied, the conversation turned to Craig's work for the Oklahoma Search and Rescue Council. He was a local member of the American Alpine Club, mountaineering his speciality.

He spent fifteen minutes relating a near-death experience on a rescue mission, during which Franky kept eyes on him, but with her mind elsewhere. Rather than listen to the business of saving lives, she was bent on the business of dispensing with one.

During the last week she'd developed her plan down to the last detail, but instead of being rewarded by the satisfaction that every detail was covered, there was always something that gave rise to doubt. Lingering and gnawing away in her mind was always the fear of the unforeseen and the unexpected.

Once more, she ran through a plan of action that would begin at Heathrow, her first task being to send an email to Boston PD. Then, on arrival at Logan International she would take a cab to Schroeder Plaza, their headquarters. There, she would make a witness statement and hopefully work alongside the PD composite artist in producing a likeness of the boy, Jason. Her next step would be to call her father on his cell phone. If he answered, she would quickly switch off and get a cab to take her to his lair, the place called home. If he failed to answer she would go back to the hotel room she intended to reserve and, from there, resume her periodic checks. On his reply she would instruct the cab driver not to go up the house but —'

'Franky, what are you doing this Christmas?'

'She opened her eyes in a fleeting panic. 'What—sorry, Craig. "What am I doing" … erm, staying home, I guess. I always do.' She took a deep breath and put her head back, deciding to leave the mental check list until she was settled, lest she confuse herself with errors.

In the meantime, she observed Tom, as he got back in conversation with Craig. She was impressed by his chameleon-like ability to shed the personality that he'd acquired while dealing with their dreadful situation. Having regained most of his urbane mannerisms, he seemed to be completely free of anxiety. His return to something like his former self should have been heartening. If *he* remained free of worry, why worry?

She thought of life after her mission was completed. With her qualifying BA degree, she would apply for the teacher preparation programme in Boston. Then, with a teaching licence, she would run away, bury herself in some harmonious community, away from Hannah … and forget?

She looked at Craig sitting in the leather armchair opposite, elbows on the side-arms and looking relaxed. How she envied him his calm, easy-going manner, his reluctance to take offence, his consideration for other people and the natural goodness he'd shown in the face of great danger.

She listened to what he was saying in answer to a question from Tom.

'No. It isn't home any longer. I'm selling the house as soon as I can. I'm staying with someone who lives in London, works for a big American law firm. They've got a London office. And since the RSC's doing *Hamlet* at the Harold Pinter theatre, I'm going to try and get in.'

'What will you be doing Tom?' said Franky.

'I shall go to my forefathers. As I always do. Folk ancient and wise. Eat and drink. Read and vegetate.'

Franky gazed out of the window at the dead garden, her eyes settling on the place where Alicia's body had lain.

Craig glanced at his watch. 'I've got a present to buy. You two?'

'I get mine at home,' said Tom. 'Less to carry.'

'Same here,' said Franky. Presents — who for? Christmas had never been a fun time of year with him money-making in his study and Yvette fidgeting over whether or not she should attend Midnight Mass, but never going.

Her mind settled on an image that she couldn't eradicate, no matter how hard she tried. Just before Hannah shut the door in her face, she'd put on a wry smile that said:

"You're beneath contempt. You know what you deserve."

Chapter Thirty-One

She was falling, head down into a black infinity, hurtling past churches, headstones and steeples, down and down.

Hannah suddenly woke up, to find herself sprawled out in front of a fire that was now nothing more than smouldering embers. She looked slowly around her, taking in familiar objects – Tom's keyboard – black fire-tools hanging on red brickwork – a plant on the windowsill, magazines on a low table …

She breathed in deeply, then eased herself upright, blinking a number of times to clear her vision. Slowly, cautiously, she rose to her feet.

Once upright, she removed her hand from the side of the armchair to test her balance. She remained perfectly still.

No longer feeling dizzy, she went into the kitchen for a drink of water.

She paused with her hand resting on the cold-water tap. That she'd befriended Franky out of compassion, someone whom she'd come to think of as a friend, but who had repaid her with an unspeakable and terrible act, was beyond all comprehension. She'd thought about it non-stop during the thirty-six hours spent in a claustrophobic cell. Why had Franky wanted Alicia dead for taking her part in a play for amateur actors and then gone on to lie to her only friend on campus, making *her* the murderer?

She poured out a glass of water and took a long drink. A number of times she'd been on the point of challenging Franky for an answer to such questions, but to what purpose? She'd tried to pray for her, as she'd been taught to pray for all sinners, but it had proved impossible.

She washed the glass, placed it back in the cupboard, then went to put on her anorak. Her last task was to select a sharp knife from the kitchen block to slip it into one of its wide, deep pockets. Then she picked up her rucksack and went outside, locking the door behind her.

She left behind on the doormat a note that she'd written. Outside, she locked the front door and slipped her house key through the letter-box.

She went to the woodshed. There, at one side of the log pile, stood a stack of bricks, surplus to the cottage extension. She placed four of them inside her rucksack, but then thought it could take one more. It failed to fit properly, leaving a gap between the zipper and the overlapping cover. She thought of removing it, but then changed her mind.

She set off down the lane, bending forward to ease the weight on her shoulders.

She was on the bus, gazing out over the sodden fields, a stark wasteland with the remains of snowdrifts lingering in the black hedgerows. She rested her head against the window frame and took herself back to one particular day, when it was warm and sunny during that magical "Indian" summer. She'd been wandering around town, taking in the sights and atmosphere, and ended up at the riverside, close to the RSC Theatre. It was the colourfully painted boats in the marina, a short distance away, that attracted her attention.

There were two boats moored up, both long and narrow. She read the explanatory board nearby. It told her that, in the pre-railway age, canals were the main routes for trade and commerce throughout much of England, moving raw materials around the industrial areas and then hauling the finished products to ports such as London, Liverpool and Newcastle for shipment to the colonies of the British Empire.

It was the narrow boat, painted in carnival colours, that interested her most. The name *Fellows, Morton & Clayton Ltd* was painted along its side, honouring its commercial predecessors. Along its flat roof stood a row of large flower pots, as well as two chained-up bicycles. A man stood on the lock-side running a hosepipe from the marina's water-point into the boat's tank.

A woman emerged from the rear cabin doors, carrying a black rubbish bag.

They both looked fit for their years, both of them wearing chinos, she with a trim figure and silvery hair, the man with grey hair and wearing a white sweater labelled "Stratford-upon-Avon Boat Club".

Seeing Hannah, the woman gave her a cheerful 'Good morning.'

'Hi,' said Hannah. 'It's a lovely boat. May I ask, do you live on it?'

'No. Only at weekends or on holiday. Two or three times a year we go out for a week or two with friends.' She placed the rubbish bag on the concrete landing, preparing to step ashore. 'You're American. Don't ask how I guessed.' She laughed a little. 'Are you with anyone – on a tour?'

'No. I'm a student. I'm at The Shakespeare Institute, here in Stratford. Do you know it?'

The woman stared at her, breaking into a big smile. 'Jack?' she turned to her husband. 'Guess what?'

Introductions being quickly made, Hannah was ordered to join them for coffee on deck.

'I'm missing the first few days of the course,' said Maggie. 'My sister's been ill, and I've had to look after her. Now why am I a student at my age? It's because I've always loved Shakespeare, and a spot of study is good for the old brain, isn't it? Use it or lose it, they say.'

Hannah laughed with her. 'I had no idea. I thought everyone would be around my age.'

'No, I got my BA at Warwick University in 1971. There's a couple of other oldies on the course. I find it wonderful. Absolutely wonderful, I really do. The best years of our lives, hey Jack?'

'The best.' Jack, having filled the water tank, hung up the hosepipe and returned to the boat. 'Now, why don't we take her for a little cruise?' he said. 'London and back.'

Maggie burst into laughter. 'London?' She turned to Hannah. 'Have you got a month to spare? No, Jack. We'll do the "toad" downriver.'

'Toad?'

'It's our name for it. You'll see.'

'It's a cruise in the sun,' said Jack.

'Hannah, if you've never been by river or canal, you'll love it.'

'Oh, I'd love to, but…' Her face dropped as she realised how she must sound. 'Oh, please! Look, I hope you don't think I barged in here trying to get a free—'

'No – yes! Yes, of course you've barged in. Except it's not a barge, it's called a narrow boat because it has to go through locks a little less than seven feet wide.' Chuckling, Maggie took the rubbish bag to the community bin. 'Lock up, Jack, let's get ourselves a picnic!' She turned to Hannah. 'Have you been to Holy Trinity yet, the church?'

'Holy … oh, you mean where Shakespeare's buried? No, I haven't, not yet.'

'Jack? We must stop there.'

'Aye-aye, skipper.'

Half an hour later, after visiting the M&S food store, they were gliding downstream on the right-hand side of the river. Jack stood at the stern of the boat, his hand on the tiller and making little steering adjustments to keep in line with the willows reaching out from the bank.

Hannah sat alongside Maggie at the bows, the boat seeming motionless, the waterscape sliding slowly towards her, her only task being to occasionally push away the soft branches of the drooping willows, many of which hung down to water level, creating cool, shady arches and shelters within. Others, more protruding, occasionally clicked along the boat windows like skeletal fingers.

The only other sounds were the muted chug from the engine compartment sixty feet back and the trickling sound of water parting at the bows. With a dragon fly darting about, it was as near to the perfect idyll as she could imagine. She wanted it to go on all day.

'Oh, look!' She gasped, pointing in delight.

A swan paddled out, gracefully, from one of the willowy arches, surrounded by her cygnets. Jack, to avoid them, thrust the throttle into reverse, but it was only a gesture as the swan was immediately away, its fluffy new-born flotilla, fast wiggling in its slip-stream.

Hannah was entranced. 'How wonderful,' she breathed. 'It's just like *Wind in the Willows.*'

'That's right,' said Maggie. 'I said we'd do a toad. That's what we call this run.'

'Oh, Maggie, it's fabulous. I could be here forever.'

'Did you know that Shakespeare created *Ophelia* here?'

Hannah stared at her open-mouthed. 'No, I didn't,' she breathed. '*Really?*'

'Yes. He based her on a girl called Katharine Hamlet. She lived in Stratford.'

'What! *Hamlet?*' Hannah's jaw dropped.

'Oh, the name was certainly Hamlet. It's in church records. She was drowned upstream in 1579, not far from where we started. Apparently, she was heartbroken after a failed love affair.'

'Oh.' Hannah winced, crestfallen. 'Poor girl.'

'Yes. When I was a girl,' said Maggie, 'we came on the river lots of times. I always imagined her floating, her dress billowing, but...' she made a gesture, 'not back there, but *here*, in this place, by these willows.'

Hannah, absorbing the tragedy and overwhelmed by the beauty of her surroundings, felt tears welling up.

'Hannah?' It was Jack calling out.

She turned to put on a smile. He was pointing to somewhere over her head. 'Look there.'

She turned quickly to see nothing but willows and water when, suddenly, she saw it, the spire of a church above the treetops where the river began a wide sweeping curve to the left.

'Yes, I see it!' she exclaimed. 'I can't see any buildings. It can't have changed since Shakespeare!'

'You're right. It can't have. Unless they moved the river.'

Hannah laughed in her excitement, turning to find Maggie smiling at her.

'Oh, Maggie. I just ... it's ... it's so amazing. It's beyond reality, isn't it?'

'Yes. I've always thought that if you're going to die, what a lovely place to do it.'

As they approached the landing stage, Maggie bent down and took hold of the coiled mooring rope, ready to step off the boat.

Jack eased the tiller to the left and, with brief reverse thrusts of the engine, slowed the boat down, allowing it to nose gently into the wooden landing stage and slide along its length. After a final burst of reverse screw, the engine stopped.

Maggie stepped off at the bows and tied the rope around the mooring bollard, while Jack did the same at the stern. They stepped on to the landing stage and climbed a flight of steps. The footpath that branched off to the church entrance was a few yards up the bank, on the left.

They entered, the noise of their footsteps echoing around the mellow stone walls.

Hannah stood still, taken by the simplicity within. 'It's the friendliest church I've ever been in!' she breathed. 'It's as though it wants you here.' She walked slowly down the aisle to the two-feet-high rail, beyond which was a simple, rustic gravestone set in the altar floor.

'I can't believe it,' she said, looking down. 'Anywhere else it would be great and ornate. It would be a tomb in mahogany and silver, wouldn't it, like Napoleon's?'

She stared down at a flagstone of modest size, no more celebratory and memorable than any of the thousands of gravestones found in English churchyards. Roughly engraved by a chisel was Shakespeare's name and his date of death. Hewed in the centre was the inscription:

GOOD FREND FOR JESVS SAKE FORBEARE
TO DIGG THE DVST ENCLOASED HEARE
BLESTE BE Ye MAN Yt SPARES THES STONES
AND CVRST BE HE Yt MOVES MY BONES

'Surprised?' Maggie smiled at Hannah's mesmerised expression, accompanied by a slow shake of the head.

'Yes—no,' she added hurriedly. 'I've just realised. He wouldn't have wanted any grand tomb. He was a man of the people. I suppose the church elders had that curse put on, knowing how famous he was, even then.'

'Yes,' said Maggie. 'I'd love to see what's buried with him, down there. What if it's his *First Folio*? Wouldn't that be marvellous?'

Hannah looked up at the large bust of Shakespeare set into the side wall of the sanctuary. He wore a red coat, white collar and an open black jerkin.

'I must say, he looks nothing like the paintings. But does it matter? It's his spirit that matters, isn't it?'

Impulsively, she turned to put her arms around Maggie's neck, breathing softly. 'Thank you so much. This is a day I'll never, ever, *ever* forget.'

Hannah alighted from the bus and walked through the busy streets with the sight, sound and smell of Christmas festivities all around. It aroused nothing in her but a deep melancholy, a feeling that she'd first had as a teenager. But instead of finding ways with which to fight it, she'd turned it into a perverse pleasure when, lying in her room, she would feel the haunting sadness that came from Barber's *Adagio for Strings*, or the mournful beauty of Albinoni's *Adagio in G minor*, or the ache of yearning love in Rachmaninoff's rapturous *Piano Concerto No. 2*.

She stopped at a shop to buy a 'Cognacaise' of brandy, one with flat sides. She stuffed it into her anorak pocket and continued walking towards the Institute.

Ahead of her, standing on the wide pavement at the junction of Scholars Lane and Church Street, was a Salvation Army band playing *Once in Royal David's City*. A small girl dressed as one of Santa's elves, held out a collection tin. As Hannah drew near, she took out a £20 note from her purse.

Then, to the band leader's astonishment, she folded it and pushed it into the tin.

'His love at Christmas,' said the girl, her mouth open, equally amazed.

'And you,' she said, a catch in her voice. 'You have a lovely smile. Don't lose it.'

The child looked at the rucksack. 'Why are you carrying bricks?'

Hannah stared at her and then with a quick smile turned away to continue plodding towards the Institute, three hundred yards ahead on her right. On her left, on the other side of the street, was Shakespeare's sixteenth-century school building, with its long oak-framed frontage.

Gradually her pace of walking became slower and slower until she stood motionless, head down, staring at a crack in the pavement. "*His love at*

Christmas". The girl's voice resonated inside her head.

Looking around to ensure she was not being watched, she drew the knife slowly out of her pocket. The band was now playing *Away in a Manger*. It took her back to when her mother played it on the piano at Christmas, when there was warmth and love all around.

With tears in her eyes she bent down awkwardly, to slip the knife between the bars of a street drain.

She stood up, gasping at the weight of bricks shifting painfully on her back. She was about to cross the road, but then hesitated, becoming motionless once more. After a long pause, her mind made up, she turned and walked back towards the band. She waited until they had finished the carol.

In the short break that followed she asked permission of the band-leader to leave the rucksack in his care, for no more than half an hour. He was only too happy to oblige.

Once free of her burden she walked quickly back towards Henley Street.

The post office was a few yards down on the right. There, she bought a pack of envelopes and some writing paper.

Using the tethered pen at the side-desk she wrote a short letter and placed it inside a self-adhesive envelope. After addressing it, she went out leaving the rest of the writing paper and envelopes behind.

From Henley Street it was a five-minute walk to Rother Street where she entered the police station and handed in the letter.

The reception sergeant, whom she had not seen before, glanced at the address. 'Who shall I say left it?' he said.

She stopped on her way out. 'Hannah Bron. The CID know me. I've signed it.'

Outside, she crossed the road to go down Scholars Lane. Ahead, the Salvation Army band was playing the final chords of *The First Noel*.

As she approached, she took out her purse and, to the girl's further astonishment, poured out the remaining cash into her hand, taking some time slipping coins into the girl's collecting tin.

Watching her, the conductor had a few quick words with the band, before raising his baton.

As she stepped off the pavement to cross the road, she was regaled with an up-tempo version of *We Wish You a Merry Christmas.*

With a melancholy smile, she raised a hand in acknowledgement and set off down Chapel Lane, the descent making it easier to carry what was now an increasingly painful load. She thought of Christ on His cross.

Reaching Southern Lane, she turned right, passing The Swan Theatre and, shortly afterwards, The Other Place. She continued to labour towards the Church of the Holy Trinity.

Entering, she looked around and stood in the silence, closing her eyes in prayer. She remained there for two minutes and then came out to walk down the steps to the riverside.

She stepped on to the grass and approached a willow arch, framed by a curtain of slender branches. Brushing them aside and lowering her head, she crouched inside, lowering herself backwards, the rucksack coming to rest against the grassy bank.

Freed of her burden, she slipped her arms out of its straps and eased herself into a more comfortable position. From a rucksack side-pocket, she withdrew a mini-iPad with earplugs. From her anorak pocket she took out the bottle of brandy.

Ready now, she switched on Puccini's '*Sono andati'* from *La Bohème.*

After its conclusion and while listening to Barber's *Adagio for Strings,* she watched a swan and its cygnets cruise serenely downstream Still drinking steadily and with tears flooding her face, came Albinoni's *Adagio in G minor.*

As the delicate mixture of pain and beauty faded into silence, and still shedding tears, she sat upright against the rucksack, slipping her arms through its straps.

Three times she tried to stand, but each time kept falling back. Finally, she succeeded in standing by bending further forward. About to topple, she said a quick prayer begging God's mercy and, with a choking sob, tumbled headfirst into the water.

At 2.12 p.m. a dog walker on the riverbank opposite the church, was feverishly making a 999 call on his mobile. He'd just seen a young woman fall into the river and remain submerged.

The emergency services sprang into action. The Stratford police, with their experience of dealing with river suicide, knew that the body, if not found within a day or two, would float to the surface due to bacterial gases inflating body tissue. They would then calculate the distance the body would travel, given that the Avon's current flow was an average of nine miles per hour. But, if they searched quickly, they had every chance of finding the body at the actual point of entry into the water.

They were quickly on-scene and located the body exactly where the dog walker had pointed, the weight of a brick-filled rucksack acting as anchor. The contents of the anorak pockets revealed an ID card.

Not long afterwards the police made a call to the Shakespeare Institute office.

'Well, I suppose I have to choose a present or two.' Craig stood up to leave the conservatory.

'And me, said Craig. 'What present can I buy,' he said, getting to his feet, 'that's light to carry home and Elizabethan. Tom, do you know?'

'A quill pen?'

'Good one. That gets you lunch. And you Franky. I owe you big time, so don't say no.'

'I won't. But I'm not present buying, because—'

She broke off as the Director, looking distraught, popped his head into the conservatory and, on seeing them, took a deep breath.

'The police,' he said, grimacing at the news he had to impart. 'They've found a body in the river. They think it's Hannah Bron.' He turned to Franky. 'Her parents are abroad and the staff aren't here. The police have her ID card, but her identity must be verified. Did any of you know her well? It's a dreadful thing to ask, but they need someone to do a formal identification.'

Chapter Thirty-Two

Hell is empty and all the devils are here
The Tempest, Act I, sc. ii

Franky stood in a brilliantly-lit windowless room, some feet away from a table on which lay a body clad in a purple robe. Only its grey-blue face was visible.

She edged nearer, fearfully. Even if she'd not volunteered to identify Hannah's remains, there would have been no escape. When the director put the question to all three of them, both Tom and Craig — even the Director himself — had looked to her in expectation. Was it in recognition of the traditional role of the female, a nod to their primitive and traditional instinct for nursing the wounded in battle, giving succour to the living – and care for the dead? There had been no way out.

She inched closer. Thankfully, Hannah's eyes were closed. Even so, the set of the mouth seemed to challenge her in an obdurate and unyielding manner. If she'd hoped that Hannah would look forgiving in death, she was disillusioned. She did not provide an iota of relief, nor did it diminish her sense of horror. She knew that Hannah, in the company of Alicia, would chase her down the years, until her own dying moment.

She looked to the open door. The pathologist had escorted her into the viewing room and then disappeared, in answer to the phone ringing in his office. But she didn't need his permission to escape, her gorge rising at the sickly smell of death, Formaline and musky-sweet Lysol.

Outside, in the cold fresh air, she put her hands on the brick wall of the mortuary and vomited, the splatter spread over the grey gravel at her feet.

She wiped her mouth with the back of her hand and went around the flat-roofed building to re-enter by the door of the mortuary office. The pathologist, listening on his phone call, saw her and put up his hand. 'Got that. I must go. Talk later. Bye.'

He replaced the phone on the handset and took in her pale face. 'Oh, I'm so sorry!' he exclaimed. 'I shouldn't have left you there. I wouldn't normally have answered, but it was a pre-planned call that I had to take. Would you like a glass of water?'

'No, thanks. It is her,' said Franky in a low voice. 'May I go now?'

'Oh dear. I have to witness you, saying that. I'm so sorry. Would you like to sit down first, and I'll get you a coffee - or water?'

'No, thank you. Let's do it.'

She was forced once again to look down at the face that shamed her. If anything, Hannah's expression seemed even more fixed, resentful and determined than before.

'It's Hannah Bron,' she said in a hoarse voice. Presented with the form to sign, she scribbled her signature and fled outside, guilt and fear pursuing her out like the very devil.

On the bus journey back to the cottage she realised that she could not spend another night there and decided she would pack immediately, then catch the next train to Heathrow where she would book a hotel for the next two nights, before flying home.

She entered the cottage to find a folded piece of note-paper lying on the hallway tiles, along with a key. She bent down to pick both up, holding her breath as she started to read the hand-written note:

> *I have sent a letter to the police, admitting my guilt and saying that no one else was involved. When you read this, I will have killed Franky because she drove me to do it. She got me drunk and said Alicia had burnt my bear when she'd done it herself. She's the true killer. Because I can't live with myself any longer, or stand the thought of prison, I'm*

going to leave this horrible life. I just want you all to know my reason. Love and God's blessing to you all. Hannah.

Franky remained motionless. After a pause, she crunched the note in her hand, then went into the living room and stuffed it into the small, glowing part of the dying fire. She waited until the paper flamed and then proceeded to call American Airlines.

She was in luck. With Christmas demand for seats outstripping supply she managed to cancel her flight and, at the same time, secure a first-class upgrade due to a cancellation on a flight departing Heathrow at 11.40, the next morning.

She booked a cab for 5.30 p.m. and then wrote the following note, addressed to Craig and Tom:

I've had to dash home in an emergency. I'm not returning for personal reasons. Bless both of you. I hope you will have a good life and try to forget what happened. I've already paid the rent for the year. Should there be any additional costs, I have left money in my account with Lloyds Bank in Bridge Street. All you need do is text me and I'll expedite it. I'm sure you will find three delighted guys or girls to share the cottage with you both. Please accept my sincere apologies for all the upsets. Franky X

She placed the note on the kitchen worktop.

Half an hour later, she came downstairs with her luggage.

She checked her watch. The cab-app told her that her ride was no more than six minutes away.

All of a sudden came the question: why hadn't Hannah attempted to kill her? Had she waited for a better opportunity, away from the Institute? Suddenly, a bolt of fear coursed through her. She had a compelling urge to leave the cottage and wait outside, escaping from the place that had promised bliss, but now was nothing more than a macabre house of horror.

But, just as her fingers gripped the front-door latch, she hesitated, let go of the latch and looked back. She remained still for a moment, then drawn by an inner compulsion she went slowly down the hallway, through the kitchen and laundry room, to stop outside Hannah's room, the door half-open.

She paused for a moment, before placing a hand on the door to push it wider.

She stepped hesitantly inside the room and looked around. Was she seeking peace of mind in this, her last visit? Or was it in the way of doing penance to help secure forgiveness, no matter how self-deluding it might be?

On the bed was an expensive-looking book, poking out of the rumpled duvet. However, picking it up she found that the hard cover was made of faux leather. Stamped in gold lettering on the front was the year 2018.

Hannah's diary.

Franky opened it slowly, with an initial sense of foreboding. From early October, the start of the semester, it was evident that the neat handwriting was not a summary of things done on a daily basis, neither was it a jumble of memos and reminders. It was a continuing analysis of how she thought of herself in relation to others.

She scanned through October until she came across the name "Franky."

Wednesday, October 26
Wonderful day. We went to view the cottage. Fabulous olde worlde. I have my own ground-floor room with an adjacent bathroom that you could die for. Franky is a little strange, I'm never quite sure what she's thinking. BUT she has put my mind at rest over Craig. She promised me he's waiting until his bereavement has eased. I am in my seventh heaven! To cap it all, tonight she's taking me out with the others for dinner at The White Swan. She's more than generous. To think that she's subsidised all four of us to the tune of thousands of dollars! I have one fear – Alicia, as a housemate. She's too overbearing for my liking. I did consider withdrawing but the temptation was too great. It has a superb inglenook! Just like the one in The Six Wives of Henry VIII on the BBC. It's like a dream!

Franky glanced at her watch. Conscious of the time, she flipped forward to a page in early December. From this date she quickly scanned through the daily entries until she found Franky's name again:

Wednesday, December 12
I don't really know myself, if I ever did. I thought Franky was the soul of generosity and kindliness, except now I'm wondering if Craig was deliberately invited so she could play around and mess me up – all that talk of pegs! Fodder for fiction? Franky is a mass of contradictions and anomalies like promising me a champagne meal and then telling me she's too busy. And this country idyll, a complete farce! She pretends to be sympathetic but that's all. I think she wants to be kind and nice, but for some reason can't get there. It's a pity because I can't help but feel sorry for her.

The doorbell rang. Taking the diary with her she went to open the door. The driver, a young man, stood there. 'Morning.'

'Morning.' She brought her luggage outside, double-locked the door and then posted a clutch of keys through the letter box.

She got into the car to the loud cawing of rooks.

As the driver stowed her luggage away her cell phone jingled. It was an email from Annabelle:

My dear Franky, I have just heard about Hannah. I am devastated. You must be suffering greatly. I've no wish to impose myself upon you at this time, but if there is any way that I can help, by talking or listening, I am here, at your disposal. I shall be in my office today after 4 p.m.

She deleted the message

THE BOSTON GLOBE

Wednesday, December 19, 2018

By Kelsie Maylam Staff Reporter

American Students released in UK

Police in Warwickshire, England, have released four American students being questioned over the brutal murder of a fellow student. The five were on a postgraduate course at The Shakespeare Institute in Stratford-upon-Avon. Detective Chief Inspector Rees, leading the inquiry, has named the victim as Alicia Somerstone from Miami. Her body was discovered in the Institute garden early on Monday morning of this week. One of the four held in custody was Françoise O'Tierney, the daughter of Fergal O'Tierney who teaches English at Boston College. The Institute, where the deceased was studying for an MA degree in Shakespearean studies, has been a favorite choice of American postgraduates ever since it opened in 1951.

Chapter Thirty-Three

Will all great Neptune's ocean wash this
Blood clean from my hand?
Macbeth, Act II, sc. ii

The train took forty-five minutes to reach Heathrow. On arrival, Franky managed to book a room at the Premier Inn, adjacent to the airport. She consoled herself in the knowledge that, the next morning she could eat a leisurely breakfast, as her flight departed around mid-day.

At 9.30 a.m. the next day, she caught a local bus to Terminal 5. Once rid of her luggage and having passed through fast-track security, she went from the exclusive Walk-Through entrance into the First Wing lounge. There, she drew cash from an ATM and then sipped a complimentary glass of champagne while trying to read the day's international edition of *The New York Times*, except she wasn't reading, merely staring.

The spider was back

It crawled and prickled up her spine to the nape of her neck. What if her careful planning was flawed in any way? She'd gone over it time and time again but now, faced with oncoming reality, she realised that the failure of any one link in the day's itinerary could be disastrous.

She looked at her watch and went to sit in one of the private booths. Using her tablet, she went straight to the website of the Boston PD and copied in her detailed account of the boy's rape, saved for this moment. She ended by giving her ETA at Logan International, together with her home address and cell phone number, adding that she would arrive by cab, direct from the airport. She ticked a box that indicated she was willing to assist the police composite-artist in creating the face of her father's victim. Having sent the message, her last task was to book a single room for the night at the Samuel Sewell Inn, in Brookline near Boston.

Having eaten, she found an empty armchair and tried to relax by doing a spell of Autogenics. As she concentrated on each part of her body, her mind drifted into a semi-trance. At first it was a pleasant experience, but then an unpleasant memory surfaced, that of her first confession. Yvette had taken her, at the tender age of eleven, into the gloom of the local church. There, feeling embarrassed, she'd chosen to sit alone in an empty pew.

A few other people were dotted about, either making their penance or waiting their turn, while listening to the echoing whispers and faint echoing tones of the priest from the nearby recess.

She remembered sitting down in the confessional with its musky smell of dusty curtains and saying, as rehearsed, *"Bless me Father, for I have sinned. This is my first confession."* But then she'd stalled, the words frozen on her lips.

It was the priest, in his soft, kind voice, telling her to close her eyes and say what she'd rehearsed. It had given her the confidence to continue, saying *"I called Helen Bookbinder a warts troll."* She felt embarrassed doing it, simply because the heavy atmosphere of the confessional was surely there for the forgiveness of weighty sins such as theft or murder, not silly things – and especially when Helen had called her worse names and all she'd done was pay her back in kind. And, because it was the only misdemeanour she could think of – she'd decided that being stingy with your spending money hardly counted – she'd stuck by it. For this sin she'd been given 'Five Hail Marys' as penance.

Back in her pew, she knelt on a cushion and recited them before re-joining Yvette.

Then came the walk outside into the bright sunlight, supposedly forgiven, but no. She felt worse than before she went in. She considered herself a fraud in not feeling any regret or sorrow when doing penance, and so felt guilty. What she'd done, according to a White Father the following Sunday, a visiting member of an evangelical group within the Church, was to take "the first step down the ladder to hell." He'd aimed it at her specifically, she was sure of that, as he'd caught her eye twice during his sermon. He'd warned her of the fiery consequences if ever she took a sacrament in vain.

Hell. What did Ariel say? "Hell is empty and all the devils are here?" It surely applied to her. She thought of the boy her father had raped. Heat rushed to her face. She'd had plenty of time in which to call the police, but failed because of her greed and the delight she had in taking his money. Could she go on telling herself that murdering Alicia had been entirely in self-defence? There was no escaping the fact that she'd hated Alicia, and Hannah had been her weapon.

Two lives destroyed. It sent a spasm of dread through her body.

How to atone? She knew of only one way – to kill her father, the one responsible.

She glanced at her watch. In twelve hours or so, she would be at peace with herself. She would have vaulted over her fantasy loops and brought justice, not in the passing fantasy of the imagination, but in hard reality.

It seemed that no more than half an hour had passed when a smiling steward was bending over her, telling her quietly that her flight had been called.

It was the first time that she'd flown first class and enjoyed the luxury of the bed and the feel of silky pyjamas. She needed sleep before the expected rigours of the day. To this end she took two Temazepam tablets in case her nerves and fear of failure kept her awake.

It was in surprise and relief that she awoke not long before the midday arrival at Logan and was thankful for those seven hours of sleep. She needed it for what was to come.

After clearing customs and immigration, a cab driver from PACS stood at arrivals with a card marked *O'Tierney*.

'Police headquarters,' she said, getting inside.

As soon as the cab moved off, she checked her cell phone for text messages. There was one from a 'Detective M Connors' telling her to give BPD her name on arrival and she'd be down to greet her.

On arrival at 1 Schroeder Plaza, she entered the large building to be checked by security, before being admitted to reception. She had a five-minute wait before Connors appeared, a slim, friendly woman who took her to the top floor, provided her with coffee, then went through her original account of witnessing the rape, before committing the basic details to print. Fergal's bloodstained note was taken for forensic examination. After checking and cross-checking, Franky signed the statement, with Connors adding her witness signature.

Only then did Franky ask the dreaded question: had any other boy from the same school at which her father worked, been raped or sexually abused in any way?

Connors was sorry, saying it was not the kind of information she was presently allowed to disclose. She would defer the question to her superior officer. He might be able to help her with that.

She was then introduced to the police composite-artist, a friendly and eager young man, who rubbed his hands, such was his enthusiasm.

'You're my real first job,' he said, escorting her into his small office.

'I'm pleased,' said Franky. 'You won't bodge it.'

'Bodge?'

'Means doing a bad job, repairing or mending something. A bodger is an old English word for a woodworker making furniture before the days of machinery.'

'Oh, nice, like it. So that's where it comes from. Okay. Now this is the latest, a great piece of kit,' he said, as they sat before the screen. The best ever. Now, close your eyes and relax, just think about the boy's face. Try and picture it. When you're ready I'll ask you questions, okay?'

He took Franky through a long list of checks and queries, each time dragging a facial item from the left of the split–screen to drop on the right. By this method he gradually worked up an approximation of the boy's face. Then his pace slowed down and, through more questioning, he refined – and kept refining – the picture, to the point where she was looking at "that boy."

'That's him,' she said. 'Jason. Definitely.'

Connors came in with her superior officer, a thickset, tough looking Detective Sergeant Halloran. Together, they stared at the screen.

Within half an hour the principal of Jason's school was looking at a monitor screen with a detective. The boy's image was then circulated among the rest of the staff, and it was confirmed that the boy was Jason Cartwright, a student at the school, now aged fifteen.

The detective was told that the boy's report card had shown 'B' on average at the age of thirteen, but over the last two years it had dropped to 'C'. Not only that, his behaviour had deteriorated, with him showing marked signs of being distrustful of adults. He had changed from being a normal and gregarious young teenager into a moody, solitary, and sometimes bad-tempered individual, but for no apparent reason.

'Okay,' said Halloran. 'You mentioned the entrance code. Where is it?'

'Side of the gates inset on the right-hand brick pillar.'

Halloran escorted her to the exit. 'You want to know if he's done it more than once. There's another kid at the same school, started to tell us, then clammed up. We tried all ways. Kid scared as hell. Nothing yet.'

Franky felt a stab of guilt. She asked when it happened.

'Oh, coupla months ago.'

It was the worst news possible. It made her task even more urgent. She remembered to call her father.

He answered within seconds.

She switched off quickly. 'He's there.' She stopped as she was about to step outside. 'Have you any idea what time you'll be round?'

'About an hour. You scared of him?'

'No. I'm not.'

Halloran looked keenly at her. 'I think you are.'

'I don't think I am. I hate him too much.'

He smiled a little. 'Okay. Keep your cell switched on. Any problems, call. You have the number.'

'Yes. And thanks.'

'Okay. Keep safe.' He turned away and then checked. 'Hey, why not stay here, come along with us?'

She thanked him, but declined, saying she had things to do, important calls to make from home.

The cab was quick to arrive.

On route, to the west of Brookline, they passed between banks of coffee-coloured and pockmarked snow piled at the roadsides. On the last quarter mile to the house, the rows of spruce trees lining the road were either white-laced or glistening with bright sparkles of hoar frost.

As they drew nearer to the house, she caught a glimpse of its snow-mantled tower above the trees.

She asked the driver to stop outside the entrance gates.

'Don't you want me to go up to the house?'

'No, that's okay.'

'Won't your feet get wet?'

'No, I'll be okay.'

'Oh thanks.' The cabby was surprised – and appreciative – when she handed him a larger tip than normal. 'You have a good day now.'

'And you.'

The cab drew away to the crackling of ice.

She pressed the four-digit code and waited for the gates to open. Stepping through, she could just see the nose of her father's car, a Range Rover Sport, parked outside the house.

With the gates closing behind her, she walked fifty yards up the driveway and then diverted quickly to cross the snow-covered parkland towards the tool shed, situated out of sight of anyone on the ground floor of the house.

Concentrating on her mission, she ignored the fact that her feet and ankles were, by now, wet and icily cold.

She entered the shed to be greeted by a smell that took her back to when she was a child. Each Christmas, she and her imaginary Grandpa would collect fir cones. He'd show her ways of turning them into Christmassy items, such as place-name markers, candle holders and even a miniature snowman with a top hat. Her greatest pleasure was in painting cones all the colours of the rainbow, then arranging them inside a triangular wooden frame that she placed in the porch next to a lantern.

Those cones, as well as those unused, were still there, packed into a cardboard box and gathering dust. It brought a lump to her throat. She'd not been in the shed for at least ten years.

She looked around the shelves for a length of coiled rope that she'd seen in the past, but was there no longer. Panicking a little, she then remembered.

Leaving her luggage behind, she went out to plod through snow into the woodland.

She came to the secret place of her childhood, a clearing where two ropes dangled from the same branch. One was made of fibre, the other polypropylene. Whereas the fibre rope had deteriorated over the years, the synthetic rope had not, being impervious to weather.

Leaping up, she grasped it in both hands and began hauling herself up, her locked feet sliding upwards with each strong pull. Breathless, she reached the point at which a branch was connected to another by a large wooden seat.

Drawing level, she managed to sit down and unclip the rope from its shackle, allowing it to drop to the ground. She then grasped hold of the old rope and launched herself from the seat. As she swung outwards her body weight set the branch arcing down, allowing her to drop easily on to the damp sponge, formed by generations of fallen leaves.

Now came the point at which she remembered her Canopy Climbers training and set about making a noose with the polypropylene rope, one that would take heavy weights.

On completion she draped it over her head and then pulled the rope, stopping at the moment the noose clung to her neck. Satisfied, she loosened it, and coiled the rest of the rope around her shoulder.

On her way out of the clearing she stood for a few moments, gazing at her name and the date carved on a tree trunk when she was twelve, still discernible in the wet bark. She thought the passing of another winter would probably see most of it gone.

She left the woodland to return to the shed, where she located a tin of machinery grease. She prised it open, plunging in two fingers to grease the length of rope that would be in contact with the running knot. She then went out, carrying the rope.

She approached the back of the house unseen, to stand against its rear wall. After a minute, relieved that she'd not been seen, she bent down to remove a loose ventilation grille from the wall. Inside the ducting was a damp-proof pouch. She unwrapped it to take out the house emergency key, after which she replaced the pouch and clipped back the grille.

She let herself into the laundry room, careful not to make any noise. She remained motionless, listening. All that could be heard, was the rumble of the central-heating boiler.

She slipped off her anorak, removed her wet shoes and opened a wall cupboard. Inside was the house circuit–breaker panel and, adjacent, a yellow switch. She flipped it down and was relieved to see a green light come on, an indication that the front gates were opening. She'd decided that she couldn't risk Halloran forgetting, or losing, the code.

She padded silently into the kitchen and from there into the wide oak-panelled hall. She could hear a piano playing *The Goldberg Variations*, the music coming from under the spacious landing. It emanated from her father's study, tucked away under its overhang.

To Bach's intricate and delicately balanced piano-track, she quickly crossed the hallway to slip up the left of the two curved staircases, onto the landing and then into her room.

Breathing hard, her heart palpitating, she snatched open a drawer looking for a pair of thin leather gloves. Rummaging around she found them and put them on. She was about to close the drawer when something caught her attention. She found herself staring at a black rosary, a necklace of beads with a crucifix. Why hadn't she thrown it away? She'd kept telling herself to get rid of it ever since she'd lapsed in the faith.

She withdrew it to study the beads. The large one, she remembered, had to be fingered when you said the "Our Father' prayer." On the ten small beads you prayed the ten "Hail Marys." But, was it followed by one, or two "Glory Be" prayers? And was the "Fatima" prayer after that?

She hesitated a moment and then placed the rosary around her neck. She carried the rope out to the landing, where she knelt down in front of the thick central post of the balustrade. Shivering, and breathing hard, she tied the rope to its base with a "figure 8 follow-through" knot.

With the noose draped around her neck and holding the tail of the rope in one hand, she bent down over the railing, her breath coming in short spasms.

'Dad?' she called out in a strained voice. She tried to relax her throat muscles. '*Dad!*' Her call was louder.

After a pause, she heard the study door open.

Then he appeared, wearing a checked shirt and jeans with a wide belt that was locked by a cow's-head buckle. He looked around the hallway.

'Franky? Is that you?'

'Up here, Dad.'

He looked upwards, at first in surprise, and then in quick-growing horror at the rope coiled round her neck.

'What…' he stammered, 'what are you doing!'

'You'd like to kill me, wouldn't you? No, let me do it for you. You've been killing me all my life. And raping children.'

'NO FRANKY!' he bellowed. 'NO!'

She swung a leg over the railing.

He raced up the stairs.

'This is my present for you dad!'

He reached the top and hurtled towards her, his arm outstretched. 'NO!'

Lunging at her.

Rope yanked tight. Smooth over roll-top.

Click of breaking neck

Amen

Stretched out on the landing, his chest heaving, he listened to the creak of taut rope, straining and slipping against woodwork.

He shifted round to face the balustrade. After a pause he began to crawl forward to press his sweaty forehead against two of its cool brown posts.

He dropped his eyes to watch the body of his daughter swing gently into view, the soft slap and click of the rope out of rhythm with that of Bach's cool music.

Painfully, he got to his knees. Then, raising a hand, he grasped hold of the banister rail and hauled himself upright.

He took a deep breath, then stepped back to examine the floor to see if anything had been dropped in his attempt to grab hold of her clothing.

Satisfied, he went into the bathroom to wash his hands thoroughly, looking at himself in the mirror. A thin smile began to cross his face.

He went downstairs to stand before her body, now almost motionless. He stared up at the rosary around her neck and frowned.

Suddenly he cocked his head at the sound of a vehicle coming up the driveway, his frown becoming more intense as it grew louder.

He wheeled round to glimpse blue flashing lights through the thick frosted glass of the front-door surround.

Racing upstairs, he seized the rope and heaved it sideways.

Shoots downstairs

Sucks in breath

Blue lights gone

Engine switched off

Thud of doors closing

Figures loom in the frosted glass

Shrill alert of doorbell

'OH MY GOD!' 'FRANKY!' 'WHY OH WHY!'

Flings open door and collapses, sobbing, to his knees …

Detective Sergeant Halloran, looking down, hesitated before striding past him into the cavernous hallway.

All to the steady, crystal-clear and metronomic notes of the Variations.

Take up the bodies. Such a sight as this
Becomes the field, but here shows much amiss

AFTERMATH

The coroner's inquest into the death of Francoise O'Tierney, heard first from Bianca Findler, a psychotherapist who had dealt with her hypersensitivity to slight, stemming from a troubled childhood. She testified how she had warned her mother of the possibility that it could develop into violent behaviour as Francoise reached adulthood. More relevant was her comment that Francoise's ever-present anxiety was due to "lack of sociability," together with feelings of self-disgust and lack of self-worth.

The next witness was a psychiatrist who found evidence that Francoise had exhibited all the signs of latent paranoid schizophrenia by admitting to smelling "unexplained acidic odours," as well as hearing strange, often loud, noises. This was corroborated by a fellow student, an elderly Margaret Wilkins, who testified that Francoise was convinced of a plot against her, led by her father and involving her tutor.

Then Detective Sergeant Halloran described what happened on his arrival at the house to come across a scene of "grand operatic tragedy." The door had been opened by a wailing Fergal O'Tierney who fell to his knees in apparent grief, while the body of his daughter hung from the landing behind him. It had led Halloran to suspect that Francoise's death had occurred "in suspicious circumstances" and was not entirely satisfied, even after an intensive and lengthy investigation.

The next witness was Dr Annabelle Lloyd, via video-link from the Shakespeare Institute in Stratford Upon Avon. As tutor and welfare advisor, she spoke of her concern for Francoise's state of mind in the weeks preceding her death. She stated that she had not only harboured thoughts of revenge for her father's appalling crime but, in so doing, had suicidal thoughts. This, plus her disturbing behaviour, had led Dr Lloyd to prevent her from acting in the annual drama production, solely out of fear for her well-being.

Having heard all the forensic evidence, the coroner took a long time to consider her verdict: Suicide.

Kelsie G. Maylam, a staff reporter on *The Boston Globe*, covered Francoise's death and, with growing fascination, the inquest. In the time leading up to Fergal O'Tierney's trial for child rape, she began research for her planned book. Not only was she gripped by the fact that his arrest occurred at the same time as his daughter's death, but also by the deaths of Francoise's two student friends back in the UK, one by homicide and the other suicide. On discovering that all three lived together while studying at The Shakespeare Institute in Stratford-upon-Avon, she felt certain that the story would resonate worldwide with readers of crime non–fiction. She was positive that the book would have a commercial USP guaranteed to grab readers, especially as the main settings were the historic Shakespeare Institute and a characterful Tudor cottage. Not only that, *three* of the five residents had died within three days of each other. What could be more fascinating than that?

Kelsie interviewed Dr Lloyd in late October 2019. There, at the Shakespeare Institute, she learnt of the events that took place during the autumn term of 2018, including an account of Françoise's behaviour and the effects that her father's crime had upon her.

She then visited Yvette O'Tierney who was living with relatives in La Rochelle, now that her husband was facing a long prison sentence. That interview led to the discovery of Hannah Bron's diary, including notes for a novel that Francoise intended to write.

The diary, Kelsie discovered, was not merely a collection of daily notes and comments, but throughout showed a sensitive monitoring and analysis of Hannah's own feelings as well as insights into Francoise and the others. She bought both the diary and Francoise's notes. Yvette, needing money, had been eager to sell them after the IRS had informed her that O'Tierney's bank account was in sequestration while they investigated his large income from trading online.

Kelsie's excitement on securing the diary was cut short on finding that an entry for week beginning Sunday 9 December was missing, the page torn out and with no satisfactory explanation from Yvette.

Kelsie managed to track down Detective Sergeant Halloran, who had just retired. He gave her an account of what he found at Fergal O'Tierney's house, thousands of computer images showing children being abused in the foulest of ways. When O'Tierney continued to deny the rape of Jason, he was shown the image of the boy, produced by a composite–artist. Halloran had then shown him the boy's statement, detailing the events of the day in question. His teacher, Fergal O'Tierney, had promised to show him a video of his favourite team in English Premiership football. It transpired that the boy was British, his father having secured a visa to work as a teacher at the *Artists for Humanity Center in Boston*. In court, Jason admitted that he had allowed himself to be taken to O'Tierney's house where the abuse took place. O'Tierney's defence attorney tried to confuse the boy about his surroundings at the crime scene. Despite Jason stating that he could remember only one staircase in the house, it gained O'Tierney nothing.

It was the publicity from this that led to another victim coming forward. In the weeks that followed, the list of O'Tierney's victims grew to nine in total, all male, the youngest ten years old.

Kelsie Maylam gave her book the title, *Murder at the Institute*. It took a year to write, and within six months it featured in the *New York Times* non-fiction bestsellers list.

A film company wanted to take a six months option, in which time they hoped to clinch a deal with *Netflix*, but were trumped by *Twentieth Century Fox* stepping in with a better offer.

O'Tierney was given life imprisonment without parole. In his tenth month of incarceration he succeeded in committing suicide by hanging himself with a strip of bedding tied to a ventilation grille in his cell.

The British inquest into Hannah Bron's death resulted in a "narrative verdict," a term meaning that no individual could be named as responsible. A pathologist declared that he had found a large amount of Varenicline in her body, a drug used in anti–smoking medication and known to provoke anger as one of its side effects. Hannah Bron had taken five times the daily maximum of the drug. That, allied to the large amount of alcohol consumed, would have greatly multiplied the chances of her becoming violent. There was no evidence to suggest that neither the drug, nor brandy, had been covertly or forcibly administered.

In Newark, Hannah Bron's home town, Craig Muirhaven and Thomas Vantusian attended her funeral. A teddy bear, sitting on top of a coffin heaped with flowers, made the journey with her to the crematorium. It had a wreath around its neck with two messages attached from her fellow students, each expressing their sadness. A third wreath, lying on top of the coffin, was signed by the director and staff of the Institute, together with a quote from Shakespeare:

But, if the while I think of thee, dear friend,
All losses are restor'd and sorrows end

Dr Lloyd remained at the Shakespeare Institute. The latest intake of students regarded her black clothing, not as a celebration of the late Elizabethan cult of melancholy, but as a symbol of mourning for the three tragic students.

Tom kept in touch with Craig, informing him that he was returning to the Institute with the intention of studying for a PhD. A week later, Craig called him to say that he'd decided to do the same. Tom suggested they shared an apartment together, to which Craig responded positively.

Tom made an early journey to Stratford ahead of the course and found a suitable two-bed flat that was comfortable, clean and warm. He took photographs at the premises and sent them to Craig. With his permission, Tom signed the rental agreement.

Tuesday, 27 September 2019

> *It is not in the stars*
> *To hold our destiny*
> *but in ourselves.*
> *Julius Caesar*, Act I, sc. ii

Tom placed his umbrella against the side of the sales counter before paying for the book that Waterstones had reserved for him. It was then he heard a familiar voice.

'Well, Moriarty, we meet again.'

He turned with a smile. 'Craig.' He reached out to clasp his hand. 'My dear fellow. You finally made it. Top man. How was the flight?'

'No problem. I picked up the key and let me say you've rented an apartment to die for. Love the power shower.'

'Good. So, we're settled.' Tom looked at his watch. 'I booked the table. We've got plenty of time.'

'What have you bought?' Craig nodded at the thick hardback in Tom's hand.

Tom showed him the front cover. *A Companion to Renaissance Drama – Blackwell Companions to Literature and Culture*

'Hmm,' Craig mused. 'Your thesis will be English Renaissance Drama and … fashioning femininity?'

'No. English Renaissance Drama, Representation of the Supernatural, from 1442 to 1530.'

'Hah. Shades of ghouls and the Gothic again. Close to your heart, Tom.'

Laughing, they walked out into a sunlit High Street.

'Decided on yours yet?' said Tom.

'I thought I had. Dr Fitch was going with something based on Wilson Knight's destruction of Hamlet, but Annabelle thought I'd be more at home with "Kingship and the Political Context of the First Tetralogy." So that's what I'm doing.'

'Annabelle hates Wilson Knight. Calls him infamous.'

'Annabelle would. Very strait-laced is Annabelle, despite her allure.'

They turned left, heading for Lambs Restaurant, situated appropriately in Sheep Street. Entering, they were led to a window table.

After taking the menus and ordering wine, they relaxed and smiled at each other.

'This time next year,' said Craig, 'where do you hope to be?'

'Well, given I get my PhD, I'm told that Bradley may have an assistant professorship going around then. I'd give it a shot.'

Craig began to chuckle. 'No, you won't. You'll go and do a Masters in nuclear physics.'

It was one of those rare moments when Tom laughed out loud. 'No, no. I've decided. I'd like to lecture for a few years then have a break directing Shakespeare – either at The Globe – or off Broadway, maybe Chicago. I saw the *Dream*, Joe Dowling's production. I was impressed. There's still a way to go though. Shakespeare doesn't have to be transgressive, but it can still be conceptual without getting the critics' dander up. Shakespeare for me is radical and still is. We'll see.'

The meal arrived. Over lunch, a breast of Gressingham duck for Craig, a pear and Stilton salad for Tom, each anticipated that edgy pause in their conversation, the point at which they'd covered everything they could think of, both knowing that the grim topic had to be addressed at some point.

They'd been chatting for twenty minutes when Craig, after a long pause and recognising that the time had come, took a deep breath. 'Well. How's it been, Tom?' he said gently.

'Hmm. "How has it been?" Well...' Tom glanced down into the street. 'It's not been anything but purgatory.' He looked back at Craig. 'You?'

'I've been on the other side of Mars.' Craig shook his head. 'I still get flashbacks ... or nightmares. I'm in a frozen wasteland with Hannah, Alicia... to think that this time a year ago we were a happy crew.'

Tom nodded. 'We were.'

They looked solemnly at each other. 'You do realise,' said Craig, 'if we'd handed Hannah in, she might still be alive?'

'Yes. You're right. We should have handed her in. I'm sorry, deeply, deeply sorry.' Tom gazed at him with a mournful expression. 'Being still under police investigation doesn't help.'

'It certainly doesn't. Do you hesitate whenever your cell goes?'

'More than hesitate. My stomach churns.'

'My stomach jumps. I've got the Olympic record for it.'

It raised a chuckle from Tom, before sighing. 'I wish I'd been more like you. Less anxious to show off my knowledge in forensics,'

'Except it worked.'

'Yes. Making me guilty.'

'And me, don't forget. I was rather surprised they gave us our passports back.'

'So was I. It was probably our social standing,' said Tom with a smile. 'Not the kind to hide in a Brazilian rain forest?'

'You may be right. Coffee?'

'No, I'm good. One back at the apartment?'

'Sure.'

They settled back in their chairs. Craig opened his mouth to speak and then hesitated.

'Go on.' Tom nodded, prompting him.

'It's just that ….' Craig paused. 'There's not a day I don't think about it.'

'Me too.'

'Tell me something. How did Franky strike you – *after* we'd been released?'

Tom raised his eyebrows. 'In what way?'

'I, erm,' Craig hesitated. 'I thought the lady did protest too much.' He picked up his glass. 'I think she's the guilty one, Tom. Not Hannah and not you.'

Tom's eyes flickered.

'Okay.' Craig shuffled his chair forward a little. 'Franky told Hannah that Alicia had burnt her bear, had seen her do it. Franky told me that, herself. She said she was frightened that Hannah might not believe her and get revenge for thinking *she'd* burnt it.' It was her constant preoccupation with it, her need to talk about it that made me suspicious. Remember the inquest? The psychotherapist thought that Franky was lacking in self-confidence, her ego continually crushed, that kind of thing? She wanted reassurance and more so after the murder.'

'Yes, said Tom. 'If I remember, she said that Franky wanted to be admired and respected.'

'Exactly.' Craig took a sip of wine. 'I also managed to talk to Brooklyn before the Christmas break. Apparently, Franky told Hannah that her father had raped her.'

'What!' Tom knitting his brows together, stared at Craig.

'It was a lie. I think Franky was seeking sympathy, presenting herself as some kind of tragic hero.'

'One moment.' Tom raised a forefinger. 'You say you were suspicious of Franky. In what way?'

'Okay.' Craig looked around to satisfy himself that he wasn't overheard. He lowered his voice a little. 'We know from the inquest that Franky had developed into a paranoid schizophrenic. She believed there was a plot led by her father, Alicia and Annabelle. She also hated Alicia for robbing her of Desdemona. I think she wanted a fall guy to kill Alicia and take the rap. And that fall-guy was Hannah. She got her drunk with brandy, then added your anti-smoking drug. It was mentioned at Alicia's inquest – what's it called? Varen …?'

'Varenicline.' Tom nodded slowly.

'Know what? At first, I thought you must have done it. But it couldn't be. So, simple deduction, Franky.'

Tom wiped the edge of his mouth with his napkin. 'I think that you and I have found the murderer — sorry, can you give us a moment?' Tom put up an apologetic hand at the waiter about to address them. He turned back to Craig. 'Franky caught me smoking outside the conservatory. I told her I'd stopped taking Varenicline because it made me angry. Later, I was missing a strip but I said nothing because I could see no motive for any of you to steal it. So, when it was mentioned at the inquest, I gave it some thought. None of you smoked. So, who needed it and why? Franky. She remembered what I said. She put it in Hannah's brandy. *Five times* the daily limit. Add the amount of alcohol?'

Craig took a deep breath. 'Yes. That's it. Got to be.'

'Yes. Just one more thing. Just before Alicia's murder I was on the landing, about to go downstairs, when I heard Hannah in Franky's room. She was sobbing and Franky wasn't sympathetic. She was accusing her of something. "*Didn't* you," she kept saying.'

Craig stared at Tom. 'Did you tell the police?'

'In a way. I put it in the box in the Great Hall. I was too much of a coward to put my name to it.'

They continued looking at each other.

Tom hesitated. 'Obviously nothing came of it. The police probably interviewed Franky about it. She'd deny it. My note had no author. I remained anonymous because I didn't want it hanging over me. And that's me being honest. Look. The more we talk about it the more guilty I feel. Do you know what I thought my thesis should be, coming back here? "Shame and Guilt – Macbeth, Othello, Hamlet." The three tragic heroes. Maybe, subconsciously, I hoped to work it out of my system.' Tom shook his head. 'What a fool I was. It would just have nailed in the guilt and remorse even further. I—'

'No Tom. You were in no way responsible for what Franky did. She killed herself because she had Alicia murdered and caused Hannah's suicide. Franky killed both of them. You killed nobody. Franky stole that Varenicline from you. You didn't hate Alicia. You didn't make Hannah a murderer.'

'Hmm. I think I'll choose you as my attorney when we come to Heaven's Gates.' Tom stared out of the window to see a large expanse of dark grey sky moving in from the west. 'You've forgotten something. My forensic pitch to you and Franky. I forced you to say you trusted me. If I hadn't done that—'

Craig put out a hand. 'Tom. I was the one who volunteered the car, remember?'

'No, Craig. You were way down the food chain.'

'I think we should stop. If we keep digging, we might regret it.' Craig's voice fell quieter. 'There's not a day goes by that I don't relive it.' He studied Tom for a moment. 'Listen. I don't have to forgive you, because you weren't to blame. We were so shocked we couldn't think straight. The cover-up was instant. I don't know, even now, how you managed to trick them. It was amazing. And, as for me, I was scared stiff all the time.'

'But I did force you into it.'

'No, you didn't.' Craig picked up the wine bottle and topped up Tom's glass. 'Okay. When we leave here, I'd like to think I can call you any time and you me. I don't want to read about you stabbing yourself with a bare bodkin. Okay?'

Tom nodded. 'Yes. Two shoulders better than one. If it does get that bad, we can Skype each other and watch the tears flow.'

'To counselling each other when needed?'

'Absolutely.'

They clinked glasses.

'To absent friends?' said Craig.

'Yes. Absent friends.'

Suddenly Craig lowered his head to hide his emotions.

Tom blinked in slight embarrassment. But there was nothing he could say or do.

They sat in silence for a moment or two.

'I'll tell you how I escaped madness,' said Tom. 'I thought the only way—for me at any rate, is to do the very best I can in whatever work I do. Things that bring joy to others.'

'Yes. Better than doing penance. Yes.' Craig, lifted his head. 'I go along with that.'

Tom wrinkled his brows. 'I forgot to tell you. As a way of salving my conscience I bought a memorial plaque for the three of them.'

'Memorial? How – where?'

'At the Institute. It's pinned on the wall, in reception.'

'How much? I'm paying half.'

'No.' Tom looked solemnly at him. 'I can never pay you back.'

'Okay. Look. I'm not going out of here without you happier. So why don't we drink to us?'

'Good idea.'

They clinked glasses with a sense of finality.

Craig insisted on paying for the drinks as well as the meal.

As they left the restaurant, the sky was a steely grey.

On the way to their apartment it began to rain.
Tom opened up his long, black umbrella.
It enclosed them both.

If you enjoyed this novel please take
a look at the next in the series
'The Stratford Trilogy'

HER THIRD SLAUGHTER

To be published in 2021

Stratford-upon-Avon

HERALD

Tuesday, 15 December 18, 2019

Body of RSC actor found with stab wounds

Detective Chief Inspector Jane Rees, of Warwickshire CID, has appealed to the general public for information regarding the murder of Rex Pennington, an RSC actor and local resident, who was found dead inside his home in Felgate Street, Old Town. Mr Pennington, in his sixties, was a well-known figure in the Warwickshire LGBT community and one of the organisers of the Pride Festival held in August this year.

Read on for an extract from this new thriller…

Detective Chief Inspector Jane Rees is at the forefront of this story. Her failure to apprehend Hannah Bron for the murder of Alicia Somerstone, weighs heavily on her conscience. She also believes, however wrongly, that she is responsible – in some measure at least – for the suicide of Franky O'Tierney. Can she make amends in her next murder investigation? Take a moment to read the opening pages. I'm hoping you will be intrigued.

On my Author Page I will let you know when it will become available.

Chapter One

Jane Rees awoke with a thick headache, feeling exhausted and slightly sick. With an aching sigh she turned her head to blink hard at the bedside clock. In the half-light of the room, its curtains drawn, she could just make out the time: 8.57 a.m.

She stretched out an arm to grab hold of the police-mobile that had woken her, lay back and held it close to her eyes. It was a text message sent from the control room at Warwickshire Police Headquarters. She was completely unaware that it had bleeped and buzzed in the last hour; not surprising since she'd found sleep only a couple of hours ago.

She re-read the message carefully. It stated that a body had been found at a house in south–west Stratford. As Detective Chief Inspector she was tasked as a Senior Investigating Officer to be on-scene as soon as possible.

The message ended with the words: "*MIR Roth.*" Decoded. it stated that "a major incident room had been established within the local police station".

She got out of bed to draw back the curtains. Although in a hurry, she was fixated for a moment by the scene outside.

In any season the sight of the Warwickshire countryside was always welcome, but on this morning in mid–December the black skeletons of trees and hedges did nothing to alleviate her fear and despair.

She turned away from the window to get dressed. She had good cause to be in such a mental and emotional stew. Something had happened the previous evening that had shocked her to the core.

She winced, closing her eyes. How does a senior police officer – how does *anyone* – deal with the discovery that they're married to a criminal? Disregarding her tiredness, how could she get through the day with *that* thought plaguing her? Nevertheless, somehow, she had to shut him out of her mind if she were to deal with the rigours of a murder investigation.

She called her deputy, Detective Inspector Drake. 'I'm on my way,' she said in a thick voice. 'Had a bad night.'

'Don't worry, I've done the "golden hour".' He was referring to that window of opportunity following the discovery of a body in which there was the best chance of arresting a suspect. 'Elderly guy,' he added. 'Stabbed in the neck, by the looks of it.'

'Okay,' she said, trying to sound alert. 'I've got my skates on.'

Ten minutes later, dressed in a white-striped shirt and a neat charcoal-grey trouser suit, she gave a final touch-up to her face and steeled herself to step out on to the landing. She could see into the spare room, the door half-open, revealing husband Charlie, asleep.

She crept downstairs, stopping in the hallway to where her cat was waiting, eagerness for food written in its large orange eyes.

'Sorry, Chippy,' she whispered. 'We're in the same boat, matey.'

She entered the kitchen, pulled open a drawer and took out a strip of Paracetamol tablets. Pressing one out of the blister pack, she bent down at the sink and swallowed it with a mouthful of tap water.

Her eyes caught the cat's, staring up at her in greedy expectation.

She picked up a pink notepad. '*Feed cat*, she scribbled. *Then go to Warwick police and hand yourself in. I don't want to see you in Stratford. If you're at home when I get back, I'll have you arrested.*

She put on a blue thermal jacket, grabbed a chocolate bar as an afterthought, and left by the back door.

She climbed into her car, clicked on the seatbelt and put her hand on the ignition key. She took a deep breath before firing the engine.

It had begun to snow as the dark blue Golf GTE crawled out of the driveway, waited for a passing cyclist and then swung into the road. A few minutes later she passed through the village of Hampton Lucy, heading for the A439 that led into Stratford. Despite her wretched state, she felt liberated.

She was putting distance between herself and *him*.

That thought alone gave her a shot of energy. The ACPO *Murder Investigation Manual* stipulated that an SIO should avoid stress and not work excessive hours. Fine, okay – but in practice? If the investigation ran into days, how would she cope? She had once solved a case and charged the suspect within six hours. She doubted she would get so lucky this time.

The snow continued to fall, prompting her to switch on the windscreen wipers. It reminded her of the last homicide case in which she'd failed to apprehend and convict the murderer, Hannah Bron, thereby killing off her chances of promotion. Snow had played a part in affecting the gathering of evidence – would it happen again this time? Could she redeem herself with this "shout?"

Suddenly she exclaimed as the wheels spun. Ice on the road. She turned the steering wheel into the slide, slowing the car down without braking.

Driving slower, a new thought entered her head, making it impossible to forget about Charlie. His crime, appalling as it was, would inevitably cause suspicion to fall upon her. It was okay being well-regarded by her superior officers, but the enormity of such a crime always led to a suspect's spouse being investigated, if only to eliminate them from suspicion.

A shiver ran down her spine.

The snowfall was thicker, plastering the windscreen.

Narrowing her eyes and driving to the fast thumping wipers, her thoughts took her back to 11 p.m. the previous night…it was when her world collapsed.

Acknowledgements

My initial thanks go to Tom Bromley, my first editor. He was quick to point out that there were two stories within the novel, each of which had merit in itself. That sorted, how could I convince the reader that the students were capable of studying for an MA or PhD in Shakespearean studies? At the world-renowned Shakespeare Institute, Professor Michael Dobson, Director, introduced me to Dr Michael Wiggins, senior lecturer, who gave me the confidence to continue. Then came Dr Chris Laoutaris who read my MS and was more than generous with his praise and advice.

I was extremely fortunate to find that I had attracted the service of Benjamin Evans, literary—critic of *The Guardian*. He found time in which to line-edit my MS, followed by a critique that was simply unbelievable. He showered the book with superlatives, for which I am more than grateful.

On the practical side, Jacqueline Abromeit provided me with book covers to love. A special word for my formatter, Jason Anderson, for his patience and concern.

I must give my long–suffering wife, Liz, a special mention. She has put up with riding my roller-coaster of joy and despair these last four and a half years. It makes her a martyr.

Finally, but not least, my love and thanks go to our daughter Jane, who, in The White Swan in Stratford – where Shakespeare is reputed to have drunk a tipple or two – gave me the idea for the book. It took place on 23 April 2016 at approximately 7 p.m. I remember it well.

Eureka.

Printed in Poland
by Amazon Fulfillment
Poland Sp. z o.o., Wrocław